BOOKS BY ELMORE LEONARD

ELMORE LEONARD'S WESTERN ROUNDUP #1

The Bounty Hunters
Forty Lashes Less One
Gunsights

ELMORE LEONARD

Delta
Trade Paperbacks

A Delta Book
Published by
Dell Publishing
a division of
Bantam Doubleday Dell Publishing Group, Inc.
1540 Broadway
New York, New York 10036

ISBN: 0-385-33322-6

Reprinted by arrangement with Dell Publishing, a division of Bantam Doubleday Dell Publishing Group, Inc.

Manufactured in the United States of America
Published simultaneously in Canada

November 1998

10 9 8 7 6 5 4 3 2 1

OPM

CONTENTS

THE
BOUNTY
HUNTERS

....

ONE

Dave Flynn stretched his boots over the footrest and his body eased lower into the barber chair. It was hot beneath the striped cloth, but the long ride down from Fort Thomas had made him tired and he welcomed the comfort of the leather chair more than he minded the heat. In Contention it was hot wherever you went, even though it was nearly the end of October.

He turned his head, feeling the barber behind him, and frowned at the glare framed in the big window. John Willet moved to his side and he saw the barber's right ear bright red and almost transparent with the glare behind it. Beneath the green eyeshade, Willet's face sagged impassively. It was a large face, with an unmoving toothpick protruding from the corner of the slightly open mouth, the toothpick seeming unnaturally small.

John Willet put his hand under the young man's chin, raising the head firmly. "Let's see how we're doing," he said, then stepped back cocking his head and studied the hairline thoughtfully. He tapped comb against scissors then moved them in a flitting automatic gesture close to Flynn's ear.

"How's it going with you?"

"All right," Flynn answered drowsily. The heat was making him sleepy and it felt good not to move.

"You still guiding for the soldier boys?"

"On and off."

"I can think of better ways to make a living."

"Maybe I'll stay in the shade and take up barbering."

"You could do worse." Willet stepped back and studied the hairline again. "I heard you was doing some prospecting . . . down in the Madres."

"For about a year and a half."

"You're back to guiding, now?" And when Flynn nodded, Willet said, "Then I don't have to ask you if you found anything."

For a few minutes he moved the scissors deftly over the brown hair, saying nothing, until he finished trimming. Then he placed the implements on the shelf and studied a row of bottles there.

"Wet it down?"

"I suppose."

"You can use it," Willet said, shaking a green liquid into his hand. "That sun makes the flowers grow . . . but your hair isn't flowers."

"What about Apaches?" Flynn said.

"What about them?"

"They don't wear hats. They have better hair than anybody."

"Sun don't affect a man that was born in hell," Willet said, and began rubbing the tonic into Flynn's scalp.

Flynn closed his eyes again. Maybe that was it, he thought. He remembered the first Apache he had ever seen. That had been ten years ago.

D. A. Flynn, at twenty the youngest first lieutenant on frontier station, took his patrol out of Fort Lowell easterly toward the Catalinas; it was dawn of a muggy July day. Before ten they sighted the smoke. Before noon they found the burned wagon and the two dead men, and the third staked to the ground staring at the sun . . . because he could not close his eyes with the lids cut off. Nor could he speak with his tongue gone. He tried to tell them by writing in the sand, but the marks made little sense because he could not see what he was writing, and he died before he could make them plainer. But out of a mesquite clump only a dozen yards from the wagon, his men dragged an Apache who had been shot through both legs, and there was all the explanation that was needed. He could not speak English and none of the soldiers could speak Chiricahua Apache, so the sergeant dragged him back into the mesquite. There was the heavy report of a revolving pistol and the sergeant reappeared, smiling.

The hell with it, Flynn thought.

He felt the barber's fingers rubbing hard against his scalp. His eyes were still closed, but he could no longer see the man without the eyelids. He heard the barber say then, "You're starting to lose your hair up front."

Willet combed the hair, which was straighter than usual with the tonic, brushing it almost flat across the forehead, then began to trim Flynn's full cavalry-type mustache. The thinning hair and dragoon mustache made him appear older, yet there was a softness to the weather-tanned face. It was thin-lined and the bone structure was small. Dave Flynn was a month beyond his thirty-first birthday, but from fifteen feet he looked forty. That's what patrols in Apache country will do.

"Hang on," John Willet said, moving around the chair. "I see a couple of wild hairs." He took a finer comb from that shelf and turning back to Flynn he looked up to see the small, black-suited man enter the shop.

"Mr. Madora."

Flynn opened his eyes.

Standing the way he was, just inside the doorway with his thumbs hooked into vest pockets, Joe Madora could be mistaken for a dry-goods drummer. He was under average height and heavy, his black suit clinging tightly to a thick frame, and the derby placed evenly over his eyebrows might have been a size too small. His mustache and gray-streaked beard told that he was well into his fifties and probably too old to be much good with the pistol he wore high on his right hip. But Joe Madora had been underestimated before, many times, by Apaches as well as white men. Most of them were dead . . . while Joe was still chief of scouts at Fort Bowie.

He stood unmoving, staring at Dave Flynn, until finally Flynn said, "What's the matter with you?"

Madora's grizzled face was impassive. "I'm trying to figure out if you got on a fancy-braid charro rig under that barber cloth."

"It takes longer than a year and a half to go Mexican." Flynn nodded to the antlers mounted next to the door. "There's my coat right there."

Madora glanced at the faded tan coat. "You're about due for a new one."

"I'm not the dude you are."

"You bet your sweet tokus you're not."

Flynn smiled faintly, watching the man who had taught him everything he knew about the Apache. The comical-looking little man who could almost read sign in the air and better than half the time beat the Apache at his own game. He had learned well from Joe Madora, and after he had resigned his commission, it was Joe who had recommended him and saw that he got a job as a contract guide.

"I hear you're back for more," Madora said.

"You know of an easier way to make money?"

"Just two. Find gold or a rich woman."

"Well, I've given up on finding gold."

"And no woman 'ud have a slow-movin' son of a bitch like you, so you don't have a choice at that."

John Willet said, "Joe, let me trim your beard. Be done here in a minute."

Madora nodded and eased himself into the other barber chair. "Where's Irv?"

"Irv went up to Willcox to get something for his wife . . . coming in on the train."

"That's good," Madora grunted. "He's a worse barber than you are." He looked at Flynn then. "I heard about your new job. Taking that kid down into the Madres . . ." He stopped, seeing Flynn glance toward the barber. "John, you keep your ears plugged."

"I never did pay attention to what you had to say," Willet answered.

To Madora, Flynn said, "How did you find out?"

"I been guiding for Deneen. I heard him talking to this Bowers kid. Did he talk it over with you yet?"

"This morning for a minute. He kept reminding me I didn't have to take it, saying, 'You can back out,' using those words. Then he said, 'Think it over and come back later.' "

Madora smiled in his beard. "What about Bowers, did you see him?"

Flynn shook his head. He said then, "In the war we had a division commander by that name."

"Maybe he's a kin."

"What kind is he?"

"If you keep him from wettin' his pants he might do."

"How old?"

"Twenty-one . . . -two."

"West Point?"

"They all are . . . that doesn't mean anything. He's been out here a year and that's Whipple Barracks. He looks brevet-conscious. He wants to move up so bad he can taste it . . . and he's afraid going away on this job might get him lost in the woods."

"It could get him a promotion."

"It could get him killed, too. But he thinks it's more a job for a truant officer than a cavalryman. He said to Deneen, 'Sir, isn't bringing an old Indian back more a task for the reservation agent?' "

"Did you tell Bowers what it's all about?"

"He didn't ask me."

Flynn shook his head. "It doesn't make sense."

"You ought to be used to that; you've worked for Deneen before," Madora said. "His naming Bowers doesn't make sense . . . though he must have a reason. But it's plain why he's sending you."

"Why?"

"You know as well as I do. He wants to make you quit again. You've done it twice before. Maybe he thinks one more will finish you for good."

"What do you think?" Flynn asked.

"I don't blame you for anything you did before. Deneen's Department Adjutant . . . with more weight than you got. When he says dance, you dance, or else go listen to a different tune. I wouldn't blame you too much if you backed out of this one. Only I think it can be done. I think you just might be able to drag Soldado Viejo—the old Indian, as the kid calls him—back to San Carlos."

"Two of us?"

"Two make less noise."

"Give me a better reason."

"Because I taught you what you know. And I'll give you one more," Madora added. "Because you might be mad enough to do this one just so you can throw it back in Deneen's face."

Flynn smiled. "You sound like you want to go."

"Maybe I should."

"Maybe you volunteered"—Flynn was still smiling—"but they said it wasn't something for an old man who looked like he was standing in a hole."

Madora shook his head. "I was wrong. You'll last down there about a day and a half."

"I've lasted ten years so far . . . plus three in the war when I didn't see you around."

"I was watchin' the frontier for you sword-clickin' bastards back East."

"About three thousand miles from Lee."

Madora was composed. "David," he said quietly. "All during that war of yours we had us a Mimbre named Soldado Viejo . . . the same one you're supposed to bring home. And I'll tell you something else. Bobby Lee, in his prime, couldn't rear-guard for Soldado if all the old Mimbre raided was whorehouses."

John Willet had looked from one to the other, trying to piece the conversation into some sense. Now he put down his comb and scissors and offered a hand mirror to Flynn.

"See how it looks," he said.

His gaze went to the window, idly, and he watched a man come out of the Republic House and start diagonally across the street toward the barbershop. Over the thick green lettering that read WILLET'S from the street side, he watched the man approach; long strides, but weaving somewhat, carrying a rifle in his right hand and saddlebags over his left shoulder. Then he recognized the man.

"God, I hope he hasn't been drinking."

Neither Flynn nor Madora had noticed him yet.

Willet spoke hurriedly, watching the man reach the plank sidewalk. "That's Frank Rellis . . . sometimes he acts funny when he's had a drink, but don't pay any attention to him."

Flynn, holding the mirror, glanced up. "What?"

But Willet was looking toward the door. "Hello, Frank . . . be with you in a minute."

Frank Rellis stood in the doorway swaying slightly, then came in and unslung the saddlebags, dropping them onto the seat of a Douglas chair next to the door. He eyed the occupied barber chairs sullenly; a man about Flynn's age, he wore range clothes: a sweat-stained hat, the curled brim close over his eyes, leather pants worn to a shine and a cotton shirt that was open enough to show thick dark hair covering his chest. His pistol was strapped low on his thigh and he still held the rifle, a Winchester, pointed toward the floor.

He looked at Willet. "Where's Irv?"

"Irv had to go to Willcox," John Willet said pleasantly. "I'll be with you in a minute . . . take a chair."

"I don't have a minute."

Willet smiled. "Frank, this being herd boss keeps you on the go, don't it?"

Rellis looked at the barber impassively. His deep-set eyes were half closed from drink and an apparent lack of sleep and a two days' beard stubble made his heavy-boned face menacing. "I said I don't have a minute."

Willet smiled, but now it was forced. "I'm finishing up, then I have to trim this here gent's beard"—he nodded to Joe Madora—"and I'll be with you."

"You can do better than that."

"Frank, I don't see any other way . . ."

"I do . . . you're taking me right now."

"Frank . . ."

"You can finish them up after."

Flynn glanced from Rellis to Madora. The chief of scouts was watching Rellis closely. "Are you in a hurry?" Madora said then.

Rellis ignored him, moving toward the first chair. He stopped at the footrest, in front of Flynn's boots. The mirror was still in his hand, but Flynn was looking over it at Rellis.

"You look prettier'n a French pimp," Rellis said. "Now get out of the chair."

Flynn felt the sudden flush of anger come over his face, but he took his time. His eyes left Rellis as he raised the mirror and studied his reflection, and he was surprised that his anger did not show. Perhaps the brown face had a reddish tint to it, but that was all. Then he said, quietly, "John, you're a little uneven right in through here"—his left hand following the part—"let's try parting it a little higher."

"Looks fine to me," Willet said uneasily. "That's the way you always wear it."

"I want to try all kinds of styles," Flynn said evenly, "before I get old and set in my ways and have to live with it the rest of my life." He looked at Rellis, whose mouth had tightened. "I've got all afternoon. You can try parting it on the other side, then in the middle, then if you run out of ideas get your book out and look up a new one."

There was a silence and suddenly a brittle tension that was ready to break. Rellis' jaw tightened and colored a deeper red beneath the beard stubble. His body was stiff as if poised to make a move.

And then Joe Madora laughed. It was a soft chuckle, but it split the silence.

Rellis turned on him. "Are you laughing at me!" His face was beet-red now.

Madora's smile straightened and suddenly his dark face was cold and dead serious. He said to Rellis, "If you're not man then you shouldn't drink that lizard-pee they pass off as whisky over at the Republic."

Rellis didn't move. Flynn felt the tension and it made him ease up straighter in the chair. He looked at Rellis standing on the edge of his nerves gripping the Winchester tightly, cradled under his arm now. Rellis' eyes were wide with disbelief, staring at the little man with the beard . . . a head smaller than he was, older, and wearing his pistol in a high, awkward position. But Madora looked back at him calmly and something stopped Rellis at the peak of his anger.

"Mister," Flynn said now, and waited until Rellis looked at him. "You don't need a shave as bad as you think you do. Maybe you better get while your luck's still holding out."

Amazement was on Rellis' face, but he was near the end of his patience and the anger was plain on his face. "What's your name?" he said.

"Flynn."

"We ever met before?"

"I doubt it."

"Are you going to get out of that chair, or do I pry you out with this?" He raised the Winchester slightly.

"You raise that another inch," Flynn said calmly, "I'll kill you."

Rellis stopped. He looked at the long barber cloth that covered Flynn to the knees, smooth striped cotton that told nothing.

"You're bluffing."

"There's one way to find out."

Rellis glanced quickly at the antlers next to the door. A tan coat hung there; a gun belt could be beneath it, but it could also be in Flynn's hand beneath the cloth.

John Willet's face turned paler under the eye shade. He said, his voice faltering, "Gentlemen, please . . ." But that was all.

Rellis moved suddenly toward the chair, but Flynn's boot kicked out in the same motion and caught him in the pit of the stomach. Rellis went back with a rip up his shirt front where Flynn's spur had slashed, and as he staggered back, Flynn came out of the chair and swung the hand mirror hard against the side of Rellis' head while his right hand wrenched at the Winchester.

The rifle barrel swung back toward Rellis, even while his hand was still on the stock, and came down across his skull. He didn't go down, but staggered backward with Flynn pushing him toward the open door, and in the doorway Flynn stopped, holding the rifle, while Rellis kept going, stumbling, until he landed in the dust on his back and rolled over. He was raising himself to his knees when his saddlebags came flying out to catch him full in the face and knock him flat again.

Flynn turned back into the shop and placed the rifle against the wall below the antlers. "Give him his rifle back when he gets some sense," he said to John Willet.

Joe Madora came out of the chair. "Some other time, John. You look a mite too nervous to be wielding scissors." He nodded to the broken glass from the hand mirror. "David, you just acquired seven years of the worst kind of luck."

Flynn paid Willet, who took the money silently, then moved to the antlers. He took down his coat, then lifted off his gun harness and passed his arm through the sling so that the holster hung well below his left armpit, the long-barreled .44 extending past his belt. He put on the tan coat, faded, bleached almost white. His light Stetson was sweat-stained around the band and he wore the stiff brim straight, close over his eyes. Putting it on, he said, "We'll see you again, John."

Willet said now, "He's not going to forget that. Dave, you don't know that man."

Madora said, "But he knows Dave now."

TWO

They rode out of Contention toward the cavalry station which was two miles north, up on the San Pedro. It was a one-troop post and Flynn wondered why it had been chosen for the meeting place. He had been working out of Fort Thomas since his return, and Bowers was from Whipple Barracks. But that was like Deneen. He'd pick it so you would wonder. Deneen, the departmental adjutant, whom he'd known for a long time. Too long. Since Chancellorsville. And there was a day at Chancellorsville that he would never forget. Madora had said once that you ought to take a good look at Deneen because he was one of the few honest-to-God full-blooded sons of bitches left.

They rode relaxed, walking the mares, Flynn on a buckskin and Madora on a chestnut. It was close to four o'clock and already the sun was low off to the left, a long crimson streak above the colorless sierra of the Catalinas.

Madora said, "Remember Anastacio Esteban?"

Flynn looked up, surprised. "Very well."

"He came through here yesterday with about the whole tribe. Four or five wagons of big and little Estebans hanging on every place you looked."

"Here? They live down in Sonora. Soyopa."

"I know it," Madora said. "They were up the line for some shindig. You know Anastacio made a lot of friends when he was packin' mules for the army. It don't take much to get him back for a celebration."

Flynn said, "I came through Soyopa. I was digging just southeast of there and stopped off on my way back. Anastacio had me spend the night at his dobe."

"He mentioned he saw you."

"His brother Hilario is the alcalde now. Least he was six months ago when I passed through."

Madora nodded. "The quiet one."

"Unlike his brother," Flynn said. "He wasn't along, was he?"

"No; his daughter was. Did you meet her?"

"I think so."

"You don't think so about her. You either did or you didn't."

"Anita?"

"Nita," Madora said. "She could stand a few more pounds, but she's much woman the way she is."

"She was along?"

"Taking her father's place. They passed through here just yesterday. You might catch up with them . . . depending when you leave."

"We might," Flynn said.

He had become acquainted with the good-natured Anastacio while still in the army, during the time Anastacio transported supplies for them; Anastacio the mule skinner, the arriero, who talked to his animals as if they were his children, and drank mescal as if it were water. But he had not met the others until he passed through the pueblo of Soyopa. They had not come up into Arizona to work as Anastacio had done. Hilario, the quiet one. And Nita, whom one remembered well. Perhaps he would see them again.

"Deneen's here already," Madora observed, as they rode into the quadrangle of Camp Contention; a scattering of cottonwoods behind a row of drab, wind-scarred adobes, a flagpole, then a long low stable shed facing the adobes.

"That's his bay over there in the end stall the trooper's wipin' down," Madora said. "When Deneen's standin' next to it you got to blink your eyes to tell which is the genuine horse's-ass, and then you can never be dead sure."

At the end of the stable shed, a dozen or more figures sat about a smoking fire. The sun was behind them and Flynn could not make out who they were until he put his hand up to shield the sun glare.

"My boys," Madora said.

Flynn recognized them then—Coyotero Apaches, working for the army as trackers. The Apaches looked toward them then and one of them stood up and waved. He wore a faded issue shirt, but it lost its regulation worn with the rest of his attire. Red cotton headband and gray breech clout, and moccasin leggings that reached his thighs.

Madora said, "You remember him?"

"Three-cents," Flynn said. "He worked with me awhile."

"That red son's better than a bloodhound," Madora said.

A sign marked the adobe headquarters. Black lettering on a whitewashed board to the right of the door: TROOP E—SIXTH U.S. CAVALRY.

A trooper who had been at parade rest by the door took their reins and they went inside.

By the left wall, an officer, holding a kepi in his hand, came up quickly off the bench that was there and Flynn knew that this was Bowers. He glanced at the sergeant seated behind the desk and nodded, then looked back at the officer. A young man—no, he looked more a boy—above medium height, red hair cropped close and a pinkish clean-lined face with a serious set to it. His dark brown eyes held the question, though it was plain he was trying to seem incurious.

"Bowers?"

The young man nodded.

"Dave Flynn. You know Joe Madora."

The officer nodded again, taking the outstretched hand. His grip was firm and he returned Flynn's close inspection as they shook hands.

"We had a divisional commander named Bowers."

"He was my father."

"Good soldier."

"Thank you."

Then Flynn beckoned to the door leading into the post commander's office. "Is Deneen in there?"

Bowers nodded. "With Lieutenant Woodside."

"Have you seen him yet?"

"Only for a few minutes."

"He hasn't explained anything, then."

"I don't see the necessity of an explanation," Bowers stated. "I've already received my orders."

"May I see them?"

Bowers hesitated.

"Look, I'm on your side."

He drew a folded paper then from inside his jacket. "You are mentioned here," Bowers said quietly. "I assumed, though, that this would be discussed in a more private manner."

"I won't tell a soul," Flynn said. He glanced at Bowers' serious face and wanted to smile, but he did not.

Madora moved next to him then, to look over his shoulder. "That's a nice hand," he said.

Flynn held it close to his face. "I don't smell any perfume on it."

"Well, don't get it too close or you're liable to smell something else," Madora said. They read the orders in silence.

From:　A. R. L. Deneen, Col.
　　　　Dept. Adjutant, Department of Arizona
　　　　In the field, Camp Contention, Arizona Terr.
To:　Regis Duane Bowers, Second Lt.
　　　　6th Cav. Reg.
　　　　Whipple Barracks, Prescott, Arizona Terr.
Subject:　Transfer and Reassignment　　　17 Oct. 1876

As of this date, R. D. Bowers is formally assigned to the office of the Departmental Adjutant, Department of Arizona, and is hereby instructed to report to Camp Contention, Arizona Terr., for detailed instructions concerning the following outlined orders:

1. Within one week, or, before 25 Oct., R. D. Bowers will have made preparations for extended patrol.
2. R. D. Bowers will contact one D. Flynn, civilian contract guide. However, herenamed contract employee is free to decline assignment. Substitute, if needed, will be selected by the office of the Department Adjutant.
3. R. D. Bowers and civilian guide will proceed to that section of Sonora (Mexico) indicated at a future date.
4. Aforementioned are to make contact, without show of arms, with one Soldado Viejo, hostile Mimbreño Apache, and return said hostile to Apache Agency, San Carlos, Arizona Terr.
5. R. D. Bowers is warned that if detained by Mexican authorities, because of the nature of the assignment he will not be recognized by the United States as a lawful agent.
6. The subject matter contained herein is of the strictest confidential nature.

The office of the Department Adjutant extends its heartiest wish for a successful undertaking.

A. R. L. DENEEN
Department Adjutant

Madora said, "That last line's the one."

Flynn returned the sheet to Bowers and moved to the bench; sitting down, hooking a boot heel on the edge, he made a cigarette and took his time lighting it, then exhaled the smoke leisurely, studying the young officer who was trying to appear composed, trying to look West Point. And it was plain that the orders meant very little as far as he was concerned.

This was the man he would take across the Rio Grande—which they would call the Bravos then—to find Soldado, a broncho Mimbre, who had been fighting longer than Bowers or he had lived. Four dollars a day to guide a new lieutenant with only one year of frontier station behind him. To take him across sun-beaten nothingness and into scrambling rock-strewn puzzling never-ending canyons in search of something that would probably not be there. But always with eyes open, because the Apache knows his business. He knows it better than anyone else. How to kill. That simple? Yes, that simple, he thought. That's what it boils down to. That's what it is from where you're standing, so that's what you call it. Four dollars a day. More than a lieutenant makes. His uniform compensates for the low pay rate . . . though he could die naked as easy as not.

He heard Madora say, "What's he got on you?"

"I beg your pardon?" Bowers said, startled.

"He must a caught you with his old lady."

Bowers looked at him steadily, but said nothing.

Flynn took his hat off, leaning back, and felt the adobe cool against the back of his head. "Mister," he said to Bowers, "what do you think?"

"About what?"

God, the calm one. He's tensed-up being calm. "About your orders."

"You almost answer your own question. They are orders. Under the circumstances I doubt if an opinion would affect them one way or the other."

Madora grinned. "Look out, Dave. You got yourself a serious one."

"I don't believe this concerns you in the least," Bowers said coldly.

There was silence. Flynn watched the lieutenant grip his hands behind his back and walk to the single window. Flynn said to the back, "Do you know what you're talking about?"

Bowers turned on him sharply. "Mr. Flynn, I assure you I am capable of interpreting a military order. It is a precise, unadorned, quite literal description fo a specific assignment which I have been trained to obey without question, without hesitation. Since my opinion is of no value, I see little reason in discussing it . . . especially with a person who is in no way related to the order in question. Is that quite clear?"

"Very clear, Mr. Bowers." Colonel Deneen stood in the doorway of the post commander's office. Lieutenant Woodside could be seen behind him. "And I might say unduly modest of you. Your opinion is worth . . . something."

He hesitated, his eyes roaming over the group in the outer office. He was a man of medium height, in his early forties, carefully dressed, from the trace of white showing above his collar to the highly polished black boots and silver spurs that chinged softly as he moved into the room. And though he took only a few steps, a faint limp was noticeable, a favoring of the right foot as he put his weight on it. One hand picked idly at the front of his tunic, as if removing invisible lint, and he looked at the three men closely, individually, as if to command their attention.

"At ease, Mr. Bowers." He nodded to Madora, who stood relaxed with thumbs in vest pockets, then his eyes went to Flynn and stopped there. Flynn had not moved his position. He leaned against the wall with a half-boot still hooked on the edge of the bench, his arm resting idly on the raised knee and the extended hand holding the stub of a cigarette. He drew on it as Deneen looked toward him.

"Don't get up, Flynn."

Dave Flynn returned his stare, looking up at the smooth features, dark hair well combed and shining. He dropped the cigarette then, but did not step on it. He glanced at Woodside, the post commander. "Don, good to see you again." Then back to Deneen—"How's the foot, Colonel?"

For a moment the face tightened and the dark eyes did not blink, holding squarely on Flynn, as if waiting for him to say more, but Flynn remained silent. The face relaxed then and Deneen said, "Very well, thank you."

There was the hint of a smile playing at the tips of Flynn's mustache. "That's good. Sometimes those old wounds start aching, especially when the weather's damp."

"Fortunately the climate is uncommonly dry."

"Fortunately."

"I can't say I expected to see you here."

"I don't imagine you did."

"You know why you were asked, of course."

"As well as you do."

"Because of your knowledge of the country. I'm told you've been on a mining venture down there for something like a year and a half. I assume it was unsuccessful, or you would not have returned to scouting. Did you see signs of Soldado Viejo?"

"There are always signs."

"And less cryptically, that means what?"

"The dead."

"I suppose the Mexican government has done little."

"On my way up I talked to a man in Soyopa who said that Porfirio Diaz was sending police to help them. They were expected any day."

"Rurales?"

Flynn nodded.

"His newly formed police. Bandits to fight bandits."

"Maybe that's the way," Flynn said.

"What about the scalp bounty?"

"The government's still paying it if you're man enough to take an Apache's hair."

"I'm told there's an American outlaw down there making something of a success of scalp hunting. Lazair. Have you heard of him?"

"He was pointed out to me once."

"Where?"

"In Guazapares, over a year ago. At that time scalps had to be taken to Guazapares for the bounty. Lazair rode in with some of his men and I saw him at a distance. I saw his face before that on wanted dodgers up here."

"How does he get along with the authorities?"

Flynn shrugged. "I don't know. Everybody seems afraid of him."

"I'm told he's now trying quite eagerly for Soldado's scalp."

"He should, it's worth five hundred pesos," Flynn said. "Are you suggesting we go to him for help?"

Deneen smiled faintly. "If you were making a business of scalping Apaches, would you think kindly of someone appearing to take them away?"

"I was going to remind you of the same thing."

"I'll take the responsibility of my own reminding."

Flynn shrugged his shoulders, saying nothing.

"I will mention again," Deneen said politely, "that you are not obligated in any way to take this assignment."

"What about Bowers?"

"That is not your concern."

"I mean nothing personal, but there are other officers with considerably more experience who might have been chosen." He glanced at Bowers as he said it and saw the young officer stiffen, as if anxious to reply.

Deneen said, "Do you imply that you won't go if Lieutenant Bowers does?"

"Of course not. I just don't see why you'd send an inexperienced man on a job like this."

"And how do you gain this experience if you never take the field?"

"Tracking Soldado in his own element isn't exactly just taking the field."

"We're not going to debate it. You either go or you don't go."

"I'd like to speak to you alone."

"I haven't the time. Are you going?"

Flynn hesitated, then nodded his head.

"You will leave in the morning. The quartermaster sergeant will issue your ammunition if you use a Springfield; otherwise you supply your own."

"I'm aware of all that."

"Then there's no reason to detain you," Deneen said, and turned abruptly to Bowers. "Lieutenant, step into the office."

The sun had dropped below the horizon line of the Catalinas and they rode back to Contention in the silent dusk, Flynn thinking, reminding himself that he was in it now, and that was that.

"He was almost half decent for a minute," Madora said. "Then the ninety-nine per cent bastard started to show."

"You've got to hand him that," Flynn said. "He's consistent." Flynn was silent, riding, following the sway of his mount. Then, "Joe, where does he get his authority for this?"

"I hadn't thought of it."

"The orders said the army wouldn't recognize us. If there was an agreement with Mexico, there'd be an expedition."

"With a lot of noise," Madora added. "And you'd never find Soldado."

"That's not the point. What does the general say about this? I don't think it's something that can be kept from him."

"Deneen's a talker," Madora said. "Maybe he can explain it so it sounds legal."

"Maybe." Flynn shrugged it off then, saying, "What are you going to do now?"

"I'm leadin' Deneen's grand tour of post inspections. With Three-cents and his Coyoteros along to add color."

"You could do worse."

"Like what?"

It was dark when they turned off Commercial Street onto Stockman, riding past the Republic House on the corner. They were both staying there and they boarded their horses at the livery stable behind the hotel, on Stockman. They dismounted in front of the wide doorway framing the darkness inside.

"I wonder where the man is?" Madora said. He stopped just inside, blinking his eyes.

Behind him, Flynn said, "Seems to me there was a lantern on a nail along the boards there."

"Over here?" Madora moved into the darkness.

"This side of the first stall."

Madora's hand went into his coat pocket and came out with a match. He scratched it against the board partition and just ahead of him Flynn saw a yellow flare and Madora's face close to the boards.

And the heavy, ringing, solid slam of the rifle report was there with the match flare. Flynn went down instinctively. The match went out and he heard Madora gasp as if he'd been hit hard in the stomach, and the sound of his weight falling against the partition.

"Joe!"

Flynn was rising. Three shots then in quick succession in the close stillness and he went down flat, hearing the horses scream, knowing they had been hit. In front of him, Madora's mare fell heavily and did not move, but his own broke away and veered out into Stockman Street. His pistol was in his hand, but there was nothing, only the darkness and the stabled mounts moving nervously, bumping the boards and nickering.

Suddenly the rear door, not more than fifty feet away, swung open with the sound of hoofs striking boards and packed earth and momentarily horse and rider were framed against the dusk, pushing through as the door swung open only part way. Flynn fired, the heavy revolver lifting in his hand, and then horse and rider were gone and he could hear the hoofbeats outside, on the street beyond the livery.

Madora was breathing with his mouth open, his chest rising and falling with a wheezing sound. Flynn's hand went over him gently until he felt the wet smear of blood just above his waist at his side.

"Joe, you'll be all right. It probably went clean through you."

Madora tried to answer, but he could not. He was breathing harder, gasping.

There were footsteps behind them.

"What happened?"

Then more steps on the packed ground and a familiar voice. It belonged to the barber, John Willet.

"Soon as I seen him I knew . . . tearing up Commercial like that. I didn't even hear the shots and I knew."

Someone said, "Who?"

"Who do you think!" Willet's voice was edged with nervousness. "Frank Rellis. My God, he's done it now. . . ."

THREE

Late in the afternoon the sky changed to pale gray and there was rain in the air, the atmosphere close and stifling, and a silence clung heavily to the flat colorless plain. The distant peaks to the east, the Dragoons, rose gigantically into the grayness, seeming nearer than they were, and the towering irregular crests were lost in the hazy flat color of the sky.

The sudden threat of rain was relief after the relentless sun glare of the morning. They had traveled through it saying little, their eyes heavy-lidded against the glare. Flynn's searching, from habit swinging a slow wide arc that took in every brush clump and rise, then lifting to the rimrock and squinting for the thin wisp of smoke that would be almost transparent in the sunlight, or the mirror flashes that no white man could read, and half expecting one or the other to be there—because you never knew. There were reservations; still, you never knew.

Flynn followed the sway of his horse loosely, a dun mare that he had bought last night, listening to the squeak of saddle leather. His hat was straight across his eyebrows and he seemed tired, listless; yet his eyes never ceased the slow swing over the valley. Often he would slip his boots from the stirrups and let his legs hang free. All things become routine. Relax, and be watchful at the same time. Relax only, and in Apache country it will kill you.

He thought about Joe Madora and he could still hear the wheezing sound of his breathing. The crowd that had formed almost out of the air. First they were alone, then there were voices, dozens of voices, and one that he recognized. John Willet's voice. He had heard John Willet very clearly say the name Frank Rellis. He had told Bowers about it before they started out that morning. Bowers said he was sorry, that was about all.

Bowers wore civilian clothes now, a gray broadcloth suit that he had worn on furlough perhaps a year or two before and now was too small for him.

The doctor had worked on Madora a long time, half the night, and stayed there the rest of it, up in the hotel room where they'd carried the wounded man. He'd stop the bleeding, then it would start again and he'd work at the wound, applying compresses. Madora was unconscious by then, his eyes closed rightly as if ready to snap open at any moment. Flynn had watched the face more than he did the doctor's hands working at the middle of Madora's body, because he expected the face to become colorless and the eyes to open. He was sure they would open, because almost every dead man he could remember had been lying with his eyes open. He had placed small stones over the eyelids when he had the time. That was a strange thing. No, that's why you remember them. There were others with eyes closed that you don't remember.

But Madora's face remained calm, and though the bearded skin was pale, it did not become drained of all its color.

Flynn slept for an hour before dawn and when he awoke and pulled on his boots and strapped on his gun, the doctor told him that the old man had a chance to live, but he wouldn't advise making any hotel reservation in his name.

They camped early because of the rain threat and rigged their ponchos into a lean-to. But the rain never came. And later on, when the moon appeared, its outline was hazy and there were few stars in the deep blackness.

Flynn lay back with his head on his saddle and lighted a thin Mexican cigar. In three and a half days we'll be there. Soyopa. And then we will watch and get to know this Apache and see if there is a pattern to the way he lives. What are his limitations? Where is his weak spot?

He stopped suddenly and blew the smoke out slowly and smiled to himself. What's the hurry? As old as he is, he'll probably be there years after you're gone. Luck doesn't last forever, you know. It stretches so far and when you're not looking there's a *pop* and it's all over and you don't know what hit you. He smiled again. But that's if you're lucky. That's how luck runs out if you're lucky.

He relighted the cigar and it was a soft glow in the corner of his mouth. Lying on his back, looking up into the darkness, his hand moved the cigar idly from one side of his mouth to the other, half biting and half just feeling the strong tobacco between his lips. He could see the girl's face clearly. Nita Esteban. He had thought of her because he had thought of Soyopa. The lines of her face were sensitive, delicate, and her lips parted slightly as she smiled. She had worn a red scarf over her slim shoulders and held the ends of it in front of her. He remembered the red scarf well. What would she be, seventeen? Not much older.

He watched the eternity of the sky. The dark was restful, but the vastness was cold and made you draw something close to you. His head rolled on the saddle and he saw Bowers' form across the small fire. He's trying to figure out what the hell he's doing here, Flynn thought.

Maybe we'll catch the Estebans. That would be good. Then we could talk about all those things Deneen brought up and be familiar with them before reaching Soyopa.

Bowers is honest, though. He doesn't like something and he shows it. He doesn't like this, but he doesn't realize what is involved. He thinks it is dull routine that will keep him out of the promotion light for too long. Probably he has been talking to Deneen and Deneen had told him to keep an eye on me because, well, even though Flynn was an officer at one time, he's not the most reliable man in the world, you see he resigned his commission because he was hotheaded and maybe a little afraid of what was to come. Those things happen.

Bowers thinks all the time and he doesn't smile.

And his dad was Division Commander over Deneen during the war. What's that got to do with Bowers being here now? Something. You can bet your best plugged peso, something.

You smiled most of the time at first, he told himself. You smiled to show you were eager. A smile shows sincerity. Warmhearted, clean-souled, open-minded . . . and inexperienced.

Flynn thought of the gray morning in April when he had crossed the Rappahannock with Averell's Brigade. Seventeen years old and a second lieutenant because his father knew somebody. He remembered Deneen, who had been his captain then, his first captain, saying, nodding to the hills, "They're up there. Those gray-coated, sorghum-eating manure spreaders are up there. We get them before they get us." He had been close to Deneen and he had smiled, because Deneen was a captain and had taken them through training and he talked like a cavalryman was supposed to talk.

They met Fitz Lee, who was part of Stuart's sabers, and almost cut him to pieces, but they couldn't finish it because the rebel pickets were too close and by then the alarm had been spread. It was a good day and he had thought: This won't be so bad.

Then Chancellorsville. The third night it had been raining hard, but it stopped a matter of minutes after their patrol came in. The rebel artillery started up shortly after this. Whitworths pouring it down from the thicketed heights.

His sergeant had appeared to him in the darkness, in the cold miserable darkness, showing the whites of his eyes with his body tensed stiffly.

"My God, I saw him do it!"

"What?"

"With his own pistol."

"What—damn it!"

The sergeant led him back into a pine stand. Deneen was sitting beneath thick, dripping branches, huddled close to the tree trunk. His pistol was in his hand. And the toe of his right boot was missing—where he had shot it away.

They carried him to the rear and said *shrapnel* to the orderly who was filling out the tag which was attached to Deneen's tunic. The remainder of the night Flynn did not smile because he was muscle-tight in the mud as A. P. Hill's Whitworths continued to slam down from Hazel Grove.

In the morning he found the sergeant dead; killed in the shelling. And he realized he was the only one who knew about Deneen.

After that he smiled when he felt like smiling.

In the army it wasn't necessary. Most of the time it helped, but it wasn't necessary. He had seen men do more than just smile to wangle a post assignment back East. He had accepted this, regarding it as something contemptible, but still, none of his business. He had accepted this and all of the unmilitary facets of army life because there was nothing he could do about them. The politics could go their smiling, boot-licking way.

There had to be men on frontier station. There had to be men who took dirty assignments and made successes of them. And when he found himself in the role—when he found himself in a part of the army which still occasionally fought, he accepted it as quickly and as readily as the politics. Somebody had to do it. Do what you can do best. That's how to make a success. Even if the success is only a self-satisfaction.

But there was an end to it.

The beginning of the end was the day a Major Deneen suddenly appeared at Fort Thomas as Post Commandant.

He said nothing to Deneen about that night at Chancellorsville; and was shocked when one day he heard Deneen refer to his wound quite proudly. Others were present, but Deneen had looked directly at Flynn as he described it, the shelling, and the damn odd place to be caught by shrapnel. Flynn was certain, then, that Deneen had been in a state of shock and was not even slightly aware of what had happened that night.

Then, suddenly, Flynn found himself with unreasonable hastily planned assignments. He had had them before—all patrols were not routine—but now they began in earnest. Bold orders that were *cavalry*, but not the way to fight Apaches. Following sign blindly because Deneen insisted on speed. Wandering, ill-provisioned decoy patrols that whittled down his men. In seven months he had lost more men than any officer at Fort Thomas.

The end came during the Tonto campaign, almost a full year to the day since Deneen had arrived as post commander. They had chased Primero and his Tonto Apaches for five weeks and toward the end, when they knew they had the war chief and his small band, Deneen took the field. He arrived in the evening as three companies were closing in on Bosque Canyon in the Mogollon country. Primero was inside, somewhere among the shadowy rock formations.

And Deneen ordered Flynn to take half of B and gallop through the narrow passage in order to draw fire. That would tell them where the damn hostiles were!

"I suggest scouting first, sir."

"You suggest nothing."

"Madora's Coyotero scouts could belly in after dark and tell us exactly where they are."

"Are you refusing an order?"

He went in at dawn with fourteen men. Yes, they drew fire . . . and it was almost noon before they were pulled out. Six of them, Flynn with an arrow wound in his thigh.

Deneen was in the tent they had rigged for him. He was not present as they brought in what was left of B, and Flynn found him there alone.

"You're killing good men to get me."

Deneen said nothing.

"You knew what you were doing at Chancellorsville. I should have realized it before this. You're afraid of me because of what I know. You're afraid I'll tell others what a yellow son of a bitch of an excuse for a man you are!"

Calmly, quietly, "When we return to Thomas, Mr. Flynn, you will be confined to your quarters. At the moment, you are in need of the surgeon's attention."

He resigned shortly after that and never again referred to Chancellorsville in Deneen's or anyone else's presence. It would do little good to tell others. Some would believe him, most would not, and either way it would accomplish nothing. He resigned hastily; too hastily perhaps, and regretted it almost immediately.

He did the next best thing—in many respects, the better thing, as he came to know his job more thoroughly—he signed up as a contract guide. He could make his own calculations and patrol officers respected his opinion. He had learned from Joe Madora and that was good enough for most. Many of these officers were new to him, for he made sure he was not assigned to Fort Thomas. But after Deneen was appointed Department Adjutant, he did work out of Thomas for almost a year—seeing Deneen occasionally, seldom speaking to him—until he was assigned to the territorial prison at Yuma. Madora fought it because it was a sheer waste of Flynn's capabilities, but he could do nothing. The order had come from the office of the Department Adjutant.

He resigned again, this time breaking all ties, and went gold prospecting down into the Sierra Madre.

Now you're back, he thought, still watching the sky. Because this is what you like to do and you hoped Deneen might have forgotten. But nothing has changed. Deneen is still Deneen. It's something in his mind. You are the only living man who saw what happened that night at Chancellorsville, which seems so long ago; something he's trying to convince himself did not happen. As if by getting you out of his sight it will cease to have ever existed.

But now you're back and he's going to a lot of trouble to make you quit again. It must be very important to him. What did Madora say: You might be mad enough to do this just so you can throw it back in Deneen's face. Does that make sense? I don't know. But this time there's no quitting. The sooner he realizes it, the better. It will either straighten him out, or drive him crazier than he already is. But it is hard to feel sorry for him.

FOUR

Early afternoon of the third day, in high timbered country, they looked out over a yellow stretch of plain to see smoke rising from the hills beyond. It lifted lazily in a wavering thin column above the ragged hillcrests.

"From here," Bowers said, "it could even be a barbecue." He put his glasses on the spot and focused, clearing the haze, drawing the thin spire closer. He studied the land silently.

"Coming from a draw beyond that first row of hills," he said then. "I would say—two miles."

"Not much more," Flynn said. "A trail cuts through the trough of the hills directly across from us."

"What's there that will burn?"

"Nothing."

"A house?"

"Not unless it was built in the last six months. It would be a jacale—and brush houses don't burn that long."

"Well, maybe it's . . ." He would have said, A wagon or wagon train, but he stopped, remembering the Esteban family that Flynn had described to him being only a day or so ahead of them; and he felt suddenly self-conscious, as if Flynn were reading his thoughts; and he said, "I don't know."

"You were going to say wagons, weren't you?"

Bowers nodded.

They had dismounted. Now they stepped into the saddles and nudged their mounts out of the timber diagonally down the slope that fell to the plain, and reaching the level they followed the base of the hill through head-high brush, keeping the plain on their left. They went on almost two miles until the plain began to crumble into depressions and the brush patches thickened, and when finally the flatness gave way to rockier ground they turned from the hill and moved across slowly so there would be no dust. They were beyond the smoke column, which had thinned, and now they doubled back more than a mile before climbing into timber again, following switchbacks single file as the hill rose steeper.

Near the crest, they tied their mounts and both drew Springfield carbines from the saddle boots.

Bowers lifted a holstered revolving pistol which hung from the saddle horn and secured it to the gun belt low on his hip. Watching him, Flynn's elbow tightened against his body to feel the heavy bulk of his own pistol beneath the coat.

"Ready?"

Bowers nodded and they moved up the remaining dozen yards of the hill, brushing the pine branches silently. At its crest the hill flattened into a narrow grove, thick with piñons. They passed through in a half-crouch and went down on hands and knees when the trees ended abruptly in a sandy slope that dropped before them more than a hundred feet. Below, the pines took up again, but here were taller and more thinly scattered. Through them, they could see patches of the trail which passed through the trough of the hill.

And directly below them, through a wide smooth-sand clearing, they saw the charred shapes of three wagons.

They were no longer wagons but retained some identity in a grotesque, blackened flimsiness; two of the wagons, their trees pointing skyward and only half burned, were rammed into the bed of the third which was over on its side. The mules had been cut from the traces and were not in sight.

Smoke from the suffocated fire hung like hot steam over the rubble of partly burned equipment—cooking gear, cases of provisions, clothing and bedding—heaped and draped about the wagons. The smoke was thinning to nothing above the wreckage, but its stench carried higher, even to the two men.

A bolt of red material, like a saber slash across the flesh-colored sand, trailed from a scorched end at one of the wagons to the base of a heavy-boled pine a few yards up the glade. And through the lower branches they saw the arm extended to clutch the end of the cloth. The arm of a woman.

A stillness clung to the narrow draw. Bowers heard a whispered slow-drawl of obscenity, but when he glanced at Flynn the scout's lean face was expressionless. He lay on his stomach looking down the short barrel of his carbine. Bowers nudged him and when Flynn glanced up the two men rose without a sound and started down the loose sand.

They came to the woman beneath the pine and Flynn parted the branches with the barrel of his carbine, then stooped quickly. Bowers saw the figure of a young girl, but Flynn was over her then and he could not see her face, though he glimpsed the sand dark with blood at her head.

Flynn came up slowly and said, "Anita Esteban's cousin," but he was thinking something else. It was in his eyes that looked past Bowers to the burned wagons. "Somebody took her hair," he said.

They separated, Flynn following the sand clearing, and came out on the trail a dozen yards apart. He looked uptrail toward Bowers, then felt his nerves jump as he saw the bodies off to the side of the road.

Two men and a young boy. Worn, white cotton twisted unnaturally. He could see the rope soles of their sandals. They lay facedown with the backs of their heads showing the blood-matted, scorched smear where they had been shot from a distance of no more than a yard. He moved toward Bowers and watched the lieutenant kneel beside another sprawled figure. As he drew closer, he saw that it was Anastacio Esteban.

Bowers looked up at him. "He's dead."

"They're all dead," Flynn said quietly. He looked past Bowers and saw other forms straggled along the side of the trail. Even from a distance he was certain they were dead. Then he knelt down next to Anastacio whom he had known a long time and he made the sign of the cross and said the Hail Mary slowly, for Anastacio and for the others.

Bowers looked at him curiously because he had not expected to see him pray, then motioned up the draw. "There are more up there." The other two wagons were roughly a hundred yards beyond and partly hidden by the brush where they stood off the trail.

He said to Flynn, "They had mules, didn't they?"

"They must have."

Flynn looked up-trail toward the two wagons. The animals that had pulled them were not in sight, but these wagons had not been burned. He heard Bowers say, "I hear 'Paches would rather eat a mule than even a horse."

In the shallow bed of the first wagon they found a woman with a child in her arms and next to her were two children clinging tightly to each other. No one was in the second wagon, but in the brush close by they found others. Most of them had been shot from close range.

Up beyond the second wagon they saw a woman lying in the middle of the trail. Her arms were spread with her fingers clawed into the loose sand. Flynn went to her quickly. Bowers watched him stoop over her then come up, shaking his head. Nita Esteban was not among the dead.

Flynn came back carrying the girl in his arms and placed her gently in the wagon. Bowers saw that she had been scalped; and his head turned to look at other things.

"They're changing their ways," Flynn said.

Bowers looked at him questioningly.

"Have you ever seen an Apache ambush?"

Bowers hesitated. "No."

"Well don't put this down as typical."

Bowers said, with embarrassment, "I'm sorry . . . about this."

"I knew Anastacio. The others I met only once."

Bowers looked up. "I thought you knew the girl well."

Flynn shook his head. "It only seems that way."

"They must have taken her."

"And perhaps others." Flynn was silent as his eyes went over the ambush—the burned wagons, the dead. "Mister, I'll tell you something. This isn't Apache."

"What other tribes are down here?"

"No other, to speak of."

"Well?"

"It isn't Indian."

"You're serious?"

"It was made to look Apache. And they did a poor job."

"I've heard that Apaches *are* known to kill."

"With bullets?"

"Why not?"

"Because they can't walk down to the corner and buy a box whenever they feel like it. Almost all the people were killed after they'd given up—*with bullets*—and that isn't Apache. On top of being hard to get, a bullet's too quick."

"I've been told not to try to figure them," Bowers said.

"That might apply to *why* they do something, but you can make sense out of how they do it." To Flynn the signs were plain. Many were plain because they were not there. A branch had been used to drag the footprints out of the sand. That wasn't Apache. The wasting of bullets. The scalping. Generally Apaches did not scalp. But they learned quickly. They have learned many things from the white man. They take the children of certain ages, to bring them up in the tribe because there was always a shortage of men. And there were many children here, dead, that an Apache would have taken.

They took Nita, and perhaps others, he thought. The taking of women is Apache—but it is hardly exclusively so.

And there were other things that he felt that told him this wasn't the work of Apaches. But it would take time to tell Bowers.

"Lieutenant," he said then. "You've got your work cut out for you. Get your tactical mind turning while I go up-trail."

Bowers began gathering the bodies, dragging them to a level sandy opening off the trail. His body was tense as he worked. He was aware of this, but he could not relax. He thought: They looked deader because their clothes are white—and because they were shot in the back of the head.

He looked up-trail, up the slight rise over which Flynn had disappeared, then to the high steep banks of the draw. A faint breeze moved through the narrowness; it brushed the pine branches lazily and carried the burned-wood smell of the wagons to the young lieutenant. The redheaded, sun-burned, slim-hipped lieutenant who had graduated fifteenth in his class from the Point and was granted his request for cavalry duty because of his high grades and because his father had been a brigadier general. His father was dead five months now. The smooth-faced, clean-featured, unsmiling lieutenant who now felt nervously alone with the dead and looked at the slopes, squinting up into the dark green, his eyes following the furrows of cream yellow that zigzagged up the crest; then, above the crest, the pale blue of the sky and the small specks that were circling lazily, gliding lower, waiting for the things that were alive to leave the things that were dead.

This was not cavalry. This was not duty his father, the brigadier, had described. A year at Whipple Barracks and he had not once worn his saber beyond the parade quadrangle. Four-day patrols hunting something that was seldom more than a flick of shadow against towering creviced walls of andesite. Patrols led by grizzled men in greasy buckskin who chewed tobacco and squinted into the sun and pointed and would seldom commit themselves. Cautious, light-sleeping men who moved slowly and looked part Indian. Every one of them did.

No, Flynn did not. That was one thing you could say for him. He

was different from most of the guides; but that was because he had
been an officer. One extreme, while the old one with the beard,
Madora, was another. That was too bad about Madora, but perhaps
he would recover. Flynn did not seem to view things in their proper
perspective. He had probably been a slovenly officer. Deneen had
said he would have to be watched, but he knows the country and
that's what qualified him for this mission. Mission! Dragging home
a filthy, runaway Indian who didn't know when he was well off. An
unreasoning savage, an animal who would do a thing like this. Flynn
is out of his mind thinking it was someone else. Get it over with.
That's all; just get it over with.

When Flynn returned he was leading two mules.

"Those must have gotten away," Bowers said.

"Or else they didn't want them."

"Not if they were Apaches," Bowers said.

Flynn nodded. "That's right. Not if they were Apaches."

They hitched the mules to one of the wagons, binding the cut
traces, and loaded the dead into the flat bed; they moved off slowly,
following the draw that twisted narrowly before beginning a curving gradual climb that once more brought them to high open country. By noon of the next day they would be in Soyopa. They would
bring the people home to be buried.

Later, as the trail descended, following the shoulder of the slope,
Flynn studied the ribbon of trail far below. It would be dark before
they reached the bottom, he knew. They both rode on the wagon
box, their horses tied to the tailgate.

First he saw the dust. It hung in the distance, filtered red by the
last of the sun. Whatever had raised it was out of sight now.

Then, below—small shapes moving out of shadow into strips of
faded sunlight—two riders, moving slowly, bringing up the rear of
whatever was up ahead. The riders seemed close, but they were not
within rifle range.

"Lieutenant, let me have your glasses."

There was something familiar about the rider on the left, even
at this distance. Flynn put the glasses to his eyes and brought the
riders close and there it was, as if looking into the future, seeing
Frank Rellis riding along with the Winchester across his lap.

FIVE

Standing in the doorway, Lieutenant Lamas Duro scratched his bare stomach and smacked his lips disgustedly. The taste of mescal was stale in his mouth. A feeling of faintness came on him, then passed just as suddenly and left him wide awake. He swallowed again as his tongue searched the inside of his mouth. And finally Lieutenant Duro decided that he did not feel too badly considering the mescal and the few hours seep. Perhaps the mescal had not worn off completely. That was it.

He looked at the corporal, who smiled at him showing bad teeth, and he thought: If he is as frightened as I know he is, why should he smile? Why should he curl his diseased mouth which makes me despise him all the more? He shrugged to himself as his hands felt the flatness of his pockets. Then he moved the few steps from the sleeping-room doorway into the front room, and drew a cigar from a packet on the cluttered desk.

The corporal, who was a small man, watched him with wide-open eyes and nervously fingered into his pocket for a match; but when he scratched it against the adobe wall it broke in his hand, unlighted.

Lieutenant Lamas Duro, chief of rurales, took a match from the desk, shaking his head faintly, and scratched it across the scarred surface of the desk. Holding it to the cigar, he looked at the corporal and the corporal's eyes shifted quickly from his own.

He moved his hand idly over the hair of his stomach and chest and the hint of an amused smile played about the corners of his sensitive mouth. The corporal, a cartridge bandoleer crossing his faded gray jacket, stood at a rigid but stoop-shouldered attention, his eyes focussed now somewhere beyond the lieutenant, seeing nothing.

"You have a good reason for hammering my door at this hour?" The lieutenant spoke calmly, yet his words seemed edged with a threat.

"Teniente, the execution," the corporal said with his eyes still on the wall beyond.

"What execution?"

"The Indian who was taken yesterday, Teniente. The one who accompanies the American."

"Oh . . ." There was disappointment in his voice.

The day before, an American had wandered into Soyopa with a glittering display of goods—kitchen utensils, cutlery, leather goods, hats, even suits of clothes. The boxes filled his Conestoga to such capacity that many of the pots and pans hung from racks along the sides. And with him was the Aravaipa Apache boy.

The boy was perhaps thirteen, certainly not older, but still an Apache. Lieutenant Duro's duty was to rid this territory of banditry, and this included Apaches. They were simple instructions with few qualifications. No exceptions. If the Apache was foolish enough to enter Soyopa, so be it. Let him make his grace with God. His scalp was worth one hundred pesos.

The trader was escorted far out of sight of the pueblo and sent on his way, after protests. The Territorial Commission would hear about this. But Lieutenant Duro could make no exceptions. It pained him that the villagers would have no opportunity to make purchases, but he must think of their protection and welfare first. He had told this to Hilario, the alcalde. Often the upholding of the law is unpleasant. One must often act against his heart.

"Why there are even things I wanted to buy," he told the alcalde, "but I could not." And while he said it, he thought of the law of compensation. The good are rewarded. He still had the Apache boy.

"Also, Teniente . . ."

"Yes!" He bellowed the word and glared, and now smiled only within himself, watching the frightened corporal. What excuses for men I have, he thought. What a magnificently stupid son of the great whore this one is.

"It is the alcalde. He desires to speak with you."

"What did you tell him?"

The corporal stammered, "I told him I would present his request."

"Have you presented it now?"

"Yes, Teniente."

"Then what keeps you here?" The corporal turned with an eagerness to be out, but Duro brought him up sharply. "Corporal!"

"Yes, Teniente ."

"Corporal . . ." He spoke softly moving back toward the sleeping room, still idly rubbing his stomach, and nodded into the room. ". . . when you go, take that cow of a woman with you . . ."

The west wall of the courtyard was bullet-riddled from one end to the other, though the pockmarks were scattered at the extreme ends. Toward the center they were more clustered and in some few places the bullet holes formed gouges—scarred patches from which the adobe had crumbled, leaving hollows.

And it appeared that the wearing away of the wall was a concern of Sergeant Santana's. He varied the position of his riflemen with a calculated deliberateness which argued reason, moving them along the wall with each execution.

At one time, perhaps the appearance of the wall had been his concern, but it had become lost in routine; so that now he moved his riflemen back and forth simply because he was able to do so. He knew that bullets would never probe completely through the thick adobe—not in his lifetime; nor did he care if they ever would.

This morning, Sergeant Santana measured the paces from the line of six riflemen to the wall. He counted twelve in time with his strides, then raised the quirt which was attached to his wrist and waved it in an indolent, sweeping motion toward the rear door of the adobe building. He lighted a cigar, leisurely, and when he looked at the door again they were bringing out the Apache boy.

Walking into the yard now, two men in front of him, two behind and one on each side, he seemed very small. Pathetically small. Santana shrugged and blew smoke out slowly. An Apache was an Apache. He had heard even the teniente say that.

They placed him close to the wall where Santana indicated with his quirt, and a rurale remained on either side of him holding his arms, though his hands were tied behind his back. The others moved away to join the line of men along the back of the house.

Santana's eyes followed them then shifted to the back door, expecting it to open, but it remained closed and again he turned to the Apache who was looking about with little show of concern.

His trousers were too large, bunched at the waist and tucked into moccasins rolled beneath his knees. His shirt was dirty, faded blue, and only his moccasins and headband indicated that he was Apache. The two rurales, in their dove-gray uniforms and crossed bandoleers, were a half-head taller than the boy who would move his chin from one shoulder to the other to look at them, studying the leather cartridge belts and the silver buttons on the soft gray jackets. And all about the courtyard were these men with their guns and so many bullets that they must have special belts to hang them over their shoulders. The boy was aware that he was going to die, but there were so many things of interest to see. He hoped they might delay it for a little while longer.

Two Americans came in through the gateway in the east wall. They strolled leisurely, smoking cigarettes, and as they approached Santana one of them called, "You better get closer, that boy's kinda small."

Both of them laughed, but Santana ignored them and looked toward the house's rear door.

They were gaunt-faced men, both needed a shave, and they wore their hats low on their foreheads against the morning sun. They stood with their thumbs in low-slung gun belts watching Santana and the rifleman. Now the one who had spoken before said, "Hey, Santy! We'll lay you even, three of the six don't hit the boy!"

They grinned, waiting for the sergeant to answer. Santana said with contempt, "Listen to the great killers of Indians."

One of the Americans said, "Well?" but Santana had turned his back to them.

Through the gateway now came a group of men dressed in white peon clothes and straw sombreros. There were six in all, but five of them walked close together, a few strides behind the older man with the bronzed face and white mustache. Hilario Esteban, the alcalde of Soyopa, walked with more dignity than the others who seemed purposely holding back, as if reluctant to enter the courtyard.

And at that moment, Lieutenant Duro came out of the back door of the adobe building. He was hatless, his jacket open, and a white scarf draped loosely about his neck. A cigar was in the corner of his mouth. Drawing on it, he glanced at Hilario Esteban who was only a few paces away. But when he saw the old man about to speak, he turned his head quickly toward Santana who was coming over from the rifle squad.

Lieutenant Duro then looked about the courtyard leisurely, from the riflemen to the Apache, then to the two Americans and the rest of his rurales in the narrow shade of the house. He ignored Hilario and his delegation of villagers. He was sick of their wide-eyed hesitancy, their halfhearted pleading on matters of no importance as they twisted the brims of their sombreros with nervous fingers. Hilario was different, he admitted to himself. But he was of the other extreme. Hilario had been with Juarez at Querétaro and had witnessed the execution of Maximilian and he retained strange ideas concerning rights. Hilario would have to be shown his place.

Santana stood before him now, idly slapping the quirt against the booted calf of his leg. Lieutenant Duro eyed the cigar in the sergeant's mouth. He took a long, sucking draw on his own then dropped it to the ground. He looked directly at the sergeant, exhaling the smoke slowly.

The sound of the quirt slapping against leather stopped.

Santana returned the lieutenant's stare, his cigar clenched in the corner of his mouth, but only for a moment. He dropped the cigar and ground it into the hard-packed sand.

Duro smiled faintly. "We are ready now?" he said.

Santana mumbled, "Ready," and turned to go back to the firing squad.

"Sergeant!"

Santana turned slowly.

"Listen. Ask your marksmen to aim lower than the head."

"Yes, Teniente."

"And take his hair neatly when it is over."

Santana nodded toward the two Americans who were watching with interest. "Perhaps one of those should do that."

Duro smiled again. "You would debate the matter?"

"I was only talking."

"Talk to your marksmen," Lieutenant Duro said.

As Santana moved off, Hilario Esteban approached Duro.

"May I ask a question, Señor Duro?"

The Lieutenant's eyes followed Santana. "What is it?"

"I would ask by what right you kill this Apache boy."

"You answer your own question. He is Apache."

"He is a peaceful Apache. The American merchant told us that he is Aravaipa, which have seldom been at war, and when they were, it was long ago. Besides, he is only a boy."

Duro looked at him with his faint smile. "Boys grow into men. Let's call these bullets the ounces of prevention."

"Señor Duro, this American will go back and tell his government . . ."

"What, that we have shot an Apache?"

Hilario shook his head and the lines of age in his face seemed
more deeply etched. "Señor Duro, this one is at peace. He assists
in the selling of the merchant's wares and entertains no thoughts
common to the Apache. The American will tell his government
what we have done and there will be ill feeling."

"Ill feeing! Old man, stop . . ."

"Señor, I am responsible for the welfare of travelers who visit
Soyopa as well as our own people. I have a trust . . ."

"Do you really believe that?" Duro looked at the old man closely.

"With all certainty."

"You believe your office to be one of honor, which involves the
bearing of grave responsibilities?"

"Señor Duro." Hilario's tone lost respect. "We are discussing
the life of a boy. One who has done nothing hostile to any of us!"

"You actually believe the alcalde resides in a seat of honor?"
The lieutenant's voice remained calm.

"Señor Duro . . ."

The lieutenant interrupted him. "Corporal!" And as the corporal hurried toward him, he said, "Since your office is of such mag-
nitude, perhaps you should remain close to it. Sit at your desk,
Alcalde, in your seat of honor, and contemplate your grave responsibilities." And then to the corporal, "Take your men and escort our alcalde to his office . . . and Corporal . . . if he puts his
head out of the door . . . shoot him."

He waited until they had taken Hilario out of the courtyard—a
rurale on each arm and others behind with their rifles at ready—
the five of the peon delegation hurrying out ahead of them. Then
he turned back to the firing squad. Santana was looking toward the
gateway.

"Sergeant!" the lieutenant called, just loud enough to be heard.
"If you please . . ." And he thought to himself: Lamas, you are an
animal. But his mind shrugged it off, because it was a long way to
Mexico City, and now he watched intently as the squad raised their
rifles.

The two rurales moved away from the Apache boy. His eyes followed one of them as the dove-gray uniform moved off toward the
house. The bullets go even all the way down the back! He heard a
command in Spanish. One word. And there are so many of them;

each man has two belts, and who knows, there might even be more stored in that great jacale. Another Spanish word broke the sudden stillness of the courtyard. Would it not be fine to have a belt with so many bullets. He heard the last command clearly . . . "Fire!"

Hilario Esteban, crossing the square, passing the slender obelisk of stone, heard the rifle fire. A short roll, a sharp, high-pitched echo that carried away to nothing. His shoulders hunched as if by reflex, then relaxed, and he sighed. A rifle barrel jabbed against his spine and only then did he realize that he had hesitated.

SIX

Lieutenant Duro strolled through the east gate and circled the two-story building which served as his headquarters. It had been someone's home when he arrived in Soyopa, but he'd forgotten whose now. On the lower floor he kept supplies—equipment, ammunition, spare rifles, all those things needed by his rurales. At the front, a stairway at each end of the ramada climbed to the floor above. This he had chosen for his living quarters. The two rooms were drab—bare, colorless adobe and board flooring that squeaked with each step. The quarters reminded Duro of the cell of a penitent monk; but in Soyopa what could one expect.

Two of his men stood in the shade of the ramada, guarding the possessions of the frontier police. They nodded as he rounded the building and straightened slightly, though their backs remained comfortably against the wall.

Duro shook his head wearily. What excuse for men, he thought. For months he had drilled, cursed and punished them into being soldiers; but it had been to no avail and now Lieutenant Duro was past caring. What did it really matter?

Mexico City was in another world, a hazy world that was becoming increasingly more difficult to conjure in his mind. He would picture himself as he had been at the Academy—and the bailes and the young girls who could not keep their eyes from the uniforms. But that had been during the short presidency of Don Sebastian Lerdo de Tejada. A few years seemed so long ago.

It was said often that the son of Don Agostino Duro, who was a personal friend of Lerdo Tejada, would rise from the Cadet Corps like a comet to a glorious career in the Army. When he received his lieutenancy, at the head of his class, Lamas Duro appeared well on the way. Unfortunately, Porfirio Diaz's political coup followed three months later.

Many of the Lerdistas disappeared, including Don Agostino Duro. His son, however, was a political enemy by blood, not by avocation; so Lamas disappeared merely from the capitol. His military training was something which could be utilized in Porfirio Diaz's new creation—the Rurales. The Frontier Police. And Soyopa was far enough from Mexico City to guard against Lamas Duro's blood interfering with his politics.

He gazed about the square now, motionless in the sunlight. Wind-scarred adobe, squat dwellings, most of them without ramadas, old looking beyond their years. The church was directly across from his headquarters—it rose sand-colored, blending with the surrounding buildings which pushed close to it, a wide door, but a belfry that was too low for the width of the building and it only vaguely resembled a church. Santo Tomás de Aquín.

Past the empty fountain with its solitary stone obelisk, Duro could see down a side street to the house of Hilario Esteban, and the two rurales lounging in the doorway. God in Heaven, how can I be given such men! He turned disgustedly then and climbed the stairs to the upstairs veranda. Before going inside, he looked out over the square again. But nothing had changed.

Curt Lazair remained in the lieutenant's chair as Duro entered from the veranda. He lounged comfortably with a boot hooked on the desk corner next to his hat and he eyed Duro curiously. The rurale lieutenant had not seen him and was still deep in thought as he closed the door; and now Lazair smiled faintly.

"It's a long way to Mexico City."

Duro was startled. He turned from the door quickly and looked at the man with astonishment.

"Well, it's no farther than Anton Chico, New Mexico," Lazair went on. "Only Anton Chico ain't a hell of a lot better than Soyopa. It's all in how you look at things."

Duro nodded. "Yes, it's all in how you look at it." His head indicated the outside. "And I cannot say that I see very much out there."

Lazair smiled again—a smile which said he believed in little and trusted in even less. He shrugged now and said, "Money."

There was little sense in talking about it. Duro had discovered that the least said to this man, the better. Nothing seemed important to him. And always he was relaxed, as if to catch you unaware and then make fun of something which should be spoken of with sincerity. He wants to make you mad, Duro thought. Tell him to go to hell. But instead, he said, quietly, "You need a shave."

"I been out working for you." Lazair passed the palm of his hand over dark, neatly combed hair. "But I slicked my hair down when I found out I had to visit the lieutenant," he said mockingly. He was a man close to forty, almost handsome, crudely handsome, and the glistening hair contrasted oddly with the beard stubble on his face. He wore soft leather pants tucked into his boots; pistols on both sides of his low-slung cartridge belt, and he slipped one of the pair up and down in the holster idly as he spoke.

His other hand dropped from the arm of the chair now and he lifted a canvas bag and swung it onto the table.

"I brought you something."

Duro made no move toward the desk, though his eyes fell on the bag. "How many women did you kill this time?"

The words had no visible effect on Lazair. "Count 'em and see."

"I'll take your word for the number. I trust though you've taken the ribbons from the hair," Duro said.

Lazair nodded. "Sure we did. Just like you wiped that little boy's nose before you shot him a while ago."

"Were you there?"

"Two of my men were. I just come in."

"You're quickly informed."

Lazair smiled. "You got to get up a hell of a lot earlier than you do."

"How many did you take?" Duro said irritably. "I don't have all day."

"Open it up and find out."

"I said I'd take your word!"

Lazair came off the chair then and pulled the sack toward him. As he untied the rawhide string he said, "You're awful goddamn squeamish about something you're making money out of."

Duro said nothing as Lazair opened the bag and held it upside-down. The scalps came out of the bag as one—a hairy mass, glistening black and matted with dried blood. Duro frowned as Lazair ran his hand through the pile, separating the scalps.

He said, "When did you take them?"

Lazair glanced at him as he lined the scalps along the edge of the desk. "What difference does it make?"

"They smell."

Lazair laughed out. "Man, these used to be the tops of heads. What do you expect!"

"Put them back. I said I'd take your word for the number!"

But Lazair would not be hurried. "Even salted 'em down." He looked up at the lieutenant then and winked. "After I greased 'em good so they'd be sure and look Indian."

Duro studied the bounty hunter silently. Within him he could feel the hatred for this man. It caused a heat over his face. But he was aware of his conscience ever more than the hate, and he said very simply, "You are the filthiest man I have known."

"But you can't get really mad, can you?" Lazair said. "Not without hurting yourself. Daylight's a bad time of the day. It shows everything plain and if you happen to look in a mirror, you even see yourself." Lazair smiled again. "But there's always night . . . and your mescal bottle. . . . Just remember one thing, soldier boy, I don't need you as bad as you think I do. If I can buy you, then there's some other goddam broken-down soldier who'll act just as dumb for money you don't have to work for."

"Maybe you had better look for this other 'broken-down soldier'!" Duro flared.

Lazair shook his head, smilingly. "I don't have to. I know you too well. You're stuck here and you don't have a choice. And every year you see government pesos coming in for the scalp bounties. Easy money to take, it looks like, only you have to balance what goes out with a scalp coming in. But when somebody comes along and offers you money in return for taking *all* scalps—no questions—then you're just doing your job. All you got to do is add and subtract . . . and you know how to do that."

Duro said, "Add scalps that are not always Apache."

"It's up to you." Lazair shrugged. "If you want to quit vouching for 'em it's up to you. Only I don't think you can. You get back ten pesos for every hundred going out. That's a lot of mescal when all you got to do is add up when the government man comes around. He isn't going to feel 'em for texture. So don't give me any goddamn talk about keeping your hands clean, because they're just as dirty as mine. Maybe dirtier," Lazair said evenly, " 'cause I don't particularly like Mexicans anyway."

"Get out!" Duro screamed.

Lazair lifted his hat from the desk. "I wouldn't want to be in your skin. You don't know who to be mad at, do you?" He went to the door, then hesitated after he had opened it. "I know there's eight hundred pesos' worth there, so let's not go juggling the books. We'll settle after you've cooled off."

Duro waited until he heard Lazair descending the stairs. He went to the desk quickly then and began sweeping the scalps into the sack that he held open below the desk edge. As he did this, he did not look down and he brushed his hand stiffly, with the fingers held tightly together so that he would not feel their texture. Yet a picture formed in his mind. A picture with the shock of a knife thrust to the stomach . . . even though it was only an almost indiscernible Mexican woman, no one he recognized, but with flowing black hair . . .

Hilario Esteban had moved the stool close to the window so that he could look out into the street. The street seemed so deserted this morning. At first he thought it strange, then one of the rurales appeared near the window and it was not strange. There was little for these frontier soldiers to do, most of them stationed far from their own villages, and often their minds would be suddenly activated by the sight of a villager passing along the street.

And as if they were a breed apart and all others were enemies, they would do unnatural things. Hilario had seen them shoot at the heels of old women to cause them to run. It was a sight to see an old woman running, then fall—they always fell—and scramble and roll in the dust shrieking. And they would think of other things to while away the hours. Sometimes they were as children. Like the morning Hilario had awakened to find the obscene word painted on the front of his house. Four red letters reaching higher than a man's head. It had taken a full day's labor to scrape the paint from the adobe, and they had stood around to laugh as the alcalde performed such work.

He leaned out of the window now and looked to the side. The two pairs of legs extended from his door stoop. The front of the brim of a sombrero showed also, but that was all he could see. Maybe they were asleep now, he thought. "God, make them sleep well and keep thoughts from their heads," he whispered.

They would not let him approach the door and earlier they had threatened him with the butts of their rifles when he wanted to open it. The house was becoming an oven and it was not good to remain in it with the door closed. Thankfully, he had the window—

not all houses had a window—but he was used to having the door open. Perhaps it is better that it does remain closed, he thought. Else they might be tempted to enter and take something. Something of Nita's. Before, one of them had asked him where Nita was, then laughed and said something obscene. "God, why do you make such as these?" And then he thought: But if there were no evil men, then how could you tell the good? He pictured his wife then, for a reason he did not know, and he was glad that she was not here to witness his being degraded. Though she would understand. Maybe she sees anyway; but she is probably talking to the saints. He thought then of Francis of Assisi because he had been a very humble man, and he wondered what St. Francis would have done had he lived in Soyopa.

St. Francis would have pleaded for the life of the Apache boy. I know that, Hilario Esteban thought. But what can be done with a man like Lamas Duro, who is in such agony with his fate that he directs his anger to those beneath him?

In the beginning, Hilario had prayed for Duro's soul. He had felt honest sorrow for him. Now his prayers were less frequent. It was easy to despise Duro, but hard not to be afraid of him. Still, he opposed Duro because his conscience directed him to. A man cannot disobey his conscience. Perhaps when Anastacio returns things will be better. It is very lonely here without Nita, he thought.

Across the narrow street, on the wall that joined Anastacio's house, a faded poster advertised a bullfight in Hermosillo. Anastacio loved the Corrida, and had posted the sheet there more than a month ago. On their way to Willcox for a reunion, he had planned to stop in Hermosillo and take the entire family to the Corrida.

From the window, Hilario read the poster again. How many times have I read that? he thought. I can see it in my mind clearly. Even that which I cannot read now. The lower part is torn, but it said at one time: *Sombra*—3 *pesos* . . . *Sol*— 1 *peso. Boletos de venta en todas partes.*

He wondered then if Anastacio had taken enough money. How much . . . three pesos times eighteen . . . so that the family could reach the Corrida from the shade. He went into the rear room then to lie down. There was nothing more to see on the street.

One of the rurales awakened at the sound of the horses, but the other remained asleep, propped against the door. He opened his eyes to see the two Americans astride the horses, looking down at him and he nudged his companion awake as he heard one of the Americans ask, "This is the house of the alcalde, isn't it?"

The rurale nodded, but did not rise.

Flynn swung down then and approached the door. "What are you, the guard of honor?"

The rurale grinned at his companion and then toward Flynn. "More the guard of dishonor," he said.

"Where is the alcalde?"

"Within."

"Would you move, so I can knock on the door?"

"No one enters," the rurale said, rising. He held his rifle diagonally across his chest. His companion rose then. "Nor does the alcalde leave."

Flynn felt a sudden anger, but he waited until it passed. "Why?" he said.

"Because the teniente orders it!" the rurale said angrily.

"What did the alcalde do?"

The rurale smiled lazily at Flynn. "You ask many questions." He glanced at his companion who moved up next to him. "He asks many questions, doesn't he?" Then to Flynn he said, "Are you another of the great hunters of Apaches? Soyopa is honored." He bowed mockingly. His companion grinned, but he moved uneasily.

Flynn studied the two rurales. Crossed bandoleers over the gray uniforms that were worn slovenly. Shirts open at the throat and wide-brimmed sombreros off their foreheads. The one stood with his hip cocked and fingered his rifle eagerly. The other was not so sure of himself; it was apparent.

"I'm going to ask you one more question," Flynn said. He unbuttoned his coat and opened it enough to show the butt of his pistol. "Are you going to get out of the way?"

For a moment the rurale only stared. Then his elbow touched his companion's arm. "Perhaps this is something for the teniente. Bring him!" He glanced after his companion as he moved off hurriedly, then back to Flynn. "Man," he said, "your pistol is not as large as you think it is."

Hilario Esteban saw the rurale pass the window, beginning to run. He looked out now, frowning, as he heard someone speak, then his entire face wrinkled into a smile.

"Señor Flín!"

The rurale was startled. He brought the rifle around abruptly.

Flynn's head turned, but there was another movement close to his chest. And abruptly the rurale's eyes widened and his face muscles went slack. First he felt the barrel press into his side, then the click of the hammer.

Close to his ear, Flynn said, "You're all through, soldier. Drop the rifle and go sit down."

Hilario disappeared from the window, but the door opened almost immediately and he was standing before them. "David!" His face beaming. "What a day this is! When did you arrive?" He saw the pistol then and the smile left his face.

"It's all right, Hilario," Flynn said. "He didn't know we were friends." He glanced at Bowers who was holding their horses. "Hilario Esteban, this is Lieutenant Bowers."

Bowers said something in a low voice and he looked at Hilario embarrassedly.

Flynn looked at Bowers curiously. Then it came to him. You forgot! he thought. How in hell could you forget! As they rode in he had been ready. Preparing himself all morning as he listened to the creaking of the wagon wheels. Now he felt suddenly self-conscious, as if Hilario was already reading it in his face.

He heard Bowers say quietly, "Why don't you two go inside and talk things over."

Flynn wanted to tell him now, quickly, with Bowers there, but the presence of the rurale bothered him oddly. "Maybe we'd better," he said.

Hilario stepped back to let Flynn enter first, his gaze following the scout with a frowning, puzzled expression. Bowers had not moved his position, but now he lifted his pistol and turned it on the rurale as the two men passed into the room.

Once, Flynn rode into Fort Thomas with four men straggling behind him. Four returning out of twelve . . . and one of the eight dead was the patrol officer; so Flynn made the report. "Major"—it had not been Deneen then—"there are eight men back there in a draw, being hacked to pieces right now, because a wet-nosed lieutenant wanted to see how fast he could make a brevet." He told it bluntly because he was angry. The major knew he was sorry—sorry for the men, and sorry because the lieutenant wasn't there to learn a lesson. And after that, young officers fresh from the Point listened to him before entering quiet, peaceful-appearing draws. The major saw to that.

Another time he listened to an officer tell a woman that her husband did not return with the patrol. He listened to the man hesitate and falter and say "I'm sorry . . ." more than a dozen times. But none of the I'm-sorrys did any good. The woman went on crying with her shoulders quivering and her mouth twisted pathetically. The two children in the next room cried because they had never heard their mother do this before.

Another time. Another soldier's wife. She waited until they left before breaking down. While he and the major were there, she cried only within, but only a little, because she was still telling herself that it could not be true.

Flynn started at the beginning, telling Hilario about missing the family in Contention. He told him everything, each detail, speaking the words quietly without hesitating. And he watched Hilario's face change—from a smile at first to a dumb stare, an expression that meant nothing. He listed those they had brought back in the wagon, painfully aware of what his words were doing to the old man; but there was no other way. He told him that it had been Apaches— because there was no sense in going into the other now—and there was a chance Nita was still alive. He didn't say maybe it would be better if she were dead. And finally, when he had finished, he said the inevitable, "I'm sorry"—for what it was worth. He thought it might be easier to tell a man, but it was the same.

Hilario did not cry. He sat staring with nothing in his eyes, telling himself that it was not true. Picturing them alive, because he didn't know how to picture them dead.

Flynn stood near the window, waiting for the old man to speak. He wanted to say again that he was sorry and he tried to think of other ways to say it; but all the words were without substance, and probably the old man would not even hear them. He looked across to the poster which advertised the bullfight in Hermosillo.

PLAZA DE TOROS
HERMOSILLO
Mañana a las 4

Tres Grandes Toreros en Competencia

VIRAMONTES (Español)
vs.
Juan Toyas y Sinaloa (Mexicanos)

Seis Hermosos Toros
De la Famosa Ganadería de don Feliz Montoya
Precios de Entrada

From there down, the poster was torn from the wall.

Flynn felt the old man next to him then.

"The part that is not there," the old man said, "tells that it would cost three pesos to sit in the shade and one peso to sit on the side of the sun."

"I was looking at it . . ."

"I hope they were able to sit in the shade." He considered this silently. Then he said, "Where are they now?"

"We left the wagon back of the church, by the graves. There's a boy watching it." Flynn hesitated. He continued in Spanish, softly, "I think we should bury them soon, Hilario."

Hilario nodded, dazedly. "Yes. I will get the priest on the way."

"Flynn!"

He went to the door quickly. Bowers glanced at him, then beckoned up the street where it led into the square. "You better get out of here!"

"Are they coming?"

"The whole Mexican Army!"

SEVEN

A dozen horsemen swung onto the square from the street siding Duro's headquarters and crossed the open area, separating at the four-sided stone shaft, bunching again to enter the narrow street with a cloud of dust billowing after them.

They swung down, all of them except Sergeant Santana, and spaced out in a ragged line along the front of the house, eager for something to happen. Just the two Americans could not offer much resistance.

From the saddle, Santana glared at the rurale who had been on guard. "Pick up your rifle!"

"I was overpowered . . ."

"Pick up your rifle!"

Flynn felt the anger return, thinking of Hilario, and now these grinning animals to make a difficult situation worse. And even though he knew they couldn't be aware of Hilario's sorrow, still their presence grated against his nerves and polite explanation wouldn't do. The rifle was in the road a few feet from the door stoop. Flynn moved to it now and placed his boot on the barrel before the rurale could reach it.

"You can order your man wherever you like," he said to Santana, "but if he stays here he doesn't need the rifle."

"Your position is not the best for suggesting orders," Santana said, half-smiling. "What is this supposed to be, an exhibition of Señor Lazair's influence? If it is, go and tell him that I am not the teniente. I order my men with my own mind."

Flynn looked at him curiously. "I don't know this Lazair," he said.

"Come now, why else would you be here? The teniente proves to the alcalde that he is governing body of Soyopa, then the hunter of Indians must prove that his power overbears the office of the teniente."

"Your words are nothing."

"Tell your leader," Santana said, "and he will explain it to you."

"Soldier, I'm not going to stand here and argue with you. If you want to order your men, order them some place else."

Santana moved his sombrero back from his forehead and looked at Flynn with amazement. "God in Heaven—how this one talks!"

From the doorway where he had been standing, Hilario moved to Flynn's side. "Señor Santana, these men do not belong to Lazair. This one I have known before, and the other is his good friend. They have come to see me."

"Many days on horseback just to see the poor alcalde of Soyopa?"

"They have come to tell me of the death of my family," Hilario said quietly.

Santana hesitated. "Your family?"

"They were killed by the Apaches as they returned home." Hilario's lips moved stiffly as he spoke the words and tried to picture what had taken place. He added, "These friends have brought them home to be buried."

"Your entire family—brothers, sisters, children?"

"I have not yet made a count."

Santana was silent for a long moment. Finally he shrugged—what can one do?—and said wearily, "Tend to your dead, old man."

He guided his horse to a turn and his rurales swung into their saddles on the signal. Let the old man alone, he thought. Along with his dead. They will guard him for the time. He pressed his heels into the horse's sides and looked up toward the square, then reined in abruptly. Lieutenant Duro was entering the street.

He approached slowly, holding his mount to a walk, and passed through the rurales, making them pull their horses out of the way. He dismounted with the same slow deliberateness.

"Leaving?" he said to Santana.

"There is nothing to be done here."

"Am I the last to know when my orders are disobeyed?"

Santana dismounted reluctantly. "I did not wish to disturb you."

"From what!"

"Your own affairs."

"Perhaps I should judge that." He looked at Flynn and then to Bowers. "What do you want here!"

"We've already done all the explaining we're going to do," Flynn said shortly.

"Hilario Esteban's family has been killed by the Apaches," Santana said bluntly. "These came to tell him of it."

"Oh. . . ." Duro's expression eased. Instinctively he said, "May I express my deep sympathy." To Flynn he said, "Did it occur near here?"

"Yesterday afternoon. About ten hours ride in the wagon."

"Oh. . . . You were on your way to Soyopa?" And when Flynn nodded, Duro said, "Perhaps on business?"

Flynn said, "You might say that." The lieutenant irritated him strangely. All of a sudden he was too friendly.

"We hope your stay in Soyopa will be a pleasant one," Lieutenant Duro said. He had already forgotten about the alcalde's family. Here was something to wonder about. Two more bounty hunters? Perhaps. And perhaps not. "We are at your service, señor . . . ?"

"Flynn. My friend's name is Bowers."

"It is a pleasure," Duro said, bowing slightly. "Perhaps you would find the time to dine with me later in the day."

Flynn glanced at Hilario. "Perhaps another time."

"Certainly . . . another time. And Hilario, if there is anything my men can do to assist you . . ."

The old man looked at the lieutenant with disbelief.

The man at the corner flicked his cigarette into the street and turned away, walking back down the row of adobe building fronts to the mescal shop. It was in the middle of the block on this, the west side of the square. A sign above the door said, Las Quince Letras—red lettering crudely done and fading as the adobe sand wore away. The man opened the screen door and put his head inside.

"Warren!"

He heard the horses behind him then and let the door swing closed and turned to see the rurales crossing the square at a trot. He watched Duro dismount in front of his headquarters and climb the stairs as his rurales passed down the side street. They would be returning to their garrison of tents on the south side of the village. Duro kept only two men with him on guard duty.

The one called Warren came out of the mescal shop adjusting his hat, squinting in the direction the rurales had gone. "They going home?"

The two men were the Americans who had witnessed the execution that morning. Now the one who had been on the corner, whose name was Lew Embree, said, "They let them go. They're not even guarding the old man any more."

"Who do you suppose they are?"

"I don't know," Lew said.

"Maybe we ought to tell Lazair," Warren said.

They looked up as Flynn and Bowers and Hilario Esteban came out of the street and crossed to the church, following the church yard back to the house in which the priest lived. The cemetery was just beyond. The two men watched them pass out of sight.

Warren said, "All of a sudden the old man can go where he wants." He tried to understand this. "Maybe Duro feels sorry for him."

"Or else he's tiptoeing till he finds out what's going on," Lew Embree said. "That younger one's got army written all over him, but that doesn't mean anything. He might of just gotten out." He shrugged. "We'll let Lazair figure it out."

They rode out of Soyopa by the south road, passing the rurales' camp area, and went on in the same direction for almost three miles before beginning a gradual swing to the east. Hours later, toward evening, they were traveling northeast and now began a winding, gradual climb into timber, scrub oak at first then cedar and sycamores and finally, when they were up high, pines. They crossed a meadow of coarse sabaneta grass and as they approached the heights on the west side, the sun barely showed over the rim-rock.

The base of the slanting rock wall was in deep shadow, and passing into the dimness, Warren said, looking up overhead, "Somebody must be asleep."

They heard the *click* close above them, sharp in the stillness— the lever action of a carbine. "Stand there!"

Lew looked up, but could not see the guard. "Who's that, Wesley?" He called out, "Wes, it's me and Warren!"

The voice answered, "What're you sneaking up for?—sing out, or you're liable to get shot!"

"Go to hell. . . ."

They passed on, entering a defile that climbed narrowly before opening again on a pocket in the rocks, walled on all sides. Four tents formed a semicircle behind a cook fire. Off to the left another fire glowed in the dusk, a smaller one, in front of a tarpaulin rigged over the entrance to a cave. The cave was Curt Lazair's. His fourteen men shared the tents.

Lew Embree handed his reins to Warren who led their horses off to where the others were picketed along the far right wall. He nodded to the men sitting around the cook fire. They looked up from tin plates, some mumbling hello, and watched him make his way over to the cave, wondering what had brought him from the pueblo, and as he reached the tarpaulin awning, Curt Lazair appeared in the entrance.

"What are you doing back?"

"Somebody hauled in a load of dead Mexicans right after you left," Lew said.

"I didn't think they'd find 'em so quick." Lazair eased into a camp chair, sucking his teeth, and propped his feet on a saddle in front of the chair. "You eaten yet?"

"No."

Lazair nodded back toward the cave entrance. "That girl ain't a bad cook . . . At least she's good for something."

"The people who found 'em weren't from Soyopa."

Lazair looked up. "Who were they?"

"A couple of Americans."

"Prospectors?"

Lew shrugged. "That's the question nobody knows."

"Well, why didn't you stay to find out?"

"I figured you'd want to know right away."

"You could've left Warren there."

"Between the mescal and that saloon whore he'd find out a hell of a lot."

"What'd they look like?"

"Like anybody else." Lew shrugged. "They weren't carrying signs."

"What!"

Lew reconsidered. "One of them looked army."

"A lot of people were in the army. What does that look like?"

"He had an army pistol holster on him . . ."

"You're about as much good as Warren."

"What did you want me to do, go up and ask 'em for their cards?"

"There're enough rum-bum rurales you could have asked!"

"How would they know?"

"Because they live in Soyopa and talk to people . . . those two aren't bringing the bodies into Soyopa 'cause they don't know any-body here! Why didn't they haul them to Rueda or Alaejos? They're just as close."

"Oh. . . ."

"Oh," Lazair mimicked him. He rolled a cigarette then, idly, considering what this could mean.

Lew said, "Maybe we shouldn't of hit that wagon string. There were too many of 'em . . . all from Soyopa."

Lazair said nothing.

"Now," Lew went on, "people right in the village have got kin and close friends to pray over and wonder about . . . and maybe they'll wonder so long they'll figure something out."

"How much they hate the Apaches," Lazair said. "That's all the figuring they'll do."

"I don't like it."

"I didn't ask you to like it! You don't get paid for your smiles!"

"Maybe those two Americans'll figure out something . . ."

"Goddamn it shut up, will you! I can't think with you crying in my ear!"

Two Americans suddenly appear with the bodies. They must have had a reason for coming down here. They stumble onto the ambush and know exactly where to cart the bodies; they knew they were from Soyopa, Lazair thought. Hell, if they knew where they were from, then they knew who they were! Why? Maybe one of the Mexicans had something on him that told what his village was. What are you getting so excited about? Probably a couple of saddle tramps looking for greener grass. Just mustered out of the Army. Maybe they heard about the scalp bounty and thought it was worth a try. You son of a bitch, you've got fourteen men with you and you worry about two. But all of a sudden people were starting to pop out of nowhere. Like the man they ran into just before the ambush *who wanted to join* the band. Well, the ambush was his test. He came out all right. If he had backed down, he'd have been left with the dead. Sure, he turned out all right. He thought now: And maybe he saw them. He must have come down the same way.

He called over to the cook fire, "Frank!"

The man was a shadowy figure crossing the camp area, taking his time until finally he appeared out of the dimness in front of the fire at the edge of the tarp awning. Frank Rellis had changed little. Dirtier, that was all.

"What?"

"When you were coming down from Contention, did you see anybody?"

"Did I see anybody?"

"Two Americans."

"What the hell kind of a question is that?" Rellis said.

Lazair swung on Lew irritably. "What did they look like!"

"One was a little taller than medium size, thin in the hips and put his boots down hard like a horse soldier. A young fella with red hair. The other one had a mustache, light-colored. He was stringier than the other fella and seemed taller. He looked peaceful enough, but his coat bulged a little like he had a six-gun under it."

Rellis said instantly, "A soldier mustache?"

Lew said, "Yeah, and the other one had an army holster on his side."

"Where are they?"

Lazair looked at Rellis curiously. "You know them?"

"Where are they?"

"Soyopa. They found those dead Mexicans and brought 'em in," Lazair said watching him closely. "I asked you if you knew them."

"I don't know. Maybe I do. One of them sounds like an old friend. Maybe I ought to go to Soyopa and find out for sure." He walked away before Lazair could ask him anything else.

Lazair watched him go back to the cook fire. The hell with it, he thought. Getting anything out of that son of a bitch is like pulling teeth. If it was something to worry about he would have said something. He looked at Lew Embree. "You want a drink?"

"Fine."

Lazair half turned and called behind him, "Honey!" There was no answer and he winked at Lew. "She's bashful."

Lew grinned, rubbing the back of his hand across his mouth. "How is she?"

"I can't even get her to smile."

"They don't have to smile."

"Honey!" Lazair called again. "Bring us out a bottle of something!"

Nita Esteban appeared in the cave opening, in half-shadow, the light of the fire barely reaching her. She held the ends of a red scarf that was about her shoulders tightly in front of her. Her features were small, delicate against the soft blackness of her hair. Her skin was pale in the light of the fire and her eyes were in shadow.

Lazair glanced at her and grinned. "A bottle of mescal, honey."

She disappeared and returned in a moment with the bottle in her hand. She approached Lazair reluctantly, handed the bottle to him and turned quickly, but as she did this he reached for her. She felt his hand on her back and dodged out of reach, twisting her body away from him. But his fingers tightened on the scarf and pulled it from her shoulders as she slipped away.

Lew grinned at his chief. "That's a step toward it."

"She likes to play." Lazair felt the material between his fingers and then tore it down the middle.

Lew said, "Maybe she's upset after seeing what you did to her kin."

Lazair folded a part of the scarf lengthwise, then tied it around his neck, sticking the ends into his shirt. "Some girls are funny that way," he said.

EIGHT

"**O** God, by whose mercy the souls of the faithful find rest, vouchsafe to bless this grave, and appoint Thy holy angel to guard it; and release the souls of all those whose bodies are buried here from every bond of sin, that in Thee they may rejoice with Thy saints forever. Through Christ our Lord."

The Franciscan made the sign of the cross in the air and sprinkled the grave with holy water.

Flynn waited patiently, though within him there was an impatience, while the priest finished his prayer over the last grave. He was anxious to be going, but the Franciscan had moved slowly from grave to grave, reciting the burial prayers reverently, a liturgy unaffected by time. There was no need to hurry.

Flynn's restlessness was not out of irreverence. He whispered his prayers with the priest, but his mind kept wandering to the news the vaquero had brought.

As they were lowering the bodies into the freshly dug graves, the vaquero had ridden in, killing his mount with the urgency of his news. He had seen Apaches! Tending his herd, a dozen miles from Soyopa, he had entered a draw after a stray—and there at the other end, trailing down from high country, were the Apaches. He had flown before they were able to see him, he told. But he had looked back once, and coming out of the draw they had traveled southeast in the direction of the deserted village of Valladolid. How many? Perhaps six or seven.

"Then it is not a raiding party," a man had said.

"Who knows the way of the Apache," the vaquero answered. He perspired, and the wide eyes told that he was still frightened.

"What about your cows?"

"My cows must protect themselves."

Flynn had listened with interest. Perhaps this was the opportunity. They could scour the hills for months without finding an Apache. Now, the Apaches had shown themselves. Scout them, he thought. Perhaps they would lead to Soldado Viejo, or, he could even be one of the six. He asked the vaquero to take them back to where he had seen the Apaches, but the vaquero steadfastly refused. Well, they could go alone.

"We might wait a long time for a trail as fresh as this one," he told Bowers.

Bowers shrugged. "Why not? That's why we're here."

A few of the villagers who had heard this looked at the Americans curiously.

They returned to the alcalde's house for their horses, then passed the cemetery again as they left Soyopa by the trail north. Hilario was still standing by the graves. He would move to the foot of a grave, recite the "Hail Mary" and drop a small stone, then move to the next. Later, the villagers would come and do this and after that any traveler entering Soyopa who knew a prayer for the dead would drop a stone.

The vaquero had told them approximately where his small herd had been grazing. Flynn remembered vaguely this country just to the north and the small village of Valladolid, half the size of Soyopa, a lonely outpost for vaqueros and their families. He had passed through it returning home. But now, he was told, Valladolid was only adobe—as lifeless as the mud it was made from. Soldado had struck the vaqueros too often and finally they had left it for larger villages—Soyopa, Rueda and others to the south; though some few herds were still grazed up there in the wild grama and toboso grass.

They rode due north through the afternoon, Flynn a few yards ahead of Bowers. Bowers would make the decisions; it was his assignment. But Flynn would show the way; it was his business.

They found the herd without difficulty, though the cattle were scattered, perhaps thirty head grazing from one end of the meadow to the other. There could be others in the hills now, hidden by the scrub trees, and up the draw which they recognized from the vaquero's description. Flynn did not doubt that the Apaches had driven off some, but until later he was not sure how many.

On the east edge of the meadow they stopped to eat—beef and tortillas which Hilario had told them to take from his house; then followed after the unshod horse tracks as they left the meadow.

At first, Flynn would step down from the saddle often to examine the prints more closely. But in less than a quarter of a mile he was sure and he said to Bowers, "The cowboy wasn't exaggerating. There are six of them. They're driving three cows." Farther on there were horse droppings in the trail. Flynn dismounted again. "They're not expecting anybody to be following."

Bowers said, "How far ahead?"

"About four hours." His eyes swung up to the high country that was before them. "They should be farther than that."

Bowers said, "They're taking their time. Maybe they've forgotten what it's like to be chased."

"What about Lazair?"

Bowers looked at him quickly, curiously, "That rurale mentioned him."

Flynn nodded. "So did Deneen. The rurale thought we worked for him, and he said something about the hunter of Indians proving to the lieutenant who was boss."

Bowers said, "Hunter of Indians."

"Bounty hunters," Flynn said.

They began climbing shortly after. The ground was high on both sides and the draw rose gradually toward thick scrub brush. Still following the tracks, they crossed a bench then climbed again, now into pine, and soon they reached the long flat crest of the rise. In the distance, the hills took up again, but more rugged—tumbling into each other, spewed with rock and brush, forming a thousand fantastic shapes. The unshod tracks continued on down the slope of the hill, and below them, deathly still in the evening light, was the village of Valladolid.

"Well?" Bowers asked it.

Flynn's eyes roamed over the adobe huts, half squinting. The first buildings were perhaps four hundred yards down the slope. The walls were wind-scarred and the bricks showed in many places where the outer plastering of adobe had crumbled off. Beyond these, a patchwork of brush rooftops, some caved in or blown away. Grass and brush grew in the streets which they could see, and the taller growth swayed gently as the wind moved through the shadowed lanes. The village seemed all the more dead, because it had once been alive.

Bowers said, "What are you thinking about?"

"All the places down here an Apache could hide," Flynn said.

They moved back into the heavier pines and tied their horses to the lowest branches so they could graze, then sat down to rest and think and check their guns. And for the next hour they smoked cigarettes cupped in their hands and spoke little. When it was almost full dark, Flynn nodded and they rose together and moved back to the slope.

Flynn was starting down the grade as Bowers touched his arm, and he stopped. "Do you really think it's worth it?" Bowers said.

Flynn shrugged. "You have something else you'd rather do?"

"You could lie down there and no one would even know about it."

"The Apaches would. . . ."

Flynn moved off then, Bowers a few yards behind him. They descended slowly, taking their time, and when they had gone almost halfway Flynn motioned to keep lower. The rest of the way they moved more cautiously, zigzagging through the shadows of the brush clumps. Flynn would move ahead, then drop to his stomach and wait for Bowers to follow, then lie motionless to make sure the silence had not changed before moving again. The brush straggled all the way down to the first building, so there was no opening to cross, and when they reached the wall they pressed close to it in the deep shadow of the roof overhang and waited a longer time now.

A cricket chirped inside the house, then another. Flynn eased to the corner of the building, and moved around it holding tight to the wall with his back. He went to a crouch then, passing beneath the small front window. As he disappeared through the doorway the crickets stopped.

Bowers waited at the corner of the house. He counted seconds mechanically, a full minute, while he strained against the silence. Then he followed.

Inside he could see nothing. To the left a window framed the night, shades lighter than the inside darkness, and through it he could make out the dim outline of the next building. He heard Flynn whisper, "Here," and moved toward the sound of his voice.

He touched Flynn before he saw him, against the wall by the window.

"Do you think they're here?"

"Almost dead sure."

"Why?"

Flynn spoke very low, close to Bowers' face. "Because you don't hear anything. Something scared off the night sounds."

The breeze moved through the streets and somewhere a door creaked. It banged—a pistol report against the warped frame—then creaked open again. They were startled by the abruptness of the sound, even though they knew it was the wind.

Flynn said, "Are you afraid?"

Bowers hesitated. "I suppose so."

"Everybody gets scared sometime," Flynn said.

"Do you?"

"Sure."

"Do Apaches?"

"I never asked one. But we might find out." He wanted to see Bowers' face, but it was too dark. "It's not so routine now, is it?"

Bowers said, "No," quietly.

"Do you think you're a better soldier than these Mimbres?"

"I don't know."

"When will you?"

"That's not it."

"It's the not seeing them, isn't it?"

Bowers nodded. "What do you want to do?"

"Take them. If they think we're a bunch they might quit without a fight. Now, they're most likely camped in the square, not chancing getting trapped inside a house. If we can get on two sides and pour it in all of a sudden, we'll catch them with their breechclouts down."

"What if they fight?"

Flynn winked and the tone of his voice meant the same thing. "You'll think of something. That's what they pay you for."

"Go on."

"We're about five houses from the square; you go up this row, I'll cross over a few rows and work around to the other side of the square. Just think of one thing: if it doesn't wear a hat, shoot it."

Bowers saw the form silhouetted in the doorway for a moment, then Flynn was gone.

The cavalryman turned to the window and his body tensed as he lifted his leg and hooked it over the window sill. He paused, sitting on one thigh, before pulling his body through. Then he was out. He moved to the next building and listened for a long minute before going through the window. As he did, the stock of the carbine scraped the inside wall. The sound was rasping, loud in the small room, and Bowers stiffened. He closed his eyes tightly. Finally, when he opened them, he thought: Dammit, hold onto yourself!

Inside, thick darkness again, and the window in the other wall framing the lighter shade of the outside. He went through to the next house, but remained there a longer time while he listened for the sounds that never came, and he tried to picture fear on the face of an Apache.

It took him longer to climb through this window, because now he was more careful. Just keep going, he thought. Don't think and keep going. He dropped to the ground and darted to the next wall keeping his head down. His hand touched the adobe, groped along the crumbling surface; his head came up quickly then and he looked both ways along the wall. But there was no window on this side of the house.

He moved to the corner and inched his face around with his cheek flat to the wall, then sank gradually to hands and knees and crawled along the front of the house, careful of the carbine. At the doorway he paused again, listening, then rose and stepped into the darkness. Instantly the smell touched his nostrils. It hung oppressively in the small room. A raw smell that made him think of blood, and of a butcher's shop.

He started to move and the toe of his foot touched something soft. He stooped then, slowly, extending his hand close to the floor until the palm touched it and told him what it was. Cowhide, and the bloated firmness of the belly. Freshly butchered . . .

Behind him there was a whisper of sound. He knew what it had to be. Turn and shoot! It flashed in his mind. Don't wait! But it was too late—a hand closed over his mouth . . . something at his throat . . . the carbine jerked from his hand then came back suddenly against his face.

Flynn waited at the rear of the livery stable, his back flat against the boards. He was in shadow, but a few feet from him the sagging door showed plainly in the moonlight. A half-moon, but there were no clouds to obscure its light and the shadows about him hung motionless. Above the doorway a loading tree jutted out dimly against the sky.

The livery stable faced on the square. In the time it had taken to work around to this side, he had heard nothing; and there was no one inside, he was certain of that now; still, they could be just beyond the front entrance. He tried to picture the square as he had once seen it. It was small, with a statue in the middle. The statue of a saint. He calculated now: Anywhere in the square they could not be more than a hundred and fifty feet away. He looked up at the loading tree again, then eased through the partly open doorway and moved along the wall until his hand touched the ladder.

He tested the rungs, the ones he could reach, and as he climbed he pulled carefully on the rungs above him before bringing up his legs. Halfway, the loft was even with his head. He raised the carbine and slid it onto the planking, then raised himself after it. Toward the front, the main loading window showed dimly—a square of night sky, starless, and it grew larger as he crept toward it, easing his weight over the planking. Now and then a squeak, a rusted nail bending—but a small sound that would not carry beyond the building. At the opening he stood to the side and looked straight down over the carbine. There was no sound. No movement.

Flynn moved back now and eased down until he was lying on his stomach. He pushed the Springfield out in front of him, the barrel nosing past the loft edge, and at that moment he saw the Apache.

The Mimbre appeared in a doorway directly across the square, then moved close along the wall until he reached the corner of the building. He crouched then and waited, facing toward the rear of the one-story structure. Flynn raised the Springfield and dropped his head slightly for his cheek to rest against the stock, then swung the barrel less than three inches to bring it against the dim figure of the Mimbre.

He hears something, Flynn thought. That animal sense of his is telling him something. His hand tightened beneath the barrel, feeling the slender balanced weight of the carbine. He wouldn't know what hit him, he thought now. Probably not even hear it. The oil smell of the breech mechanism was strong with his face so close and two inches away his finger crooked over the trigger guard. His thumb raised. Pull it back easy, he thought. He wouldn't hear it, but pull back easy. The thumb closed over the hammer and cocked it.

The figure moved then and the barrel followed him as he glided across the narrow street to the corner of the next house. Flynn saw now that he carried a rifle and was pointing it toward the house behind the one he had just left. It was in the row Bowers would be moving up.

They know he's there, Flynn thought. They must have known it for some time. That's why they aren't in the square. But where are the others? His eyes inched along the adobe fronts across the square. Nothing moved. He swung back to the Apache on the corner. They've filtered back among the buildings and this one is waiting in case he breaks free.

Maybe they've taken him already. And maybe they haven't. But if he breaks for the street, the one on the corner will get him. This went through his mind quickly as he aimed at the Apache, realizing almost at the same time that there was no choice. He must kill the Apache on the chance Bowers wasn't already taken. "Look around," he whispered to the Apache, "then it will be easier." But the figure remained motionless, his back hunched into a round target, as Flynn inhaled slowly, stopped, squeezed the trigger, felt the shock jab against his shoulder, smelled the powder and heard the report echo through the deserted streets. He saw that the Apache had turned as he was hit and was facing him now, lying on his back.

NINE

The wind rose, bringing clouds to dim the moonlight, and the wind moved through the streets with a low hissing sound, bending the brush clumps and splattering invisible sand particles against the adobe. The wind moved over the dead Apache, spreading his hair, fanning it into a halo about his head. But this was all, only the wind.

As morning approached, Flynn could see the Apache more plainly. The sun came up behind the stable and a shaft of cold light filtering between the stable and the next building fell directly across the Apache. The shirt would move gently as the breeze stirred, but the curled moccasin toes which pointed to the sky, and the extended arms, palms up, did not move.

Flynn thought: Your friends are probably looking at you at this same moment. One of them saying, "Poor . . ."—something that ends in *i-n* or *y-a* and has a guttural sound to it. Or else something the Mexicans named you. Juan Ladron. Joselito. Or a name like Geronimo which a few years ago was Gokliya. And now they are begging U-sen not to make you walk in eternal darkness, because it wasn't your fault, Flynn continued to think. I'm sorry I killed you at night. It was not the way a warrior should die. But you would have killed me. That's the way it goes. I wish I could light a cigarette.

Where are they, in that house the Mimbre was pointing toward? Probably. With Bowers. Perhaps one has worked his way around and is entering the livery. Flynn rolled to his side and looked back toward the ladder, then to the loft opening again. Just don't start imagining things, he told himself. They'll show sooner or later. It's their move now.

Shortly after he thought this, it came.

His eyes were swinging along the ramada fronts when he caught the movement in the corner of his vision. His eyes slid back instantly to the street where the dead Apache lay. Bowers was standing at the corner of the building. His hands were behind his back.

Flynn watched him, surprised. He had not admitted it, but now he realized that he had supposed Bowers dead.

The cavalryman staggered out from the building suddenly, off balance, and Flynn saw the two Apaches then. One of them pushed Bowers again, staying close behind him, urging him on until they reached the middle of the square and stopped next to the statue. The other Apache followed and now the three of them looked up at the livery stable first, then to the buildings on either side. The Apache behind Bowers jabbed him with his carbine barrel.

Moving his head slowly along the building fronts, Bowers yelled out, "They want me to say something!"

You don't have to say it, Flynn thought. He watched one of the Apaches point the carbine at Bowers' head and pull back the hammer. Give up, or they'll kill him. That doesn't need words. But how do they know I'm still here? And that I'm alone? He thought of their horses then, picketed on the hill. They found the horses. They move fast and they're very thorough, and they know a man wouldn't run off without his horse. Not in this country.

"Flynn . . . don't come out!"

He moved from the opening back to the ladder and climbed down it wearily. He walked out the wide front door of the stable toward the three figures at the statue. Beyond them, now, he saw two other Apaches standing in the shadow of a wooden awning. The square was dead-still.

The second Apache stepped forward to meet him and he handed the carbine to him, then reached into his coat and drew the pistol and handed this to him.

He said to Bowers, "Well, we tried. What happened?" He saw the bruised cheekbone and the swelling above his right eye.

"I walked into the house where they were butchering a steer," Bowers said. "They were on me before I knew it."

"Red, don't back away from them. Stay calm and we'll get out of this."

Bowers looked at him quickly. It was the first time he had been called that since before the Point. And it had come unexpectedly from Flynn.

The guide looked at the Apache next to him. He said roughly, in Spanish, "What are you called?"

The Apache eyed him narrowly. "Matagente." Then he said in hesitant, word-spaced Spanish, "I do not know you."

"Nor I, you," Flynn said. "But I know you are Mimbreño—and at this time very far from the land of the Warm Springs. But you will come to know us very well. At San Carlos you will see us often."

Matagente's expression did not change as he listened. Now he said, "San Carlos is not for the Warm Springs Apache."

"This is something which ones above us have ordered," Flynn said. "There is no profit in talking about it with you. Where is Soldado? Our words are for him."

"You will see him," Matagente said. He motioned with the carbine, saying no more, directing them toward the house where the others stood. They had carried the dead Apache from the street and now he was under the ramada near the doorway. Matagente looked at him as he prodded the two men into the house, but still he said nothing.

They sat on the packed-dirt floor with their legs crossed and their backs to the wall and waited. For what, they did not know, wondering why they were not taken to the Apaches' ranchería.

Matagente brought them meat, then sat near the doorway with one of the Springfields across his lap. His hand moved over the smooth stock idly. Before this he had used a Burnside .54 which needed percussion caps and powder, and often it misfired.

When they had eaten the meat, Flynn said, "Take us to Soldado now."

"You will see him," Matagente said, and again lapsed into silence. This new gun was in his mind—this pesh-e-gar—and he was thinking how good it would be to fire it.

Through the doorway Flynn could see the other Apaches standing in front of the house, talking to each other in low tones he could not hear. Then he saw them look up. One of them moved off and the others watched after him. In a moment he was back and he called in to Matagente, in the Mimbreño dialect. "They are here."

Matagente rose and moved to the doorway as mounted Apaches suddenly appeared in front of the house. These dismounted as others continued to enter the square from the side street, walking their ponies. The sound of this came to Flynn, but he could see nothing until Matagente stepped back from the doorway. He saw the Apaches now, at least twenty, probably more, milling in front of the house, then his view was blocked again as a figure moved into the doorway.

Matagente said, "Now you see Soldado. Tell him your story, American."

Bowers looked at him with open surprise, and now wondered why he had expected this Apache to look different than any other, though he was old for an Apache still active. Wrinkled face and eyes half closed beneath the bright red headband. And skinny— filthy clothes, ill-fitting to make him seem smaller. A buttonless cavalry jacket, a bandoleer crossing his chest holding the jacket only partly closed, and cotton trousers stuffed into curl-toed moccasins that reached to his knees where they folded and tied. He rested one hand on the butt of a cap-and-ball dragoon pistol in his waistband. But the hand only rested there; it was not a threat.

Flynn watched his face as he sat down in front of them crossing his legs. The cavalry guide had expected nothing. A man is some things and he is not others. A Mimbre Apache is not a fashion plate. He is ragged and dirty and has the odor of an unwashed dog and at night in his ranchería drinks tizwin until it puts him to sleep or sends him after a woman. He has many faults—by white standards. But he is a guerrilla fighter, and in his own element he is unbeatable. That's the thing to remember, Flynn thought. Don't underestimate him because he smells. He isn't chief because his dad was. And a broncho chief doesn't get to be as old as he is on his good looks.

He said now, in Spanish, "Do you speak English?"

The Apache shook his head.

"Lieutenant, you can take that for what it's worth. He might speak it better than we do." Then to Soldado he said, "We did not come here to fight your men. The fight could not be avoided."

"But one of them is dead," Soldado said.

"I did not wish him to die the way he did, but it could not be helped. It is not the way a Mimbreño should die."

The old chief looked at him intently. "Who of us have you known?"

"I have known Victorio and Chee and Old Nana."

"What are you called?"

"Davíd Flín." He pronounced the name slowly.

"I have not heard of you."

"This country is wide."

The Apache said quietly, "Yet you would force us to live in one small corner of it."

"What I do," Flynn said, "is not entirely of my mind."

"Then perhaps you are a fool."

"It is only foolish when you fight against what is bound to happen," Flynn said. "I see the days of the Mimbreño numbered . . . as well as the Chiricahua, Coyotero, Jicarilla and the Mescalero. The Tonto and Mojave have already been given their own land."

"And who is this that gives land which he does not own?" the Apache asked.

Damn him, Flynn thought. He said, "The chief of the Americans, who owns it because of his power. Let me tell you something, old man, for your wisdom to absorb: your days remaining are few. If you give yourself up now, you will be given good land which still abounds in those things to keep you alive. And you will be under the protection of our government."

Soldado said seriously, "And if I were to find my woman lying with someone else and I cut off her nose, what would happen to me?"

"You would be taken before the agent," Flynn said, feeling foolish saying the words.

"For what reason?"

"For your offense."

"And when our women see that they can lie with any man they wish and only the husband is punished if he objects, what will your government do then?"

"Your women are your own problem," Flynn said.

"Man, we have many problems which we would keep our own."

Flynn shook his head wearily. What a sly old bastard, he thought. He makes you sound like a damn fool. Maybe you can't be a big brother. Maybe the only kind of respect they know is a kick in the face. He intimated so just now with that about the women. Only you're not in a very good spot to do any kicking. All you can do now is bluff—and if it doesn't work, which it probably won't, you haven't lost anything.

He said now to Soldado, "I tell you this as a friend: If you fight, you will be defeated, and being remembered with distaste you will be treated ill and perhaps be put into prison."

Soldado said, "What is the difference in meaning between these words prison and reservation?"

"You ask many questions."

"I only wish to borrow from the wisdom of the American," Soldado said.

"You may scoff at these words," Flynn said, "but what happens, happens. It is above you and me and will come about regardless of what you do, but I am wise enough to see it."

"Are you wise enough to see your own fate, American?"

"I speak to you as a people."

"And I speak to you as a man. What does this spirit of yours say will happen to you?"

"I could die at this moment," Flynn said. "So could you."

"But who would you say this is more likely to happen to?"

You're not doing this very good, Flynn thought to himself. He always has the last word and makes you feel like a green kid who doesn't know what he's doing. Bowers touched his arm then and as he looked at him Bowers said, "How does he know why we're here?"

"What?"

"You've told him nothing. We could be scalp hunters for all he knows, yet he talks about the reservation. How does he know we came to see him?"

Soldado said, "The silent one wonders how I know of your mission."

In English, Flynn said quickly, "How did you know what he said?"

Soldado shook his head. *"No comprendo."*

Flynn repeated the question in Spanish and the old Indian smiled faintly. "His question was on his face. It did not need words; though I have been waiting for you to ask it."

"Then you have known of us for some time," Bowers said.

"Since the day you gathered the bodies of the *Nakai-yes* and returned them to their village. This was not an act of the killers of Indians."

Flynn concealed his amazement. Now he said, "You were very thorough. No one was left alive."

Soldado studied him silently before saying, "Do you believe these words you use?" and when Flynn did not answer, he said, "No, you do not believe them, but you would hear it aloud that we did not kill the *Nakai-yes*. There is no need however to explain these things to the wise American who is able to see the future."

But it was the past Flynn was seeing as the old Indian spoke.

Burned wagon and the lifeless bodies in a narrow draw, and he tried to picture white men having done this. Before, he had been almost certain that this was not the work of Apaches. Still, he could not bring himself to believe that it had been white men. "How do you know who did this?" he said now.

Soldado smiled faintly. "Once, at night, I sat before my jacale and in front of me there was a mound of stones. There were red stones and white stones, which I could see by the light of the fire. And I played this game with myself, taking all of the red stones and placing them here," he said, gesturing with his hands, "and soon, all of the stones remaining before me were white." His smile broadened. "That is how I look into the past, American."

"These men will be punished for their deeds," Flynn said.

"By your government?"

"Yes, by my government. By men who act in its behalf."

"And who are these men?"

"I speak of this one whom I serve," Flynn said, nodding to Bowers, "and myself."

Soldado said, "Yet the one who serves is the spokesman."

"I speak when the ones before us are not worthy of his voice."

"But only worthy of his wonder," the Apache said confidently.

"You will be the one to wonder, soon, when you are a witness to his power."

"And what if you are already dead?"

"Your threat is nothing against the power of this man who is silent. And remember these words well, old man. As the hunters of Indians are destroyed, so will you be. They have already aroused his vengeance, which is what you are doing now. For I swear by the sacred pollen which you carry to ward off evil, that if you do not follow us in peace, you will be dragged to San Carlos behind our horses."

The Apache's face was expressionless. The eyes half closed, sleepily. He stared at Flynn a long moment, then his gaze swung to Bowers and as it did he drew the dragoon pistol from his waistband. He raised it slowly, cocking it, then straightened his arm, aiming the long barrel at Bowers and said, "Where is his power now, American?"

Flynn said nothing.

The Apache lowered the gun, looking toward Flynn again. He said, "Do you speak in the tongue of the Mimbreño?"

Flynn was surprised, but he nodded. "I speak some."

"Good. Then you will come to the ranchería." To Matagente, he said, "You will conduct them with three men. The rest of us will come at night tomorrow when this raid is terminated." He said to Flynn, as explanation, "We have only stopped here for meat."

Flynn was puzzled. He said, "And why is it necessary that I speak Mimbre?"

Soldado smiled, showing yellowed teeth. "So that you may tell our children your story."

TEN

"I'm leaving now," Rellis said.

Lazair was looking toward the tarp shelter of the cave, following the girl's movements as she gathered the tin plates, scraping and stacking them, and as she picked them up she glanced toward Lazair then turned away quickly when she saw that he was watching her. The two men were standing by the cook fire; Rellis, with his bay mare behind him.

"I said I'm leaving," Rellis repeated, impatiently.

"Well, go on." Lazair still watched the cave, though the girl had gone in now.

"I'm taking some men with me."

Lazair looked at him now. "Are you asking me or telling me?"

"Take it any way you want."

Lazair smiled faintly. "You're pretty tough, aren't you?"

"I get by."

"You'll get by with four men today," Lazair said quietly. "Lew and Warren are going back. Tell Lew to bring two more." He waited, but Rellis made no reply.

"Doesn't that suit you?"

Rellis shrugged lazily, but his eyes were hard on the other man's face. "They tell me you're the boss."

"You don't sound like you're sure of it."

He shrugged again. "You can't believe everything you hear."

There was a silence. Then Lazair said quietly, "Believe it, Frank. Even if you never believe anything else." He turned away then and moved off toward the cave, taking his time.

Rellis mounted the bay, then looked after Lazair a long moment before calling to the men standing off by the horses. They stared up at him idly.

"Lew, you and Warren . . . and two more!"

Lew Embree nodded to two of the men and one of them said, "We got us another boss." Rellis was moving off and did not hear him. They mounted then, resignedly, and followed Rellis down through the defile to the meadow.

Lew glanced up to the rocks and shouted, "Wesley, you keep awake, now!" to the guard, and then laughed. Warren laughed with him. They crossed the meadow at a trot, but slowed to a walk as the grass sloped over into the pines, beginning the long winding descent. Down farther, where the trail widened, Lew spurred to ride next to Rellis.

"Curt's going to get that girl yet, you wait and see." Lew grinned.

"I don't give a damn who he gets," Rellis answered shortly. Then he said, "How far to the pueblo?"

"About three, four hours," Lew said. "Depending how fast you go."

"I want to get there quick."

"The country ain't built for going too fast. She closes in on you and you can't see ahead in some places."

"I'm not looking for anything."

"But the 'Paches might be looking for you."

Rellis turned on one hip to look at Lew. "You scared of them?"

"Much as anybody else is," Lew said. "It's when you can't see 'em but can feel 'em is when I'm scared. Like just seeing their smoke curling up in the hills and then when you get on ahead there's another smoke rise and you know they're passing the word that you're coming. We was over deeper in the Madres once and we seen this smoke, but we kept going and soon there was this canyon that was still as a tomb—just rocks that went up and up and up and then sky. There wasn't a sound but the horses. Then if you'd listen close, you'd hear the wind playing over the rocks. You'd stretch your neck looking up those walls and there was just that dead stillness . . . and the hum of the breeze, which you didn't count because it would be there even if nobody was about.

"We moved down the middle, about fifty yards from both sides. Then all of a sudden I heard this swish and a thud and right next to me Wesley's brother . . . you know that boy that was on guard? . . . Wes's brother falls out of the saddle with a arrow sticking out of his neck. Mister, we got out of there fast."

"Was Curt there?" Rellis said.

"Sure he was there."

"You feel any 'Paches now?"

"I feel 'em most every time I ride to the pueblo."

"Maybe you should've stayed back there with Curt."

"Maybe I'd like to have."

Rellis said now, "He doesn't care much what happens to you or the rest, does he?"

"What do you mean?"

"He would've sent you and Warren back alone if I hadn't been going out and said something."

"We rode in alone."

"That's what I mean," Rellis said. "He knows there's 'Paches around. How come you and Warren got to ride back and forth alone?"

"You can get used to anything," Lew said, looking at Rellis closely now, "even a feeling."

"Just sits there working up his nerve to grab chiquita and lets you do all the work."

"You don't like it?"

"Hell no."

"Why don't you get out then?"

Rellis looked at him. "Just keep your goddamn nose where it belongs."

"You do a lot of pushing for one man."

"You going to do anything about it?"

Lew said nothing.

"Then keep your mouth shut."

"A man's got to talk about something."

Rellis did not answer. He rolled a cigarette and drew on it without taking it from his mouth, watching the trail.

For a short while, Lew remained silent, then he said, "I'm going up ahead a ways and look around." Rellis shrugged and Lew said, half turning in the saddle, "Warren, come on."

Rellis watched them move off, bearing to the right, climbing to higher ground, parallel with the trail but into the pines where they could watch the country below without being seen.

He pinched the cigarette stub from his mouth and ground it out between his fingers, crumbling tobacco and paper, then let the breeze take the particles from his open palm. His eyes, light colored, mild, and contrasting oddly with the coarseness of his features, were focused on the trail ahead, because you had to be careful. And partly because he was thinking and did not want distractions. Thinking about what he would do to a tall, thin man with a light mustache who wore a shoulder rig and who thought he was so goddamn smart. You should have pulled the trigger. What the hell was wrong with you! he thought. Well, you won't back down next time. Then he thought: I didn't back down! The son of a bitch had something under the cloth. He wouldn't have been so smart if he hadn't. You played it careful, that's all. He won't have a chance to get anything ready this time. And it's him, all right. It's his description. And I can even feel it's him, the son of a bitch.

He thought of the things he could do to Flynn. Get him when he's turned around and go up behind him and say something like . . . "Aren't you going to say hello to your old friend?" And when the son of a bitch turns around, jam the pistol into his gut and let go . . . and watch the expression on his face . . . He smiled thinking of this. And if that other one's with him, he'll get his, too. Like that old man with the beard who thought he was so smart laughing all the time.

Then Warren was standing just off the trail in a small clearing. His horse was not in sight. He held one hand palm-toward-them and the other hand was to his mouth.

Rellis dismounted and led his horse toward him. "What's the matter?"

" 'Paches."

"Where?"

"Down below. Going into a draw that comes out just up a ways from where Lew is now."

"How many?"

"Six. But two of them have got hats on."

They left their horses and followed Warren up through the pines, then, just ahead, they could see Lew belly-down behind the rocks, his carbine pointing down the draw. Farther back, the trough between the hills was dense with trees, but here the trees thinned as the draw climbed into a rise, its steep sides falling gradually away. Lew's carbine pointed to where the riders would come out of the trees. He glanced around as he heard the others come up.

"Don't make a sound."

Rellis eased down next to him and the other spread out along the rocks.

"We ought to have somebody over on the other side," Lew said, "But it's too late now."

"Where are they?" Rellis said.

"They'll show any minute." Lew pointed with the carbine barrel. "Come out right over there and pass within a hundred feet."

Rellis said, "Five against six," considering this.

"They won't have a chance."

"What's this about two of them wearing hats?"

"They was way off when I spotted them but that's what it looked like."

"I never heard of that."

Lew said, "I seen reservation 'Paches wearing hats." He raised himself on his elbows and looked toward the others down the line then to Rellis, "If we do this right," he said, "we got us six hundred pesos in the bank."

Rellis said nothing. He had both a carbine and a shotgun with him, and now he was examining the shotgun. At this range the shotgun would be better, especially if they rode close together.

Suddenly he heard Lew whisper, "Here they come. Get ready."

A lone Apache came out of the trees slowly, cautiously. He rode directly up the middle of the draw, holding his pony to a walk. Near the rise, he angled toward the far side and as he reached the slope, two more appeared from the trees coming out into the open. They scanned both sides of the draw as they drew closer to the rise. One of them rode straight ahead, urging his pony up the rise. The other followed for a short distance, then veered abruptly, coming toward the near side. He stopped suddenly and his eyes crawled over the rimrock.

Rellis whispered to Lew, "Take him. I'll get the one on the rise." His head turned to Warren. "The one on the other side. Tell the others."

"That's only three of them," Lew whispered hoarsely.

"We can't wait forever . . . take him!"

Lew squinted down the short barrel as Rellis swung the shotgun toward the Apache who had stopped at the crest of the rise.

Flynn felt his horse's head jerk suddenly and saw that the Apache was leading them off to the side toward the hill slope. A line trailed from the Apache's horse, back through the bit ring of Flynn's bridle to Bowers' and was tied there. Their hands were lashed to the saddle horns. Ahead, they could see Matagente and the two other Apaches disappearing into the trees.

Bowers said, "Did you make out what he told them?"

"He said they'd go on up to that rise . . . see it way up there over the trees? . . . and signal for us to follow."

"Doesn't take any chances."

"They never do," Flynn said.

The Apache, with one of their Springfields across his lap, was looking intently toward the rise. He glanced toward them then and muttered gutturally.

Bowers said, "What was that?"

"Mimbre for shut-up," Flynn said.

They kept their eyes on the rise. It was perhaps a quarter of a mile above them, but seemed much closer because of the height. Then one of the Apaches was visible past the dense tops of the trees, a small speck moving gradually up the slope. They watched him reach the crest and stop there, and he seemed to wait there uncertainly before turning his mount to face back down the draw.

He sat erect on the pony's back and raised his hand to shield the glare from his eyes, looking over the trees below him. Then the other hand raised a carbine high overhead and waved it once in a long sweeping motion. And as if on the signal, gunfire cut the stillness, echoing down the draw.

The Apache clung low to the pony and started to move off, but he was sliding to the side and as the horse broke he fell, grabbing wildly for the mane, and rolled down out of sight. There were more shots, but from below they could see no one.

The Mimbre did not hesitate. Flynn swore. Bowers yelled as he cut past them suddenly. The lead rope turned their horses abruptly, jerked from standstill to dead-run as he swerved out into the draw and back down the way they had come. They dodged after the Mimbre through the scattering of trees and brush scraping mesquite thickets, riding head-down, unable to raise their arms against the branches. The lead rope would slacken, then tighten suddenly to stagger their mounts off balance, though neither of them went down. When they reached open country the Mimbre paused to listen, but now there was no sound of firing. And he moved off again at a sharp right angle, skirting the base of the hills. Soon, though, he angled into the hills again, now leading them much slower.

"You never know, do you?" Bowers said.

"Not in this country."

"It's either rurales or this Lazair," Bowers considered, and when the scout nodded, he said, "Where's he going now?"

"He'll want to take a look before running for home."

"With us along?"

"Maybe he's got plans for us," Flynn said.

They moved up into high country behind the Apache who would stop frequently to listen; climbing slowly because there was no trail, winding into natural switchbacks where the ground rose steeper, transforming itself into jagged rock formations. But always there were dense pines scattered, straggling over the slopes, and they kept to the dimness of the trees most of the time. The sunlight clung to the open areas, coldly reflecting on the grotesque stone shapes—shadowed crevices and the brush clumps that stirred lazily when the wind would rise.

And over it all, a stillness.

For a time, as they climbed, the cry of a verdin followed them. But when they looked up into the trees the bird was never there— hidden against the flat shade of a tree limb. A thin, bodiless cry in the stillness. Just before they stopped they saw the verdin suddenly rise from a cholla bush and disappear into the glare, and they did not hear him again.

The Mimbre led them into a hollow that was steep on three sides with shelf rock, ending abruptly only a dozen yards beyond the brush fringe of the entrance. He dismounted, dropping the Springfield, and approached Flynn's horse.

He looked up at the scout steadily for a moment then moved in close and quickly unstrapped the latigo. He grabbed Flynn's leg suddenly and pulled, dragging him down with his saddle. He moved to Bowers then and did the same thing, and now both of them were on the ground still astride their saddles. If they were to move, they would have to drag the saddles between their legs. The Mimbre picked up the Springfield, then glanced at them once more before disappearing through the brush.

Rest easy, Flynn thought. He saw Bowers begin to strain at the rawhide that was squeezing his wrists and he said quickly, "Not yet!" Bowers looked up and he added quietly, "He's watching us. Give him time to calm down and get out."

"How do you know?"

"Wouldn't you?" Flynn said.

Bowers relaxed, squatting hunched over the saddle, and his fingers moved idly against the saddle horn. It would be easy to drag the saddle over and untie Flynn's hands, since his fingers were free, and he could not understand this. Finally he said, "We can get out of this. Why didn't he tie us to a tree?"

"Because he'd have to free our hands to do it," Flynn said. "He didn't want to take a chance, and this is the next best thing. He's more concerned with those others over in the draw—close friends, maybe a brother."

"Why didn't he kill us?"

"I don't know. Maybe for the same reason Soldado did not."

Bowers frowned. "Which was what?"

"You'd have to ask an Apache," Flynn said.

Bowers said nothing now, listening to the silence, staring up at the shelf rock and the sky directly above them and over the brush fringe at the entrance. The hollow was in deep shadow because now the sun was off to the west. After a time he shook his head wearily.

"It's a god-awful poor way to fight a war," he said.

Flynn looked at him. "What war?"

"Whatever you want to call it then," Bowers said irritably.

"No cannons."

"You can keep the cannon."

"It's a good thing that old Apache doesn't have any."

"Or the rurales . . . or this Lazair," Bowers said. "I'm trying to make up my mind who's the worst of the three."

Flynn said quietly, "I don't think there's any doubt."

Bowers thought of the wagon train now, and of the girl and what the old Apache had said about the red stones and the white stones and he knew what Flynn meant. And he said nothing. But after a while, after he had thought of Flynn and the girl and Flynn's never mentioning the girl, he became angry and he thought; He's been fighting Apaches so long he acts like one. No emotions. Just a stoicism—like a rock.

They waited for almost two hours, talking in low tones when they did talk, and now there was little light showing over the brush fringe. Then, "It's about that time," Flynn said matter-of-factly. "Let's get out of here."

Bowers looked at him as the cavalry guide rose and dragged over his saddle and pushed it tight against Bowers. His fingers strained away from the rawhide until he touched Bowers' hand, then the fingers worked at the rawhide slowly because the knots were stiff and he did not have the full strength of his hands to use.

But finally the thong loosened and Bowers was free. He untied the guide's hands. They passed through the brush cover and moved off in a general southwest direction toward Soyopa.

But when it was full dark, they stopped. A niche in the rocks would protect them from the wind. There was no fire; and before lying down, Flynn placed a semicircle of loose stones out a few yards from the niche. Then they slept; even with the chill and the wind moaning over the rocks. The Apaches had prevented sleep entirely the night before. And the dead had made it fitful the night before that.

They moved off again with the first light, past the circle of stones that were still in place.

"We're above that draw now," Flynn said. "The Mimbre brought us almost clear around it to the other side." He pointed far off over the trees to the wild country that fell below them. "It's down in there somewhere. If we head about that way we'll cross it . . . maybe find out what happened."

As they moved on, working their way down, Bowers said suddenly, "You've got the biggest capacity for doing things of any man I know."

"It's a big country. Everything in it's big," Flynn said. "The sun's big, the mountains, the deserts, even the bugs. You got to strain to keep up with it, that's all."

"What are you going to get out of this?" Bowers said.

"Sore feet."

"You know what I mean."

"Four dollars a day."

"What else?"

"What do you want, Red, a medal for everything you do?"

"I want a good reason, that's all!"

"Isn't that colonel reason enough?"

"You haven't answered my question."

Flynn's eyes lifted from Bowers and moved along the wall of rocky slope that rimmed this end of the clearing they had entered minutes before. He glanced off in the other direction, at the flat meadow that offered no cover, then back to the rocks and he saw it again—remaining fixed now, a sliver of light pointing out from a crevice in the rocks—like sun reflecting on a gun barrel.

"Mister, you'll have to ask me some other time," he said. "I think we're walking into something."

ELEVEN

"**H**old it there!"

It came abruptly then to stop them fifty feet from the sloping rock wall. Bowers' eyes went over the slope and Flynn said, "About ten o'clock, just above those two boulders." He saw it now, the gun barrel hanging motionless, pointing down through the crevice. No one showed behind it.

"Throw your guns away!"

Flynn's eyes stayed on the crevice. "We're unarmed!"

"I'll give you five seconds."

"We don't have any!"

A silence followed. Then, "Take off your coats and walk slow with your hands in the air."

They did this and as they reached the slope, the man appeared. He descended part way until he was only a few yards above them. He stopped here, squatting on a shelf, with a double-barreled shotgun pointing down toward them.

"What do you want?"

"We're on our way to Soyopa," Flynn said.

"Just out for a little stroll?"

"You're close."

The man grinned, raising the shotgun. "You better say something that makes sense."

Bowers said impatiently, "We need horses, does that make sense?"

The man nodded, taking his time, "But I want to know what you're doing here."

Flynn said, "Get off that rock and take us to Lazair and quit wasting everybody's time." The man looked at him startled and he knew he had guessed it right.

"How do you know he's here?"

"You going to take us, or d'you want me to start yelling for him?"

The man studied them silently, then shrugged, as if he had carried it as far as he could. He said, "Move on into that pass yonder and follow it up." And as they entered the defile he came down and stayed a few feet behind them until the pass opened up into the pocket high in the rocks.

The camp seemed deserted—no one about the four tents, the cook fire dead and over by the cave the only movement was the tarp awning moving gently with the breeze. The guard mumbled, "Where the hell is everybody . . ." Then he saw them, seven or eight men off beyond the tents, standing idly before a patch of young aspen. "They're over there," he said, and motioned them to go on.

The men looked toward them as they approached. One of them had his back turned, squatting at the base of an aspen and he looked over his shoulder but did not get up. The man with the shotgun yelled, "Somebody fetch Curt!"

For a moment no one moved and someone said, "What's the matter with you?" Then one of them walked off toward the tarp shelter. The others stood where they were, staring at the newcomers, and the one who had been squatting rose now to study them also. Something was behind him, huddled at the base of the aspen—a shoulder, and an arm bent back to the tree trunk.

The guard said, "You still at it?"

"What does it look like?"

Another one said, "The son of a bitch won't even groan."

He stepped aside to reveal the half-naked figure of a man, a dark man with hair to his shoulders, a breechclout and curl-toed moccasins. His upper body sagged limply from the white bark, head-down, hands bound behind the trunk. And he sat heavily with his legs extended, the left thigh bloody, dried blood and a gaping raw wound. His upper body and head showed bruises and in many places the blood ran down his body.

Flynn leaned closer to him, and as if the Indian could feel his presence he looked up slowly. It was Matagente, his face beaten almost beyond recognition.

Flynn said gently, in Mimbreño, "What do they do to you?" But the head went down and the Apache did not answer.

He heard someone say, "Who are they?" and he looked up to

see the guard shrug his shoulders; then, past him, he saw a man standing in the cave entrance, holding the blanket covering aside, watching them. Flynn rose and now saw the blanket hanging smooth again and the man was not there. But in a moment he reappeared and now came from the shelter toward them.

Lazair said nothing, studying them, then glanced toward the guard. "Who's on watch?"

"I am."

"You ain't going to see a hell of a lot from here." He waited until the guard moved off before returning his gaze to Bowers and Flynn. "Well?" he said.

Flynn nodded to Matagente. "What happened to the others?"

"Dead," Lazair said. He eyed them coldly, his face shadowed beneath a willow-root straw. The brim curled, pointed low over his thin nose. He stood in a half-slouch, his shirt open almost to the waist, but the bright red kerchief tight about his throat. He said, "How'd you know there were any more?"

"That one had us when you hit him," Flynn said.

"Small goddamn world. My boys brought him in yesterday."

"What are you doing to him?"

"Why?"

"Just curious."

"Asking him where the old chief lives."

"You don't expect him to tell you?"

Lazair shrugged. "No skin off my tail. It's up to him. He tells or he wakes up dead."

"I hear the old man's got five hundred pesos on his head," Flynn said.

"You heard wrong. It's eight hundred now." Lazair nodded toward Matagente. "His lieutenant's got three hundred." He smiled faintly. "The price of fame, eh?"

Flynn said quietly, "How much is your hair worth?"

Lazair studied him. "You can talk plainer than that."

"I've seen your picture somewhere . . . on a dodger."

"Where would that be?"

"Cibucu, Fort Thomas, somewhere like that."

Lazair grinned. "You're Army, eh? Goddamn Lew was right . . . for once in his life. You're a little out of your territory."

Bowers said now, "So are a few Mimbreño Apaches."

Lazair looked him up and down, noticing the issue belt and holster and the high boots. "Where's your uniform?" he said. He smiled again pushing back the straw from his forehead. "They sent the two of you all the way down here after Apaches?" He shook his head, still grinning. "That's the goddamnedest thing I ever heard. What do you expect to do?"

Flynn said, "Talk that old Mimbre into being a farmer."

Lazair shifted his eyes to him. "You think he'll mind?"

"He might."

Lazair shook his head again, because he still couldn't believe it. "You mean to tell me they sent just two of you?"

Bowers said, "That's right."

"Christ, I've got fourteen men and we've never laid eyes on him!"

"He's seen you, though," Bowers said. "He was talking about it yesterday."

"Where?"

"Not far from here," Bowers said.

"If your men weren't so gun-happy," Flynn said, "they could have followed that one," he nodded toward Matagente, "right to the ranchería." He looked at the men standing off from him. "He had my guns with him—a Springfield swing-block and an altered .44, the ramrod and lever off, with an ejector on the right side of the barrel."

Lazair's men returned his stare silently, hostilely.

He looked at Lazair. "D. F. was carved on the stock of the Springfield. Do I look for them, or do you tell somebody to hand them over?"

Lazair picked a cigar from his shirt pocket and as he lighted the end his eyes remained on Flynn. He exhaled the smoke leisurely. "Maybe we'd better wait," he said.

"Long as I get them."

"Where'd the old man say he was going?"

"He didn't."

"But he was going to come home and tend to you later, eh?" Flynn nodded.

"Maybe," Lazair said grinning, "I ought to just follow you around if I want to find old Soldado."

Bowers looked surprised. "You're not holding us?"

"Why?"

"We might be cutting into your business."

"Do I look worried to you? Hell, you can go any place you like . . . even give you a couple of mounts to use. Anything to help the Army." He smiled sardonically, his teeth clenched on the cigar. "Goddamnedest thing I ever heard of. You're down here hunting him against the law 'cause you're on the wrong side of the fence, and I do the same thing and get paid for it 'cause I'm in a legitimate business."

"We'll have to have a drink over that sometime," Flynn said.

"Next time I'm in Soyopa."

Flynn glanced toward the cave. "Don't you have anything?"

"Not today," Lazair said. "You going back now?"

Flynn nodded.

"There's a friend of yours in town," Lazair said. "Matter of fact he was the one ambushed those Indians yesterday. Brought in this one 'cause he was still alive, then rode out this morning for Soyopa. One of the boys saw you in town and this one thinks he might know you." He watched Flynn slyly. "Name of Rellis. That ring any bells?"

Flynn hesitated and his face showed a natural surprise. "Frank Rellis . . . I'd like to see him again."

Lazair prompted, "He didn't say where he knew you."

"In Contention."

"Nice place . . . I've been there." Lazair glanced at his men. "Who's got this man's guns?"

No one spoke.

His eyes went over them. "Sid?"

The man said nothing.

"Goddamn it I'm talking to you!"

The one called Sid, heavy-set, with a stubble of red beard, stepped out reluctantly and drew Flynn's pistol from his belt. "The carbine's in the tent," he mumbled.

"Here, let's see it," Lazair said. He weighted the pistol in his hand. "Just a mite long in the barrel. Likely it's accurate, though." His arm swung quickly thumbing the hammer and he fired the pistol in the motion.

Sid jumped quickly. "Hey!"

But no one was looking at him. Matagente sagged forward, his chin against his chest, unmoving, and below his chin was the small hole Lazair's bullet had made.

"Damn accurate," Lazair said.

A silence followed. Flynn studied him coldly. "You trying to prove something?"

Lazair shrugged. "He wasn't doing anybody much good. Hair's

worth more'n his carcass. See, we don't exactly make farmers out of them, but we help the crops . . . turn them under, like manure."

He handed the pistol to Flynn. "You ought to cut that barrel down. Sid," he said over his shoulder, "you saddle up two mounts and fetch that carbine along and if anybody's got this other soldier's gun, fork over." He nodded to Bowers and Flynn. "You boys take it easy now." He turned and walked off toward the cave.

It was past noon when they reached Soyopa, entering by the way they had gone out two days before. And now the cemetery was silent. Rows of wooden crosses, but no one kneeling to remember the dead. Later on, when the shadows lengthened behind the church, the women would come. Always someone came.

The newer graves were near the road and already these were beginning to resemble the others, though the wooden crosses were not yet graved by the weather; small stones spread over the low mounds—a stone for a prayer for the repose of the soul.

Flynn dismounted stiffly and walked to the grave of Anastacio Esteban. Bowers followed him. A square of wood was nailed to the arms of the cross and it bore the inscription:

> *Aquí yace Anastacio María Esteban*
> *Vencino de Soyopa*
> *Matado por los barbaros*
> *el dia 26 de Octubre del año 1876*
> *Ora por el, Christiano, por Dios.*

Flynn said in English, "Killed by the barbarians. . . . Christian, for the sake of God, pray for his soul." Then he said again, *"Matado por los barbaros. . . ."* He looked at Bowers. "A barbarian with a willow-root straw and a red neckerchief."

Bowers eyed him curiously. "You're sure?"

"Absolutely."

"The Indian could have been lying."

"It's not what Soldado said."

Bowers looked at him, but said nothing.

"Then you didn't see her," Flynn said, ". . . just for a moment in the cave entrance. Nita Esteban."

TWELVE

A breeze moved over the square, raising dust swirls about the stone obelisk.

Two rurales lounged asleep in the shade of Duro's headquarters, and in front of Las Quince Letras a row of horses stood at the tie rack—a dun swished its tail lazily and the flanks of a big chestnut quivered to shake off flies. A dog yelped somewhere beyond the adobe fronts. And a woman, a black mantilla covering her head and shoulders, passed without sound into the shadowed doorway of Santo Tomás de Aquín. In the heat of the afternoon it was best to remain within.

From the doorway that opened onto the balcony, Lamas Duro watched the man leave the mescal shop and cross the square to the adobe whose sign read Comida. He walked leisurely, carrying a bottle of something.

"One of the American filth," Duro said half aloud.

As the figure passed from view he saw two riders then enter the square from the street that bordered the church, and as they passed the mescal shop Duro moved back into the room, buttoning his shirt. He smoothed his hair with his fingers as his eyes went on the desk to see the mescal bottle and glass. Hastily now he gathered them up, finishing the inch of colorless sweet liquid in the glass, and disappeared into the bedroom. He was back in a moment and arranged the papers on his desk in a semblance of order before returning to the doorway. The two riders were almost directly below.

He stepped out onto the balcony and called down, "Señores, please come up!" his smile as white as his shirt.

The taste of mescal was sour in his mouth and he lighted a cigar as he listened to the double tread on the stairs. Then they were on the balcony and he stepped aside allowing them to enter the room first.

"You do me an honor, Señor Flín and Lieutenant Bowers."

Bowers looked at him quickly.

Duro smiled. "This is a small pueblo, Lieutenant. The news does not have far to travel. Perhaps the alcalde tells a close friend . . . or someone overheard you speaking. He tells a friend. It enters Las Quince Letras and *pop* . . . it is out."

"Our identity was not intended to be kept secret," Bowers said.

"Of course not." Duro smiled. "But I wouldn't blame you if you did intend it so. Sometimes there is a problem in crossing into another country to perform a mission of a government nature. Often such matters must be handled with discretion. Of course, here you have nothing to fear. As a representative of Porfirio Diaz, I am at your command."

"That's very kind of you," Bowers said woodenly.

"Not at all." Duro held up his hand as if he would not think of accepting gratitude. "I know His Excellency, Porfirio, would have instructed that I aid your mission in every way . . . had he been informed of it. After all, the menace of the Apaches is a reason for the existence of our rurales. Actually then, you are giving assistance to us. Though I cannot say I envy your task." He said this as one soldier to another.

Bowers said, "But as a military man you know one cannot question his orders."

"Certainly." Duro bowed.

Flynn's eyes went over the room and returned to the rurale. "Have you ever made contact with Soldado Viejo?"

Duro shook his head. "Not with that elusive one. A few times, though, we have taken others of his tribe. The day you arrived we executed one." He sighed. "Sometimes such an act seems without heart but," his eyes shifted to Bowers, "one cannot question his orders."

Flynn crooked a knuckle to stroke his mustache idly. "I suppose not," he said. "You don't have to pay out much bounty money then."

"Occasionally." Duro shrugged.

"We were talking to a man named Lazair this morning—"

"Oh—"

"He was telling us about the fifteen scalps he brought in the other day."

"Fifteen!"

"Isn't that right?"

"I don't recall the exact number."

"That was a good haul."

"Yes, but it does not happen often."

Flynn eyed him steadily. "I was wondering how often it does happen. This Lazair must be pretty good to take that many at one time. He only has about a dozen men."

"I suppose," Duro said, "he knows many tricks in the tracking of Indians."

"I suppose," Flynn said.

"Would you care for a drink?" Duro said now, looking from one to the other.

Flynn said, "Fine," and Bowers nodded.

Duro went into the next room and returned with the bottle of mescal and three tumblers. "I have this for special guests," he said confidingly.

Flynn watched him place the glasses on his desk and pour mescal into them. "He had a Mimbre brave in his camp," he said.

Duro looked up. "This Lazair?"

Flynn nodded. "He'll be bringing you the scalp pretty soon."

"Oh . . . he was dead."

"He was after a while."

Duro shrugged. "Lazair is a businessman. A live Apache is worth nothing to him."

Bowers said quietly, "You get the feeling a live anything is worth nothing to him."

"Except perhaps a woman," Flynn added.

Duro handed them each a glass and said offhandedly, "He has a woman with him?"

"Didn't you know that?" Flynn asked.

"I have never visited his camp."

They sipped at the mescal, saying nothing. It was not a tension, but an uneasiness. After a moment Flynn said, "How do his men get on in the village?"

Duro shrugged. "As well as can be expected. They are, of course, sometimes primitive in their ways. As men would have to be who live as they do, by fighting Indians. But I have asked our people to treat them with courtesy since they are rendering our government a service." He sighed. "But sometimes they eye our women too covetously and with this my men are prone to raise objections."

"In other words," Flynn said, "they don't get along."

"Not all of the time, no."

"Lieutenant," Bowers said, "one of the reasons we came . . . I wonder if I could talk you into selling me a gun from your stores. I lost both of mine yesterday. That's if you have any extras."

"I could not possibly sell you one," Duro said stiffly, then smiled. "But I would be honored if you would select any gun you wish, as a gift."

They finished their drinks and descended to the equipment room. Bowers chose a Merrill carbine, and then a .44 Remington handgun which Duro insisted that he take. And though again he offered to pay for the arms, Lieutenant Lamas Duro would have none of this.

Flynn said, "Let us buy you a drink now."

But Duro refused painfully. "I'm sorry . . . a volume of paper work awaits me. You would not believe that only thirty men can do so much to expand the records." He bowed. "Perhaps another time."

They walked off toward Las Quince Letras, leading their horses, as Duro mounted the stairs.

"Well," Bowers said wearily, "what does he know?"

"One thing I'm willing to bet on," Flynn answered, "—the difference between a Mimbre and a Mexican scalp."

From the sunlight they entered the dimness of Las Quince Letras, Flynn half expecting to see Frank Rellis, half hoping and ready, but Rellis was not there though four Americans were toward the other end of the bar at a front table. Three girls were with them. They looked up as Flynn and Bowers moved to the bar. Here and there were men of the village, older men, sipping their wine or mescal slowly to make it last and they looked up only for a moment.

"Those four weren't at Lazair's camp," Bowers said. The men with the girls at their table were still looking toward them.

"No, I didn't see them," Flynn said. He held up two fingers to the mustached Mexican behind the bar and said, "Mescal." Then to Bowers, "Let's sit down."

They brought bottle and glasses with them to a table. Bowers poured the mescal and pushed a glass toward the cavalry scout. His eyes held on the sandy mustache, waiting for Flynn to say something. Bowers was in charge—that's what the orders read—but it wasn't that simple. Just putting a man in charge doesn't make it so. Bowers was realizing this.

He said finally, "Now what?"

Flynn was making a cigarette. He lighted it and blew smoke and through the smoke said, "I'm going back to Lazair's camp."

"When?"

"As soon as I see Hilario."

"Alone?"

"I think it would be better." Looking at Bowers he added, "If there are no objections."

"Of course not."

Flynn leaned closer. "Have you been figuring this?"

"How does it stand?"

"I know which is the worst now. I think Soldado is in second place, then the rurales."

Flynn added, "None very pleasant, and all of them hating each other. What does that suggest?"

"The obvious. Get them against each other."

"You want to work on it?"

"I'm not sure about going about it."

"Santana, Duro's sergeant, I think he's the one to start on. Tell him about all the Mexican girls in Lazair's camp. Concentrate on Santana. Make up whatever you like; whatever he wants to believe; something that would take time to prove."

"And Duro?"

Flynn said thoughtfully, "And Duro—He's in with Lazair, that stands to reason since he's paying for scalps he knows damn well aren't Apache. Santana against Duro . . . that makes sense . . . if you can work it."

Abruptly, seriously, Bowers said, "Why was I sent on this?"

"Somebody had to go."

"You told Deneen he should have picked a man with more experience."

"I shouldn't have said that."

"Why did he pick me?"

"I don't know. How well does he know you?"

"I met Deneen in Contention for the first time."

"Your dad was division Commander over both of us in the war. Maybe you knew, Deneen was a captain then. I've known him off and on for thirteen years."

"Well?"

Flynn shrugged. "Maybe he admired your father so, he knew you'd make a good soldier."

Bowers glanced up from his mescal, but said nothing.

"Look, what difference does it make?" Flynn said. "We're here now."

"He dislikes you," Bowers said, glancing at him again. "That's apparent."

"You can't like everybody."

"It's more than that."

"Why not just think about the job you have to do?"

"All right."

Flynn finished the mescal in his glass and rose. "I'm going to see Hilario now. Look for me the day after tomorrow. But if I don't come then, wait a few more days before you do anything."

"You don't want me to go with you?"

"If it doesn't work with one, it wouldn't work with two."

"You make it sound like taking a walk in the park."

The corners of Flynn's eyes creased as he smiled; then the eyes were serious. "Look, I'd like to help you . . . but there isn't any pattern to these things. You can't open *Cooke's Cavalry Tactics* and get the answer. Much of this is patience. But having time to think, you end up worrying about what you're going to do first, then about why you were sent and you even worry whether or not Apaches become afraid." Flynn smiled. "I meant that as no offense."

Bowers said, "That's all right."

Flynn sat down again. "Let's get it out in plain sight. You know Deneen doesn't have one ounce of authority to send us down here?"

"He's Department Adjutant. I'd say that was enough."

"In Arizona. This is Mexico, somebody else's country. Remember, the orders said the army would not recognize us as lawful agents if we were held for any reason."

"He explained that to me in Contention," Bowers said. "He said so far it was a verbal agreement with Mexico. We can cross their border so many miles and they can enter the United States, if it means running down hostiles. He said he had to put that not responsible business in the orders as a formality. The agreement was supposed to be in writing soon, he said probably before we'd get here."

"But Duro said *if his government had known about it . . .*" Flynn said. "That doesn't sound like an agreement."

"Then why are we here?" Bowers said.

Flynn hesitated. "You're here because you're obeying an order." He added, "Because you're not in a position to question authority." Now go easy, he thought, and said, "I'm here because I want to be. It's that simple."

"Yet you say neither of us have any business being here." He wanted to ask Flynn what was between him and Deneen, but it wouldn't be in order.

Flynn smiled again. "All right, but what would you be doing if you weren't here? Parade drills . . . patrols that never find anything . . . mail-run escort—"

Bowers nodded.

"So . . . why don't we do the world a good turn and kick Soldado's Apache tail back to San Carlos. And if problems come along we'll meet them one at a time and not worry about everything at once. Right?"

Bowers nodded, thoughtfully. "All right." He watched Flynn rise and move to the door, then nodded as Flynn did. The screen banged.

He took a sip of the mescal and putting the glass down he saw the four Americans watching him.

The street of the house of Hilario Esteban was quiet. There were sounds from other streets, but here was only sun glare on sand-colored adobe and a thin shadow line close to the houses extending down both sides of the street. The bullfight poster near the deserted home of Anastacio Esteban was hanging in small shreds now and only a few words were readable.

A small boy ran out of the house next to Hilario's.

"I will hold your horse!"

Flynn swung down and handed him the reins. "Carefully."

"With happiness," the boy smiled.

It was a woman who opened the door to his knock. Stooped, beyond middle age, a black scarf covered her shoulders and her dress beneath that was black. Hilario appeared behind her and his eyes brightened.

"Davíd!"

"How does it go?"

"Well," the alcalde answered. He motioned the woman and Flynn past him into the room.

The woman moved to the fireplace and sat on the floor there. She began stirring a bowl of atole and did not look at Flynn. With her head down, her figure was that of a child who weighed less than ninety pounds.

Hilario indicated the woman and said, "La Mosca. She is a herb woman, but now she prepares atole for me out of kindness. If there were a wound on my body, La Mosca would apply to it seeds of the guadalupana vine each marked with the image of the Virgin and soaked in mescal . . . or a brew of pulverized rattlesnake flesh if I were afflicted with the disease which the gachupines introduced to the women of our land . . . but she can do nothing for me now."

"Listen, Hilario," Flynn said. "I have not much time. I've come to tell you that your daughter is alive. I saw her."

He heard the soft rough sound that cloth makes and La Mosca, the curandera, was next to him.

"I have felt this," she said, "and have already told our alcalde of it."

Flynn said, "All right. Then I'm confirming what you have already told."

Hilario's voice was barely above a whisper, breathing the words in disbelief. "Is it true? Where?"

"If I told you that, you would go there hastily—"

"With all certainty!"

"And that would not be wise." He touched the old man's arm. "Look. I am going there now, with a plan. It is a matter of trusting me. If I told you where I was going perhaps others would find out—"

"Not from me."

"Perhaps not. But this not telling you is an additional safeguard."

The curandera said then, "She is being held by a man."

Hilario looked at her. "This comes to you?"

La Mosca nodded. "The man is not Indian. That I also know."

She can figure that out without looking into the future, Flynn thought.

"Is this true, David?"

"My companion, the one I came with, will remain here. He knows about this and will help you if for a reason I cannot come back."

Quietly Hilario said, "All right."

La Mosca said now, "You will come back." Her wrinkled face looked up at Flynn. "This comes to me now. You will return by the beginning of *Día de los Muertos*—the festival of the dead—and you will bring with you the daughter of this man."

THIRTEEN

He studied the place for a long time, his gaze holding on the shape that was barely visible through the trees at the bottom of the shallow slope.

Someone was there. Not a movement, but something resembling a human form, though from this distance it was hard to tell. Flynn was on his stomach in the coarse grass that grew among the pines here. His horse was yards behind him, below the line of the hill.

Above the tree that he watched, a cliff rose shadowed with crevices and grotesque chimneys; pink cantera stone fading pale as the threat of rain washed the sky gray. High above the thickening clouds was an eruption of sunlight, a cold light that fanned upward away from the rain that was to come.

Minutes passed and the shape did not move.

Flynn eased back from the crest to his mount and pulled the Springfield from its scabbard. He crouched at the crest again studying the shape, then rose and moved slowly, cautiously down the slope into the trees.

There it was. And he saw now why there had been no movement.

It was Matagente. He was hanging from the twisted limb of a juniper by a short length of rawhide that squeezed into the flesh of his throat. Matagente no longer wore his headband . . . the crown of his head had been hacked off for its scalp.

It's a warning, Flynn thought, meant for Soldado. But probably the buzzards would have found him before Soldado.

And then it occurred to him: But where are they? If there are no buzzards then he was just hung there . . . within the hour probably. Because Lazair shot him this morning you assumed he was put here then. But if he'd been here all day there wouldn't be much left of him—

He went back up the slope and returned to his mount, drawing a clasp knife from his pocket, and from the height of the McClellan saddle had to raise himself only a little more to reach the rawhide and cut it. He held the Apache about the body as he did this, feeling hard flesh and caked blood that crumbled against his hand and as he felt the full weight he tried to bend Matagente across the pommel of his saddle. But the body was stiff with death.

He used the rawhide line then, piecing it together, and dragged the Mimbre behind the horse carefully through the evergreens until he reached the sandy cantera cliff. There was no other way to do it.

He carried Matagente then, when he was closer to the wall, and laid his body into a hollow of the base. There were hundreds of cracks, hollows and niches here, sharply shadowed black seams rising with the heights of the pink façade. Then he placed rocks over the hollow and within minutes Matagente was a part of the cliff.

Flynn retraced his steps then, smoothing the marks Matagente's dragged body had made.

Let's go slow now, he told himself. Let's think it out before jumping into anything. Their camp is beyond the cliff and even up another climb farther on. If they were to ride to Soyopa they would pass this place. They could have hung him here on their way . . . but I would have seen them . . . Not necessarily. You could have passed in timber. You could have missed them easily and there would not have been a dust rise in the trees.

He looked at the sky now. It's going to rain before dark. I can't picture Lazair's men riding out into the rain unless ordered to, unless he was there to make them.

Tracks. It occurred to him then. With the rain there will be no tracks tomorrow of where they went today. They can hang Matagente and Soldado cannot trace the sign to Lazair's camp.

He rode back to the juniper from which Matagente had been hanging and looked at the ground. The tracks, half-moon impressions of steel-shod hooves, went east . . . not to Soyopa, nor back to Lazair's camp. There had been no attempt to cover the tracks.

That's it, Flynn thought, they're counting on the rain. They're riding because it's going to rain and they're not going to all this trouble for anybody else but Soldado. Setting up an ambush at a logical place . . . along some trail they think the old Indian would have to take some time or another . . . and they don't want their tracks to warn him and turn the ambush around. And if this is true, then there would not be many at Lazair's camp now.

He went on, and even though he could feel an excitement inside of him now he traveled at the same careful pace, watching four directions as he skirted the steep slant of cliff wall and began climbing again, now into dwarf oaks. He would stop and wait and listen, then go on. You never knew for sure, so why take a chance?

Finally he reached the meadow and by this time it was beginning to drizzle. It was not yet dark and a gray mist hung over the sabaneta grass that would bend silently in a wave as the wind stirred. The rain made a sound, but it was a soft hissing whisper that was not there after you listened to it long enough.

He would move when it was dark. He'd cross the meadow and climb the slope there two hundred yards away and find the guard before the guard found him. If the rain keeps up it will help, he thought.

Then he would find out if he'd guessed right. He had planned to watch here until the band of scalp hunters rode out . . . even if it might take a few days . . . but now he was almost certain they were not in camp, and waiting to make sure would only waste time.

It took longer for full darkness to creep over the meadow, because Flynn was waiting for it, but finally it settled and with it the rain seemed louder.

Pretend you're Mimbreño, he thought as he left the cover of the trees and started across the meadow. This would be easy for one of Soldado's boys. It would be nothing. But think of the guard now; he was up in the rocks before; that doesn't mean he'll be there now. It's raining. If he's taken cover you'll have to be careful; but at least he won't hear you with the rain. Think like an Apache. But don't kill him, he thought then. Not if you can help it.

Faintly he could see the shape of the rock rise against the sky. We were over more to the right, he thought, remembering the outline of the crest as it had looked to him the first time. The first and only time . . . this morning. And that's hard to believe that it was this morning. The guard had been to the left then. Now he would be directly in front of you if he's in the same place.

Flynn moved to the right, now, holding the detail of the rock rise in his memory and now estimating where the defile would be. He moved closer, threading into the rocks and there it was just above him slanting darkly into the slope.

He eased himself up over the rocks, crawled, lay flat to listen, then crawled again to the pass opening and rose, looking up to the ledge where the guard had been that morning.

He's not there. Flynn's gaze came back to the define which was totally dark as far as he could see—*or* maybe he's in there using an overhang for shelter. But maybe there isn't any guard— and if there isn't, then you *know* Lazair's gone. That's the way it would be—nobody bothering to take watch if Lazair wasn't there to make him.

But you have to be sure.

He moved in a little farther, listening. Then went the rest of the way through without hesitating, crouched low to one wall, and at the other end he went down into the wet grass, feeling it cold against his hands and face, and looked out at the camp.

Across the open area he could make out the horses. They had drifted into the aspens, and now he heard one of them whinny, a faint shrill sound in the darkness.

The rain made a splattering sound against the tents. The ties of one had unfastened and the flaps billowed and then popped as the wind rose to sweep stinging into the camp. Three of the tents were deserted. The fourth stood ghostlike in the darkness—a lantern inside illuminating the pale, wet canvas outline.

No light showed from the cave entrance.

A man's voice came from the lighted tent. The sound of a word, then laughter, faint sounds far away.

Flynn raised himself slowly and edged along the rock outcroppings that rimmed the pocket. Nearing the cave, a vertical crack of light now showed along one edge of the blanket that covered the entrance. And then he was up the slight rise under the shelter.

Now, very quietly, he thought. Take all the time you want because you'll do this just once. He put his hands into his coat and dried them against his shirt. He wiped his face with a bandana then drew his pistol and wiped it carefully.

The voice sound came from the tent again and Flynn could feel it inside of him tightening his chest. He pictured the men in the tent. He pictured four of them for some reason. I could go down there and empty this into the canvas and get all of them, he thought. Then: Don't be foolish. Come on now.

Cocking the pistol he brushed aside the blanket covering and the next moment was inside the cave—in high, room-size dimness, a line with clothes hanging from it, bedding along one wall, and in a corner, crouched beside the coal-oil lamp turned low, was Nita Esteban.

Flynn put one finger to his mouth. Then, "Don't speak out loud," he said softly.

The girl looked up at him, her body tensed. She was kneeling on a blanket, sitting back on her feet. Her hands held the blanket tightly and no part of her body moved.

Close to her, Flynn dropped to one knee. "Nita." He put his hand on her shoulder and took it away feeling her body shudder. "I'm not one of them." He touched her again, gently. "Do you remember, six months ago I came through Soyopa and stayed at the house of your uncle. I was a friend of his, *David Flin*."

Her eyes held his—searching, deep black eyes that were not sure. And then they were sure. Then they remembered and the dark eyes in the drawn face were suddenly glistening with tears. Flynn brought her to him gently and heard and felt the muffled sob against his chest. Her shoulders quivered and he held her close to him, awkwardly with one hand because the pistol was there, now moving the other hand up to stroke her hair, with much the same feeling you stroke a child's head.

Lowering his face he said to her ear, "How many are there?"

The sobbing stopped. "Most of them left during the afternoon. There would not be many now. One of them came here not long ago. I thought you were he when you entered."

"There is a light in only one tent."

"They are the only ones," she said. "Perhaps three, or four or five. The one who was here came for a bottle of something to drink." She hesitated. "He said I should go with him, but I refused and he said that when he came back I would be sorry."

Flynn rose, bringing her up with him. She wore a skirt to her ankles and a man's shirt buttoned high and the shirttail hanging to where her knees would be.

"Lazair keeps his clothes here, doesn't he?"

She nodded, but did not look at his face.

"Put another shirt on."

He moved to the blanket covering as she did this and stood listening. There it was again; one of them laughing. Then another sound—close!

He had time to warn the girl only with his eyes. She saw him flatten against the wall. A leather coat was hanging there from a nail and he drew the coat in front of him, though he still could be seen.

Then the blanket cover was whipped back and a man stood in the entrance, weaving, his eyes narrowing on Nita Esteban, then smiling.

"You must a been coming to see us. Nowhere else you could go." Mescal was in his voice and in the half-open eyes. He had come from the tent bareheaded and now his hair was shining, plastered close to his skull. He had brought no hat, but he was armed. He chuckled and turned to the wall where Lazair's gear was, where the mescal was kept.

He was about to say something more to the girl but the words caught in his mouth. He could see Flynn, and the pistol pointed toward him.

The man wheeled. In split-second surprise he wheeled toward the cave entrance.

Flynn held back, then there was no choice and he felt the .44 jerk with the exploding sound.

The scalp hunter stumbled, rolling to his side. His hand waved, slapped against his holster . . . the glint of metal coming up with the hand . . . then a second report, ear-splitting in the closeness, and the man fell back and did not move.

They were over him, past him, almost the same moment. Flynn holding the girl's arm, brushing aside the blanket, then out into darkness running for the scattered rimrocks. And as they reached cover the other men were coming out of the tent, furiously at first—the canvas shaking, something kicked over, glass breaking, curses—then the light was extinguished and the men were outside. Now they made no sound. Now it was realization of what they had to do and they approached toward the cave slowly, fanning out, as Flynn and the girl crept to the defile and made their way through the blind narrowness of it.

There were four of them—it went through Flynn's mind—now only three, but you can count on them coming, coming quick!

His hand was tight clutching Nita's arm and he ran with her through the swishing wet wound of the sabaneta grass, holding himself to run at the girl's speed.

There was his mount, where he had left it. Hide glistening wet, skittering nervously at the abruptness of their coming into the trees. Flynn mounted, now reached for the girl and swung her up behind him and felt her arms holding as he wheeled the horse off through the trees. They descended, following the trail in his memory, crossed a flat stretch on the dead run then climbed again into timber before stopping to listen.

At first it was only the sound of Nita's breathing, then far off, faintly, he could hear the horses.

They're close, he thought, straining to listen, now conscious of his own breathing. They've figured it out. Somebody from Soyopa since it was not Apaches. So they're running hard in the direction of Soyopa. If they don't overtake someone they'll double back and in the morning spread out and start looking.

The sound of running horses was louder now. They had reached the flat stretch below them. Still mounted, unmoving, with the girl's arms tightening about him, they heard the horses pass, carrying their sound with them into the distance again. The girl's arms relaxed.

"We'll have to wait until it's light," Flynn said. "In the darkness we could run into them." He looked over his shoulder and saw her head nod.

Higher up in the timber they dismounted. Flynn kindled a low burning fire, without worrying about it being seen. A brush rimmed pocket shielded them on three sides. The fire might be visible from the fourth, but a man would have to be standing less than twenty feet away to see it and if he were that close, fire or no fire he'd know they were there.

They sat close over the mesquite twig fire letting their clothes dry on them. The girl's were not so wet, but Flynn's were stuck cold to his body and it was some time before the fire warmth penetrated enough for him to feel it on his body.

Later on, they lay close to each other to sleep.

"Nita."

The girl's face turned to his and was only a few inches away.

He said in Spanish, softly, "I offer my sorrow for what has happened, though the words do little good."

"There is nothing one can say," the girl answered.

"Your father is well."

"Will you take me to him?"

"Of course. When it is light. When we can go without the fear of coming onto those without seeing them."

She's calm, Flynn thought. Even after all she's been through she has control of herself and can speak without her voice giving it away. She's a woman of Mexico, used to the sight of death—but that's a lot of nonsense. No, it's not callousness. It's faith. God is God and He lets things happen and that's all there is to it. But He has reasons, and His reasons for something happening would be more important than a man's reason for questioning whatever it might be. That's how she has probably looked at it and it has taken some of the sting out. Not all, some.

Flynn said now, "I have thought of you often since the time in Soyopa."

Nita had closed her eyes. Now she opened them. "I remember you well. At first I did not, because in my mind I was expecting the other, but now I do."

He said abruptly, though gently, "Did Lazair cause you pain?"

"With his eyes," the girl answered. "He did not molest me because he wanted me to consent. He would touch me, but that was all."

Flynn said, "I'm sorry," quietly, almost with embarrassment.

And then, as if they had been speaking of it before, the girl began: "The firing came suddenly from above, from both sides of the road and I saw my Uncle Anastacio fall from his horse. Others fell. There was screaming then and the mules began to go faster, but the wagons became entangled because the road was narrow and as this happened the men came down from the slopes firing their guns. One of them pulled me from the wagon and on the ground, beneath it, he tore open my dress and began to touch me, but the one called Lazair appeared and ordered him away. He took me up the slope to his horse and from there we watched what took place after"—she paused—"the scalping of those who had been killed, and some who had not been killed. Then he rode down the slope, holding me in front of him on the saddle, and ordered the men to cut loose the mules and burn the wagons. But after only two of them were burning he said to not bother with the others as it was time to go. Then four men rode through dragging saplings to obliterate the signs that were there. Then I saw one of my cousins being carried on another horse. She tore herself from the man who carried her and ran back toward the burning wagons, and the man shot her as she ran. One of those with the saplings dismounted and was drawing his knife as Lazair turned and rode off with me."

Nita said no more. She lay facing him, but her eyes were closed and her soft, shadowed features seemed relaxed now. Flynn put his arm around her gently. Through the night they lay close together and neither spoke again.

With first light they were moving down through the timber, through the gray mist that clung to the trees, left behind by night. Flynn carried the Springfield, leading the horse. Nita was mounted. Moving, winding slowly with the squeaking of straining leather and the crisp cracking rustling of hoofs in dried leaves.

Then they were crossing sand that muffled the hoofs; through mesquite and catclaw that tangled both sides of a draw, and there was ocotillo that yesterday had been thorned stalks but now blazed scarlet with the rain. The sky told there would be more rain and Flynn could smell it coming on the sultry wind.

The draw began to slope, gradually at its beginning, cutting between sweeping slopes, and as they followed the rise it narrowed, curving high up into the hills. In timber again, in the shadowy silence of it, they looked back down the way they had come. Far below, three riders were entering the draw.

They've found the tracks, Flynn thought. And now they know there are only two of us. One man and one woman. They probably aren't very worried and are thinking now it's getting interesting. He pictured them grinning at each other.

The girl had been watching them and now she looked at Flynn, asking the question with her eyes.

He said, "We can't run, because they can move faster. They would overtake us. The only thing to do is show them that we are aware of them and try to make them go slower." And he added, in his mind: Or stop them from going at all.

He moved the girl deeper into the trees then crept out among the rocks that overhung the steep-falling slope here. Dropping to his stomach he pushed the Springfield out between the rocks and looked down the barrel.

There they were, closer now, out of sight passing through jackpines, then reappearing. From his pocket Flynn brought out two brass cartridges and put them on the ground, on the spot where his hand would drop after swinging open the breech.

Five hundred yards, he thought. Take your time, they'll get closer. His eyes moved ahead of them, up the draw to where it narrowed and began to curve. But you'll have to hit them before they reach there. They'd have cover then and be able to sneak up through the brush if you miss with your first shot. So you'll fire from three hundred yards. It's a good thing it's downhill. They make them short in the barrel for shooting from horseback, but for long range you might just as well spit.

Now it was four hundred yards. They were single-file, taking their time.

Hit the first one. First things first. Let them get up to that open spot, so they won't be able to break for cover. But you won't get them all. You know that.

Close over the barrel he watched them come. The Springfield was cocked. His finger fondled the trigger lightly, feeling the spring tightness of it. The front sight covered the first rider. A little closer now, he thought.

All right.

His trigger hand tightened, squeezed closed. The shot rang, ripping thin air, echoing down canyon. The first horse was down. The man was on the ground. But now he was up, running. The second rider made a tight circle and leaned to help him up as the third one streaked away. He swung up behind the cantle and they were moving down the draw as Flynn fired again. The man went back, rolling off the horse's rump.

He threw open the breech and shoved in the third cartridge and fired as he lowered his head. The second horse went down. The rider hit and rolled and scrambled for cover. The third rider was out of range now.

Flynn looked back to the man he had hit. He was lying facedown. The other one was crawling toward him now. He knelt next to him and stayed there and Flynn thought: He must be alive.

Flynn had inserted another cartridge. He lowered his head, looking down the barrel at the man's back; then looked up again. He's got enough troubles now, Flynn thought, and backed away from the rocks.

They moved on through what was left of the morning, riding double now, running the horse when they would reach level stretches; but most of the time their travel was slow, following the maze of canyons and sweeping climbing draws that gouged the foothills, lacing in all directions. They bore a general direction west toward Soyopa, keeping the looming gray mass of the Sierra Madre behind them, the Mother Mountain that towered into the overcast sky losing her crested shapes gray against gray.

It was after noon, shortly after, when they stopped again, having come down into a ravine thick with aspen to a stream that was running with yesterday's rain.

When she had finished drinking, Nita Esteban sat on the grassy bank watching Flynn water the horse.

"We might reach Soyopa by nightfall," he said, looking toward her. Flynn spoke in Spanish. She had leaned back, resting on her arm. "You're tired, aren't you?"

"Knowing that we are going home takes much of the tiredness out of this."

She smiled then and Flynn thought, watching her: Now she's a girl again. This is the first time she's smiled. Before she was a woman. In her eyes the worn look of a woman who has seen an entire lifetime turn rotten. But now she's a girl again because she can look forward to something. Home.

"But from now on we'll have to use more caution."

She looked at him with surprise. "Those others are far behind."

"Two of them are. Perhaps all three, but we have no assurance of that. The third one is still mounted. He might have remained with his companions. He could be following us . . . or he might have circled to cut us off." He added gently, "I tell you this so you won't relax your guard entirely."

They moved on and it stayed in Flynn's mind now and he hoped the girl was thinking about it, being ready. The Springfield was across his lap and his gaze edged inching up over the brush on both sides of the ravine. The sides were steep and high up were pines. But being ready didn't lessen the shock when it came.

The shot broke the stillness, coming from nowhere. It ricocheted off rock above their heads, whining into the air. The second shot hit lower, but they were off the horse then, Flynn pushing the girl, running crouched, jerking the horse after them. Two shots followed them to cover and then stillness again.

Why didn't he wait, Flynn thought. Maybe he's jumpy. Or else that was his best shot and he took it. If it was he couldn't be closer than a hundred yards. He leaned close to Nita.

"He fired from the left slope, high up."

She waited for him to say more, her eyes wide, the pupils dilated an intense black..

"He has us . . . until we find him." He said then, "Do you know how to fire this?" handing her the Springfield.

"Once I did, but it was long ago."

He pointed it out in front of her and cocked it. "All you do is pull the trigger now. But don't fire unless he is close . . . if he should come. Keep it low; then if he should come onto you, wait until he is from here to there"—he pointed out just beyond the rocks—"then fire."

He moved quickly then, surprising the girl; up over the rocks, through the brush into the open; the sound of his running across the ravine, then a bullet spanged kicking dust behind him; his head was up watching for it and there it was, the almost transparent dissolving puff of powder smoke high up, farther down. Then he was into the brush going up the slope.

Now you know, Flynn told himself. But so does he.

At the top he kept to the pines, making a wide circle to where the scalp hunter would be. Three times he stopped to listen, but there was no sound. He went on, inching into the rocks. There was his horse! Then it would be close, right ahead, he thought, looking up beyond and back along the ravine. He moved closer, cautiously, with the pistol in front of him. There—

Three cigarette stubs. Boot scuff marks in the sand. But he's gone—

Flynn was over the rocks, scrambling down the brush slope, sliding with the shale that crumbled under his boots; at the bottom he crouched, hesitated, then started back to where Nita was, quickly, keeping to cover. And he saw the man before he was halfway.

The scalp hunter was moving in a crouch, half crawling up the ravine. Now he straightened, bringing up a Winchester, and walked slowly toward the rocks where Nita was hidden.

Flynn raised the pistol, aiming—two hundred feet at least, that's too far—then beyond the man's shoulder something else, a movement. It was Nita. He could see her head, now her shoulders, and suddenly the scalp hunter was running toward her. He was almost to the rocks, almost to Nita, when he stopped in his stride and hung there as a thin report flattened and died. He fell then, rolling on his back.

Nita still held the Springfield, looking at the man she had shot.

"It's over now," Flynn said gently, taking the carbine from her. He looked at the scalp hunter, recognizing him as the one Lazair had called Sid. The red-bearded one who had had his pistol. Sid stared back at him with the whites of his eyes and his jaw hung open in astonishment, though he had died the moment the bullet struck his chest.

They did not halt at dusk to make camp but went on, making better time now that both were mounted. Still, it was after midnight when they passed the cemetery and rode into the deep shadow of Santo Tomás.

A much smaller shadow glided out from the steps of the church as they came in the square. A woman. The face of La Mosca looked up at them from the blackness of the shawl covering her head.

"Man, it is as I said. You have returned. And now commences The Day of the Dead—"

FOURTEEN

Mescal, like tequila, is a juice of the maguey. As colorless as water unless orange peelings or pieces of raw chicken are dropped in while it's standing. When you see mescal a rich yellow, you'll know that's what it is, chicken or orange peels.

Who told him that? A straining, groaning authoritative voice in a stagecoach trying to out-shout axles that hadn't taken grease in forty miles of alkali . . . coming into somewhere.

Lieutenant Regis Duane Bowers poured himself another drink.

He drank well, because he had a good stomach; though he would have tried to drink as much if he didn't have a stomach, because it was part of being a cavalryman. You can tell a cavalryman by his walk and the way he wears his kepi and by the amount of whisky he can drink like a gentleman. These as much a part of being cavalry as a saber.

Now he was sitting. He wore neither kepi nor saber. And he was drinking mescal. It doesn't matter. It's something inside. Those things help: a slanted kepi and a saber, but they are only badges; you are a cavalryman because you think like one and feel like one and then you know you're one. That's all. Just one of those things you know . . . and don't let anybody say different.

One of the Mexican girls was looking at him now, a smile softening her mouth as he glanced at her. She was at the table with the four Americans.

His eyes lowered and he sipped at the sweet liquor. There was a lot to think about. But Flynn makes everything sound simple. He looks at things in their proper perspective, things one at a time, and doesn't worry about something that's supposed to happen next week because there's no assurance there will be a next week. That's a good way to look at things, but it takes some doing. Saying, well, we're here; we might as well do the job. That's the easy way to look at things. No it isn't. It's the hard way . . . when you don't have any business being here. If what he says is true, it's natural to want to go back to Deneen and tell him to go to hell and next time find some authority. Staying on anyway takes humility, doesn't it? It takes something. Something that wasn't handed out with *Cavalry Tactics*. But that's assuming Deneen doesn't have the authority, and you don't assume anything.

Flynn can almost convince you that he's right even before he says one word. It's his manner. The way he goes about things. He doesn't get excited. He seems absolutely perfectly honest with himself; that's why you believe what he says. After being with him only a few days part of him rubs off. The feeling you've known him a long time. Relaxing. Maybe he's right about Deneen overstepping his bounds . . .

Don't get carried away. Maybe he is; and maybe he isn't. Remember, you're talking about a colonel with fifteen years and a war behind him. They don't generally make mistakes like that. There's something between him and Flynn, something personal, so naturally Flynn is against him. But I'm glad Flynn's here. He speaks quietly and sometimes you get the idea he's lazy and doesn't care, but I wouldn't want to be fighting against him.

He wanted to be a good friend of Dave Flynn's, and often since leaving Contention, he wondered if Flynn ever thought about their first meeting, at the cavalry post before Deneen came in. He had been aloof then, maybe snobbish in Flynn's eyes. It bothered him, because he hadn't meant to seem a snob. It was just that he wanted to show them he wasn't a kid, that he knew what it was all about. He wanted Flynn's respect . . . even if he wasn't sure how right Flynn was about Deneen's authority.

He noticed the Mexican girl get up: the one who had been watching him. The man next to her said something and put his hand on her arm, but she jerked away from his grasp and the next moment was coming toward Bowers.

"May I sit with you?"

Bowers half rose, self-consciously, glancing at the other table. Then: The hell with them. She can go wherever she wants. They don't own her.

"I am enchanted."

She smiled. "You speak our language well."

"That was only a word."

"Now you've said five, equally well."

Bowers smiled. "I have learned in the past year to understand some of what is said, but it is yet difficult to speak. Most of the words I don't yet know."

"You need someone to accompany you, to make interpretations." She looked at him slyly from under dark lashes and smiled.

"I would never learn the language that way."

"Perhaps you would learn other things."

He felt them looking at him. "What about your friend?"

She glanced coldly over her shoulder. "He is not my friend; nor any of them there. I amuse myself with them only." Her glance returned quickly as one of the men rose and came toward their table.

It was Lew Embree. He bumped the next table unsteadily. A two days' beard growth darkened his face; mescal showed in his glazed, watery eyes and in the way his mouth was parted, sticky wet in the corners, loose in his bearded jaw.

The girl refused to look at him.

"Honey, I didn't come to see you, but your friend. When I come for you you'll know it." The sleepy eyes went to Bowers.

"I wondered if you knew your friend Frank was here?"

Bowers hesitated. "Frank who?"

"Frank Rellis."

"I don't know anyone by that name." But he remembered it. As he said it he pictured the two riders through the field glasses and the one on the left with the Winchester; then tying that in with what Flynn had told him before. Frank Rellis. The man who shot Joe Madora. Then Lazair mentioning him.

"Frank told how he knew you and your partner. In Contention, as I recollect."

"I've never met Frank Rellis."

The girl pretended to shudder and shook her head. "That one!"

"Well, he says he knew you and your partner."

"He must be mistaken."

"Frank doesn't say much, so when he does it's something he's sure of 'cause he's had all that silent time to think about it."

"If he's not mistaken then you misunderstood what he said."

"I heard him plain as your face tell Curt that he knew you."

Bowers said nothing and looked at his glass.

"He's over eatin'. He'll be back shortly; why'nt you wait to see him?"

"If I'm still here when he comes then most likely I'll see him."

"He said it was in Contention—"

"Look, I've never met Frank Rellis!" He looked at the man steadily now wondering if he was really drunk, even though it was on his face. The girl was suddenly looking beyond him and now he heard the door and the ching of heavy Mexican spurs. Sergeant Santana stopped at the bar.

Lew Embree looked at him a long moment and then glanced at the girl. "Come on, honey."

"I like it where I am."

"You be nice now."

"Go stick your head in it!"

"Honey, Warren's back there at the table cryin' his eyes out for you."

The girl did not say anything now.

Shaking his head Lew Embree looked at Bowers. "Don't these biddy-bitches get uppity though. She suspects you got more money than Warren, which could be a case." He was standing next to her chair. His hand moved to the cane back rest then idly up to the girl's neck, and suddenly, his fingers gripping the white cotton, he jerked his hand down, ripping the loose-fitting blouse away from her back. She was up out of the chair, screaming, holding the front of the blouse to her breasts, running toward the rear of the mescal shop, past the table where Warren and the others were, trying to dodge an arm that reached for her and caught a shred of material. It pulled her off balance, jerking the front of the blouse from her hands and now she made no attempt to cover herself, standing, cursing Embree with every indecent word she knew before running crying through the rear door.

Warren called to Lew, "She looks like she can't hardly wait!"

Still grinning, Lew Embree looked from Santana to Bowers then turned his back to them indifferently and started for the other table. "For a girl that throws it around like she does," Lew was saying, "she acts awful kittenish."

Bowers watched Embree until he reached the other table, then he looked toward Santana.

"Will you sit here?"

The rurale sergeant pushed back his straw Chihuahua hat, shaking his head faintly. "I will be here only a moment."

Bowers stood and moved to the bar carrying the mescal bottle. "Let me buy you a drink." He said then, "I was wondering what that man's name was."

Santana accepted the bottle that Bowers extended and poured a glass half full. "I've never listened for his name."

"That was something he did to the girl, eh?"

"She had her clothes off in his presence before."

"I had the feeling he did it for my benefit," Bowers said, watching the rurale.

Santana shrugged, then drank. He wiped his mouth and said, "He misses no opportunity to show they have bought these women well. But it makes little difference since the women *are* bought; it's hardly a winning of their affection."

Bowers said idly, "But it would seem to me to be a matter of principle. I don't know if I could just let these men come in and take over all the women. That's if it was up to me."

Santana was watching the ones at the table. "This is not something that will go on always."

"I should think you'd have enough men that you wouldn't have to stand for such nonsense going on. Those are Lazair's men, aren't they?"

Santana nodded.

"Then you must have about three to one on him."

"We have been instructed to treat him with courtesy."

Bowers half smiled. "Where do you draw the line? If a guest at your home made advances to your wife, would courtesy hold you back from dealing with him?"

"There is a difference."

"You live in Soyopa. The women are yours, of your land. Then these come and take whatever they like and make themselves comfortable. Was it your lieutenant who said this about courtesy?"

Santana nodded. "That one."

"He hasn't been to Lazair's camp, has he?"

"No."

"I'm told there were some women there. Not like the ones that work here, but good girls, from another pueblo. Alaejos, somewhere like that. What they were doing to them I've heard called many things . . . but courtesy wasn't one of them."

"Where did you hear this?"

"From one of the men of the village. Now I'm not sure, that might have been a time ago and now they are gone."

Santana sipped his mescal; he was thinking, and it was even something physical, tightening his swarthy face. His eyes were small in his face and now they did not show as he squinted to make things plainer in his mind.

"When I heard that," Bowers said, "I couldn't help but be angry myself; but one man cannot do anything against all of them."

"What of your companion?"

"That would make two of us."

"No, I meant where is he?"

Bowers shrugged. "Probably at the house of the alcalde, or visiting others. He also cannot understand this immunity that seems to have been granted them."

"Lieutenant Duro—"

"Yes, Lieutenant Duro . . . who is forced to associate with them only when paying the scalp bounty. The rest of the time he is alone in his comfortable house with little to do—"

"Not always alone."

"But while you perform his work. I have heard that," Bowers said.

"What?"

"Everyone speaks of it. You're modest. It's said about that Duro would accomplish nothing if it were not for Sergeant Santana."

"That is said?"

"You are modest; for you know this better than I. How often does he come from his house into the sun?"

"Little."

"Perhaps for pleasure, but never for work, eh?"

Santana nodded, thoughtfully.

"It seems such a waste. Yet he is the one who insists that you be courteous to the men of Lazair. Has he led you against the Apaches?"

"That one? That son of the great whore would sooner cut his arm off."

Bowers said, sympathetically, "You can find little respect for a man like that."

"None. Just the sight of him is an abuse."

Bowers said nothing, watching him.

Santana said, "In the army it isn't uncommon to find men such as he. I know that for I have served. As a boy I was present at the battle of Cinco de Mayo, where at Puebla, under Zaragoza and this same Diaz we now have, we defeated the army of France."

"That was a long time ago."

"Fifteen years," Santana answered. "But with the clearness of yesterday in my mind."

"And you have served all of this time?"

"Most of it."

"I didn't know you were a veteran of such long service."

"But this is not the army," Santana said.

"More a police force?"

"More an association of bandits. Listen . . . almost every one of my men has lived his entire life outside of the law. These you meet in all armies, but not in such proportion as here. To organize this, Diaz must have thrown open the jails."

"Then there is a problem making them obey orders."

"Listen." Santana looked at Bowers intently. "There is no problem. These that were conceived in stables and have seasoned in prisons . . . there is not one of them I cannot handle. If it were not for that pimp of a lieutenant, much more would be accomplished here. Lieutenant Duro sometimes believes he is much man, but it is only his rank that tells him so. Inside of him live worms."

Bowers shook his head. "That's too bad. Here you are, a military man, years of experience and with a force you could probably turn into a fine fighting corps . . . and they saddle you with an officer who has no feeling for service. I would venture that you could have taken your men even against this Soldado Viejo long before this if it were not for Duro."

"With certainty, even though they are not trained properly for the fighting of Indians; that is, as a body, which is the only way to defeat them."

"Taking them into the hills after Soldado would not be wise then."

"No. We have not been given trackers. How would we find them? And if we did, how would we assault them? Firing, puffs of the powder smoke high up, but when you climb to the place, nothing. Then you carry down your dead. It is always thus with the Apaches."

"But to get them in the open, eh?" Bowers prompted. He pushed the mescal bottle toward Santana, watching the sergeant light a cigar, puff hard, hurrying to light it.

"*Aiii*—to get them in the open. Listen, when that day comes we will flood them; we will sweep through their ranks and you will see riding you thought was not possible. There are many vaqueros

among us; these will sweep them, firing, stinging like a thousand
ants, then roping them to be dragged behind the horses. Then, instead of scalps, we will take the entire heads and secure them to
poles and place each pole a certain distance apart, all the way to
Hermosillo."

"If you get them in the open."

"Yes." Santana's voice was lower, the word part of his breath.
Then he said, again excitedly, "Listen, tomorrow with the sun I am
taking a patrol toward the pueblo of Alaejos. That is a good direction for Apaches. You come with us. Then, if we see Apaches down
from the hills, I'll show you something, man, to tell them back
home."

"How long would we be gone?"

"We would return the following day . . . in time for the fiesta.
Día de los Muertos—"

Santana took one more drink, repeating that he had only a moment, then left the mescal shop.

Red Bowers exhaled slowly, a long sigh. Flynn had it right,
Bowers thought. Santana arouses easily, and he hates Lazair's
men. This could be all right. This could work, if it's handled properly. Just take it slowly. This could be like war from a general's
saddle—moving troops, but only hearing the gunfire in the distance. Here's some practice for you. And then there's Duro . . .
something for his ear.

He paid the bartender and started for the door.

"Boy . . . you goin' to wait for Frank!"

Bowers glanced back at the table where Embree and the other
sat. He hesitated, then went out without bothering to answer.

He crossed the square toward Duro's house, leading his mount,
hoofs clopping behind a thin shadow with legs twice as long as
they should be. The square was still vacant; the two rurales who
had been in front of Duro's were not in sight.

He mounted the stairs heavily, slowly. If he were interrupting
anything Duro would hear him and have time to clear away whatever it, or she, might be. That was the gentlemanly thing to do. But
when he reached the veranda there was no sound from within. He
called the lieutenant's name through the partly opened door. He
waited, then pushed in when there was no answer. Calling again,
he moved to the bedroom doorway—

Duro was on the bed, sprawled on his back. A fly buzzed close
to his face, close to his open mouth. The mescal bottle was on the

floor, but Duro still clutched the glass he'd been holding when he passed out.

"Officer and gentleman," Bowers said half aloud. He left then.

Lazair counted the scalps again as they returned to camp. He knew there were eight, but there was no harm in a recount. His hunch had paid off. With the rain the streams had filled. He had located his men at three watering places on the chance Soldado's people would come to one of them. And they had.

The second evening they came—seven women and two old men to protect them. And now they had eight scalps. One woman had gotten away. It was almost dark, but best to return to camp now than wait for a war party to come storming back for revenge. You could always pick off a few if you found the right water holes, that was the way to do it; but God, don't try and hit the whole bunch!

He'd sent a man to gather the ones at the other two places, and some men were bringing up the rear to cover sign as best they could in the fast-falling dark. Well, it was a worthwhile two days. He'd get a good rest, maybe have a little talk with Nita, and take the scalps in in the morning. A good day to go to town . . . there was supposed to be some kind of fiesta.

FIFTEEN

We are all afraid of death, Lamas Duro thought, but one admits it only to himself. He was standing on the veranda of his headquarters, watching the straggle of villagers coming now and then from the side streets, crossing the square in the direction of the cemetery.

In company we can be brave. We proclaim this festival, *Día de Los Muertos*, to celebrate on the grave stones and joke at death and tell him we aren't afraid . . . but these are only outward signs. With some of the people it takes a full bottle of mescal before they are at ease in his presence. And with others it takes even more. And he thought: Like yourself . . . it takes a bottle every day. Did you know that? For you, every day is *Día de Los Muertos*.

Looking across the square, he watched one group pass into the midmorning shadow of the church. They moved along the west wall, carrying their homemade wine and mescal, and lunches of bread—small loaves baked in the shapes of death's heads for the occasion.

Take a bite of death on the grave of your father.

Death and the devil are one. Show him you aren't afraid and he'll stay in hell where he belongs. But take another drink before it wears off and he comes leaping out.

Lamas Duro smiled. Children of the ignorant whore Superstition. But he thought: You believe in nothing, now; yet you conduct yourself in this manner every day. What does it mean?

He looked out over the square, at the shadow of the obelisk which was the only thing about the square that ever changed, and made the scene seem more monotonous because the change itself was a dull, inching thing that wasn't worth thinking about.

It means you're sick of life . . . but afraid of death, so you take the in-between, and that's mescal. You didn't begin that way. Even a year ago there was no fear, but that was before Diaz . . . and his rurales . . . his bandits, which is what they are.

It came suddenly, and he wasn't aware of the reason—though it must have been the picture of himself as he had once been, for that flashed in his mind, differently than it had the many times before, for consciously now he saw himself as he had been and, at the same time, as he was now—and he knew then that he would leave.

And the plan of what he would do fell into place quickly . . . remembering the bounty money in his possession and Lazair away from the pueblo and Santana due in from patrol that morning but being weary should be in the mescal shop or at camp and the entire population of Soyopa celebrating *Día de Los Muertos*. . . . No one, no one would notice a lone rider leaving Soyopa!

He would ride north . . . across the border. That was it. Living among the Americans would be something to get used to, but at least the bounty money would make the getting used to it less unbearable. And it now seemed so simple, so elementary, that he wondered why it had not occurred to him before this. He inhaled deeply, feeling his shirt tighten against his chest, then moved away from the veranda railing and went into the office.

A half-full mescal bottle that he had started only that morning was on the desk. He picked it up by the neck and was smiling as his arm swung wide and let it go. The bottle smashed against the far wall—shattering, flying glass and the liquid burst of it beginning to run down to the floor.

Entering the square, Bowers glanced at Santana. "What was that?"

Santana smiled through the sweat-streaked dust on his face. "This is a feast day. Many bottles are opened, some of them are dropped."

They were passing Duro's house, less than a hundred feet away, and nodding toward it Bowers said, "Sounded like it came from there."

Santana answered, "Lieutenant Duro has never dropped a bottle in the entirety of his life."

They stopped in front of Las Quince Letras, Bowers and Santana, with a few of the rurales pulling even with them now. Most of the rurales had swerved from the square down the street leading to their camp.

Bowers came off the saddle stiff-legged. It seemed a long time since dawn; riding steadily for hours with nothing happening made it seem like days. There were no Apaches, not even a pony sign all day yesterday or that morning. But the thought was in Bowers' mind all during the patrol that probably it was just as well. Santana wouldn't have been ready for Apaches had they appeared. He allowed his patrol to stretch thin. There was more than just talking in ranks—loud laughter, even drinking. Almost, it seemed to Bowers, as if their purpose was to ride through the brush to flush out game for a hunting party ahead. Santana failed to send out flankers. He kept two men riding advance, but each time the twenty-man patrol caught up with them they were dismounted, lying in the shade, if there was shade, or else with sombreros tilted over their faces. When they reached Alaejos, two men were missing. The two straggled in almost an hour later, and Santana said nothing to them. In more than a dozen places along the way, three Apaches could have annihilated a good half of the patrol. Bowers kept his thoughts to himself. By the time they had reached Alaejos, that afternoon, he realized it wasn't a lack of discipline; Santana didn't know what he was doing . . . in spite of his years in the army. He thinks he's a soldier, Bowers had thought, but he isn't even close to being one.

When they left Alaejos, a man in white peon clothes was with them. He rode between two rurales and his hands were tied to the saddle horn. A middle-aged man with tired eyes that looked at nothing. Santana said he was a thief and one purpose of the patrol was to bring him back to Soyopa to be tried by Duro. "What did he steal? I don't know. What difference does it make? I have the name and this is the man who answers to it."

A few miles out of Alaejos Bowers noticed Santana nod to one of the men next to the peon. The rurale dropped back half a length and suddenly slapped the peon's mount across the rump. Santana waited, deliberately. No one had moved. Bowers looked at Santana quickly, with astonishment that turned to shock as Santana smiled, waiting, then with the smile in the tone of his voice shouted for his men to stop him.

A dozen rurales fired, and when the man was on the ground motionless some of them were still firing.

"Why do they always try to escape?" Santana had said, then shrugged. "*Ley fuga.* It saves the cost of a trial."

They had made camp later on and started for Soyopa again with the first light.

Now it was midmorning as they entered Las Quince Letras.

"Mescal?" Santana asked, and when Bowers nodded he said, "This time on me."

Bowers waited as Santana paid for the bottle. He was more than a little tired of Santana now, after a full day and a half of him, but if he wanted to buy a drink that was all right. After, he would go to Hilario's house and wait for Flynn. Today was supposed to be the day.

He was surprised at the amount of people in the shop and then he remembered that this was a festival day. There was a hum of talking spotted with laughter and the sounds of glasses and bottles. And going over the room his eyes hesitated on the table where the four Americans sat. The same table as before. One of them was the man who had torn the girl's dress off. God, he must live here. And with the same three friends. No, one of them wasn't here the other day. His eyes moved on and came back to the bar and Santana was coming toward him with bottle and glasses. There was a vacant table in front of them and they sat down at it.

"Good crowd," Bowers said, "for before noon."

Santana smiled. "Preparing themselves for the graves."

"Part of the festival?"

"The big part. *Día de Los Muertos* lasts these three days. On this the first day, the graves of ancestors are visited. They are mourned, toasted and finally eaten over before the day is through. By the third day death is convinced that we aren't afraid of him."

Now they did not speak. As if there was nothing more in common between them which they had not already spoken of. Bowers, out of politeness, thought for something to say, but the things that occurred to him weren't worth talking about. There was the mescal to drink and many faces about and movements in the room to attract attention, so talk wasn't necessary. Bowers sank back into the cane-bottomed chair and sipped the sweet liquor, now and then thinking about the peon. "Why do they always try to escape?" Santana had said that, smiling. Bowers thought: If they were going to hang the man anyway, what difference does it make? But it did make a difference. It didn't seem right. Two men and a girl laughing at the next table and the girl saying something as she laughed, a phrase she repeated three, four times. The words had almost a musical sound and Bowers repeated the phrase in his mind trying to translate it. It's an idiom that you can't translate word for word. You have to concentrate, pick up the idioms, if you get those you've got the language. There's no reason in the world why you should

think that peon was treated unfairly. He was a thief. He would have
been tried and hanged. Their justice is somewhat more harsh, and
they cut corners administering it. Now he heard the girl's voice at
the next table again. He glanced that way, but a man's legs and
stomach and chest were there. Two, three feet away, standing, and
now Bowers looked up at him, recognizing the new man he had
seen at the Americans' table and at the same quick moment he
knew who the man was . . . though the first and only time he had
seen him had been through field glasses focused on the man's back
as he rode out of the canyon shadow.

"Where's your partner?" Frank Rellis said.

Bowers shrugged. "I don't know."

"Why don't you know?"

Bowers hesitated. "That's a funny question."

"I don't see anybody laughin'."

Bowers sat up straighter, slowly. "I said before I don't know
where he is. I don't see how I can help you."

Rellis was holding a glass in his left hand. He raised it, finishing what he was drinking, then moved to the bar and brought the
glass down hard on the polished surface. He was half watching
Bowers as he did this and now he turned, leaning his elbows on the
bar behind him. He stared for long seconds, staying in this position, motionless but relaxed, then he stirred. He began making a
cigarette. Behind him, the bartender filled his glass with mescal.
Rellis was hatless, hair hanging low on his forehead, and he
needed a shave. It was evident that he had been drinking most of
the morning: it showed in his eyes, though not in his voice. He was
armed: a pistol hanging low on his right hip.

Rellis said, "You shouldn't a let him out of your sight. He probably run for home."

Bowers had looked away. Now his eyes returned to Rellis. "I'm
not worried about that."

"What are you worried about?"

"Nothing."

"Does your partner know I'm here?"

Bowers shrugged. "I don't even know your name."

"Frank Rellis."

Bowers waited. "That doesn't mean anything to me."

"He never mentioned my name to you?"

"Why should he?"

"You're a goddamn liar if you say he hasn't."

It was in Rellis' mind, planted firmly, that Flynn was in Soyopa because he had followed him down after what happened in Contention, somehow learning of his having joined Lazair. Two men coming down to locate Soldado and his band made no sense at all. That was a cover-up. Lazair had a mule's ass for brains if he believed that. Rellis turned sideways to the bar and drank off part of the mescal.

It was going through his mind that this couldn't be better: the shavetail coming in alone . . . don't count the rurale . . . yeah, that was all right, too. Teach him a lesson he won't forget.

Bowers could see it. The tone of Rellis' voice and the right hand hanging free. He was angry, watching Rellis, seeing what he was doing, but he knew it was exactly what Rellis wanted. Jump up, drawing, at an insult . . . and not having a chance . . . so he sat still and let the anger start to pass off. His own pistol was wedged between his thigh and the chair arm rest, and the holster flap was snapped. And you had to miss the table edge bringing up the gun. Rellis has done this before, you haven't. The objections were there to calm him, to make him go slow, but they brought with them a fear, a small nervous fear, and planted it in the pit of his stomach.

His voice sounded loud in his ears as he said to Rellis, "I don't keep tab on him. If you want him, go out and start looking."

Rellis dragged on his cigarette and blew the smoke out slowly. "What's your name?"

"Bowers."

"Bowers what?"

"Lieutenant Bowers."

Rellis' lips curled, grinning. "Well goddamn . . ." He said then, still grinning, "I was looking for you the other day. I came back from eatin' and they said you'd run off."

"You mean I'd left."

"You heard what I said."

"Why would I run away from you?"

Rellis lowered his head and drew on the cigarette, not taking his elbow from the bar. His head raised and the fingers holding the cigarette flicked out. The cigarette shot in a low arc and landed on the table in front of Bowers.

Bowers' eyes held on the man, feeling the heat on his face, wanting to do something, but . . . he was conscious of stillness . . . a sound close to him then: Santana mumbling an obscenity in his breath . . . and the sound of the screen door closing, but not seeing anyone come in because his eyes were on Rellis and Rellis, elbow on the bar, his hand hanging limp above his pistol butt, was returning the stare.

"Mostly," Rellis said now, "when I see a piss-ant like you I just step on him."

"Rellis—" It came unexpectedly, but without alarm.

Bowers' face relaxed, that was the effect, that suddenly, even without looking. But Rellis had to turn his head, sharply, and as he did the grin died on his face.

Flynn stood in from the doorway. He came on a few strides and stopped, his eyes on Rellis, his right hand unbuttoning his coat.

"Frank, I understand you've been looking for me."

Rellis wasn't loose now, though he was in the same position, elbows on the bar. Now he might have been nailed there.

"I . . . was just asking where you were."

"I heard you asking."

"Listen." Rellis straightened. "I want to get clear with you what happened in Contention. I might have talked out of turn in that barbershop—I'd been drinking and was anxious to ride out." He added quickly, "And that's what I did right after. I rode out a long ways to let my head clear, then camped by water and slept from early right through the night."

"And now you want to buy me a drink."

"That's right."

"You want to drink to what happened at the livery."

"Listen, I didn't have any part of that."

"What?"

"Shootin' that man."

"If you left Contention, how did you know about it?"

"News travels."

"All the way to Sonora?"

"It don't take long."

"Frank," Flynn said quietly, "you're a liar."

"You got no cause to say that."

Flynn moved toward Rellis. "It's said." He paused, watching Rellis' eyes. "I'm going outside. I'll expect to see you within the next few minutes . . . with your gun in your hand."

Rellis' face was stiff. Then it smiled, forcing the smile wide. "Now wait a minute. You're jumping to conclusions. I swear to God I wasn't near that livery!"

Flynn's eyes stayed on Rellis, though he did not speak. He

stared, watching Rellis trying to appear unconcerned, and he became more confident because he knew then that Rellis was half afraid to fight. Rellis would bully Bowers, he thought, because Bowers was young, too new to have experience. Maybe Red could take him with his fists, but he wouldn't have gotten all the way out of the chair to try. This was different. This was something Rellis would want his own way or not at all, and Flynn thought: And you know how that would be. All right, let him have his way. Give him his chance.

He moved toward Rellis until only a stride separated them and suddenly, abruptly, he swung a fist up hard against Rellis' jaw. A brittle smacking sound, boot scuffing, Rellis hitting the bar, sliding back off balance, but not going down. An arm caught the bar edge. The hand moved down, but jerked back and he hung there, breathing with his mouth open, watching Flynn.

"I'll say it once more," Flynn said. "You're a liar. If you don't come out in five minutes I'll come back inside to kill you."

Flynn turned and moved toward the door. Now it's coming. Wait for Bowers. He was tensed. You'll hear it. One word. One word is all it will be and . . .

"Dave!"

He wheeled, drawing, thumbing the hammer, aiming with his eyes, firing. He fired once.

Rellis went to his knees, holding his chest, the uncocked pistol dropping from his other hand and he was dead as his face struck the floor.

SIXTEEN

Lew Embree placed his palms flat on the table, looking past Warren who was too drunk to know what had happened; then Lew pushed his weight on his hands, rising unsteadily. He moved between the tables, chairs scraping in the semi-stillness to make way for him, and when he stopped he was looking down at Frank Rellis.

Flynn's pistol pointed at Lew momentarily as he slipped it into the shoulder holster. "Take your friend out of here," Flynn said.

Embree looked up. "He's no friend of mine."

"Take him out anyway."

Embree shrugged. "If you hadn't done that, somebody else would've. The only trouble is somebody's got to bury the son of a bitch."

"You've buried men before, haven't you?"

Embree looked up again. "Sure."

"Then no one has to tell you how."

Flynn looked at Bowers who was next to him now. He motioned Bowers ahead of him and they went out of the mescal shop, then along the adobe fronts toward Hilario's street, Bowers leading his horse.

"I'm glad that's over," Flynn said. "It was one of those things that had to come and now I'm glad it's over with."

"It took some nerve to do it that way," Bowers said.

Flynn glanced at him, the smile at the corners of his eyes. "Red, I was counting on you for the signal."

"What if I'd been looking the other way?"

Flynn hesitated. "You can't think of everything at once." He said then, "How did you make out with Santana?"

"He's no soldier," Bowers answered. "He doesn't know the first thing about conducting a patrol . . . but he hates the bounty hunters. And he hates Duro even more."

Flynn nodded thoughtfully. "Santana's our man."

"But hating them," Bowers said, "doesn't make him sympathetic. I saw something called *ley fuga*. I don't know what it means, but I saw it . . . coming back from Alaejos."

"It's not something new . . . the law of flight. If a prisoner attempts to escape, take the opportunity to shoot him . . . it saves the cost of a trial."

"That's what Santana said."

"He was explaining the practical side."

"I suppose *forcing* the man to escape is practical, too."

"As far as Duro is concerned it is," Flynn said. "But it's happened too often now . . . even right here in Soyopa at Duro's direction. These people have taken a lot from him . . . one injustice after another since the day he arrived. His men are bad, but it's easier to hate one man . . . the one who gives the orders. And now they're going to do something about it."

Bowers looked quickly. "What do you mean?"

"Hilario has figured it out. He says Duro must have known the scalps Lazair gave him were not Apache . . . that time, or times before. He blames Duro more than he does Lazair because Duro is Mexican, even if he is a rurale. I asked him to wait until I'd located you and then we'd talk about it. He has some people at his house; they're ready now to face. Now," Flynn said thoughtfully, "if Santana were to throw his weight against Duro . . ."

"Only that would be mutiny," Bowers said. "If it didn't work, he'd be shot."

"What do you think would happen to Hilario?" Flynn went on. "Put yourself in his place . . . his entire family was massacred, his daughter was forced to live with the men who did the killing. Lazair is out in the hills somewhere, that's something to think about later; but Duro, the one who *bought* the scalps, is here, probably on his bed drunk. Now what would you do?"

"I don't know. I suppose look for some guns."

Flynn half smiled. "They need more than guns. Right now they're up in the air. Hilario's been talking to his friends all morning. Between them they've got a few old pieces that wouldn't shoot across the square; but that doesn't matter now. What happened to

Hilario's family does. They'd throw rocks if that's all that was handy. Still, more than guns they need timing, and somebody looking at this who isn't so close to the forest . . ."

It was clear to Bowers the moment they entered Hilario's adobe.

. Hilario Esteban with the tightness in his face—sharp-featured now, the look of an old man gone from his eyes—and his hand holding the rusted Burnside .54 muzzle up, the stock resting on the floor. Hilario stood by the window. Five, six other men were there—threadbare white peon clothes and rope-soled shoes, patient faces that were now tired of being patient, but knew no other expression. Three of them were armed with old model rifles, older than Hilario's whose carbine had seen at least twenty years of service; and the remaining three carried knives—long-bladed knives ideal for cutting mesquite branches for cook fires, but knives that could hack through other things equally well. An old woman in black, her head covered, stooping in front of the hearth, stirring atole . . . because even when men made war, even when they were at the end of their patience, they still had to eat. A young girl was next to the old woman. That must be Nita. And as she looked up, hearing them enter the room, Bowers thought: No wonder Flynn went back alone to get her.

La Mosca stood up now in front of the smoke-blackened hearth. She looked at Flynn and said, "During the night I examined Hilario's daughter. There is no sign that she was molested and she is in good health."

Flynn noticed Bowers' quick, surprised glance, and feeling the warm flush over his face he saw the others looking at him also. Why the devil is she telling me that! The curandera, he thought, must be looking into the future again. He nodded to La Mosca and then looked quickly toward Hilario, saying, "I'm glad you haven't done anything yet. Now we can talk it over and do the right thing."

Hilario shook his head. "We waited because you asked us to. But the time for that has passed. We have been waiting a long time for this Duro to become a human being; now we have proof it could never happen to him."

"Duro has a force behind him, well armed," Flynn answered. "That's why I say wait and go about this cautiously."

Hilario nodded to one of the men. "At the home of Ramón's brother, others are waiting, most of them with arms. In the space of minutes we can call dozens more." He shook his head doggedly. "This has been going on too long, Davíd."

Flynn nodded. "All right. But losing more lives is not the way to avenge those already dead."

"Listen," Hilario said. "We have been thinking about this. It isn't something of a rash moment." He went on, carefully, as if to make sure the men present would remember. "Listen. I am going to Duro's house. To his face I'll accuse him of what he's done and ask him to surrender to the people of Soyopa. Now our men will be watching from the square. If he demonstrates in any way, or, if I do not return, then our men will attack the arsenal beneath Duro's quarters. Then we will be ready for Duro's rurales should they object. After this, the first thing will be ridding Soyopa of the men of Lazair." He said this very simply as if it involved merely asking them to leave.

Flynn was about to speak, but Hilario held up his hand and said, "Now you would ask, 'But what of the government? What will they do?' All right. Porfiristas will come from Mexico City to investigate. What will we tell them? The truth. What Duro is doing is unlawful. Stopping him would be acting in behalf of the government."

Flynn said quietly, "All right. But you're not going to see Duro alone."

"Davíd, this is my problem, as alcalde."

Flynn smiled. "You make things sound more simple than they are. I would say there are other interests involved now." He looked at Nita Esteban who was watching him and their eyes met and held. He had said it naturally, thinking the words only as he said them, as if instinctively, and he thought, smiling within: Maybe La Mosca has cast a spell. Well—

He heard Hilario say, "All right. First we will eat and then we will finish with this."

Hilario leaned the Burnside against the wall and turned nodding to Nita and La Mosca to serve the atole and as he did this they heard the shot. It sounded muffled, far away, from off the square somewhere.

Bowers looked up and at Flynn. "What was that?"

"A pistol."

There was silence in the room. Then, as they moved toward the door there was a flurry of shots—muffled, then louder, echoing through the square and with the gunfire the sound of a running horse.

They were outside now, all of them except the women who

stood in the doorway. The sound of horses reached them again a minute later, but none were seen passing the end of the street.

A man rounded the corner from the square and ran toward them. Nearing them, he cried, "It is done! The rurales and the hunters of Indians are at war!"

Hilario said, "Man, speak calmly now and tell what happened."

The man was breathing hard with the excitement of what he was about to tell and now he inhaled slowly to calm himself, taking his time, because waiting for news makes it the more delicious when it comes.

"The one this man shot," he said, indicating Flynn, "was carried out of the shop by two of his friends, but one remained, the one called War-ren, because he was too drunk to move."

Hilario interrupted, "Who was this you shot?"

"I'll tell you after," Flynn said. And to the man, "Go on."

"The one called War-ren remained, lying with his head on the table, unable to raise it, it seemed." The man smiled as he said, "Now Sergeant Santana was there and he noticed this one. He looked at him for some time and you could see that he was thinking. Some of his rurales were there and he told one of them to bring a riata from his saddle and when he was back with it, they took the one called War-ren, who was still not conscious, to the small closet in the rear of the room, and somehow, with the rope, they secured him upright so that he appeared to be standing up, though his arms and his head hung limp."

The man's smile broadened, saying, "Now Sergeant Santana returned to a table and within a few minutes the two friends of War-ren returned. They couldn't have buried the one who was shot, they returned so soon, but must have thrown his body somewhere. They stood at the bar, unmindful that War-ren was no longer present and now Sergeant Santana approached the one called Loo and he said, 'Listen'—the man attempted to imitate Santana's tone of voice— 'that American was a good shot . . .' meaning you, señor," he said to Flynn. "Then Santana said, 'Are all Americans that capable with firearms?' Now these two Americans winked at one another and the one called Loo said, 'I saw your men shoot that Apache boy in the courtyard. If I could not outshoot any of them I would quit.'

"Now Santana said, 'Listen. You didn't see me shoot the day. I think I am better than the others.' And the one called Loo replied, 'I doubt it, but if you want a little match, let us go outside.' And Santana said, in a tone which was a monument to tranquility, 'Why not have it right here, out of the sun's heat?' To which the American agreed.

"Now Santana boldly walked to the end of the room, bringing a chair and a tumbler with him. He placed the chair with its back rest against the closet door and balanced the tumbler so that it rested on the chair but leaned against the door. Then, walking back to the American he said, 'After you . . .' with the politeness of a gachupín caballero. The American nodded and with that, raised his pistol, aimed and fired."

The man paused, looking around the group. Dramatically, hushed, he said, "The glass shattered."

"That was the first of the shots we heard," Hilario said.

The man scowled at the alcalde, the scowl turning to a smile as he said, "Now listen. Santana turned to the man congratulating him and then said, 'Perhaps we should look in the closet to make sure there is nothing breakable inside of it.' The one called Loo said, 'What difference does it make?' And Santana shrugged saying, 'Merely as a courtesy to the owner of Las Quince Letras.'

"Now we watched closely as they approached the closet. Santana's gun was out of its holster for he was to shoot next. He moved the chair. The one called Loo opened the door and at that moment you should have seen the look on his face! He had holstered his pistol and suddenly he attempted to draw it, but Santana's pistol was pointed directly at this one's stomach and with a coolness that made us shudder, he pulled the trigger once and then again as the man fell.

"The other American was still toward the front at the bar. He drew his pistol and fired, missing, then ran for the door. Santana and his rurales followed him to the door, firing their pistols, but that one reached his horse and escaped.

"Then Santana began gathering bottles of mescal from the bar, telling his companions to do the same, all of the time shouting, 'Now it is done! The time has come! First the gringos and then Duro!' And then he described Duro in the vilest language saying, repeating, his time had come. They rode away then and I saw them stop before the Lieutenant Duro's house, but they remained there only for a moment, taking a horse which the rurale who was on duty there mounted and rode after them down the street toward their camp . . . I assume, now, to gather the others."

The man had finished. Looking at Hilario, Flynn said quietly, "Santana has said it for us. The time has come—"

SEVENTEEN

Curt Lazair reined in, holding his mount within the shadow of Santo Tomás' east wall, and from there watched the rurale patrol swing into the square, seeing most of the horsemen riding out again by way of the street that led to their camp. He saw Bowers then, dismounting with those who had remained, in front of Las Quince Letras.

Flies buzzed at the canvas bag that hung from Lazair's saddle horn. He waved his hand at them idly and, still watching the men in front of the mescal shop, he sniffed as the rancid odor of the scalps rose from the bag. He did this instinctively, as an animal sniffs the air, still, he was not fully aware that he had done so. There was a question in his mind and the answer to it could be a hell of a lot more dangerous than the smell of day-old scalps. And now, suddenly, he thought he was looking at the answer—

A rurale patrol . . . been out in the hills . . . that shavetail with them . . . he knew where the camp was, because he'd been there. That must be it!

Lazair had been thinking about it all the way in . . . calmly at first, because that was the best way to go about things like this; go over it slow and everything will fall into place . . . then he had found Sid's body—not all of it because the buzzards had found Sid first—and the calm thinking ended then and there.

Two dead, one wounded. And not even the wounded man—who was shot clean through a lung and wouldn't last another day—or the man who had brought him in, the only one of the four who was still healthy, had seen who had done the shooting. That didn't happen every day: three men shot up and not even knowing who did it.

But now it was plain to Lazair. Bowers and the rurale patrol . . . it couldn't be anyone else!

He crossed the square along the east side, following the adobe fronts around to Duro's house. The rurale guard sat leaning against the door to the arsenal. He was asleep and did not look up even as Lazair rode up close to him and dismounted.

Lamas Duro jumped with the abrupt sound of the door opening. Sitting behind the desk he stiffened, looking up with startled wide-eyed surprise, and a roll of silver coins spilled from his fingers to the desk top. The coins scattered, rolling into silver pesos already stacked in neat columns on the desk, ten coins to a column, 100 pesos in each.

Lazair stood in the doorway, confidently, defiantly, the way a man stands who has two Colts strapped to his thighs. One hand rested idly on the handle of the right pistol; the fingers of the other hand were curled in the drawstring of the canvas sack. His eyes held on Duro, coming to conclusions then and there, seeing the money, the look on Duro's face, the way he was dressed—ready to travel—jacket, scarf, gun belt and the Chihuahua hat at one end of the desk.

"Where're you going?"

It was still on Duro's face, the shock of seeing Lazair suddenly in front of him, but now he tried to smile. "It's time for a patrol."

"Your sergeant just come off one."

"This is a different kind." Duro smiled. "I am going to ride out alone. Perhaps one man can find out more than twenty."

"About what?"

"Apaches."

Lazair was silent, his eyes remaining on Duro. Suddenly, "You've had enough, so now you think it's time to haul out."

"What are you talking about?"

"You should have waited for a report before you started counting your money."

"I was just putting aside the amount owed to you from the last time," Duro explained.

"Not when you never expected to see me again you weren't." Lazair moved toward the desk, his hand still on the pistol butt. "That boy-cavalry-soldier told you where we lived . . . so you got it in your head: Hit 'em . . . sometime after it's dark and it will save passing out *muchos pesos*." Lazair said again, "You should have made sure before counting your money."

"That makes no sense," Duro said slowly and now the question furrowing his forehead was genuine. "Who hit your camp?"

Lazair smiled faintly. "You're getting better." He said then, "Your sergeant'll be coming in pretty soon . . . he's over to the cantina now. When he gets enough brave juice in him he'll come and tell you how they got only two for sure 'cause somebody couldn't hold his nerves and started shooting before they found out hardly nobody was home."

"I don't follow you," Duro said, still frowning. "Got two of what?"

"Two of my boys!"

Duro's features relaxed with amazement. "No!" and then the smile began forming slowly, curling the corners of his mouth. "Santana did that!" The smile widening, "I can't believe it. He wouldn't have the nerve."

"He got it somewhere," Lazair said. "My men followed and he ambushed them."

Duro shook his head slowly, considering this. "No . . . it could not have been Santana."

"You know goddamn well it was!"

"I swear I know nothing of this!"

"Who else is there?"

"Apaches."

"They'd a been messier."

Duro was silent, his eyes roaming the room slowly, but picturing other things. He said suddenly, bringing his palm down slapping the desk. "The other American! He's not been here for two days!"

"One man couldn't have raised all that hell."

"Maybe we don't know him," Duro said thoughtfully.

Lazair half smiled. "But I know you . . . and I've got eyes . . . counting your money . . . all dressed up for a trip. . . ."

"Listen . . . I swear on the grave of my mother I know nothing of this! I am counting this now to pay you what is owed . . . putting it aside to have it ready for you . . . you come at odd times, so I considered: The next time he comes it will be ready—" Duro hesitated and smiled at Lazair confidently. "Look . . . this is silly what you've been thinking. Let's have a drink now, together, and then I'll finish counting this."

He nodded to the sack in Lazair's hand. "You have more. Good. I'll pay you for those too; and then the account will be up to date. How many do you have there? No—wait until after we have a drink. This is a feast day, we should have a drink together." He looked suddenly in the direction of the square then back to Lazair. "Was that a shot?"

Lazair did not move. "That one was off somewhere. It's the one that rings in your ear for half a second that you worry about. Then it's all over." He said it with his hand on the gun butt and the meaning was clear.

"Everyone talks of death today," Duro said, and made himself laugh. "But look, even with the talking of death there is an equal amount of drinking." He said then, winking, "You know you can frighten the devil only so long. When there is no more mescal he comes and inserts a demon in your head. Now the demon hates this confinement and he runs from one side to the other butting at the sensitive walls of one's head." He raised a hand to his forehead and the fingers spread over the shape of it delicately. "Señor," he said, smiling through a frown which was meant to indicate a headache, "would you kindly consent to a glass of something?"

Lazair did not smile. He looked at Duro silently and his contempt for the rurale lieutenant was in his eyes, in the features that did not move, and grimly evident in the hard line of his mouth. "Get your drink," he said curtly. Duro started from the desk and Lazair added, "I'm right behind you."

He stood in the doorway to the sleeping room and watched Duro take a fresh bottle of mescal from the cupboard next to the bed, then stepped aside as Duro passed him, going to the desk again. Duro sat down and as he opened the desk drawer, Lazair said, "If you're smart you'll just come out with glasses."

Duro looked up. "Of course."

They drank in silence, Duro filling the glasses quickly as they were emptied; Lazair watching him, in no hurry, wondering what Duro would do, willing to take all the time necessary to find out.

Duro looked up suddenly. "Did you hear it? Another one!"

Lazair was half sitting with his left hip on the edge of the desk, resting the mescal glass on his thigh. He looked down at Duro calmly. "You hear all kinds of noises during a fiesta."

But with the sudden bursts of gunfire that followed, Lazair came off the desk. He moved to the door quickly, still holding his drink, still half watching Duro, and as the rurale lieutenant started to rise, Lazair snapped, "Stay where you are!"

He opened the door and the sound of a running horse rose from the square. He saw the rider, one of his men, reaching a side street and the rurales in front of the cantina firing after him.

The glass flew out of Lazair's hand shattering against the desk and in that instant a pistol was in his right hand pointed at Duro. "You didn't know!"

He wanted to pull the trigger. It rushed to his mind, but a judgment was already there; it had prevented him from killing Duro before and now it was there again with its cold reason making him slow down, making him grip the pistol tighter. If he killed Duro he would be through. Not just in this part of Sonora, but everywhere in Mexico. He'd have to go back to the States, where he was wanted, and spend the rest of his life on the dodge. He'd have to take his chances in the States because if he were caught he'd be better off than if he were pulled in by the Mexican authorities. That's what stopped him. Don't throw away a good thing: a safe place to live and a profitable business just because of one man. But it occurred to Lazair then, at that moment, that Duro was through. The only thing was, this wasn't the time or the place.

More calmly he said to Duro, "You didn't know, eh . . . ?"

"I swear to Almighty God I didn't! What happened out there?" Duro was rising again.

"Stay put!" Lazair snapped. He looked at Duro and then out again. He kept his eyes on the front of the mescal shop and when Santana and two rurales came out, shouting, mounting their horses, Lazair pulled the door quickly, almost closed, and watched them through an inch opening. They came toward the house, shouting something. When they were directly below, Lazair could not see them, but he heard Duro's name and suddenly they were riding away—four of them now, the last one, the rurale who had been on guard, on Lazair's mount.

Lazair looked at Duro and his gaze held steadily. "Something's going on. Santana and the two with him had a jug of mescal in each hand. They stopped here then rode off toward the rurale camp."

"They always drink after a patrol," Duro said.

"They were hollering something about you."

"What?"

"I couldn't make it out."

"Perhaps calling out to me."

"Does he do that often?"

Duro hesitated. "No . . ."

"Something's going on," Lazair said again. He waited, watching the square, feeling a tension that he could not understand. After a few minutes it occurred to him to run over to the mescal shop to see what had happened, then keep going to camp and move it someplace else before doing anything. There would be time enough to pay back Duro.

Looking out over the square he saw them as soon as they appeared from the side street and started across the openness. He was not sure how many there were at first, because they seemed to be all wearing peon clothes with so much white blending together, from this distance a crowd of white cotton cloth with darker spots that were faces and straw sombreros. Then he realized there were not as many as he thought. Perhaps ten altogether. And—the two cavalrymen! He squinted, watching them come closer, making sure, and when he was certain they were coming here he glanced at Duro.

"Come here . . . you've got company."

Duro rose, hesitantly now. "Who? I don't hear anyone."

"You will."

"Who is it?"

"See for yourself."

Lazair opened the door, taking Duro's arm, and pushed him suddenly out to the veranda. He closed the door again, seeing Duro, seeing Duro's eyes as he turned. Lazair pushed his pistol threateningly through the door opening and Duro turned back toward the square.

Hilario pointed with the Burnside. "There he is."

Bowers said curiously, "Was that someone behind him?"

"It looked like it," Flynn said. He looked up, watching Duro, noticing the man's hesitancy, his reluctance to stand at the rail and look down at them.

"He seems afraid," Hilario whispered.

"He should be," Flynn said. "If he heard Santana."

Watching Duro, Hilario said, "If I were to raise this barrel two inches, and pull the trigger, it would be accomplished."

Flynn said, "You know better than that."

"I wish I did not," Hilario answered. And now he called out, "Señor Duro, we would speak with you."

They heard Duro's voice faintly. "Come back another time."

"This will not keep," Hilario called. "Already too much time has passed."

Duro hesitated. Then rested his hands firmly on the railing and looking down now he seemed suddenly more sure of himself, as if the mescal he had drunk was now making his head lighter, his senses keener. He said, "Listen, alcalde, when I want to speak to you, I'll send rurales. You'll come at that time and at no other. Now go home . . . and take your friends with you." He started to turn.

"Duro!" Flynn called the name sharply and the rurale lieutenant turned back again. "We'd like to speak to you."

Duro looked down at them coldly. To Flynn he said, "I have invited you before to come to my house, thinking you would come as a gentleman . . . but when you accompany animals, then perhaps you should be treated as one."

Flynn could feel the sudden heat on his face, but he restrained the impulse to raise his voice and he said mildly, "What happened to your manners?"

"There's no need for them since you are neglecting to use your own."

Flynn smiled to himself. Now it comes out: the real Duro. But why the change of face all of a sudden? Maybe Santana scared him into reality. He's so busy thinking what he's going to do next, there's no time for the polite front. He heard Bowers saying, in a low voice, "He doesn't want us to come up there."

Flynn called up, "Hilario Esteban has something to say. He'll do all the talking."

"Then why are you here," Duro returned, "if this doesn't concern you? And if I choose not to speak to him at this time, that doesn't concern you either." Flynn felt his patience ebbing; but he would try it once more. He began, "Lieutenant . . ." but that was all—

The gunfire came suddenly, a scattering of rifle shots off beyond Duro's house. Flynn looked at the others; they were standing still, wondering; then some were moving hurriedly to the head of the street that led to the rurale camp. Now, from the other direction, came faintly screams and shouts and a few people were reaching the square coming from the streets on both sides of the church, some of the people who had been celebrating the fiesta at the cemetery. They were calling something. The sound of horses now from the street siding Duro's house and a half-dozen rurales were galloping into the square. their cries were shrill, unintelligible with the sharp clatter of the hoofs . . . then one word was clear . . . and it was a shriek that hung hot in the air like a knife blade raised in the sunlight—

"APACHES!"

EIGHTEEN

It is always the same when you hear it . . . a feeling you can't describe . . . and right away you are picturing them, even if you've never seen one, and nine times out of ten the cry comes after they've gone—*Apaches!* . . . A dust cloud in the distance if you're quick, if you get there soon after; but usually the sign is cold and the man lying there, the survivor, cannot tell you which way they went . . . not with the sun scalding fire-red inside of his head because the Apaches have taken his eyelids . . . and other parts of him. First patrol . . . and the heavy flat sound of the sergeant's revolving pistol finishing off the buck who had been shot through the legs.

Apaches! Again and again and again . . . and the instantaneous tight throb that the word brings never changes because it is not something a man gets used to. But the reaction that comes a split second later, that changes. In a short time it changes from natural panic to trying to remember everything you know about the Apache in a few seconds; and after a half dozen years of it, when it's your business, your reaction instantly eliminates what will not help you here and now and you think of the Apache as pertaining only to this particular place, this particular time.

And that's what Flynn was doing—picturing the south side of Soyopa, where the rurale camp was, where the firing was coming from—it was open country for miles, stretching, curving east and west. So the main threat was not here, even though the firing was coming from that direction now. No, the north side, beyond the cemetery, there it was close with brush, uneven country.

And now, running to the head of the street where most of the others were, Flynn glanced across the square and saw more people coming hurriedly along both sides of the church.

Now it's Soldado's turn—it went through Flynn's mind. Something has stirred him up good.

Past the end of the street, beyond a rise a good two hundred yards off, the bleached tops of the tents were visible. There was smoke and scattered gunfire and suddenly, coming up the rise, up into the street, were the rurales, Santana with them, and as they rode into the square Santana was shouting for them to fan out in a circle, on all sides of the pueblo.

"Sergeant Santana!" Hilario ran close in front of the sergeant's horse as he reined in. "What is it?"

"The Anti-Christ! What do you think!"

"But how did they come?"

"Suddenly . . . as they always do!"

"Did you lose men?"

"Several," Santana answered, swinging down, breathing hard, watching his men disappear down the streets on all sides of the square. "They struck suddenly, riding almost directly through our camp; then they were gone, leaving some of the tents afire, moving out, away, but seeming to circle to the other side of the pueblo."

Flynn said, "You're going after them?"

"After them! Soldado Viejo is here in force. He would like us to come out after him . . . so he can cut us to pieces. He is here with men! Something has happened to his thinking. Before he would raid perhaps smaller pueblos, but most of the times herders and then with never more than two dozen men. Now he has over a hundred!"

"See that your men are circling the entire village," Hilario told him, looking about anxiously.

"I know my job!"

Bowers was looking across the square toward the church where more people were entering the square. "You hear them? They're yelling Apache. God, they must be close . . ."

"That's the side," Flynn said. "They can come up close because of the brush . . . that's where most of them will be. The strike at the rurale camp was to finish them off quick, but it didn't work."

Hilario's head turned about, wide-eyed. "We should go over there, then."

"What about Duro?" Flynn asked, turning, looking up at him. The lieutenant stood holding tight to the railing, looking, staring across the square.

"Ah, Señor Duro," Hilario said. "I remember his own words

once . . . let me see . . ." And then he called out, "Duro!" The lieutenant's gaze dropped down to Hilario, surprised, as if he had forgotten they were there. "Duro! Stay in your house until we return.
There will be a man here. If he sees your head come out of the
door, he will shoot it!"

As they passed the church, many of the people were crowding
into its wide doorway which the Franciscan padre stood holding
open. Flynn saw him wave to them as they passed and then they
were hurrying down the side wall shadow of the church and
beyond, deserted now, they could see the cemetery—the rows of
wooden crosses and mounds of stones and scattered here and there
the remains of the fiesta which would not be finished today: mescal
bottles, ollas, plates of pottery and on three or four of the crosses
hung sombreros. These moved. As the faint breeze came down
from the hills it stirred the wide hat brims, turning them lazily, and
this was the only movement now in the deserted cemetery.

Beyond, scattered mesquite thickets began their creeping in
from the wild country and beyond the brush were piñon and scrub
oak, then jackpine as the ground rose to deep-green and brown-
green hills and over all of this nothing moved.

He's smart, Flynn thought, thinking of Soldado. If a white man
had the upper hand he'd stand out there showing himself, defying
you to come out. Soldado's smart. He makes you think he's gone,
and when you go out . . . then he has you.

They stood in the backyard of the adobe which was across the
road from the church, looking out over a low wall. Bowers' eyes
were half closed as his head swung slowly, squinting into the brush
shadows, seeing nothing. "They're gone," he said finally.

Hilario shook his head, disagreeing. "Why should they go?"

Bowers said, "Dave, what do you think?"

"I think Hilario answered it," Flynn replied. "Why should
they go?"

"You don't see them!"

"When did you ever?" Flynn spoke quietly, staring out at the
thickets. "Something has aroused Soldado . . ." He hesitated.
"Maybe Lazair stumbled onto his rancheria while the men were
away . . . whatever the reason, it must be a good one to make him
throw his men at an entire village. He attacked when he was hot,
and it wasn't successful, but now he's cooled off. Whatever he
came for, he must still want, because he didn't get anything.
There's no one here who's going to go out after him, so there's no

reason for him to leave. He has all the time in the world . . . good cover . . . and he's Apache. Now you tell me what he'll do."

Bowers said, after a silence, "And what are we going to do?"

"Wait."

"For how long?"

"That's up to Soldado," Flynn said. "Probably nothing will happen tonight, but in the morning something might." Bowers looked at him curiously and he added, "That rider of Lazair's that Santana chased out of town . . . he's on his way to their camp now, if Soldado didn't spot him. By morning he should be rushing back here with the rest of them, yelling for rurales, but they'll find Apaches instead."

Bowers' face brightened. "Then that's our chance!"

Flynn shook his head. "Soldado will know about them before they know about him."

They separated soon after this, stringing out in the backyards of the adobes, watching the brush and the trees and the shadows that crept toward them as the sun began to fade. Then there were the evening sounds which seemed quieter than day sounds, and the smell of wood fires. Mesquite burning. Bowers was in the next yard, a hundred feet from Flynn, Hilario was beyond him, in his own yard. And now it was getting dark quickly.

There was Nita, coming out of the back door, moving across the yard toward her father. She was carrying something and Flynn thought: Probably atole. We eat and Soldado eats, but that's all we have in common with him. He watched Nita go to Bowers next and as she came closer he could see her face more clearly. Then she was approaching him with the atole—the flour gruel—carrying it in a tin pot, her other hand carrying pottery bowls, and he felt an excitement inside of him. And telling himself it was silly, repeating it quickly as she drew closer, did not make it go away.

"Are you hungry?"

He shook his head. "No. But it would be best to eat something."

"There was not time to prepare anything better than this." She kept her eyes down most of the time, but when she did look at Flynn, when their eyes met, they would hold and there was no other living soul on the earth.

"I don't mind atole, I've had it many times before."

He said, unexpectedly then, "If it were darker, I think I would kiss you."

Her eyes rose to his. "If it were darker, I think I would let you."

They looked at each other in silence, then she rose and moved toward the next yard with the pot of atole.

Later, after it had been dark almost an hour, a man came to him. It was Ramón who had been in Hilario's house with the others.

"We think they are approaching."

"Where?"

"Directly out from my yard"—he waved his arm in the darkness—"which is the other side of Hilario's. Before it was dark we saw this Apache who seemed to be showing himself purposely, making strange signs, as if tempting us to come out. Then for a while he was gone. Then, after the darkness came, we heard faint sounds. They have stopped now, but you'd better come."

Hilario and Bowers were there, crouched behind the low stone wall.

Ramón asked in a whisper that was nervously harsh, "Has anything occurred?"

Bowers nodded to them. Hilario looked up and said quickly, "He is close now, but out of sight. A moment ago there was a sound, it seemed a hiss, but I'm sure it was a word."

Flynn said, *"Si-kisn?"*

"Yes, that was it!" Hilario whispered excitedly.

"He was telling you," Flynn said, "that he's a brother, a friend."

"It is a ruse," Hilario whispered.

"Perhaps," Flynn said. "But when an Apache fights at night, it is because he has no other choice. Soldado has time. He has more of it than we have."

Bowers said, "And maybe he's planning on your thinking that way."

He's learning fast, Flynn thought, and said, "You never know them so well you don't have to take chances." He knelt close to the wall now and cupping his hands to his mouth he called in a low, drawn-out hiss, *"Si-kisnnnn."*

There was dead silence. Then the word came back from not far away. Again silence, and suddenly the dim shape of an Apache was standing across the wall from them. He said, "Flín?"

Flynn rose, and hesitated so there would be no surprise in his voice that would make him speak out loud. Then he said, "Three-cents." He glanced at Bowers and at Hilario. "This is Three-cents, Joe Madora's head Coyotero tracker."

Bowers said, "What!" and clamped his mouth shut because the word was sharp in the stillness.

"Come over," Flynn said to the Coyotero.

"There is another with me," Three-cents said in Spanish, and almost as he said it, he was gone.

"I thought they made army trackers wash," Bowers whispered. "He's filthy."

"The dirt's on purpose," Flynn said. "He wiped saliva on his body and then sand on top of that. That's why we didn't see him."

A moment later, Three-cents was back and behind him another figure was coming, crouched low. Then he rose, and as he spoke, even before he spoke, Flynn was smiling.

The words came as a hoarse whisper—"David, you son of a bitch, I've got to pull you out of another one."

"Joe!" Flynn whispered, and grabbed the man's arm to help him over the wall.

"Let go! You'll rip open the hole!"

"How is it?"

"I'm standing in front of you."

"I never expected to see you again, Joe."

"That's why I can't figure they sent a shortsighted bastard like you on this trip." Madora looked at Bowers then. "How you doin', Red?"

Self-consciously, Bowers said, "All right."

Madora turned from him abruptly. "David, I'm hungrier 'n a bastard. What've you got?"

Hilario said, "Nita will bring something."

But Flynn said, "We'll go in and get it. Joe, you and your boy come along and I'll fix you up."

When they were near the house, Madora said, "Those boys were dyin' for news. They won't take kindly to you rushin' me away."

Flynn ignored this, saying quickly, "Where's Deneen?"

"He's out there."

Flynn relaxed somewhat. "I had a hunch he was. With how many?"

"Counting Coyoteros?"

Flynn nodded. "Yes."

"Ten."

"Ten! How many are scouts?"

"Ten."

"No . . ." Flynn groaned, but there was a humor to this and it struck Flynn and he could not help but smile now. "All right. What happened?"

"About the time Deneen got back to Whipple from his tour, the genral'd found out what he'd done." They had entered the adobe and now, close to the firelight, Madora was smiling. "That was something. The genral dressed hell out of him and the first thing you know Deneen's got a Mexico assignment of his own."

"How'd you find out?"

"Hell, it's all over. Some of it was overheard firsthand . . . a friend of mine. Anyway, your pal was relieved of his adjutant's job and the genral kicks his tail down to Sonora to find a Lieutenant Duro of the rurales . . . cuz the genral says, All right, goddamn it, if we're going to do it, then we're going to do it right. Get your ass down to Mexico and get some permission and if you don't get it, don't come back." Madora added, "Now some say genrals don't talk like that, but my friend says it's gospel."

"But why only ten men?"

"We ain't a war party. The genral told him no soldiers, else it'd be considered invasion of a foreign country, but he said you can take all the trackers you want cuz for cry-sake there's enough goddamn Apaches down there now that nobody's going to notice a few goddamn more."

"I never heard the general talk like that."

"What's that, atole? That's the only thing that's almost not better than nothing."

"Where's Deneen now?"

"About a mile off."

"Apaches spot you?"

"Hell no."

"I'd better go talk to him."

"Somebody better. He like to wet his pants when Three-cents come in and told about Soldado." Madora looked at Flynn quickly, seriously. "This is the first time I've seen him in a tight spot. He can't take it, can he?"

"Why ask me?" Flynn said.

"Because you were in the war with him where there were lots of tight spots." Madora paused and half smiled. "That's what's between you two. You caught him in a jackpot cryin' for his mama."

"You don't get to be colonel that way."

"That's what everybody thinks."

"But that isn't what's bothering us here and now."

"You want to see Deneen. All right, I'll take you to him."

"Maybe he'll come in," Flynn suggested. "It would be safer for him here."

"He won't move."

"All right, then we'll go out."

"In one minute." Madora took heaping spoons of the atole, scraping the plate clean. Three-cents had been eating as they spoke and now they went outside, back to the low wall. Bowers was alone.

"Where's Hilario?" Flynn asked.

"He went to relieve the man watching Duro's house. Dave, what is it?"

"Deneen is here, but with only a few trackers. He was on his way to talk to Duro about a border campaign when they ran into the Apaches."

"He's fighting them?"

"No, holed up. I'm going out and talk to him. When I get back I'll tell you all about it."

"What if you don't get through?"

Flynn smiled. "If this old man can do it, anybody can."

Madora said mildly, "David, when they passed out proper respect you must've been scratchin' your butt with both hands."

Bowers watched them go over the wall and fade into the darkness. He asked himself: Could you do that? Sure, if you've been doing it as long as they have. What about the first couple of times? He was squinting into the darkness, expecting a sound. You either get used to it, or you don't get used to it. That's the way to look at things like that. He knew this was easy to say and he told himself: Who said anything about getting used to it being easy!

He had thought before that this was not an assignment for a soldier, but now he knew conclusively that he had been wrong. And thinking of soldiers, oddly, he thought of Santana and how Santana considered himself one and boasted that if ever his rurales got the Apaches in open country, then he'd see some soldiering; that's what Santana had intimated.

After this he thought of many things, faraway things, but slowly his thoughts came back to the present. Now . . . and then the morning, a few hours away. What would happen then? Flynn said Lazair's men might come back in the morning, he thought.

That's how it started in his mind, the plan. Just from remembering something Flynn had said, and in the next few minutes the plan began to develop, began to grow into something that might work.

A man crouched next to him in the darkness, startling him.

"What passes?" the man said. "Hilario Esteban relieved me and told me to come here."

Bowers nodded, "It is still quiet," and then quickly, unexpectedly, he asked, "Have you seen the rurale, Santana?"

NINETEEN

The alcalde, Hilario Esteban, stood beneath the veranda of Lamas Duro's house, and with the Burnside .54 cradled in his arm he looked out over the dark stillness of the square. Far across loomed the dim outline of Santo Tomás and creeping in a wide circle toward him on the two sides were the low, shadowed adobe fronts of the buildings that faced the square. There were no horses in front of Las Quince Letras.

This is the first time in six months that the cantina has been empty, Hilario thought. The time before was the day everyone remained in their houses. The day the rurales came.

But it was just the one day that there was no business, his thoughts continued, for the rurales were inside the cantina as soon as their camp was erected. And soon after, within three days, the people were beginning to go there again; quietly at first, once in a while, then soon with the same frequency as before . . . having adjusted themselves to our new neighbors.

A man can adjust himself to anything.

Still, there is a limit. He thought, now we have reached the limit. We could go on pretending that Lamas Duro is not here, but in doing so we would also be pretending that such a thing as honor still remained. If a man must make excuses for himself, continually argue with himself that he is a man, then he is better off dead. And then he thought: Why do I think about this one man when our worst enemy now surrounds the village? He shook his head faintly. No, Lamas Duro is more the Anti-Christ than Soldado Viejo. He whispered, half aloud, "Saint Francis, help us."

Now and then his eyes would go up the stairways that came down from both ends of the veranda above him, angling toward the center where he stood.

He would look up as the sound came from the room: walking, a squeaking board, and sometimes he thought he heard talking; but he told himself, if so Lamas Duro was talking to himself to keep his spirits up.

And finally it occurred to Hilario: Why not talk to him now? Waiting until Soldado left would be reasonable if you were occupied elsewhere, but here you stand. Go up and talk to him . . . no, tell him . . . and get it over with.

He started up the stairs on the left. Halfway up he stopped, holding himself still. The door above had opened. Slowly, with a long, low squeak. He heard footsteps on the veranda now. Three steps, then silence. Now three more, moving to the other side of the veranda.

Hilario turned slowly, crouching, and eased down until he was sitting on the steps. He raised the Burnside carefully and pointed it toward the opposite stairway. Cocking it will make a noise, he thought, hearing and feeling his heart beating through his body. So don't cock it until you are ready to fire . . . if firing is necessary. But, Saint Francis, don't make it necessary. Make Señor Duro go back inside.

He heard the footsteps again, at the top of the stairs now. Then they were coming down. Hilario held himself tense, squinting in the darkness, and now he could see the dim outline of a man. He waited, holding his breath, watching the figure reach the bottom. Then another sound, above . . . another man was on the stairs!

Two of them . . . how can that be!

His eyes fought the darkness, studying the second dim shape almost at the bottom of the stairs now. That one is Duro! I know it is!

Hilario Esteban rose suddenly, bringing up the Burnside, pulling back the hammer. "Señor Duro—stand where you are!"

And with the suddenness of this the first man was running. Hilario ignored him. Duro stood at the bottom of the stairs looking across and up at him.

"Who is it!"

"Hilario Esteban!"

He could hear the sound of the other man on the hard-packed square and suddenly the shadowy form of Duro was not in front of him, but running, sprinting into the open darkness of the square.

"Señor Duro!"

Quick, rapid-sharp boot steps in the openness . . .

"Señor Duro! Halt!"

A dim form growing dimmer . . . fifty, sixty, seventy feet . . .

The Burnside came up, cheek level. "Señor Duro! . . ."

Eighty . . .

"Saint Francis help me!" And with it the heavy dull explosion of the Burnside.

Lamas Duro took six more strides, though he was not conscious of them . . . for he was dead the instant the heavy ball slammed into his back.

"Here he comes," Madora said.

"He's half animal," Flynn whispered, belly-down next to Madora in a shallow gully, watching the dim form creeping noiselessly toward them through the brush.

"He's all animal," Madora grunted and rolled to his side to face Three-cents as the Coyotero dropped into the gully with them. They were returning the same way Madora and the Coyotero had come—Three-cents going ahead to see that the way was clear, then either signaling them on or crawling back to get them if he considered an audible animal-sound signal dangerous. This way, if they ran into Soldado's Apaches, Three-cents would meet them first, and there was the chance they would think him one of their own. Even recognizing him as not a Mimbreño would take time and Three-cents would have his chance to act.

In his own language, but with a word here and there of Spanish, he informed them that Mimbres were just ahead.

"There are three," he told them. "They stand listening. Then two will move in opposite directions, but always one remains in the same place."

"Like army pickets," Flynn whispered.

Madora muttered, "They've been doing it for five hundred years." They were silent then, thinking, but finally Madora said, "Well, let's go take him."

"Who's doing the honors?"

"Whoever sees him first."

They crawled out of the gully one at a time, Three-cents leading, and kept to the brush patches as they went over the flat ground. Just ahead now they could make out the dense blackness of trees, a soft crooked line against the night sky, and when Three-cents glanced back at them they knew that there the Mimbre waited.

They moved up on both sides of the Coyotero and he said, with his mouth close to the ground, "Thirty paces into the trees he stands. The two come out to the edge before going opposite ways." They were silent again, watching, and then Three-cents muttered, "There," pushing his arm out in front of him on the ground.

It was visible for a moment, like an off-white speck of shadow and then gone.

"He's sure of himself," Madora grunted, "wearing a white breech-clout at night." They waited several minutes, giving the two Mimbre vedettes time to move off, out of hearing; then they crawled toward the trees.

Pines. The scent was heavy. Flynn could feel the needles in the sand beneath his hands and knees, and now a branch brushed his face. He had not brought the Springfield. It would be in the way. But he could feel his pistol under his left arm and a clasp knife was in his pocket.

Watch Three-cents now, Flynn thought. He'll call it. They waited for the Mimbre to move, to cause a sound that would tell where he was, but no sound came and as the minutes passed they knew they would have to bring the Mimbre to them.

Three-cents rose silently and moved off from them a dozen steps before sinking down, huddling close among pine branches. A low moan came from him then, in the stillness a long low gasp of pain.

Flynn waited. Come on. That's one of your brothers in trouble. Come on and find him. Still there was no sound, but at that moment he felt the movement; he sensed it and from the corner of his eye there he was, the Mimbre, crouched low, moving toward Three-cents. Wait. Nothing sudden. Let him get past you. Joe's seen him too. Joe probably smelled him.

The Mimbre stopped. In the moaning tone, a word in the Mimbreño dialect came from Three-cents. And in the corner of Flynn's eye the Mimbre moved again. All right, get him.

But as he rose, Madora was suddenly, silently behind the Mimbre and the next moment his arms were around him, forearm vise-like against the throat and hand clamped over the mouth, dragging the warrior to the ground with him. Three-cents stood over them. Without hesitating he pushed his knife into the Mimbre's chest.

They went on, carrying the Apache, for he could not be left there for the others to find. When it's light, Flynn thought, they'll read the signs. That will make it harder to get back. But what might happen after sunup was something to think of then. They moved on through the darkness.

Three-cents signaled when they neared the place where the others were. A soft low whistle . . . silence . . . then an answering whistle and within a minute there were Coyotero scouts all around them.

"Where is he?" Flynn said to Madora. Here was another pine stand and in the darkness he could see only the Coyoteros standing close by.

Madora pointed. "He was right over there before."

"You'd think three men walking in at night would interest him."

"He's got enough troubles without looking for more."

"Joe, there's another problem now we didn't count on before." He indicated the dead Mimbre. "Tonight they'll miss him; tomorrow they'll be getting in each other's way looking for him."

Madora nodded. "I agree."

"So," Flynn went on, "if we're going back to the village, it's got to be tonight or not at all."

"But," Madora said, "you got to convince Deneen crawling through their line's the thing to do—anytime."

"I'll convince him," Flynn said, and looked at the Mimbre again. "We'd better get rid of him."

"We'll bury him."

"When we go back it should be in two or three groups. What do you think?"

Madora nodded. "I'll work it out with Three-cents, you go talk to Horse's-ass."

Colonel Deneen was lying down, head on his saddle bag and a blanket covering him as Flynn entered the small clearing Deneen had reserved for himself; but in one abrupt movement the blanket was thrown back and he was sitting up, pointing a pistol at Flynn.

"Who is it?"

"Flynn." He started to explain, "Madora brought me out . . ." but he stopped. God, he should know that much.

"Well, goddamn it, sit down! I don't care for you standing there looming over me!"

"I didn't mean to frighten you."

"You didn't frighten me, I assure you. Where's Bowers?"

"Soyopa."

"Why didn't he come?"

"It wasn't necessary."

Sitting down, Flynn studied the man, trying to see the face clearly in the darkness. The face had changed, but he could not make out details other than it being in need of a shave, perhaps drawn. Bluntly now, Flynn asked, "What are you going to do?"

"I haven't decided."

"It's less than four hours to daylight."

"So?"

"We killed a Mimbre on the way out. As soon as it's light they'll be looking for him."

"So?"

"So we'll have to start back to the village now while it's still dark," Flynn said patiently.

"And since I happen to command, and don't choose to go to the village, what then?"

"It would be better if you went."

"Are you threatening me, Flynn?"

God, he's sitting on the edge of his nerves! "Of course I'm not threatening. I'm reminding you that with the sun something's bound to happen. It would be too late then to get back to the village and those people might need all the help they can get."

Abruptly then, in a tone intended to sound calm, natural, Deneen said, "I suppose you were surprised to find me here."

Flynn nodded. "Somewhat."

"The general decided I had better look into this myself, since it has possibilities of an extensive border campaign. It's been my argument right along, one push from both sides of the border will squeeze every Apache man, woman and child out of the hills right where we want them." As he said this, his voice sounded natural.

He's been rehearsing this one, Flynn thought.

Deneen went on, "I'm contacting the local rurale officer first . . . at my own time. Do you know him?"

Flynn nodded.

"There in that village?"

Flynn nodded again.

"Well goddamn it speak up! What's his authority!"

"Do you really want to know?"

"What!"

Flynn's voice was calm. "Look, there are only a few hours until light. I think it would be wise if we started back right now instead of sitting here playing games. I know why you're here. Everyone does, and you know it. And I'll tell you this . . . I don't give a good damn what happened between you and the general. That's past history, to me it's as dead as what happened that night at Chancellorsville. You've made that one live on even when I was trying to forget it, and now you throw this border campaign nonsense in my face and expect me to swallow it, pretending you're on a secret mission . . . like I've been doing with Bowers for the past week— trying to act like this is an honest-to-God assignment; half wanting to help him keep his faith in the army, half wanting to tell him what a real son of a bitch you really are, but not having the heart because to him a colonel, even you, is a rank that takes time, guts and a military mind." Flynn stopped, but abruptly he added, "Why did you send him?"

Deneen stared with the rage plain in his face, even in the darkness, and he was not able to speak.

"Maybe I can answer it myself," Flynn said, watching Deneen closely. He started out slowly, "Bowers' father, the brigadier, was there. Maybe he saw you do it . . . or he was in the medical tent after and could tell gunshot from shrapnel and had time to figure where a doctor there wouldn't. Either way, you were aware of his knowing. Perhaps you'd forgotten it over the years, but when the boy showed up at Whipple there it was again and you took it for granted the brigadier had told his boy about the cowardly act of a Captain Deneen one night at Chancellorsville. If Bowers knows about it, he's not saying, but the chances are remote that he even does, because his father wasn't the kind of man to let it get beyond him. But maybe he should have told . . . and had you drummed out of the service. No, you should have resigned yourself. But instead you stuck it out, because after the war there wouldn't be any more Chancellorsvilles . . . and now some men have paid with their lives because you're a rotten officer and not honest enough to admit it . . . because two men you think know about a mistake you once made, you conclude the only thing to do is get rid of them before *everybody* knows." Flynn paused. "Your big mistake was pointing that pistol at your foot—you were about five feet too low."

"Is that all you have to say, Flynn?" Deneen kept his voice calm.

"One other thing."

"What is that?"

"You're going to the village."

"At the point of a gun?" Deneen half smiled. "I think not. And we'll stay as long as I choose to."

"If you do, you'll stay alone."

"Madora is under my command. If I stay, he'll stay . . . and with all of his men!"

Turning to go, Flynn said quietly, "Ask him."

TWENTY

They waited in the darkness crouched low in the mesquite, watching the pines off across the clearing. Clouds had formed in the night sky and now the moonwash was a soft haze that barely outlined the dense shape of the trees.

Madora said, "How long now?"

"About twenty minutes," Flynn answered.

"That's not so good."

"Maybe they're close and he can't move."

Deneen, crouched at Flynn's right, moved his leg and his boot scraped the loose sandy rock.

Madora's head turned. "Why don't you ring a bell?"

Deneen began, "Madora, you'll be sorry you ever . . ."

"Damn it—shut up!"

Indicating the pines across the clearing, Flynn said, "That's where the Mimbre was killed . . . maybe he's run into something."

"Like the other two," Madora said.

Flynn glanced at Madora. "If he doesn't show soon, we'd better start thinking. What about the rest of your trackers?"

"They'll wait a good hour before following: give us plenty of time. If something happens, they're on their own."

But a moment later, Three-cents appeared, crawling, squirming into the mesquite. He told them that two Mimbreños were among the trees looking for the one who had disappeared, feeling through the pines carefully. "They will look only a short time more, searching a wider area. Then they will go to inform the others."

"Which means," Flynn said, "we go now or never."

"What did he say?" Deneen whispered, demanding, not merely asking.

"He said it's empty; we could drive a wagon through," Madora told him.

"That's not what he said!"

Madora did not bother to reply; he moved out and they crawled single file after him across the clearing, moving more quickly through shoulder-high brush hands and knees again across another open stretch and then into the pines. They waited, listening to the silence, then deeper among the trees they could hear crickets. They sing if nothing's disturbing them, Flynn thought. But even a cricket wouldn't hear a Mimbre. They moved on, creeping through the trees, brushing pine needle branches, holding them from swishing . . . and three of them gritted their teeth and felt needles down their spines as Deneen's boot snapped a rotted tree limb. They stopped where they were and dead silence followed.

Three-cents looked at Madora and when the scout nodded he moved off, disappearing into the darkness.

The clasp knife is in the left side pocket, Flynn thought, and his hand moved against the cloth feeling the shape of it. He could feel the weight if the pistol beneath his left arm. But no shooting, he reminded himself. He smelled the cold fresh smell of the pines and suddenly he realized there was no longer the sound of crickets. A movement in the tree darkness flicked in his vision.

He saw it again, a short quick shadow movement, and held his gaze on it, waiting for it to show again. When it did, he knew that it was a man, and almost instinctively he knew it was not Three-cents.

He glanced at Deneen. He hadn't seen him. The shadow moved again, coming closer cautiously, taking the definite shape of a man. It went through Flynn's mind: Joe's closest. It's up to him. Now he could see the shoulder-length hair and the colorless gray of the breechclout. He knew Madora, a few feet in front of him, was ready; but now he thought of Deneen, behind, slightly to the side, and he wanted to warn him not to move, but he knew it was too late. Joe—get the mouth. Whatever you do, don't let him yell. Let him take a few more steps—

"Oh God!" and the pistol shot slamming the stillness on top of the words.

Deneen held the pistol out in front of him . . . the Apache was on the ground . . . but suddenly another shape was coming out of the trees . . . his thumb hooked the hammer and he fired at it . . . the figure hung motionless and he pulled the trigger twice again until the shape dropped to the ground.

Madora's voice suddenly—hoarse, urgent, "Stop him!"

Flynn was moving . . . one hand gripped the gun barrel, wrenching it from clawed fingers . . . the other tightened in uniform cloth to drag Deneen to the ground.

"Get off of me!"

The face beneath him was tight with panic, ready to scream again. Flynn pushed his palm down viciously over the mouth, holding it there, seeing the eyes stretched open—

Madora was next to him. "He shot Three-cents!"

"What!"

"The second one . . . It was Three-cents! The crazy son of a bitch killed him!"

Looking down, seeing the eyes, Flynn's hand tightened over the jaw. And one of the flashes in his mind, coming through the shock of Madora's words, said: This would be easy. But it was momentary. Ten years on the frontier was telling him something else, something undeniable, urgent . . . and he leaped up to follow Madora who was already moving, running through the trees. They reached the end of the trees together and paused, drawing their pistols. Then they were in the open—five, six, seven strides—and suddenly the gunfire broke, coming from three sides, pin-point bursts of flame, stopping them in their tracks, forcing them back crawling, lunging into the cover of the trees.

Minutes later, after the firing had stopped, Deneen appeared. He said it once. "Goddamn it they all look alike. How did I know who it was?" That, by way of an apology.

Flynn could still feel the hot anger and he thought: Now that he's said that, he can forget about it. He's explained and apologized in one. Life is very simple. Why do you let it get so complicated— just look at it the way Deneen does. And within the first few minutes he also thought: Take your anger and use it now against these Mimbreños. But he felt the closeness of the trees. No, it would be all right if you were fighting them in the open, with fists; but there's no place for anger here. They'll come at dawn and if you're still excited, two minutes later you'll be dead.

They moved a few yards to where there was more protection— the brush was heavier and a fallen tree formed a natural barrier on the side that faced deeper into the trees, and out from it there was a fifteen foot clearing to help some. The other side looked out on the open meadow they had started to cross. Flynn remembered that the next trees were about two hundred yards off, with Soyopa's cemetery beyond them. The threat was not from the open side.

Madora moved next to Flynn.

"They'll come soon as there's a hint of light."

Flynn nodded.

"How would you figure it?" Madora said.

"Come from the inside, through the trees. If they can count to five three times they've got us."

"Be all over before we could reload."

"Did you take Three-cents' gun?" When Madora nodded he said, "That'll help some. How many rounds you got?"

"About thirty, plus the loads in Three-cents' gun."

Flynn patted his coat pocket. "That's about what I got. Will they count shots?"

"Hell yes. What side do you want?"

Flynn was closest to the fallen tree. He said, "Well, now that I'm here." He glanced at Deneen who looked away quickly.

"Then you get this," Madora said, handing him the extra pistol. "If you want to use it sometime, it's all right."

"Maybe next week," Madora said.

Now Flynn was looking out past the fallen tree, his eyes probing the darkness and the trees. There! Did you hear it? There must be a lot of them if they make a noise. The Coyoteros will be pinned down; there aren't enough of them to do anything. Twice he thought he saw movements, but he held his fire. Wait for the real thing, that will come soon enough. The time was passing and he knew it would not be very long and he was as certain as he could be that he would die within the next hour. You have to have time to reload. O my God I'm heartily sorry for having offended Thee. I detest all my sins because I dread the loss of heaven and the pains of hell; but most of all because they offend Thee, my God, Who art all good and deserving of all my love. I firmly resolve with the help of Thy grace—

There!

His left pistol came up and fired. Count them! One. Another shape coming across the clearing, stumbling with the report. Two. A Mimbre darted from one tree to another and he missed him. Three. Don't throw them away! The same one came on, in view for a longer time, and he knocked him flat. Four. Madora's firing the other way. Don't look around. There . . . off left! The slamming report and powder smell. Five. Now wait . . . you're starting to reload . . . here they come!

He stood up suddenly, pointing the other pistol, firing, seeing them go down . . . four blasts from the pistol and two Mimbres dropped, one hit twice. Others were coming out of the trees! No . . . split-second indecision and they were going back in. Hurry up, reload! He inserted two cartridges, looked up, and when there was no movement he loaded three more; then the other gun.

The firing had stopped on both sides. "What did you have, Joe?"

"Ponies. Didn't you hear them?"

Flynn shook his head.

"They were for attention," Madora said. "Your side's the one."

"Don't tell me."

"You want to trade off?"

"I'm used to it now."

Turning toward Deneen, Madora said, "You want to help out next time?" He stopped, his eyes narrowing into a frown. "You feel all right?"

Flynn looked over. Deneen was crouched with his back against the base of a pine, half hidden by the branches, clutching the pistol in a tight-knuckled, close-to-chest, protecting way as if it were the only thing that stood between him and the end of his world. And the picture of that night at Chancellorsville flashed through Flynn's mind—the darkness and the dripping pines and almost the same tight-jawed wide-eyed expression frozen on his face—and Flynn looked away, back to Madora.

"We're not going to get any help from him," the scout said. He looked out over the meadow in the dawn light. Flynn moved back to the fallen tree, but as he did Madora called, "David, look-at over there."

His eyes followed Madora's outstretched arm through the early morning haze, out across the meadow. There, at the edge of the trees two hundred yards off, stood three Mimbreños. They were looking toward the pines; then one of them motioned and others appeared, carrying something.

"David . . . that's a man."

Flynn studied them, watching two warriors drag the limp form of a man between them. They held him upright then while another Mimbre threw a line over a tree limb above them. Flynn saw now that one end was fastened to the man's wrists and as the Mimbreños walked off holding the free end, the line tightened, drawing the man's arms up over his head and the next moment he was hanging above the ground.

Madora said, "Do you recognize him?"

Flynn shook his head. "His head's down."

"Get Deneen's glasses."

Deneen was staring at Flynn as he turned toward him. "What is it!"

"Take it easy. Let me have your glasses."

Deneen's left hand felt the case hanging at his side. "I'll look first!"

Flynn shrugged. "You won't like it." And he thought: He's not as bad as at Chancellorsville. Maybe he thinks there's still a way out.

Deneen looked through the glasses. When he brought them down his face was drawn tighter than before and for a moment Flynn thought he was going to be sick. Madora jerked the field glasses from his hands without ceremony. "He told you," the scout said, and handed the glasses to Flynn; and after he had given Flynn time to study the man he asked, "Who is he?"

Flynn lowered the glasses, handing them back to Madora. "I don't know. His head's still down . . . what's left of it."

Looking through the glasses Madora said, "Scalped. And nekked as a jay-bird." He was silent. Then, "He's alive, David."

"You're sure?"

"Positive."

"What's that?" Flynn watched the Mimbres nearing the man again.

"They got knives," Madora said. He grunted. "You see that?"

"Enough," Flynn said quietly.

"They cut the tendons in his arms." Madora waited, and winced holding the glasses to his eyes. "Now both his legs."

Deneen turned away.

Flynn said, "That's for our benefit."

"You bet it is." Madora lowered the glasses. "They're telling us what's coming up about an hour from now."

"Next time they'll rush until they get us," Flynn said.

Madora nodded up and down. "The first time they found out what they wanted to know . . . though it cost them more than they figured. Your side was the natural, cuz of the cover, just fooled around mine. Next time they'll come mounted, all of them . . . like a twister and run right through us."

Flynn didn't know what to say, but he said, "Well . . ." and in his mind, rapidly: . . . but most of all for having offended Thee, my God, who art all good and deserving of . . . "Joe, what if we run?"

"Which way?"

"Back." He nodded into the trees.

"We wouldn't get ten feet." Mildly, Madora said, "David, the only thing we can do now is think about all the things we shouldn't of done before."

Flynn half smiled now, thinking of Nita. "And all the things you'd like to have done."

"What would you do, David, besides kick his francis from here to Prescott?" He nodded toward Deneen.

Flynn said vaguely, "Maybe stay around here."

"And prospect?"

"Maybe."

"For what?"

Flynn smiled. "She's a nice girl."

"I thought so," Madora said. "Well . . . it'd be a nice living." He looked at Deneen again. "And I wouldn't see how you'd have anything further to prove as far as he's concerned."

Flynn said, "Only nothing like that will happen now." Still, he thought of Nita Esteban, until she was forced suddenly from his mind—

"David . . . here they come!"

Flynn had time to recognize Soldado, though it was a quick, fleeting glimpse—first Soldado, then his warriors riding out of the trees, coming out bunched, separating in the open, the rumble of their ponies, dust rising—then he was whirling back to face the dense pines. He heard a pistol shot close behind him, but it went in and out of his mind for he was tensed waiting for something else, then Madora's voice—

"David!"

Nothing moved in the trees. He glanced around quickly seeing Madora and beyond him the Mimbreños swerving their ponies, racing down through the wide aisle between the pines and the trees they had come out of.

"They don't want *us!*"

And off to the left, far out, were mounted men. They had been coming along the road that, ahead, would skirt the cemetery, but now momentarily they stood holding their horses, almost a dozen riders, watching the Apaches bearing down on them . . . then as one they spurred, breaking for the village off beyond the trees.

"They were waiting for them all the time!"

"Joe, that's Lazair's men!"

"God Almighty they don't have a chance!"

"Joe!"

Madora's head jerked toward Flynn, seeing him pointing off to the right, the other direction, and as he followed Flynn's gaze his eyes opened in amazement.

"God Almighty . . . *rurales*!"

Flynn screamed through the din of the horses that had swerved around from the right side of the trees, "And Bowers! Look at him!"

And there it was. Cavalry! Cavalry out of the Manual. Charging, full-glory cavalry used the way it should be, the way you dream about it but seldom see it. Something out of *Cooke's Tactics*. And it was all there as Flynn had seen it before—only here were straw Chihuahua hats and the full-throated battle screams were in Spanish. Flynn felt the excitement in him and screamed at them as they rode by bearing down on the Apaches who were milling, turning in confusion and not all the way around when Bowers hit them. He hit them with gunfire, carbine butts, sabers and a will . . . a rawhide cavalry will to hit the enemy, slash him hard in the first few seconds and use the rest that makes up a minute to mop up, chase the stragglers, run them to the ground.

And as suddenly as it had started, it was over. Some Apaches, perhaps a dozen, had broken free and were streaking off in the distance; many were on the ground, horses and men, scattered over the meadow; and there were those who had given up. They sat their ponies sullenly with their hands raised in the air, herded into groups, rurales circling each group with carbines ready.

Then Bowers was coming toward them, holding his mount to an easy trot, the saber flashing in the sunlight; but he saw the naked figure hanging from the tree and he guided the left rein in that direction.

Madora was grinning broadly in his gray-streaked beard. "Where'd he get that saber? David, I think he might do."

Flynn was smiling, but then he turned quickly remembering Deneen . . . there, by the tree. "Colonel . . ." The word hung by itself with none to follow. Flynn stared, feeling the cold shock of what he saw, then gradually realizing what had happened—remembering the pistol shot right after Madora had yelled that the Mimbreños were coming.

That was enough, just knowing they were coming, and knowing what they would do from seeing the man strung up across the meadow. That finished him, Flynn thought. At Chancellorsville it was a shelling. That had been bad. But what the Mimbreños had in mind would have been much worse. So . . .

"Joe . . . look here."

Madora was silent for some time looking at Deneen slumped against the tree. The face was beyond recognition, the pistol barrel still jammed into his mouth, his hand still on the trigger. Then Madora shook his head slowly. "When did he do that?"

"Right after you yelled. I remember hearing a shot close, but I thought it was you."

Madora shook his head again. "Just think, if he'd a put that off one minute he'd be bitchin' at us for something right now."

"Maybe," Flynn said, "he's done everybody a favor."

Madora said, looking up, "Here comes Bowers," and moved out to the edge of the trees.

Flynn started to follow, but he stopped, glancing back at Deneen thinking of Bowers. What good would it do him to see that? Flynn thought. Throwing it in his face that Deneen was a coward . . . *a Colonel, United States Cavalry*. And suddenly he had hurdled the fallen tree trunk and was dragging back the nearest of the dead Mimbreños, lifting him over the trunk, dropping him to the other side, dragging him up face-down over Deneen's body. He pried Deneen's hand open, closed the Mimbre's fist around the gun butt and placed the barrel back—gently—against the gaping teeth-shattered expressionless hole.

Madora was calling, "Red, where in hell did you get that sword?"

Bowers was dismounting as Flynn reached him. He pushed the sword point into the ground, taking the extended hand, grinning, feeling the glory of it, but not wanting to show his excitement.

Flynn smiled back at him, saying, "There was no room for cavalry, but it was cavalry that won after all. How'd you do it with Santana?"

Bowers smiled half self-consciously, even in his cavalry pose, hand resting on the sword hilt. "Santana and I talked for a long time last night," he said. "We discussed again the battle of Cinco de Mayo at Puebla. We talked of Santana's military ability—about which he wasn't the least bit restrained—then we got around to Gettysburg—the second day, if the memory of my father's words serves me correctly—and I told him about an incident during the Culp's Hill skirmish."

Bowers squinted. "Now I think it was Geary's division of Slocum's XII Corps holding the hill, with Ewell's rebel division pinning them down. Ewell couldn't climb his division up the hill, but neither could Geary get out . . . and Meade, that's General George G. Meade, wanted part of Geary's division over to reinforce Sickles' end of Cemetery Ridge where Longstreet was hammering. Now there was a fellow named Gregg with some cavalry sent to help out Geary, but he couldn't see how to get at Ewell, until, from the hill, they spotted a supply train coming up along Rock Creek. They knew Ewell's scouts would tell him about it and from then on it was timing. Ewell started for the supply wagons and Gregg hit him while his pants were down with umpteen troops of Union Cavalry." Bowers' eyes were alive, smiling. "I've always considered that would have been some sight to see." He said then, "Now just casually I mentioned to Santana, 'If Lazair's men were to come down that road in the morning, Soldado would sniff him and it would be pretty much the same maneuver, wouldn't it? And for a military man of your ability, it would be easy as walking.' That did it. He even dug sabers out of Duro's storeroom. We knew the Mimbres were in the trees . . . no other place they could be; so we waited until there was a sign of Lazair's men far out, then swung out a side street and barreled around that grove of trees."

"How did Duro react?" Flynn said.

"Duro's dead. He ran for it during the night. Hilario was watching then . . . he told him to stop, but Duro kept going, so he shot him. Hilario said someone else ran out ahead of Duro. We've been trying to figure out who it could be." Bowers jerked his thumb over his shoulder vaguely pointing across the meadow. "We didn't even think of him, but that's who it must have been."

From Flynn, "Who is it?"

"Lazair."

Flynn paused, surprised. "Is he dead?"

Bowers nodded. "Dead as a stone."

Madora half smiled in his beard, noticing the new, sure-of-himself tone of Bowers' voice along with the hip-cocked cavalry way he stood. He said, "Red, you might do at that . . . with a little seasoning."

Bowers smiled, though he was thinking: Damn, how you have to listen to old men and smile just because they are old men. As if a few more years just naturally makes them wiser. Then he said, because he had to say something, "I hope so, Mr. Madora. I do hope so." And then, remembering, Bowers said, "Where's the colonel?"

Flynn stepped aside and nodded into the trees and followed Bowers as he walked in among the pines.

"My God—"

Flynn said nothing. And suddenly, watching Bowers' face, he was more than glad he had done this—seeing the young lieutenant looking at a soldier's death—no, more than that, looking at a *colonel of cavalry* killed in action. When a colonel dies, it's a bigger thing, Flynn thought. No matter how he dies.

Bowers was saying, "This will head the report," his voice heavy with respect, "for it isn't often that a colonel dies this way."

Flynn looked at him quickly, but only awe and respect were on Bowers' face and Flynn said, "No, thankfully, it isn't often."

Madora came up behind them. He glanced at Flynn after looking down at Deneen, but he said nothing to him. Then to Bowers, "I see Soldado survived . . . him and about two dozen others. Counting his women up in the hills somewhere, you'll have about seventy people all told. Red, how do you propose to get 'em to San Carlos?"

"I was thinking of talking Santana into helping as far as the border . . . have cavalry come down to meet us there." Bowers smiled. "Hell, Joe, all the fight's out of those Mimbres. The three of us could take them up, for that matter."

"You mean the two of us."

"Two?"

"David here's talking about doing some prospecting."

Flynn smiled, but he didn't deny it.

FORTY
LASHES
LESS
ONE

....

ONE

The train was late and didn't get into Yuma until after dark. Then the ticket agent at the depot had to telephone the prison and tell them they had better get some transportation down here. He had three people waiting on a ride up the hill: a man he had never seen before who said he was the new prison superintendent, and another man he knew was a deputy sheriff from Pima County and he had a prisoner with him, handcuffed, a big colored boy.

Whoever it was on the phone up at the prison said they had sent a man two hours ago and if the train had been on time he would have met them. The ticket agent said well, they were here now and somebody better hurry with the transportation, because the Southern Pacific didn't care for convicts hanging around the depot, even if the boy was handcuffed.

The Pima deputy said hell, it wasn't anything new; every time he delivered a man he had to sit and wait on the prison people to get off their ass. He asked the big colored boy if he minded waiting, sitting in a nice warm train depot, or would he rather be up there in one of them carved-out cells with the wind whistling in across the river? The Pima deputy said something about sweating all day and freezing at night; but the colored boy, whose name was Harold Jackson, didn't seem to be listening.

The new prison superintendent—the new, temporary superintendent—Mr. Everett Manly, heard him. He nodded, and adjusted his gold-frame glasses. He said yes, he was certainly familiar with Arizona winters, having spent seven years at the Chiricahua Apache Mission School. Mr. Manly heard himself speak and it sounded all right. It sounded natural.

On the train Mr. Manly had exchanged a few words with the deputy, but had not spoken to the colored boy. He could have asked him his name and where he was from; he could have asked him about his sentence and told him that if he behaved himself he would be treated fairly. He could have asked him if he wanted to pray. But with the Pima deputy sitting next to the colored boy—all afternoon and evening on the wicker seats, bumping and swaying, looking out at the sun haze on the desert and the distant, dark brown mountains—Mr. Manly had not been able to get the first words out, to start a conversation. He was not afraid of the colored boy, who could have been a cold-blooded killer for all he knew. It was the idea of the deputy sitting there listening that bothered him.

He thought about starting a friendly conversation with the ticket agent: ask him if he ever got up to the prison, or if he knew the superintendent, Mr. Rynning, who was in Florence at the present time seeing to the construction of the new penitentiary. He could say, "Well, it won't be long now, there won't be any more Yuma Territorial Prison," and kidding, add, "I suppose you'll be sorry to see it closed." Except maybe he wasn't supposed to talk about it in idle conversation. It had been mentioned in newspapers—"Hell-Hole on the Bluff to Open Its Doors Forever by the Spring of 1909"—pretty clever, saying *opening* its doors instead of closing them. And no doubt the station agent knew all about it. Living here he would have to. But a harmless conversation could start false rumors and speculation, and before you knew it somebody from the Bureau would write and ask how come he was going around telling everybody about official government business.

If the ticket agent brought up the subject that would be different. He could be noncommittal. "You heard the old prison's closing, huh? Well, after thirty-three years I imagine you won't be too sorry to see it happen." But the ticket agent didn't bring up the subject.

A little while later they heard the noise outside. The ticket agent looked at them through his barred window and said, "There's a motor conveyance pulling into the yard I reckon is for you people."

Mr. Manly had never ridden in an automobile before. He asked the driver what kind it was and the driver told him it was a twenty-horsepower Ford Touring Car, powerful and speedy, belonged to the superintendent, Mr. Rynning. It was comfortable, Mr. Manly said, but kind of noisy, wasn't it? He wanted to ask how much a motor rig like this cost, but there was the prison above him: the walls and the guard towers against the night sky, the towers, like little houses with pointed roofs; dark houses, nobody home. When the gravel road turned and climbed close along the south wall, Mr. Manly had to look almost straight up, and he said to the guard driving the car, "I didn't picture the walls so high." And the guard answered, "Eighteen feet up and eight feet thick. A man can't jump it and he can't bore through neither.

"My last trip up this goddamn rock pile," the Pima deputy said, sitting in the back seat with his prisoner. "I'm going to the railroad hotel and get me a bottle of whiskey and in the morning I'm taking the train home and ain't never coming back here again."

The rest of the way up the hill Mr. Manly said nothing. He would remember this night and the strange feeling of riding in a car up Prison Hill, up close to this great silent mound of adobe and granite. Yuma Territorial Prison, that he had heard stories about for years—that he could almost reach out and touch. But was it like a prison? More like a tomb of an ancient king, Mr. Manly was thinking. A pyramid. A ghostly monument. Or, if it was a prison, then one that was already deserted. Inside the walls there were more than a hundred men. Maybe a hundred and fifty counting the guards. But there was no sound or sign of life, only this motor car putt-putting up the hill, taking forever to reach the top.

What if it did take forever, Mr. Manly thought. What if they kept going and going and never reached the prison gate, but kept moving up into stoney darkness for all eternity—until the four of them realized this was God's judgment upon them. (He could hear the Pima deputy cursing and saying, "Now, wait a minute, I'm just here to deliver a prisoner!") It could happen this way, Mr. Manly thought. Who said you had to die first? Or, how did a person know when he was dead? Maybe he had died on the train. He had dozed off and opened his eyes as they were pulling into the depot—

A man sixty years old could die in his sleep. But—and here was the question—if he was dead and this was happening, why would he be condemned to darkness? What had he done wrong in his life?

Not even thinking about it very hard, he answered at once, though quietly: What have you done right? Sixty years of life, Mr. Manly thought. Thirty years as a preacher of the Holy Word, seven years as a missionary among pagan Indians. Half his life spent in God's service, and he was not sure he had converted even one soul to the Light of Truth.

They reached the top of the bluff at the west end of the prison

and, coming around the corner, Mr. Manly saw the buildings that
were set back from the main gate, dim shapes and cold yellow
lights that framed windows and reflected on the hard-packed yard.
He was aware of the buildings and thought briefly of an army post,
single- and two-story structures with peaked roofs and neatly painted
verandas. He heard the driver point out the guard's mess and recre-
ation hall, the arsenal, the stable, the storehouses; he heard him
say, "If you're staying in the sup'rintendent's cottage, it's over yonder by the trees."

Mr. Manly was familiar with government buildings in clean-
swept areas. He had seen them at the San Carlos reservation and at
Fort Huachuca and at the Indian School. He was staring at the
prison wall where a single light showed the main gate as an oval
cavern in the pale stone, a dark tunnel entrance crisscrossed with
strips of iron.

The driver looked at Mr. Manly. After a moment he said, "The
sally port. It's the only way in and, I guarantee, the only way out."

Bob Fisher, the turnkey, stood waiting back of the inner gate
with two of his guards. He seemed either patient or half asleep, a
solemn-looking man with a heavy, drooping mustache. He didn't
have them open the iron lattice door until Mr. Manly and the Pima
deputy and his prisoner were within the dark enclosure of the sally
port and the outer gate was bolted and locked behind them. Then
he gave a sign to open up and waited for them to step into the yard
light.

The Pima deputy was pulling a folded sheaf of papers out of his
coat pocket, dragging along his handcuffed prisoner. "I got a boy
name of Harold Jackson wants to live with you the next fifteen
years." He handed the papers to the turnkey and fished in his pants
pocket for the keys to the handcuffs.

Bob Fisher unfolded the papers close to his stomach and glanced
at the first sheet. "We'll take care of him," he said, and folded the
papers again.

Mr. Manly stood by waiting, holding his suitcase.

"I'll tell you what," the Pima deputy said. "I'll let you buy me a
cup of coffee 'fore I head back."

"We'll see if we got any," Fisher said.

The Pima deputy had removed the handcuffs from the prisoner
and was slipping them into his coat pocket. "I don't want to put

you to any trouble," he said. "Jesus, a nice friendly person like you."

"You won't put us to any trouble," Fisher answered. His voice was low, and he seemed to put no effort or feeling into his words.

Mr. Manly kept waiting for the turnkey to notice him and greet him and have one of the guards take his suitcase; but the man stood at the edge of the yard light and didn't seem to look at any of them directly, though maybe he was looking at the prisoner, telling him with the sound of his voice that he didn't kid with anybody. What does he look like, Mr. Manly was thinking. He lowered his suitcase to the ground.

A street car motorman, that was it. With his gray guard uniform and gray uniform hat, the black shiny peak straight over his eyes. A tough old motorman with a sour stomach and a sour outlook from living within the confinement of a prison too many years. A man who never spoke if he didn't have to and only smiled about twice a year. The way the man's big mustache covered the sides of his mouth it would be hard to tell if he ever smiled at all.

Bob Fisher told one of the guards to take the Pima deputy over to the mess hall, then changed his mind and said no, take him outside to the guard's mess. The Pima deputy shrugged; he didn't care where he got his coffee. He took time to look at Mr. Manly and say, "Good luck, mister." As Mr. Manly said, "Good luck to you too," not looking at the turnkey now but feeling him there, the Pima deputy turned his back on them; he waited to get through the double gates and was gone.

"My name is Everett Manly," Mr. Manly said. "I expect—"

But Fisher wasn't ready for him yet. He motioned to the guards and watched as they led the prisoner off toward a low, one-room adobe. Mr. Manly waited, also watching them. He could see the shapes of buildings in the darkness of the yard, here and there a light fixed above a doorway. Past the corner of a two-story building, out across the yard, was the massive outline of a long, windowless adobe with a light above its crisscrossed iron door. Probably the main cellblock. But in the darkness he couldn't tell about the other buildings, or make any sense of the prison's layout. He had the feeling again that the place was deserted except for the turnkey and the two guards.

"I understand you've come here to take charge."

All the waiting and the man had surprised him. But all was

forgiven, because the man was looking at him now, acknowledging his presence.

"I'm Everett Manly. I expect Mr. Rynning wrote you I was coming. You're—"

"Bob Fisher, turnkey."

Mr. Manly smiled. "I guess you would be the man in charge of the keys." Showing him he had a sense of humor.

"I've been in charge of the whole place since Mr. Rynning's been gone."

"Well, I'm anxious to see everything and get to work." Mr. Manly was being sincere now, and humble. "I'm going to admit though, I haven't had much experience."

In his flat tone, Fisher said, "I understand you haven't had any."

Mr. Manly wished they weren't standing here alone. "No *prison* experience, that's true. But I've dealt with people all my life, Mr. Fisher, and nobody's told me yet convicts aren't people." He smiled again, still humble and willing to learn.

"Nobody will have to tell you," Fisher said. "You'll find out yourself."

He turned and walked off toward the one-room adobe. Mr. Manly had no choice but to pick up his suitcase and follow—Lord, with the awful feeling again and wishing he hadn't put so many books in with his clothes; the suitcase weighed a ton and he probably looked like an idiot walking with quick little steps and the thing banging against his leg. And then he was grateful and felt good again, because Bob Fisher was holding the door open for him and let him go inside first, into the lighted room where the colored boy was jackknifed over a table without any clothes on and the two guards were standing on either side of him.

One of the guards pulled him up and turned him around by the arm as Fisher closed the door. "He's clean," the guard said. "Nothing hid away down him or up him."

"He needs a hosing is all," the other guard said.

Fisher came across the plank floor, his eyes on the prisoner. "He ain't worked up a sweat yet."

"Jesus," the first guard said, "don't get close to him. He stinks to high heaven."

Mr. Manly put down his suitcase. "That's a long dusty train ride, my friend." Then, smiling a little, he added, "I wouldn't mind a bath myself."

The two guards looked over at him, then at Fisher, who was still facing the prisoner. "That's your new boss," Fisher said, "come to take Mr. Rynning's place while he's gone. See he gets all the bath water he wants. This boy here washes tomorrow with the others, after he's put in a day's work."

Mr. Manly said, "I didn't intend that to sound like I'm interfering with your customs or regulations—"

Fisher looked over at him now, waiting.

"I only meant it was sooty and dirty aboard the train."

Fisher waited until he was sure Mr. Manly had nothing more to say. Then he turned his attention to the prisoner again. One of the guards was handing the man a folded uniform and a broad-brimmed sweat-stained hat. Fisher watched him as he put the clothes on the table, shook open the pants and stepped into them: faded, striped gray and white convict pants that were short and barely reached to the man's high-top shoes. While he was buttoning up, Fisher opened the sheaf of papers the Pima deputy had given him, his gaze holding on the first sheet. "It says here you're Harold Jackson."

"Yes-suh, captain."

The Negro came to attention as Fisher looked up, a hint of surprise in his solemn expression. He seemed to study the prisoner more closely now and took his time before saying, "You ain't ever been here before, but you been somewhere. Where was it you served time, boy?"

"Fort Leavenworth, captain."

"You were in the army?"

"Yes-suh, captain."

"I never knew a nigger that was in the army. How long were you in it?"

"Over in Cuba eight months, captain. At Leavenworth four years hard labor."

"Well, they learned you some manners," Fisher said, "but they didn't learn you how to stay out of prison, did they? These papers say you killed a man. Is that right?"

"Yes-suh, captain."

"What'd you kill him with?"

"I hit him with a piece of pipe, captain."

"You robbing him?"

"No-suh, captain, we jes' fighting."

Mr. Manly cleared his throat. The pause held, and he said quickly, "Coming here he never gave the deputy any trouble, not once."

Fisher took his time as he looked around. He said, "I generally talk to a new man and find out who he is or who he believes he is, and we get a few things straightened out at the start." He paused. "If it's all right with you."

"Please go ahead," Mr. Manly said. "I just wanted to say he never acted smart on the trip, or was abusive. I doubt he said more than a couple words.'

"That's fine." Fisher nodded patiently before looking at Harold Jackson again. "You're our last nigger," he said to him. "You're the only one we got now, and we want you to be a good boy and work hard and do whatever you're told. Show you we mean it, we're going to help you out at first, give you something to keep you out of trouble."

There was a wooden box underneath the table. Mr. Manly didn't notice it until one of the guards stooped down and, with the rattling sound of chains, brought out a pair of leg-irons and a ball-peen hammer.

Mr. Manly couldn't hold back. "But he hasn't done anything yet!"

"No, sir," Bob Fisher said, "and he ain't about to with chains on his legs." He came over to Mr. Manly and, surprising him, picked up his suitcase and moved him through the door, closing it firmly behind them.

Outside, Fisher paused. "I'll get somebody to tote your bag over to Mr. Rynning's cottage. I expect you'll be most comfortable there."

"I appreciate it."

"Take your bath if you want one, have something to eat and a night's sleep—there's no sense in showing you around now—all right?"

"What are you going to do to the colored boy?"

"We're going to put him in a cell, if that's all right."

"But the leg-irons."

"He'll wear them a week. See what they feel like."

"I guess I'm just not used to your ways," Mr. Manly said. "I mean prison ways." He could feel the silence again among the darkened stone buildings and high walls. The turnkey walked off toward the empty, lighted area by the main gate. Mr. Manly had to step quickly to catch up with him. "I mean I believe a man should have a chance to prove himself first," he said, "before he's judged."

"They're judged before they get here."

"But putting leg-irons on them—"

"Not all of them. Just the ones I think need them, so they'll know what irons feel like."

Mr. Manly knew what he wanted to say, but he didn't have the right words. "I mean, don't they hurt terrible?"

"I sure hope so," Fisher answered.

As they came to the lighted area, a guard leaning against the iron grill of the gate straightened and adjusted his hat. Fisher let the guard know he had seen him, then stopped and put down the suitcase.

"This Harold Jackson," Fisher said. "Maybe you didn't hear him. He killed a man. He didn't miss Sunday school. He beat a man to death with an iron pipe."

"I know—I heard him."

"That's the kind of people we get here. Lot of them. They come in, we don't know what's on their minds. We don't know if they're going to behave or cause trouble or try and run or try and kill somebody else."

"I understand that part all right."

"Some of them we got to show right away who's running this place."

Mr. Manly was frowning. "But this boy Harold Jackson, he seemed all right. He was polite, said yes-sir to you. Why'd you put leg-irons on him?"

Now it was Fisher's turn to look puzzled. "You saw him same as I did."

"I don't know what you mean."

"I mean he's a nigger, ain't he?"

Looking up at the turnkey, Mr. Manly's gold-frame spectacles glistened in the overhead light. "You're saying that's the only reason you put leg-irons on him?"

"If I could tell all the bad ones," Bob Fisher said, "as easy as I can tell a nigger, I believe I'd be sup'rintendent."

Jesus Christ, the man was even dumber than he looked. He could have told him a few more things: sixteen years at Yuma, nine years as turnkey, and he hadn't seen a nigger yet who didn't need to wear irons or spend some time in the snake den. It was the way they were, either lazy or crazy; you had to beat 'em to make 'em work, or chain 'em to keep 'em in line. He would like to see just one good nigger. Or one good, hard-working Indian for that matter. Or a Mexican you could trust. Or a preacher who knew enough to keep his nose in church and out of other people's business.

Bob Fisher had been told two weeks earlier, in a letter from Mr. Rynning, that an acting superintendent would soon be coming to Yuma.

Mr. Rynning's letter had said: "Not an experienced penal administrator, by the way, but, of all things, a preacher, an ordained minister of the Holy Word Church who has been wrestling with devils in Indians schools for several years and evidently feels qualified to match his strength against convicts. This is not my doing. Mr. Manly's name came to me through the Bureau as someone who, if not eminently qualified, is at least conveniently located and willing to take the job on a temporary basis. (The poor fellow must be desperate. Or, perhaps misplaced and the Bureau doesn't know what else to do with him but send him to prison, out of harm's way.) He has had some administrative experience and, having worked on an Apache reservation, must know something about inventory control and logistics. The bureau insists on an active administrator at Yuma while, in the same breath, they strongly suggest I remain in Florence during the new prison's final stage of preparation. Hence, you will be meeting your new superintendent in the very near future. Knowing you will oblige him with your utmost cooperation I remain . . ."

Mr. Rynning remained in Florence while Bob Fisher remained in Yuma with a Holy Word Pentacostal preacher looking over his shoulder.

The clock on the wall of the superintendent's office said ten after nine. Fisher, behind the big mahogany desk, folded Mr. Rynning's letter and put it in his breast pocket. After seeing Mr. Manly through the gate, he had come up here to pick up his personal file. No sense in leaving anything here if the preacher was going to occupy the office. The little four-eyed son of a bitch, maybe a few days here would scare hell out of him and run him back to Sunday school. Turning in the swivel chair, Fisher could see the reflection of the room in the darkened window glass and could see himself sitting at the desk; with a thumb and first finger he smoothed his mustache and continued to fool with it as he looked at the clock again.

Still ten after nine. He was off duty; had been since six. Had waited two hours for the preacher.

It was too early to go home: his old lady would still be up and he'd have to look at her and listen to her talk for an hour or more. Too early to go home, and too late to watch the two women convicts take their bath in the cook shack. They always finished and were gone by eight-thirty, quarter to nine. He had been looking forward to watching them tonight, especially Norma Davis. Jesus, she had big ones, and a nice round white fanny. The Mexican girl was smaller, like all the Mexican girls he had ever seen; she was all right, though; especially with the soapy water on her brown skin. It was a shame; he hadn't watched them in about four nights. If the train had been on time he could have met the preacher and still got over to the cook shack before eight-thirty. It was like the little son of a bitch's train to be late. There was something about him, something that told Fisher the man couldn't do anything right, and would mess up anything he took part in.

Tomorrow he'd show him around and answer all his dumb questions.

Tonight—he could stare at the clock for an hour and go home.

He could stare out at the empty yard and hope for something to happen. He could pull a surprise inspection of the guard posts, maybe catch somebody sleeping.

He could stop at a saloon on the way home. Or go down to Frank Shelby's cell, No. 14, and buy a pint of tequila off him.

What Bob Fisher did, he pulled out the papers on the new prisoner, Harold Jackson, and started reading about him.

One of the guards asked Harold Jackson if he'd ever worn leg-irons before. Sitting tired, hunch-shouldered on the floor, he said yeah. They looked down at him and he looked up at them, coming full awake but not showing it, and said yes-suh, he believed it was two times. That's all, if the captain didn't count the prison farm. He'd wore irons there because they liked everybody working outside the jail to wear irons. It wasn't on account he had done anything.

The guard said all right, that was enough. They give him a blanket and took him shuffling across the dark yard to the main cell block, then through the iron-cage gate where bare overhead lights showed the stone passageway and the cell doors on both sides. The guards didn't say anything to him. They stopped at Cell No. 8, unlocked the door, pushed him inside, and clanged the ironwork shut behind him.

As their steps faded in the passageway, Harold Jackson could make out two tiers of bunks and feel the closeness of the walls and was aware of a man breathing in his sleep. He wasn't sure how many were in this cell. He let his eyes get used to the darkness before he took a step, then another, the leg chains clinking in the silence. The back wall wasn't three steps away. The bunks, three decks high on both sides of him, were close enough to touch. Which would make this a six-man room, he figured, about eight feet by nine feet. Blanket-covered shapes lay close to him in the middle bunks. He couldn't make out the top ones and didn't want to feel around; but he could see the bottom racks were empty. Harold Jackson squatted on the floor and ducked into the right-side bunk.

The three-tiered bunks and the smell of the place reminded him of the troopship, though it had been awful hot down in the hold. Ten days sweating down in that dark hold while the ship was tied up at Tampa and they wouldn't let any of the Negro troops go ashore, not even to walk the dock and stretch their legs. He never did learn the name of that ship, and he didn't care. When they landed at Siboney, Harold Jackson walked off through the jungle and up into the hills. For two weeks he stayed with a Cuban family and ate sugar cane and got a kick out of how they couldn't speak any English, though they were Negro, same as he was. When he had rested and felt good he returned to the base and they threw him in the stockade. They said he was a deserter. He said he came back, didn't he? They said he was still a deserter.

He had never been in a cell that was this cold. Not even at Leavenworth. Up there in the Kansas winter the cold times were in the exercise yard, stamping your feet and moving to keep warm; the cell was all right, maybe a little cold sometimes. That was a funny thing, most of the jails he remembered as being hot: the prison farm wagon that was like a circus cage and the city jails and the army stockade in Cuba. He'd be sitting on a bench sweating or laying in the rack sweating, slapping mosquitoes, scratching, or watching the cockroaches fooling around and running nowhere. Cockroaches never looked like they knew where they were going. No, the heat was all right. The heat, the bugs were like part of being in jail. The cold was something he would have to get used to. Pretend it was hot. Pretend he was in Cuba. If he had to pick a jail to be in, out of all the places—if somebody said, "You got to go to

jail for ten years, but we let you pick the place"—he'd pick the
stockade at Siboney. Not because it was a good jail, but because it
was in Cuba, and Cuba was a nice-looking place, with the ocean
and the trees and plenty of shade. That's a long way away, Harold
Jackson said to himself. You ain't going to see it again.

There wasn't any wind. The cold just lay over him and didn't go
away. His body was all right; it was his feet and his hands. Harold
Jackson rolled to his side to reach down below the leg-irons that
dug hard into his ankles and work his shoes off, then put his hands,
palms together like he was praying, between the warmth of his
legs. There was no use worrying about where he was. He would
think of Cuba and go to sleep.

In the morning, in the moments before opening his eyes, he
wasn't sure where he was. He was confused because a minute ago
he'd have sworn he'd been holding a piece of sugar cane, the pur-
ple peeled back in knife strips and he was sucking, chewing the
pulp to draw out the sweet juice. But he wasn't holding any cane
now, and he wasn't in Cuba.

The bunk jiggled, strained, and moved back in place as somebody got down from above him. There were sounds of movement
in the small cell, at least two men.

"You don't believe it, take a look."

"Jesus Christ," another voice said, a younger voice. "What's he
doing in here?"

Both of them white voices. Harold Jackson could feel them
standing between the bunks. He opened his eyes a little bit at a
time until he was looking at prison-striped legs. It wasn't much
lighter in the cell than before, when he'd gone to sleep, but
he could see the stripes all right and he knew that outside it was
morning.

A pair of legs swung down from the opposite bunk and hung
there, wool socks and yellow toenails poking out of holes. "What're
you looking at?" this one said, his voice low and heavy with sleep.

"We got a coon in here with us," the younger voice said.

The legs came down and the space was filled with faded, dirty
convict stripes. Harold Jackson turned his head a little and raised
his eyes. His gaze met theirs as they hunched over to look at him,
studying him as if he was something they had never seen before.
There was a heavy-boned, beard-stubbled face; a blond baby-boy
face; and a skinny, slick-haired face with a big cavalry mustache
that drooped over the corners of the man's mouth.

"Somebody made a mistake," the big man said. "In the dark."

"Joe Dean seen him right away."

"I smelled him," the one with the cavalry mustache said.

"Jesus," the younger one said now, "wait till Shelby finds out."

Harold Jackson came out of the bunk, rising slowly, uncoiling and bringing up his shoulders to stand eye to eye with the biggest of the three. He stared at the man's dead-looking deep-set eyes and at the hairs sticking out of a nose that was scarred and one time had been broken. "You gentlemen excuse me," Harold Jackson said, moving past the young boy and the one who was called Joe Dean. He stood with his back to them and aimed at the slop bucket against the wall.

They didn't say anything at first; just stared at him. But as Harold Jackson started to go the younger one murmured, "Jesus Christ—" as if awed, or saying a prayer. He stared at Harold as long as he could, then broke for the door and began yelling through the iron-work, "Guard! Guard! Goddamn it, there's a nigger in here pissing in our toilet!"

TWO

Raymond San Carlos heard the sound of Junior's voice before he made out the words: somebody yelling—for a guard. Somebody gone crazy, or afraid of something. Something happening in one of the cells close by. He heard quick footsteps now, going past, and turned his head enough to look from his bunk to the door.

It was morning. The electric lights were off in the cell block and it was dark now, the way a barn with its doors open is dark. He could hear other voices now and footsteps and, getting louder, the metal-ringing sound of the guards banging crowbars on the cell doors—good morning, get up and go to the toilet and put your shoes on and fold your blankets—the iron clanging coming closer, until it was almost to them and the convict above Raymond San Carlos yelled, "All right, we hear you! God Almighty—" The other convict in the cell, across from him in an upper bunk, said, "I'd like to wake them sons of bitches up some time." The man above Raymond said, "Break their goddamn eardrums." The other man said, "No, I'd empty slop pails on 'em." And the crowbar clanged against the door and was past them, banging, clanging down the passageway.

Another guard came along in a few minutes and unlocked each cell. Raymond was ready by the time he got to them, standing by the door to be first out. One of the convicts in the cell poked Raymond in the back and, when he turned around, pointed to the bucket.

"It ain't my turn," Raymond said.

"If I want you to empty it," the convict said, his partner close behind him, looking over his shoulder, "then it's your turn."

Raymond shrugged and they stood aside to let him edge past them. He could argue with them and they could pound his head against the stone wall and say he fell out of his bunk. He could pick up the slop bucket and say, "Hey," and when they turned around he could throw it at them. Thinking about it afterward would be good, but the getting beat up and pounded against the wall wouldn't be good. Or they might stick his face in a bucket. God, he'd get sick, and every time he thought of it after he'd get sick.

He had learned to hold onto himself and think ahead, looking at the good results and the bad results, and decide quickly if doing something was worth it. One time he hadn't held onto himself—the time he worked for the Sedona cattle people up on Oak Creek—and it was the reason he was here.

He had held on at first, for about a year while the other riders—some of them—kidded him about having a fancy name like Raymond San Carlos when he was Apache Indian down to the soles of his feet. Chiricahua Apache, they said. Maybe a little taller than most, but look at them black beady eyes and the flat nose. Pure Indin.

The Sedona hands got tired of it after a while; all except two boys who wouldn't leave him alone: a boy named Buzz Moore and another one they called Eljay. They kept at him every day. One of them would say, "What's that in his hair?" and pretend to pick something out, holding it between two fingers and studying it closely. "Why, it's some fuzz off a turkey feather, must have got stuck there from his headdress." Sometimes when it was hot and dry one of these two would look up at the sky and say, "Hey, chief, commence dancing and see if you can get us some rain down here." They asked him if he ever thought about white women, which he would never in his life ever get to have. They'd drink whiskey in front of him and not give him any, saying it was against the law to give an Indian firewater. Things like that.

At first it hadn't been too hard to hold on and go along with the kidding. Riding for Sedona was a good job, and worth it. Raymond would usually grin and say nothing. A couple of times he tried to tell them he was American and only his name was Mexican. He had made up what he thought was a pretty good story.

"See, my father's name was Armando de San Carlos y Zamora. He was born in Mexico, I don't know where, but I know he come up here to find work and that's when he met my mother who's an American, Maria Ramirez, and they got married. So when I'm born here, I'm American too."

He remembered Buzz Moore saying, "Maria Ramirez? What kind of American name is that?"

The other one, Eljay, who never let him alone, said, "So are Apache Indins American if you want to call everybody who's born in this country American. But anybody knows Indins ain't citizens. And if you ain't a citizen, you ain't American." He said to Raymond, "You ever vote?"

"I ain't never been where there was anything to vote about," Raymond answered

"You go to school?"

"A couple of years."

"Then you don't know anything about what is a U. S. citizen. Can you read and write?"

Raymond shook his head.

"There you are," Eljay said.

Buzz Moore said then, "His daddy could have been Indin. They got Indins in Mexico like anywhere else. Why old Geronimo himself lived down there and could have sired a whole tribe of little Indins."

And Eljay said, "You want to know the simple truth? He's Chiricahua Apache, born and reared on the San Carlos Indin reservation, and that's how he got his fancy name. Made it up so people wouldn't think he was Indin."

"Well," Buzz Moore said, "he could be some part Mexican."

"If that's so," Eljay said, "what we got here is a red greaser."

They got a kick out of that and called him the red greaser through the winter and into April—until the day up in the high meadows they were gathering spring calves and their mammas and chasing them down to the valley graze. They were using revolvers and shotguns part of the time to scare the stock out of the brush stands and box canyons and keep them moving. Raymond remembered the feel of the 12-gauge Remington, holding it pointed up with the stock tight against his thigh. He would fire it this way when he was chasing stock—aiming straight up—and would feel the Remington kick against his leg. He kept off by himself most of the day, enjoying the good feeling of being alone in high country. He remembered the day vividly: the clean line of the peaks towering against the sky, the shadowed canyons and the slopes spotted yellow with arrowroot blossoms. He liked the silence; he liked being here alone and not having to think about anything or talk to anybody.

It wasn't until the end of the day he realized how sore his leg was from the shotgun butt punching it. Raymond swung down off the sorrel he'd been riding and limped noticeably as he walked toward the cook fire. Eljay was standing there. Eljay took one look and said, "Hey, greaser, is that some kind of one-legged Indin dance you're doing?" Raymond stopped. He raised the Remington and shot Eljay square in the chest with both loads.

On this morning in February, 1909, as he picked up the slop bucket and followed his two cellmates out into the passageway. Raymond had served almost four years of a life sentence for second-degree murder.

The guard, R. E. Baylis, didn't lay his crowbar against No. 14, the last door at the east end of the cellblock. He opened the door and stepped inside and waited for Frank Shelby to look up from his bunk.

"You need to be on the supply detail today?" R. E. Baylis asked.

"What's today?"

"Tuesday."

"Tomorrow," Shelby said. "What's it like out?"

"Bright and fair, going to be warm."

"Put me on an outside detail."

"We got a party building a wall over by the cemetery."

"Hauling the bricks?"

"Bricks already there."

"That'll be all right," Shelby said. He sat up, swinging his legs over the side of the bunk. He was alone in the cell, in the upper of a double bunk. The triple bunk opposite him was stacked with cardboard boxes and a wooden crate and a few canvas sacks. A shelf and mirror hung from the back wall. There was also a chair by the wall with a hole cut out of the seat and a bucket underneath. A roll of toilet paper rested on one of the arms. The convicts called the chair Shelby's throne. "Get somebody to empty the bucket, will you?" Looking at the guard again, Shelby said, "You need anything?"

R. E. Baylis touched his breast pocket. "Well, I guess I could use some chew."

"Box right by your head," Shelby said. "I got Mail Pouch and Red Man. Or I got some Copenhagen if you want."

R. E. Baylis fished a hand in the box. "I might as well take a couple—case I don't see you again today."

"You know where to find me." Shelby dropped to the floor, pulled on half-boots, hopping a couple of times to keep his balance, then ran a hand through his dark hair as he straightened up, standing now in his boots and long underwear. "I believe I was supposed to get a clean outfit today."

"Washing machine broke down yesterday."

"Tomorrow then for sure, uh?" Shelby had an easy, unhurried way of talking. It was known that he never raised his voice or got excited. They said the way you told if he was mad or irritated, he would fool with his mustache; he would keep smoothing it down with two fingers until he decided what had to be done and either did it himself or had somebody else do it. Frank Shelby was serving forty-five years for armed robbery and second-degree murder and had brought three of his men with him to Yuma, each of them found guilty on the same counts and serving thirty years apiece.

Junior was one of them. He banged through the cell door as Shelby was getting into his prison stripes, buttoning his coat. "You got your mean go-to-hell look on this morning," Shelby said. "Was that you yelling just now?"

"They stuck a nigger in our cell last night while we was asleep." Junior turned to nail the guard with his look, putting the blame on him.

"It wasn't me," R. E. Baylis said. "I just come on duty."

"You don't throw his black ass out, we will," Junior said. By Jesus, this was Worley Lewis, Jr. talking, nineteen-year-old convict going on forty-nine before he would ever see the outside of a penitentiary, but he was one of Frank Shelby's own and that said he could stand up to a guard and mouth him if he had a good enough reason. "I'm telling you, Soonzy'll kill the son of a bitch."

"I'll find out why—" the guard began.

"It was a mistake," Shelby said. "Put him in the wrong cell is all."

"He's in there now, great big buck. Joe Dean seen him first, woke me up, and I swear I couldn't believe my eyes."

Shelby went over to the mirror and picked up a comb from the shelf. "It's nothing to get upset about," he said, making a part and slanting the dark hair carefully across his forehead. "Tonight they'll put him someplace else."

"Well, if we can," the guard said.

Shelby was watching him in the mirror: the gray-looking man in the gray guard uniform, R. E. Baylis, who might have been a town constable or a deputy sheriff twenty years ago. "What's the trouble?" Shelby asked.

"I mean he might have been ordered put there, I don't know."

"Ordered by who?"

"Bob Fisher. I say I don't know for sure."

Shelby turned from the mirror. "Bob don't want any trouble."

"Course not."

"Then why would he want to put Sambo in with my boys?"

"I say, I don't know."

Shelby came toward him now, noticing the activity out in the passageway, the convicts standing around and talking, moving slowly as the guards began to form them into two rows. Shelby put a hand on the guard's shoulder. "Mr. Baylis," he said, "don't worry about it. You don't want to ask Bob Fisher; we'll get Sambo out of there ourselves."

"We don't want nobody hurt or anything."

The guard kept looking at him, but Shelby was finished. As far as he was concerned, it was done. He said to Junior, "Give Soonzy the tobacco. You take the soap and stuff."

"It's my turn to keep the tally."

"Don't give me that look, boy."

Junior dropped his tone. "I lugged a box yesterday."

"All right, you handle the tally, Joe Dean carries the soap and stuff." Shelby paused, as if he was going to say something else, then looked at the guard. "Why don't you have the colored boy empty my throne bucket?"

"It don't matter to me," the guard said.

So he pulled Harold Jackson out of line and told him to get down to No. 14—as Joe Dean, Soonzy, and Junior moved along the double row of convicts in the dim passageway and sold them tobacco and cigarette paper, four kinds of plug and scrap, and little tins of snuff, matches, sugar cubes, stick candy, soap bars, sewing needles and thread, playing cards, red bandana handkerchiefs, shoelaces, and combs. They didn't take money; it would waste too much time and they only had ten minutes to go down the double line of eighty-seven men. Junior put the purchase amount in the tally book and the customer had one week to pay. If he didn't pay in a week, he couldn't buy any more stuff until he did. If he didn't pay in two weeks Junior and Soonzy would get him in a cell alone and hit him a few times or stomp the man's ribs and kidneys. If a customer wanted tequila or mescal, or corn whiskey when they

had it, he'd come around to No. 14 after supper, before the doors
were shut for the night, and pay a dollar a half-pint, put up in medicine bottles from the sick ward that occupied the second floor of
the cell block. Shelby only sold alcohol in the morning to three or
four of the convicts who needed it first thing or would never get
through the day. What most of them wanted was just a day's worth
of tobacco and some paper to roll it in.

When the figure appeared outside the iron lattice Shelby said,
"Come on in," and watched the big colored boy's reaction as he entered: his gaze shifting twice to take in the double bunk and the
boxes and the throne, knowing right away this was a one-man cell.

"I'm Mr. Shelby."

"I'm Mr. Jackson," Harold said.

Frank Shelby touched his mustache. He smoothed it to the sides
once, then let his hand drop to the edge of his bunk. His eyes remained on the impassive dark face that did not move now and was
looking directly at him.

"Where you from, Mr. Jackson?"

"From Leavenworth."

That was it. Big time con in a desert prison hole. "This place
doesn't look like much after the federal pen, uh?"

"I been to some was worse, some better."

"What'd you get sent here for?"

"I killed a man was bothering me."

"You get life?"

"Fifteen years."

"Then you didn't kill a man. You must've killed another colored
boy." Shelby waited.

Harold Jackson said nothing. He could wait too.

"I'm right, ain't I?" Shelby said.

"The man said for me to come in here."

"He told you, but it was me said for you to come in."

Harold Jackson waited again. "You saying you the man here?"

"Ask any of them out there," Shelby said. "The guards, anybody."

"You bring me in to tell me about yourself?"

"No, I brought you in to empty my slop bucket."

"Who did it before I come?"

"Anybody I told."

"If you got people willing, you better call one of them." Harold
turned and had a hand on the door when Shelby stopped him.

"Hey, Sambo—"

Harold came around enough to look at him. "How'd you know that was my name?"

"Boy, you are sure starting off wrong," Shelby said. "I believe you need to be by yourself a while and think it over."

Harold didn't have anything to say to that. He turned to the door again and left the man standing there playing with his mustache.

As he fell in at the end of the prisoner line, guard named R. E. Baylis gave him a funny look and came over.

"Where's Shelby's bucket at?"

"I guess it's still in there, captain."

"How come he didn't have you take it?"

Harold Jackson stood at attention, looking past the man's face to the stone wall of the passageway. "You'll have to ask him about that, captain."

"Here they come," Bob Fisher said, "Look over there."

Mr. Manly moved quickly from the side of the desk to the window to watch the double file of convicts coming this way. He was anxious to see everything this morning, especially the convicts.

"Is that all of them?"

"In the main cell block. About ninety."

"I thought there'd be more." Mr. Manly studied the double file closely but wasn't able to single out Harold Jackson. All the convicts looked alike. No, that was wrong; they didn't all look alike.

"Since we're shutting down we haven't been getting as many."

"They're all different, aren't they?"

"How's that?" Bob Fisher said.

Mr. Manly didn't answer, or didn't hear him. He stood at the window of the superintendent's office—the largest of a row of offices over the mess hall—and watched the convicts as they came across the yard, passed beyond the end of a low adobe, and came into view again almost directly below the window. The line reached the door of the mess hall and came to a stop.

Their uniforms looked the same, all of them wearing prison stripes, all faded gray and white. It was the hats that were different, light-colored felt hats and a few straw hats, almost identical hats, but all worn at a different angle: straight, low over the eyes, to the side, cocked like a dandy would wear his hat, the brim funneled, the brim up in front, the brim down all around. The hats were as different as the men must be different. He should make a note of that. See if anything had been written on the subject: determining

a man's character by the way he wore his hat. But there wasn't a
note pad or any paper on the desk and he didn't want to ask Fisher
for it right at the moment.

He was looking down at all the hats. He couldn't see any of
their faces clearly, and wouldn't unless a man looked up. Nobody
was looking up.

They were all looking back toward the yard. Most of them turning now so they wouldn't have to strain their necks. All those men
suddenly interested in something and turning to look.

"The women convicts," Bob Fisher said.

Mr. Manly saw them then. My God—two women.

Fisher pressed closer to him at the window. Mr. Manly could
smell tobacco on the man's breath. "They just come out of the latrine, that adobe there," Fisher said. "Now watch them boys eyeing
them."

The two women walked down the line of convicts, keeping about
ten feet away, seeming at ease and not in any hurry, but not looking at the men either.

"Taking their time and giving the boys sweet hell, aren't they?
Don't hear a sound, they're so busy licking their lips."

Mr. Manly glanced quickly at the convicts. The way they were
looking, it was more likely their mouths were hanging open. It
gave him a funny feeling, the men dead serious and no one making
a sound.

"My," Fisher said, "how they'd like to reach out and grab a
handful of what them girls have got."

"Women—" Mr. Manly said almost as a question. Nobody had
told him there were women at Yuma.

A light-brown-haired one and a dark-haired one that looked to
be Mexican. Lord God, two good-looking women walking past
those men like they were strolling in the park. Mr. Manly couldn't
believe they were convicts. They were *women*. The little dark-
haired one wore a striped dress—smaller stripes than the men's
outfits—that could be a dress she'd bought anywhere. The brown-
haired one, taller and a little older, though she couldn't be thirty
yet, wore a striped blouse with the top buttons undone, a white
canvas belt and a gray skirt that clung to the movement of her hips
as she walked and flared out as it reached to her ankles.

"Tacha Reyes," Fisher said

"Pardon me?"

"The little chilipicker. She's been here six months of a ten-year sentence. I doubt she'll serve it all though. She behaves herself pretty good."

"What did she do? I mean to be here."

"Killed a man with a knife, she claimed was trying to make her do dirty things."

"Did the other one—kill somebody?"

"Norma Davis? Hell, no. Norma likes to do dirty things. She was a whore till she took up armed robbery and got caught holding up the Citizens' Bank of Prescott, Arizona. Man with her, her partner, was shot dead."

"A woman," Mr. Manly said. "I can't believe a woman would do that."

"With a Colt forty-four," Fisher said. "She shot a policeman during the hold-up but didn't kill him. Listen, you want to keep a pretty picture of women in your head don't get close to Norma. She's serving ten years for armed robbery and attempted murder."

The women were inside the mess hall now. Mr. Manly wanted to ask more questions about them, but he was afraid of sounding too interested and Fisher might get the wrong idea. "I notice some of the men are carrying buckets," he said.

"The latrine detail." Fisher pointed to the low adobe. "They'll go in there and empty them. That's the toilet and wash house, everything sewered clear out to the river. There—now the men are going into mess. They got fifteen minutes to eat, then ten minutes to go to the toilet before the work details form out in the exercise yard."

"Do you give them exercises to do?"

"We give them enough work they don't need any exercise," Fisher answered.

Mr. Manly raised his eyes to look out at the empty yard and was surprised to see a lone convict coming across from the cellblock.

"Why isn't that one with the others?"

Bob Fisher didn't answer right way. Finally he said, "That's Frank Shelby."

"Is he a trusty?"

"Not exactly. He's got some special jobs he does around here."

Mr. Manly let it go. There were too many other things he wanted to know about. Like all the adobe buildings scattered around, a whole row of them over to the left, at the far end of the mess hall. He wondered where the women lived, but didn't ask that.

Well, there was the cook shack over there and the tailor shop, where they made the uniforms. Bob Fisher pointed out the small one-story adobes. Some equipment sheds, a storehouse, the reception hut they were in last night. The mattress factory and the wagon works had been shut down six months ago. Over the main cellblock was the hospital, but the doctor had gone to Florence to set up a sick ward at the new prison. Anybody broke a leg now or crushed his hand working the rocks, they sent for a town doctor.

And the chaplain, Mr. Manly asked casually. Was he still here?

No, there wasn't any chaplain. The last one retired and they decided to wait till after the move to get another. There wasn't many of the convicts prayed anyway.

How would you know that? Mr. Manly wanted to ask him. But he said, "What are those doors way down there?"

At the far end of the yard he could make out several iron-grill doors, black oval shapes, doorways carved into the solid rock. The doors didn't lead outside, he could tell that, because the top of the east wall and two of the guard towers were still a good piece beyond.

"Starting over back of the main cellblock, you can't see it from here," Bob Fisher said, "a gate leads into the TB cellblock and exercise yard."

"You've got consumptives here?"

"Like any place else. I believe four right now." Fisher hurried on before Mr. Manly could interrupt again. "The doors you can see—one's the crazy hole. Anybody gets mean loco they go in there till they calm down. The next one they call the snake den's a punishment cell."

"Why is it called—"

"I don't know, I guess a snake come in through the air shaft one time. The last door there on the right goes into the women's cell block. You seen them. We just got the two right now."

There, he could ask about them again and it would sound natural. "The one you said, Norma something, has she been here long?"

"Norma Davis. I believe about a year and a half."

"Do the men ever—I mean I guess you have to sort of watch over the women."

"Mister, we have to watch over everybody."

"But being women—don't they have to have their own, you know, facilities and bath?"

Fisher looked right at Mr. Manly now. "They take a bath in the cook shack three, four times a week."

"In the cook shack." Mr. Manly nodded, surprised. "After the cooks are gone, of course."

"At night," Fisher said. He studied Mr. Manly's profile—the soft pinkish face and gold-frame glasses pressed close to the window pane—little Bible teacher looking out over his prison and still thinking about Norma Davis, asking harmless sounding questions about the women.

Fisher said quietly, "You want to see them?"

Mr. Manly straightened, looking at Fisher now with a startled expression. "What do you mean?"

"I wondered if you wanted to go downstairs and have another look at Norma and Tacha."

"I want to see everything," Mr. Manly said. "Everything you have here to show me."

THREE

When Frank Shelby entered the mess hall he stepped in line ahead of Junior. In front of him, Soonzy and Joe Dean looked around.

"You take care of it?" Junior asked him.

"He needs some time in the snake den," Shelby said.

Soonzy was looking back down the line. "Where's he at?"

"Last one coming in."

"I'll handle him," Junior said.

Shelby shook his head. "I want somebody else to start it. You and Soonzy break it up and get in some licks."

"No problem," Junior said. "The spook's already got leg-irons on."

They picked up tin plates and cups and passed in front of the serving tables for their beans, salt-dried beef, bread, and coffee. Soonzy and Joe Dean waited, letting Shelby go ahead of them. He paused a moment, holding his food, looking out over the long twelve-man tables and benches that were not yet half filled. Joe Dean moved up next to him. "I see plenty of people that owe us money."

"No, I see the one I want. The Indin," Shelby said, and started for his table.

Raymond San Carlos was pushing his spoon into the beans that were pretty good but would be a lot better with some ketchup. He looked up as Frank Shelby and Junior put their plates down across from him. He hurried and took the spoonful of beans, then took another one more slowly. He knew they had picked him for something. He was sure of it when Soonzy sat down on one side of him and Joe Dean stepped in on the other. Joe Dean acted surprised at seeing him. "Well, Raymond San Carlos," he said, "how are you today?"

"I'm pretty good, I guess."

Junior said, "What're you pretty good at, Raymond?"

"I don't know—some things, I guess."

"You fight pretty good?"

It's coming, Raymond said to himself, and told himself to be very calm and not look away from this little boy son-of-a-bitch friend of Frank Shelby's. He said, "I fight sometimes. Why, you want to fight me?"

"Jesus," Junior said. "Listen to him."

Raymond smiled. "I thought that's what you meant." He picked up his coffee and took a sip.

"Don't drink it," Shelby said.

Raymond looked directly at him for the first time. "My coffee?"

"You see that colored boy? He's picking up his plate." As Raymond looked over Shelby said, "After he sits down I want you to go over and dump your coffee right on his woolly head."

He was at the serving table now, big shoulders and narrow hips. Some of the others from the latrine had come in behind him. He was not the biggest man in the line, but he was the tallest and seemed to have the longest arms.

"You want me to fight him?"

"I said I want you to pour your coffee on his head," Shelby answered. "That's all I said to do. You understand that, or you want me to tell you in sign language?"

Harold Jackson took a place at the end of a table. There were two men at the other end. Shifting his gaze past them as he took a bite of bread, he could see Frank Shelby and the mouthy kid and, opposite them, the big one you would have to hit with a pipe or a pick handle to knock down, and the skinny one, Joe Dean, with the beard that looked like ass fur off a sick dog. The dark-skinned man with them, who was getting up now, he hadn't seen before.

There were five guards in the room. No windows. One door. A stairway—at the end of the room behind the serving tables—where the turnkey and the little man from the train were coming down the stairs now: little man who said he was going to be in charge, looking all around—my, what a fine big mess hall—looking and following the turnkey, who never changed his face, looking at the grub now, nodding, smiling,—yes, that would sure stick to their ribs—taking a cup of coffee the turnkey offered him and tasting it. Two of the guards walked over and now the little man was shaking hands with them.

That was when Harold felt somebody behind him brush him, and the hot coffee hitting his head was like a shock, coming into his eyes and feeling as if it was all over him.

Behind him, Raymond said, "What'd you hit my arm for?"

Harold wiped a hand down over his face, twisting around and looking up to see the dark-skinned man who had been with Shelby, an Indian-looking man standing, waiting for him. He knew Shelby was watching, Shelby and anybody else who had seen it happen.

"What's the matter with you?" Harold said.

Raymond didn't move. "I want to know why you hit my arm."

"I'll hit your mouth, boy, you want. But I ain't going to do it here."

Raymond let him have the tin plate, back-handing the edge of it across his eyes, and Harold was off the bench, grabbing Raymond's wrist as Raymond hit him in the face with the coffee cup. Harold didn't get to swing. A fist cracked against his cheekbone from the blind side. He was hit again on the other side of the face, kicked in the small of the back, and grabbed by both arms and around his neck and arched backward until he was looking at the ceiling. There were faces looking at him, the dark-skinned boy looking at him calmly, people pressing in close, then a guard's hat and another, and the turnkey's face with the mustache and the expression that didn't change.

"Like he went crazy," Junior said. "Just reared up and hit this boy."

"I was going past," Raymond said.

Junior was nodding. "That's right. Frank seen it first, we look over and this spook has got Raymond by the neck. Frank says help him, and me and Soonzy grabbed the spook quick as we could."

The turnkey reached out, but Harold didn't feel his hand. He was looking past him.

"Let him up," Fisher said.

Somebody kicked him again as they jerked him to his feet and let go of his arms. Harold felt his nose throbbing and felt something wet in his eyes. When he wiped at his eyes he saw the red blood on his fingers and could feel it running down his face now. The turnkey's face was raised; he was looking off somewhere.

Fisher said, "You saw it, Frank?"

Shelby was still sitting at his table. He nodded slowly. "Same as

Junior told you. That colored boy started it. Raymond hit him to
get free, but he wouldn't let go till Junior and Soonzy got over
there and pinned him."

"That's all?"

"That's all," Shelby said.

"Anybody else see it start?" Fisher looked around. The convicts
met his gaze as it passed over them. They waited as Fisher took his
time, letting the silence in the room lengthen. When he looked at
Harold Jackson again there was a moment when he seemed about
to say something to him. The moment passed. He turned away and
walked back to the food tables where Mr. Manly was waiting, his
hands folded in front of him, his eyes wide open behind the gold-
frame glasses.

"You want to see the snake den," Bob Fisher said. "Come on,
we got somebody else wants to see it too."

After breakfast, as the work details were forming in the yard,
the turnkey and the new superintendent and two guards marched
Harold Jackson past the groups all the way to the snake den at the
back of the yard.

Raymond San Carlos looked at the colored boy as he went by.
He had never seen him before this morning. Nobody would see
him now for about a week. It didn't matter. Dumb nigger had done
something to Shelby and would have to learn, that's all.

While Raymond was still watching them—going one at a time
into the cell now—one of the guards, R. E. Baylis, pulled him out
the stone quarry gang and took him over to another detail. Raymond couldn't figure it out until he saw Shelby in the group and
knew Shelby had arranged it. A reward for pouring coffee on a
man. He was out of that man-breaking quarry and on Shelby's detail because he'd done what he was told. Why not?

As a guard with a Winchester marched them out the main gate
Raymond was thinking: Why not do it the easy way? Maybe things
were going to be better and this was the beginning of it: get in with
Shelby, work for him; have all the cigarettes he wanted, some
tequila at night to put him to sleep, no hard-labor details. He could
be out of here maybe in twenty years if he never did nothing to
wear leg-irons or get put in the snake den. Twenty years, he would
be almost fifty years old. He couldn't change that. Or he could do
whatever he felt like doing and not smile at people like Frank

Shelby and Junior and the two convicts in his cell. He could get his
head pounded against the stone wall and spend the rest of his life
here. It was a lot to think about, but it made the most sense to get
in with Shelby. He would be as dumb as the nigger if he didn't.

Outside the walls, the eight-man detail was marched past the water
cistern—their gaze going up the mound of earth past the stone-
work to the guard tower that looked like a bandstand sitting up
there, a nice shady pavilion where a rapid-fire weapon was trained
on the main gate—then down the grade to a path that took them
along the bluff overlooking the river. They followed it until they
reached the cemetery.

Beyond the rows of headstones an adobe wall, low, and uneven,
under construction, stood two to three feet high on the river side of
the cemetery.

Junior said, "What do they want a wall for? Them boys don't
have to be kept in."

"They want a wall," Shelby said, "because it's a good place for
a wall and there ain't nothing else for us to do."

Raymond agreed four year's worth to that. The work was to
keep them busy. Everybody knew they would be moving out of
here soon, but every day they pounded rocks into gravel for the
roads and made adobe bricks and built and repaired walls and lev-
ees and cleared brush along the river bank. It was a wide river with
a current—down the slope and across the flat stretch of mud beach
to the water—maybe a hundred yards across. There was nothing
on the other side—no houses, only a low bank and what looked to
be heavy brush. The land over there could be a swamp or a desert;
nobody had ever said what it was like, only that it was California.

All morning they laid the big adobe bricks in place, gradually
raising the level string higher as they worked on a section of wall
at a time. It was dirty, muddy work, and hot out in the open. Raymond couldn't figure out why Shelby was on this detail, unless he
felt he needed sunshine and exercise. He laid about half as many
bricks as anybody else, and didn't talk to anybody except his three
friends. It surprised Raymond when Shelby began working on the
other side of the wall from him and told him he had done all right
in the mess hall this morning. Raymond nodded; he didn't know
what to say. A few minutes went by before Shelby spoke again.

"You want to join us?"

Raymond looked at him. "You mean work for you?"

"I mean go with us," Shelby said. He tapped a brick in place with the handle of his trowel and sliced off the mortar oozing out from under the brick. "Don't look around. Say yes or no."

"I don't know where you're going."

"I know you don't. You say yes or no before I tell you."

"All right," Raymond said. "Yes."

"Can you swim?"

"You mean the river?"

"It's the only thing I see around here to swim," Shelby said. "I'm not going to explain it all now."

"I don't know—"

"Yes, you do, Raymond. You're going to run for the river when I tell you. You're going to swim straight across and find a boat hidden in the brush, put there for us, and you're going to row back fast as you can and meet us swimming over."

"If we're all swimming what do you want the boat for?"

"In case anybody can't make it all the way."

"I'm not sure I can, even."

"You're going to find out," Shelby said.

"How wide is it here?"

"Three hundred fifty feet. That's not so far."

The river had looked cool and inviting before; not to swim across, but to sit in and splash around and get clean after sweating all morning in the adobe mud.

"There's a current—"

"Don't think about it. Just swim."

"But the guard—what about him?"

"We'll take care of the guard."

"I don't understand how we going to do it." He was frowning in the sunlight trying to figure it out.

"Raymond, I say run, you run. All right?"

"You don't give me any time to think about it."

"That's right," Shelby said. "When I leave here you come over the wall and start working on this side." He got up and moved down the wall about ten or twelve feet to where Soonzy and Junior were working.

Raymond stepped over the three-foot section of wall with his mortar bucket and continued working, facing the guard now who was about thirty feet away, sitting on a rise of ground with the Winchester across his lap and smoking a cigarette. Beyond him, a hundred yards or so up the slope, the prison wall and the guard tower at the northwest corner stood against the sky. The guard up there could be looking this way or he could be looking inside, into the yard of the TB cell block. Make a run for the river with two guns within range. Maybe three, counting the main tower. There was some brush, though, a little cover before he got to the mud flat. But once they saw him, the whistle would blow and they'd be out here like they came up out of the ground, some of them shooting and some of them getting the boat, wherever the boat was kept. He didn't have to stay with Shelby, he could go up to the high country this spring and live by himself. Maybe through the summer. Then go some place nobody knew him and get work. Maybe Mexico.

Joe Dean came along with a wheelbarrow and scooped mortar into Raymond's bucket. "If we're not worried," Joe Dean said, leaning on the wall, "what're you nervous about?"

Raymond didn't look up at him. He didn't like to look at the man's mouth and tobacco-stained teeth showing in his beard. He didn't like having anything to do with the man. He didn't like having anything to do with Junior or Soonzy either. Or with Frank Shelby when he thought about it honestly and didn't get it mixed up with cigarettes and tequila. But he would work with them and swim the river with them to get out of this place. He said to Joe Dean, "I'm ready any time you are."

Joe Dean squinted up at the sun, then let his gaze come down to the guard. "It won't be long," he said, and moved off with his wheelbarrow.

The way they worked it, Shelby kept his eye on the guard. He waited until the man started looking for the chow wagon that would be coming around the corner from the main gate any time now. He waited until the guard was finally half-turned, looking up the slope, then gave a nod to Junior.

Junior jabbed his trowel into the foot of the man working next to him.

The man let out a scream and the guard was on his feet at once, coming down from the rise.

Shelby waited until the guard was hunched over the man, trying to get a look at the foot. The other convicts were crowding in for a look too and the man was holding his ankle, rocking back and forth and moaning. The guard told him goddamn-it, sit still and let him see it.

Shelby looked over at Raymond San Carlos, who was standing now, the wall in front of him as high as his hips. Shelby nodded and turned to the group around the injured man. As he pushed Joe Dean aside he glanced around again to see the wall empty where Raymond had been standing. "What time is it?" he said.

Joe Dean took out his pocket watch. "Eleven-fifty about."

"Exactly."

"Eleven-fifty-two."

Shelby took the watch from Joe Dean as he leaned in to see the clean tear in the toe of the man's shoe and the blood starting to come out. He waited a moment before moving over next to the wall. The guard was asking what happened and Junior was trying to explain how he'd tripped over the goddamn mortar bucket and, throwing his hand out as he fell, his trowel had hit the man's shoe. His foot, the guard said—you stabbed him. Well, he hadn't meant to, Junior told the guard. Jesus, if he'd meant to, he wouldn't have stabbed him in the foot, would he?

From the wall Shelby watched Raymond moving quickly through the brush clumps and not looking back—very good—not hesitating until he was at the edge of the mud flats, a tiny figure way down there, something striped, hunched over in the bushes and looking around now. Go on, Shelby said, looking at the watch. What're you waiting for? It was eleven fifty-three.

The guard was telling the man to take his shoes off, he wasn't going to do it for him; and goddamn-it, get back and give him some air.

When Shelby looked down the slope again Raymond was in the water knee-deep, sliding into it; in a moment only his head was showing. Like he knew what he was doing, Shelby thought.

Between moans the injured man said Oh God, he believed his toes were cut off. Junior said maybe one or two; no trowel was going to take off all a man's toes, 'less you come down hard with the edge; maybe that would do it.

Twenty yards out. Raymond wasn't too good a swimmer, about average. Well, that was all right. If he was average then the watch would show an average time. He sure seemed to be moving slow though. Swimming was slow work.

When the chow wagon comes, the guard said, we'll take him up in it. Two of you men go with him.

It's coming now, somebody said.

There it was, poking along close to the wall, a driver and a helper on the seat, one of the trusties. The guard stood up and yelled for them to get down here. Shelby took time to watch the injured man as he ground his teeth together and eased his shoe off. He wasn't wearing any socks. His toes were a mess of blood, but at least they all seemed to be there. He was lucky.

Raymond was more than halfway across now. The guard was motioning to the wagon, trying to hurry it. So Shelby watched Raymond: just a speck out there, you'd have to know where to look to find him. Wouldn't that be something if he made it? God Almighty, dumb Indin probably could if he knew what to do once he got across. Or if he had some help waiting. But he'd look for the boat that wasn't there and run off through the brush and see all that empty land stretching nowhere.

Eleven fifty-six. He'd be splashing around out there another minute easy before he reached the bank.

Shelby walked past the group around the injured man and called out to the guard who had gone part way up the slope, "Hey, mister!" When the guard looked around Shelby said, "I think there's somebody out there in the water."

The guard hesitated, but not more than a moment before he got over to the wall. He must have had a trained eye, because he spotted Raymond right away and fired the Winchester in the air. Three times in rapid succession.

Joe Dean looked up as Shelby handed him his pocket watch. "He make it?" Joe Dean asked.

"Just about."

"How many minutes?"

"Figure five anyway, as a good average."

Junior said to Shelby, "What do you think?"

"Well, it's a slow way out of here," Shelby answered. "But least we know how long it takes now and we can think on it."

Mr. Manly jumped in his chair and swiveled around to the window when the whistle went off, a high, shrieking sound that ripped through the stillness of the office and seemed to be coming from directly overhead. The first thing he thought of, immediately, was, *somebody's trying to escape*! His first day here . . .

Only there wasn't a soul outside. No convicts, no guards running across the yard with guns.

Of course—they were all off on work details.

When he pressed close to the window Mr. Manly saw the woman, Norma Davis, standing in the door of the tailor shop. Way down at the end of the mess hall. He knew it was Norma, and not the other one. Standing with her hands on her hips, as if she was listening—Lord, as the awful piercing whistle kept blowing. After a few moments she turned and went inside again. Not too concerned about it.

Maybe it wasn't an escape. Maybe it was something else. Mr. Manly went down the hall and opened the doors, looking into empty offices, some that hadn't been used in months. He turned back and, as he reached the end of the hall and the door leading to the outside stairway, the whistle stopped. He waited, then cautiously opened the door and went outside. He could see the front gate from here: both barred doors closed and the inside and outside guards at their posts. He could call to the inside guard, ask him what was going on.

And what if the man looked up at him on the stairs and said it was the noon dinner whistle? It was just about twelve.

Or what if it was an exercise he was supposed to know about? Or a fire drill. Or anything for that matter that a prison superintendent should be aware of. The guard would tell him, "That's the whistle to stop work for dinner, sir," and not say anything else, but his look would be enough.

Mr. Manly didn't know where else he might go, or where he might find the turnkey. So he went back to his office and continued reading the history file on Harold Jackson.

Born Fort Valley, Georgia, September 11, 1879.

Mr. Manly had already read that part. Field hand. No formal education. Arrested in Georgia and Florida several times for disorderly conduct, resisting arrest, striking an officer of the law. Served eighteen months on a Florida prison farm for assault. Inducted into the army April 22, 1898. Assigned to the 24th Infantry Regiment in Tampa, Florida, June 5. Shipped to Cuba.

He was going to read that part over again about Harold Jackson deserting and being court-martialed.

But Bob Fisher, the turnkey, walked in. He didn't knock, he walked in. He looked at Mr. Manly and nodded, then gazed about the room. "If there's something you don't like about this office, we got some others down the hall.

"Caught one of them trying to swim the river, just about the other side when we spotted him." Fisher stopped as Mr. Manly held up his hand and rose from the desk.

"Not right now," Mr. Manly said. "I'm going to go have my dinner. You can give me a written report this afternoon."

Walking past Fisher wasn't as hard as he thought it would be. Out in the hall Mr. Manly paused and looked back in the office. "I assume you've put the man in the snake den."

Fisher nodded.

"Bring me his file along with your report, Bob." Mr. Manly turned and was gone.

FOUR

Harold Jackson recognized the man in the few moments the door was open and the guards were shoving him inside. As the man turned to brace himself Harold saw his face against the outside sunlight, the dark-skinned face, the one in the mess hall. The door slammed closed and they were in darkness. Harold's eyes were used to it after half a day in here. He could see the man feeling his way along the wall until he was on the other side of the ten-by-ten-foot stone cell. It had been almost pitch dark all morning. Now, at midday, a faint light came through the air hole that was about as big around as a stovepipe and tunneled down through the domed ceiling. He could see the man's legs good, then part of his body as he sat down on the bare dirt floor. Harold drew up his legs and stretched them out again so the leg-iron chains would clink and rattle—in case the man didn't know he was here.

Raymond knew. Coming in, he had seen the figure sitting against the wall and had seen his eyes open and close as the sunlight hit his face, black against blackness, a striped animal in his burrow hole. Raymond knew. He had hit the man a good lick across the eyes with his tin plate, and if the man wanted to do something about it, now it was up to him. Raymond would wait, ready for him—while he pictured again Frank Shelby standing by the wall and tried to read Shelby's face.

The guards had brought him back in the skiff, making him row with his arms dead-tired, and dragged him wet and muddy all the way up the hill to the cemetery. Frank Shelby was still there. All of them were, and a man sitting on the ground, his foot bloody. Raymond had wanted to tell Shelby there wasn't any boat over there, and he wanted Shelby to tell him, somehow, what had gone wrong. He remembered Shelby staring at him, but not saying anything with his eyes or his expression. Just staring. Maybe he wasn't picturing Shelby's face clearly now, or maybe he had missed a certain look or gesture from him. He would have time to think about it. Thirty days in here. No mattress, no blanket, no slop bucket, use the corner, or piss on the nigger if he tried something. If the nigger hadn't done something to Shelby he wouldn't be here and you wouldn't be here, Raymond thought. Bread and water for thirty days, but they would take the nigger out before that and he would be alone. There were men they took from here to the crazy hole after being alone in the darkness too long. It can happen if you think about being here and nothing else, Raymond said to himself. So don't think about it. Go over and hit the nigger hard in the face and get it over with. God, if he wasn't so tired.

Kick him in the face to start, Harold was thinking, as he picked at the dried blood crusted on the bridge of his nose. Two and a half steps and aim it for his cheekbone, either side. That would be the way, if he didn't have on the irons and eighteen inches of chain links. He try kicking the man, he'd land flat on his back and the man would be on top of him. He try sneaking up, the man would hear the chain. 'Less the man was asleep and he worked over and got the chain around the man's neck and crossed his legs and stretched and kicked hard. Then they come in and say what happen? And he say I don't know, captain, the man must have choked on his bread. They say yeah, bread can kill a man all right; you stay in here with the bread the rest of your life. So the best thing would be to stand up and let the man stand up and hit him straight away and beat him enough but not too much. Beat him just right.

He said, "Hey, boy, you ready?"

"Any time," Raymond answered.

"Get up then."

Raymond moved stiffly, bringing up his knees to rise.

"What's the matter with you?"

"I'll tell you something," Raymond said. "If you're any good, maybe you won't get beat too bad. But after I sleep and rest my arms and legs I'll break your jaw."

"What's the matters with your arms and legs?"

"From swimming the river."

Harold Jackson stared at him, interested. He hadn't thought of why the man had been put in here. Now he remembered the whistle. "You saying you tried to bust out?"

"I got across."

"How many of you?"

Raymond hesitated. "I went alone."

"And they over there waiting."

"Nobody was waiting. They come in a boat."

"Broad daylight—man, you must be one dumb Indin fella."

Raymond's legs cramped as he started to rise, and he had to ease down again, slowly.

"We got time," Harold Jackson said. "Don't be in a hurry to get yourself injured."

"Tomorrow," Raymond said, "when the sun's over the hole and I can see your black nigger face in here."

Harold saw the chain around the man's neck and his legs straining to pull it tight. "Indin, you're going to need plenty medicine before I'm through with you."

"The only thing I'm worried about is catching you," Raymond said. "I hear a nigger would rather run than fight."

"Any running I do, red brother, is going to be right at your head."

"I got to see that."

"Keep your eyes open, Indin. You won't see nothing once I get to you."

There was a silence before Raymond said. "I'll tell you something. It don't matter, but I want you to know it anyway. I'm no Indian. I'm Mexican born in the United States, in the territory of Arizona."

"Yeah," Harold Jackson said. "Well, I'm Filipina born in Fort Valley, Georgia."

"Field nigger is what you are."

"Digger Indin talking, eats rats and weed roots."

"I got to listen to a goddamn field hand."

"I've worked some fields," Harold said. "I've plowed and picked cotton, I've skinned mules and dug privies and I've busted rock. But I ain't never followed behind another convict and emptied his bucket for him. White or black. *No*body."

Raymond's tone was lower. "You saw me carrying a bucket this morning?"

"Man, I don't have to see you, I know you carry one every morning. Frank Shelby says dive into it, you dive."

"Who says I work for Frank Shelby?"

"He say scratch my ass, you scratch it. He say go pour your coffee on that nigger's head, you jump up and do it. Man, if I'm a field nigger you ain't no better than a house nigger." Harold Jackson laughed out loud. "Red nigger, that's all you are, boy. A different color but the same thing."

The pain in Raymond's thighs couldn't hold him this time. He lunged for the dark figure across the cell to drive into him and slam his black skull against the wall. But he went in high. Harold got under him and dumped him and rolled to his feet. They met in the middle of the cell, in the dim shaft of light from the air hole, and beat each other with fists until they grappled and kneed and strained against each other and finally went down.

When the guard came in with their bread and water, they were fighting on the hard-packed floor. He yelled to another guard who came fast with a wheelbarrow, pushing it through the door and the short passageway into the cell. They shoveled sand at Harold and Raymond, throwing it stinging hard into their faces until they broke apart and lay gasping on the floor. A little while later another guard came in with irons and chained them to ring bolts on opposite sides of the cell. The door slammed closed and again they were in darkness.

Bob Fisher came through the main gate at eight-fifteen that evening, not letting on he was in a hurry as he crossed the lighted area toward the convicts' mess hall.

He'd wanted to get back by eight—about the time they'd be bringing the two women out of their cellblock and over to the cook shack. But his wife had started in again about staying here and not wanting to move to Florence. She said after sixteen years in this house it was their *home*. She said a rolling stone gathered no moss, and that it wasn't good to be moving all the time. He reminded her they had moved twice in twenty-seven years, counting the move from Missouri. She said then it was about time they settled; a family should stay put, once it planted roots. What family? he asked her. Me and you? His wife said she didn't know anybody in Florence and wasn't sure she wanted to. She didn't even know if there was a Baptist church in Florence. What if there wasn't? What was she supposed to do then? Bob Fisher said that maybe she would keep her fat ass home for a change and do some cooking and baking, instead of sitting with them other fatties all day making patchwork quilts and bad-mouthing everybody in town who wasn't a paid-up member of the church. He didn't honestly care where she spent her time, or whether she baked pies and cakes or not. It was something to throw at her when she started in nagging about staying in Yuma. She said how could anybody cook for a person who came home at all hours with whiskey stinking up his breath? Yes, he had stopped and had a drink at the railroad hotel, because he'd had to talk to the express agent about moving equipment to Florence. Florence, his wife said. She wished she had never heard the name—the same name as her cousin who was still living in Sedalia, but now she didn't even like to think of her cousin any more and they had grown up together as little girls. Bob Fisher couldn't picture his wife as a little girl. No, that tub of fat couldn't have ever been a little girl. He didn't tell her that. He told her he had to get back to the prison, and left without finishing his coffee.

Fisher walked past the outside stairway and turned the corner of the mess hall. There were lights across the way in the main cell-block. He moved out into the yard enough to look up at the second floor of the mess hall and saw a light on in the superintendent's office. The little Sunday school teacher was still there, or had come back after supper. Before going home Fisher had brought in his written report of the escape and the file on Raymond San Carlos. The Sunday school teacher had been putting his books away, taking them out of a suitcase and lining them up evenly on the shelf. He'd said just lay the report on the desk and turned back to his books. What would he be doing now? Probably reading his Bible.

Past the latrine adobe Fisher walked over to the mess hall and tried the door. Locked for the night. Now he moved down the length of the building, keeping close to the shadowed wall though moving at a leisurely pace—just out for a stroll, checking around, if anybody was curious. At the end of the building he stopped and looked both ways before crossing over into the narrow darkness between the cook-shack adobe and the tailor shop.

Now all he had to do was find the right brick to get a free show. About chin-high it was, on the right side of the cook-shack chimney that stuck out from the wall about a foot and would partly hide him as he pressed in close. Fisher worked a finger in on both sides of the brick that had been chipped loose some months before, and pulled it out as slowly as he could. He didn't look inside right away; no, he always put the brick on the ground first and set himself, his feet wide apart and his shoulders hunched a little so the opening would be exactly at eye level. They would be just past the black iron range, this side of the work table where they always placed the washtub, with the bare electric light on right above them.

Fisher looked in. Goddamn Almighty, just in time.

Just as Norma Davis was taking off her striped shirt, already unbuttoned, slipping it off her shoulders to let loose those round white ninnies that were like nothing he had ever seen before. Beauties, and she knew it, too, the way she stuck them out, standing with her hands on her hips and her belly a round little mound curving down into her skirt. What was she waiting for? Come on, Fisher said, take the skirt off and get in the tub. He didn't like it when they only washed from the waist up. With all the rock dust in the air and bugs from the mattresses and sweating under those heavy skirts, a lick-and-a-promise, armpits-and-neck wash wasn't any good. They had to wash theirselves all over to be clean and healthy.

Maybe he could write it into the regulations: Women convicts must take a full bath every other day. Or maybe every day.

The Mexican girl, Tacha Reyes, appeared from the left, coming from the end of the stove with a big pan of steaming water, and poured it into the washtub. Tacha was still dressed. Fisher could tell by her hair she hadn't bathed yet. She had to wait on Norma first, looking at Norma now as she felt the water. Tacha had a nice face; she was just a little skinny. Maybe give her more to eat—

Norma was taking off her skirt. Yes, *sir,* and that was all she had. No underwear on. Bare-ass naked with black stockings that come up over her knees. Norma turned, leaning against the work table to pull the stockings off, and Bob Fisher was looking at the whole show. He watched her lay her stockings on the table. He watched her pull her hair back with both hands and look down at her ninnies as she twisted the hair around so it would stay. He watched her step over to the tub, scratching under one of her arms, and say, "If it's too hot I'll put you in it."

"It should be all right," Tacha said.

Another voice, not in the room but out behind him, a voice he knew, said, "Guard, what's the matter? Are you sick?"

Twisting around, Bob Fisher hit the peak of his hat on the chimney edge and was straightening it, his back to the wall, as Mr. Manly came into the space between the buildings.

"It's me," Fisher said.

"Oh, I didn't know who it was."

"Making the rounds. I generally check all the buildings before I go to bed."

Mr. Manly nodded. "I thought somebody was sick, the way you were leaning against the wall."

"No, I feel fine. Hardly ever been sick."

"It was the way you were standing, like you were throwing up."

"No, I was just taking a look in here. Dark places you got to check good." He couldn't see Mr. Manly's eyes, but he knew the little son of a bitch was looking right at him, staring at him, or past him, where part of the brick opening might be showing and he could see light coming through. "You ready to go," Fisher said, "I'll walk you over to the gate."

He came out from the wall to close in on Mr. Manly and block his view; but he was too late.

"What's that hole?" Mr. Manly said.

"A hole?"

"Behind you, I can see something—"

Bob Fisher turned to look at the opening, then at Mr. Manly again. "Keep your voice down."

"Why? What is it?"

"I wasn't going to say anything. I mean it's something I generally check on myself. But," Fisher said, "if you want to take a look, help yourself."

Mr. Manly frowned. He felt funny now standing here in the darkness. He said in a hushed tone, "Who's in there?"

"Go ahead, take a look."

Through the slit of the opening something moved, somebody in the room. Mr. Manly stepped close to the wall and peered in.

The light glinted momentarily on his glasses as his head came around, his eyes wide open.

"She doesn't have any clothes on!"

"Shhhh." Fisher pressed a finger to his heavy mustache. "Look and see what they're doing."

"She's bare-naked, washing herself."

"We want to be sure that's all," Fisher said.

"What?"

"Go on, see what she's doing."

Mr. Manly leaned against the wall, showing he was calm and not in any hurry. He peered in again, as though looking around a corner. Gradually his head turned until his full face was pressed against the opening.

What Norma was doing, she was sliding a bar of yellow soap over her belly and down her thighs, moving her legs apart, and coming back up with the soap almost to her breasts before she slid it down again in a slow circular motion. Mr. Manly couldn't take his eyes off her. He watched the Mexican girl bring a kettle and pour water over Norma's shoulders, and watched the suds run down between her breasts, Lord Jesus, through the valley and over the fertile plain and to the dark forest. He could feel his heart beating and feel Bob Fisher close behind him. He had to quit looking now; Lord, it was long enough. It was too long. He wanted to clear his throat. She was turning around and he got a glimpse of her behind as he pulled his face from the opening and stepped away.

"Washing herself," Mr. Manly said. "That's all I could see she was doing."

Bob Fisher nodded. "I hoped that was all." He stooped to pick up the brick and paused with it at the opening. "You want to look at Tacha?"

"I think I've seen enough to know what they're doing," Mr. Manly answered. He walked out to the open yard and waited there for Fisher to replace the brick and follow him out.

"What I want to know is what you're doing spying on them."

"Spying? I was checking, like I told you, to see they're not doing anything wrong."

"What do you mean, wrong?"

"Anything that ain't natural, then. You know what I mean. Two women together without any clothes on—I want to know there ain't any funny business going on."

"She was washing herself."

"Yes, sir," Fisher said, "that's all I saw too. The thing is, you never know when they might start."

Mr. Manly could still see her, the bar of yellow soap moving over her body. "I've never heard of anything like that. They're both *women*."

"I'll agree with you there," Fisher said, "but in a prison you never know. We got men with no women, and women with no men, and I'll tell you we got to keep our eyes open if we don't want any funny business."

"I've heard tell of men," Mr. Manly said—the sudsy water

running down between her breasts—"but *women*. What do you suppose they do?"

"I hope I never find out," Fisher said. He meant it, too.

He got Mr. Manly out of there before the women came out and saw them standing in the yard; he walked Mr. Manly over to the main gate and asked him if he had read the report on the escape attempt.

Mr. Manly said yes, and that he thought it showed the guards to be very alert. He wondered, though, wasn't this Raymond San Carlos the same one the Negro has assaulted in the mess hall? The very same, Fisher said. Then wasn't it dangerous to put them both in the same cell? Dangerous to who? Fisher asked. To *them*, they were liable to start fighting again and try and kill each other. They already tried, Fisher said. They were chained to the floor now out of each other's reach. Mr. Manly asked how long they would leave them like that, and Fisher said until they made up their minds to be good and kind to each other. Mr. Manly said that could be never if there was a grudge between them. Fisher said it didn't matter to him, it was up to the two boys.

Fisher waited in the lighted area as Mr. Manly passed through the double gates of the sally port and walked off toward the superintendent's cottage. He was pretty sure Mr. Manly had believed his story, that he was checking on the women to see they didn't do queer things. He'd also bet a dollar the little Sunday school teacher wouldn't make him chink the hole up either.

That was dumb, taking all his books over to the office. Mr. Manly sat in the living room of the superintendent's cottage, in his robe and slippers, and didn't have a thing to read. His Bible was on the night table in the bedroom. Yes, and he'd made a note to look up what St. Paul said about being in prison, something about all he'd gone through and how one had to have perseverance. He saw Norma Davis rubbing the bar of soap over her body, sliding it up and down. No—what he wished he'd brought were the file records of the two boys in the snake den. He would have to talk to them when they got out. Say to them, look, boys, fighting never solved anything. Now forget your differences and shake hands.

They were different all right, a Negro and an Indian. But they were alike too.

Both here for murder. Both born the same year. Both had served

time. Both had sketchy backgrounds and no living relatives anybody knew of. The deserter and the deserted.

A man raised on a share-crop farm in Georgia; joined the army
and, four months later, was listed as a deserter. Court-martialed,
sentenced to hard labor.

A man raised on the San Carlos Indian reservation; deserted by
his Apache renegade father before he was born. Father believed
killed in Mexico; mother's whereabouts unknown.

Both of them in the snake den now, a little room carved out of
stone, with no light and hardly any air. Waiting to get at each other.

Maybe the sooner he talked to them the better. Bring them both
out in ten days—no matter what Bob Fisher thought about it. Ten
days was long enough. They needed spiritual guidance as much as
they needed corporal punishment. He'd tell Fisher in the morning.

As soon as Mr. Manly got into bed he started thinking of Norma
Davis again, seeing her clearly with the bare light right over her
and her body gleaming with soap and water. He saw her in the
room then, her body still slippery-looking in the moonlight
that was coming through the window. Before she could reach the
bed, Mr. Manly switched on the night-table lamp, grabbed hold of
his Bible and leafed as fast as he could to St. Paul's letters to the
Corinthians.

For nine days neither of them spoke. They sat facing each other,
their leg-irons chained to ring bolts that were cemented in the
floor. Harold would stand and stretch and lean against the wall and
Raymond would watch him. Later on Raymond would get up for a
while and Harold would watch. They never stood up at the same
time or looked at each other directly. There was silence except for
the sound of the chains when they moved. Each pretended to be
alone in the darkness of the cell, though each was intently aware of
the other's presence. Every day about noon a guard brought them
hardtack and water. The guard was not allowed to speak to them,
and neither of them spoke to him. It was funny their not talking, he
told the other guards. It was spooky. He had never known a man in
the snake den not to talk a storm when he was brought his bread
and water. But these two sat there as if they had been hypnotized.

The morning of the tenth day Raymond said, "They going to let
you out today." The sound of his voice was strange, like someone
else's voice. He wanted to clear his throat, but wouldn't let himself

do it with the other man watching him. He said, "Don't go anywhere, because when I get out of here I'm going to come looking
for you."

"I be waiting," was all Harold Jackson said.

At midday the sun appeared in the air shaft and gradually faded.
Nobody brought their bread and water. They had been hungry for
the first few days but were not hungry now. They waited and it was
early evening when the guard came in with a hammer and pounded
the ring bolts open, both of them, Raymond watching him curiously but not saying anything. Another guard came in with shovels
and a bucket of sand and told them to clean up their mess.

Bob Fisher was waiting outside. He watched them come out blinking and squinting in the daylight, both of them filthy stinking dirty,
the Negro with a growth of beard and the Indian's bony face hol-
lowed and sick-looking. He watched their gaze creep over the yard
toward the main cellblock where the convicts were standing
around and sitting by the wall, most of them looking this way.

"You can be good children," Fisher said, "or you can go back in
there, I don't care which. I catch you fighting, twenty days. I catch
you looking mean, twenty days." He looked directly at Raymond.
"I catch you swimming again, thirty days and leg-irons a year. You
understand me?"

For supper they had fried mush and syrup, all they wanted. After, they were marched over to the main cellblock. Raymond
looked for Frank Shelby in the groups standing around outside, but
didn't see him. He saw Junior and nodded. Junior gave him a dead-
pan look. The guard, R. E. Baylis, told them to get their blankets
and any gear they wanted to bring along.

"You putting us in another cell?" Raymond asked him. "How
about make it different cells? Ten days, I'll smell him the rest of
my life."

"Come on," Baylis said. He marched them down the passageway and through the rear gate of the cellblock.

"Wait a minute," Raymond said. "Where we going?"

The guard looked around at him. "Didn't nobody tell you? You
two boys are going to live in the TB yard."

FIVE

A work detail was making adobe bricks over by the south wall, inside the yard. They mixed mud and water and straw, stirred it into a heavy wet paste and poured it into wooden forms. There were bricks drying all along the base of the wall and scrap lumber from the forms and stacks of finished bricks, ready to be used here or sold in town.

Harold Jackson and Raymond San Carlos had to come across the yard with their wheelbarrows to pick up bricks and haul them back to the TB cellblock that was like a prison within a prison: a walled-off area with its own exercise yard. There were eight cells here, in a row facing the yard, half of them empty. The four tubercular convicts stayed in their cells most of the time or sat in the shade and watched Harold and Raymond work, giving them advice and telling them when a line of bricks wasn't straight. They were working on the face wall of the empty cells, tearing out the weathered, crumbling adobe and putting in new bricks; repairing cells that would probably never again be occupied. This was their main job. They worked at it side by side without saying a word to each other. They also had to bring the tubercular convicts their meals, and sometimes get cough medicine from the sick ward. A guard gave them white cotton doctor masks they could put on over their nose and mouth for whenever they went into the TB cells; but the masks were hot and hard to breathe through, so they didn't wear them after the first day. They used the masks, and a few rags they found, to pad the leg-irons where the metal dug into their ankles.

The third day out of the snake den Raymond began talking to the convicts on the brick detail. He recognized Joe Dean in the group, but didn't speak to him directly. He said, man alive, it was good to breathe fresh air again and feel the sun. He took off his hat and looked up at the sky. All the convicts except Joe Dean went on working. Raymond said, even being over with the lungers was better than the snake den. He said somebody must have made a mistake, he was supposed to be in thirty days for trying to escape, but they let him out after ten. Raymond smiled; he said he wasn't going to mention it to them, though.

Joe Dean was watching him, leaning on his shovel. "You take care of him yet?"

"Take care of who?" Raymond asked him.

"The nigger boy. I hear he stomped you."

"Nobody stomped me. Where'd you hear that?"

"Had to chain him up."

"They chained us both."

"Looks like you're partners now," Joe Dean said.

"I'm not partners with him. They make us work together, that's all."

"You going to fight him?"

"Sure, when I get a chance."

"He don't look too anxious," another convict said. "That nigger's a big old boy."

"I got to wait for the right time," Raymond said. "That's all."

He came back later for another wheelbarrow load of bricks and stood watching them as they worked the mud and mixed in straw. Finally he asked if anybody had seen Frank around.

"Frank who you talking about?" Joe Dean asked.

"Frank Shelby."

"Listen to him," Joe Dean said. "He wants to know has anybody seen Frank."

"I got to talk to him," Raymond said. "See if he can get me out of there."

"Scared of TB, huh?"

"I mean being with the black boy. I got enough of him."

"I thought you wanted to fight him."

"I don't know," Joe Dean said. "It sounds to me like you're scared to start it."

"I don't want no more of the snake den. That's the only thing stopping me."

"You want to see Frank Shelby," one of the other convicts said, "there he is." The man nodded and Raymond looked around.

Shelby must have just come out of the mess hall. He stood by the end-gate of a freight wagon that Junior and Soonzy and a couple of other convicts were unloading. There was no guard with them, unless he was inside. Raymond looked up at the guard on the south wall.

"I'll tell you something," Joe Dean said. "You can forget about Frank helping you."

Raymond was watching the guard. "You know, uh? You know him so good he's got you working in this adobe slop."

"Sometimes we take bricks to town," Joe Dean said. "You think on it if you don't understand what I mean."

"I got other things to think on."

As the guard on the south wall turned and started for the tower at the far end of the yard, Raymond picked up his wheelbarrow and headed for the mess hall.

Shelby didn't look up right away. He was studying a bill of lading attached to a clipboard, checking things off. He said to Junior, "The case right by your foot, that should be one of ours."

"Says twenty-four jars of Louisiana cane syrup."

"It's corn whiskey." Shelby still didn't look up, but he said then, "What do you want?"

"They let me out of the snake den," Raymond said. "I was suppose to be in thirty days, they let me out."

Shelby looked at him now. "Yeah?"

"I wondered if you fixed it."

"Not me."

"I thought sure." He waited as Shelby looked in the wagon and at the clipboard again. "Say, what happened at the river? I thought you were going to come right behind me."

"It didn't work out that way."

"Man, I thought I had made it. But I couldn't find no boat over there."

"I guess you didn't look in the right place," Shelby said.

"I looked where you told me. Man, it was work. I don't like swimming so much." He watched Shelby studying the clipboard. "I was wondering—you know I'm over in a TB cell now."

Shelby didn't say anything.

"I was wondering if you could fix it, get me out of there."

"Why?"

"I got to be with that nigger all the time."

"He's got to be with you," Shelby said, "so you're even."

Raymond grinned. "I never thought of it that way." He waited again. "What do you think?"

"About what?"

"About getting me back with everybody."

Shelby started fooling with his mustache, smoothing it with his fingers. "Why do you think anybody wants you back?"

Raymond didn't grin this time. "I did what you told me," he said seriously. "Listen, I'll work for you any time you want."

"I'm not hiring today."

"Well, what about getting me out of the TB yard?"

Shelby looked at him. He said, "Boy, why would I do that? I'm the one had you put there. Now you say one more word Soonzy is going to come down off the wagon and break both your arms."

Shelby watched Raymond pick up his wheelbarrow and walk away. "Goddamn Indin is no better than a nigger," he said to Junior. "You treat them nice one time and you got them hanging around the rest of your life."

When Raymond got back to the brick detail Joe Dean said, "Well, what did he say?"

"He's going to see what he can do," Raymond answered. He didn't feel like talking any more, and was busy loading bricks when Harold Jackson came across the yard with his wheelbarrow. Harold wore his hat pointed low over his eyes. He didn't have a shirt on and, holding the wheelbarrow handles, his shoulders and arm muscles were bunched and hard-looking. One of the convicts saw him first and said to Raymond, "Here comes your buddy." The other convicts working the adobe mud looked up and stood leaning on their shovels and hoes as Harold Jackson approached.

Raymond didn't look at him. He stacked another brick in the wheelbarrow and got set to pick up the handles. He heard one of the convicts say, "This here Indian says you won't fight him. Says you're scared. Is that right?"

"I fight him any time he wants."

Raymond had to look up then. Harold was staring at him.

"Well, I don't know," the convict said. "You and him talk about fighting, but nobody's raised a hand yet."

"It must be they're both scared," Joe Dean said. "Or it's because they're buddies. All alone in that snake den they got to liking each other. Guard comes in thinks they're rassling on the floor—man, they're not fighting, they're buggering each other."

The other convicts grinned and laughed, and one of them said, "Jesus Christ, what they are, they're sweethearts."

Raymond saw Harold Jackson take one step and hit the man in the face as hard as he could. Raymond wanted to say no, don't do it. It was a strange thing and happened quickly as the man spun toward him and Raymond put up his hands. One moment he was going to catch the man, keep him from falling against him. The next moment he balled up a fist and drove it into the man's face, right out in the open yard, the dumbest thing he had ever done, but doing it now and not stopping or thinking, going for Joe Dean now and busting him hard in the mouth as he tried to bring up his shovel. God, it felt good, a wild hot feeling, letting go and stepping into them and swinging hard at all the faces he had been wanting to smash and pound against a wall.

Harold Jackson held back a moment, staring at the crazy Indian, until somebody was coming at him with a shovel and he had to grab the handle and twist and chop it across the man's head. If he could get room and swing the shovel—but there were too many of them too close, seven men in the brick detail and a couple more, Junior and Soonzy, who came running over from the supply detail and grabbed hunks of lumber and started clubbing at the two wild men.

By the time the guard on the south wall fired his Winchester in the air and a guard came running over from the mess hall, Harold lay stunned in the adobe muck; Raymond was sprawled next to him and neither of them moved.

"Lord," Junior said, "we had to take sticks this time to get them apart."

Soonzy shook his head. "I busted mine on that nigger, he went right on fighting."

"They're a scrappy pair," Junior said, "but they sure are dumb, ain't they?"

Bob Fisher told the guard to hose them off and throw them in the snake den. He told Soonzy and Junior and the men on the brick detail to get back to work. Chained? the guard wanted to know. Chained, Fisher said, and walked off toward the stairs at the end of the mess hall, noticing the convicts who had come out of the adobe huts and equipment sheds, brought out by the guard's rifle fire, all of them looking toward the two men lying in the mud. He noticed Frank Shelby and some convicts by the freight wagon. He noticed the cooks in their white aprons, and the two women, Norma and Tacha, over by the tailor shop.

Fisher went up the stairs and down the hall to the superintendent's office. As he walked in, Mr. Manly turned from the window.

"The same two," Fisher said.

"It looked like they were all fighting." Mr. Manly glanced at the window again.

"You want a written report?"

"I'd like to know what happened."

"Those two start fighting. The other boys try to pull them apart and the two start swinging at everybody. Got to hit 'em with shovels to put 'em down."

"I didn't see them fighting each other."

"Then you must have missed that part." Past Mr. Manly's thoughtful expression—through the window and down in the yard—he saw a convict walking toward the tailor shop with a bundle under his arm. Frank Shelby. This far away he knew it was Shelby. Norma Davis stood in the door waiting for him.

"Soon as I heard the shots," Mr. Manly said, "I looked out. They were separated, like two groups fighting. They didn't look close enough to have been fighting each other."

Bob Fisher waited. "You want a written report?"

"What're you going to do to them?"

"I told them before, they start fighting they go back in the snake den. Twenty days. They know it, so it won't be any surprise."

"Twenty days in there seems like a long time."

"I hope to tell you it is," Fisher said.

"I was going to talk to them when they got out the other day. I meant to—I don't know, I put it off and then I guess some other things came up."

Fisher could see Shelby at the tailor shop now, close to the woman, talking to her. She turned and they both went inside.

"I'm not saying I could have prevented their fighting, but you never know, do you? Maybe if I *had* spoken to them, got them to shake hands—you understand what I mean, Bob?"

Fisher pulled his gaze away from the tailor shop to the little man by the window. "Well, I don't know about that."

"It could have made a difference."

"I never seen talking work much on anybody."

"But twenty days in there," Mr. Manly said, "and it could be my fault, because I didn't talk to them." He paused. "Don't you think, Bob, in this case, you ought to give them no more than ten days?

You said yourself ten days was a long time. Then soon as they come out I'll talk to them."

"That Indian was supposed to be in thirty days," Fisher said, "and you changed it to ten. Now I've already told them twenty and you want to cut it down again. I tell a convict one thing and you say something else and we begin to have problems."

"I'm only asking," Mr. Manly said, "because if I could have done something, if I'm the one to blame, then it wouldn't be fair to those two boys."

"Mister, they're convicts. They do what we tell them. Anything."

Mr. Manly agreed, nodding. "That's true, we give the orders and they have to obey. But we still have to be fair, no matter who we're dealing with."

Bob Fisher wondered what the hell he was doing here arguing with this little four-eyed squirt. He said, "They don't know anything about this. They don't know you meant to talk to them."

"But I know it," Mr. Manly said, "and the more I think about it the more I know I got to talk to them." He paused. "Soon."

Fisher saw it coming, happening right before his eyes, the little squirt's mind working behind his gold-frame glasses.

"Yes, maybe you ought to bring them in tomorrow."

"Just a minute ago you said ten days—"

"Do you have any children, Bob?"

The question stopped Fisher. He shook his head slowly, watching Mr. Manly.

"Well, I'm sure you know anyway you got to have patience with children. Sure, you got to punish them sometimes, but first you got to teach them right from wrong and be certain they understand it."

"I guess my wife's got something wrong with her. She never had any kids."

"That's God's will, Bob. What I'm getting at, these two boys here, Harold and Raymond, they're just like children." Mr. Manly held up his hand. "I know what you're going to say, these boys wasn't caught stealing candy, they took a life. And I say that's true. But still they're like little children. They're grown in body but not in mind. They got the appetites and temptations of grown men. They fight and carry on and, Lord knows, they have committed murder, for which they are now paying the price. But we don't want no more murders around here, do we, Bob? No, sir. Nor do we want to punish anybody for something that isn't their fault. We got two murderers wanting to kill each other. Two mean-looking boys we chain up in a dungeon. But Bob, tell me something. Has anybody ever spoke kindly to them? I mean has anybody ever helped them overcome the hold the devil's got on them? Has anybody ever showed them the path of righteousness, or explained to them Almighty God's justice and the meaning of everlasting salvation?"

Jesus Christ, Bob Fisher said—not to Mr. Manly, to himself. He had to get out of here; he didn't need any sermons today. He nodded thoughtfully and said to Mr. Manly, "I'll bring them in here whenever you want."

When Junior and Soonzy came back from clubbing the Indian and the colored boy, Frank Shelby told them to get finished with the unloading. He told them to leave a bottle of whiskey in the wagon for the freight driver and take the rest of it to his cell. Soonzy said Jesus, that nigger had a hard head, and showed everybody around how the hunk of wood was splintered. Junior said my, but they were dumb to start a fight out in the yard. This old boy over there called them sweethearts and that had started them swinging. If they wanted to fight, they should have it out in a cell some night. A convict standing there said, boy, he'd like to see that. It would be a good fight.

Shelby was looking at Norma Davis outside the tailer shop. He knew she was waiting for him, but what the convict said caught in his mind and he looked at the man.

"Which one would you bet on?"

"I think I'd have to pick the nigger," the convict said. "The way he's built."

Shelby looked around at Soonzy. "Who'd you pick?"

"I don't think neither of them look like much."

"I said who'd you pick."

"I don't know. I guess the nigger."

"How about in the mess hall," Shelby said. "The Indin showed he's got nerve. Pretty quick, too, the way he laid that plate across the boy's eyes."

"He's quick," Junior said.

"Quick and stronger than he looks," Shelby said. "You saw him swimming against the river current."

"Well, he's big for an Indin," Junior said. "Big and quick and, as

Frank says, he's got some nerve. Another thing, you don't see no marks on him from their fighting in the snake den. He might be more'n the nigger can handle."

"I'd say you could bet either way on that fight," Shelby said. He told Junior to hand him the bundle for the tailor shop—a bolt of prison cloth wrapped in brown paper—and walked off with it.

Most of them, Shelby was thinking, would bet on the nigger. Get enough cons to bet on the Indin and it could be a pretty good pot. If he organized the betting, handled the whole thing, he could take about ten per cent for the house. Offer some long-shot side bets and cover those himself. First, though, he'd have to present the idea to Bob Fisher. A prize fight. Fisher would ask what for and he'd say two reasons. Entertain the cons and settle the problem of the two boys fighting. Decide a winner and the matter would be ended. Once he worked out the side bets and the odds.

"Bringing me a present?" Norma asked him.

Shelby reached the shade of the building and looked up at her in the doorway. "I got a present for you, but it ain't in this bundle."

"I bet I know what it is."

"I bet you ought to. Who's inside?"

"Just Tacha and the old man."

"Well, you better invite me in," Shelby said, "before I start stripping you right here."

"Little anxious today?"

"I believe it's been over a week."

"Almost two weeks," Norma said. "Is there somebody else?"

"Two times I was on my way here," Shelby said, "Fisher stopped me and sent me on a work detail."

"I thought you got along with him."

"It's the first time he's pulled anything like that."

"You think he knows about us?"

"I imagine he does."

"He watches me and Tacha take a bath."

"He comes in?"

"No, there's a loose brick in the wall he pulls out. One time, after I was through, I peeked out the door and saw him sneaking off."

Shelby grinned. "Dirty old bastard."

"Maybe he doesn't feel so old."

"I bet he'd like to have some at that." Shelby nodded slowly. "I just bet he would."

Norma was watching him. "Now what are you thinking?"

"But he wouldn't want anybody to know about it. That's why he don't come in when you're taking a bath. Tacha's there."

Norma smiled. "I can see your evil mind working. If Tacha wasn't there—"

"Yes, sir, then he'd come in."

"Ask if I wanted him to soap my back."

"Front and back. I can see him," Shelby said. "One thing leads to another. After the first time, he don't soap you. No, sir, he gets right to it."

"Then one night you come in"—Norma giggled—"and catch the head guard molesting a woman convict."

Shelby shook his head, grinning.

"He's trying to pull his pants on in a hurry and you say, Good evening, Mr. Fisher. How are tricks?"

"God *damn*," Shelby said. "that's good."

"He's trying to button his pants and stick his shirt in and thinking as hard as he can for something to say." Norma kept giggling and trying not to. "He says, uh—"

"What does he say?"

"He says, 'I just come in for some coffee. Can I get you a cup, Mr. Shelby?' And you say, 'No, thank you. I was just on my way to see the superintendent.' He says, 'About what, Mr. Shelby?' And you say, 'About how some of the guards have been messing with the women convicts.' "

"It's an idea," Shelby said, "but I don't know of anything he can do for me except open the gate and he ain't going to do that, no matter what I get on him. No, I was wondering—if you and him got to be good friends—what he might tell you if you were to ask him."

Norma raised her arm and used the sleeve to wipe the wetness from her eyes. "What might he tell me?"

"Like what day we're supposed to move out of here. If we're going by train. If we're all going at once, or in groups." Shelby spoke quietly and watched her begin to nod her head as she thought about it. "Once we know when we're moving we can begin to make plans. I can talk to my brother Virgil, when he comes to visit, get him working on the outside. But we got to know *when*."

Norma was picturing herself in the cook shack with Fisher. "It would have to be the way I asked him. So he wouldn't suspect anything."

"Honey, you'd know better than I could tell you."

"I suppose once I got him comfortable with me."

"You won't have any trouble at all."

"It'll probably be a few times before he relaxes."

"Get him to think you like him. A man will believe anything when he's got his pants off."

"We might be having a cup of coffee after and I'll make a little face and look around the kitchen and say, 'Gee, honey, I wish there was some place else we could go.' "

"Ask him about the new prison."

"That's what I'm leading to," Norma said. "I'll tell him I hope we'll have a better place than this. Then I'll say, like I just thought of it, 'By the way, honey, when are we going to this new prison?' "

"Ask him if he's ever done it on a train?"

"I'll think of a way. I bet he's a horny old bastard."

"So much the better. He's probably never got it off a good-looking woman before in his life."

"Thank you."

"You're welcome."

"The only thing is what to do about Tacha."

"I'll have to think on that," Shelly said.

"Maybe he'd like both of us."

"Honey, he don't even have dreams like that anymore."

Tacha Reyes looked up from her sewing machine as they came into the shop and Shelby dropped the bundle on the work table. The old man, who had been a tailor here for twenty-six years since murdering his wife, continued working. He sat hunched over with his legs crossed, sewing a button to a striped convict coat.

Norma didn't say anything to them. She followed Shelby into the back room where the supplies and bolts of material were kept. The first few times they went back there together she said they were going to inventory the material or look over the thread supply or count buttons. Now she didn't bother. They went into the room and closed the door.

Tacha sat quietly, not moving. She told herself she shouldn't listen, but she always did. Sometimes she heard Norma, the faint sound of her laughing in there; she never heard Frank Shelby. He was always quiet.

Like the man who owned the café in St. David. He would come up behind her when she was working in the kitchen and almost before she heard him he would be touching her, putting his hands on her hips and bringing them up under her arms, pretending to be counting her ribs and asking how come she was so skinny, how come, huh, didn't she like the cooking here? And when she twisted away from him—what was the matter, didn't she like working here?

"How can he come in," Tacha said, "do whatever he wants?"

The tailor glanced over at the stock-room door. He didn't look at Tacha. "Norma isn't complaining."

"She's as bad as he is."

"I wouldn't know about that."

"She does whatever he wants. But he's a convict, like any of them."

"I'll agree he's a convict," the tailor said.

"You're afraid to even talk about him."

"I'll agree to that too," the tailor said.

"Some people can do whatever they want. Other people have to let them." Tacha was silent again. What good was talking about it?

The owner of the café in St. David thought he could do whatever he wanted because he paid her seven dollars a week and said she didn't have to stay if she didn't want to. He would kiss her and she would have to close her eyes hard and hold her breath and feel his hand coming up over her breast. Her sister had said so what, he touches you a little. Where else are you going to make seven dollars a week? But I don't want him to, Tacha had said. I don't love him. And her sister had told her she was crazy. You don't have to love a man even to marry him. This man was providing for her and she should look at it that way. He gave her something, she should give him something.

She gave him the blade of a butcher knife late one afternoon when no one was in the café and the cook had gone to the outhouse. She jabbed the knife into him because he was hurting her, forcing her back over the kitchen table, smothering her with his weight and not giving her a chance to speak, to tell him she wanted to quit. Her fingers touched the knife on the table and, in that little moment of panic, as his hand went under her skirt and up between her legs, she pushed the knife into his stomach. She would remember his funny, surprised expression and remember him pushing away from her again with his weight, and looking down at the knife handle, touching it gently with both hands then, standing still, as if afraid to move, and looking down at the knife. She remembered saying, "I didn't mean to—" and thinking, Take it out, you can do whatever you want to me, I didn't mean to do this.

"Some people lead," the tailor said, "some follow."

Tacha looked over at him, hunched over his sewing. "Why can Frank Shelby do whatever he wants?"

"Not everything, he can't."

"Why can he go in there with her?"

"Ask him when he's through."

"Do you know something?" Tacha said. "You never answer a question."

"I've been here—" the tailor began, and stopped as the outside door opened.

Bob Fisher stepped inside. He closed the door quietly behind him, his gaze going to the stock room, then to Tacha and past her to the tailor.

"Where's Norma at?"

Tacha waited. When she knew the tailor wasn't going to answer she said, "Don't you know where she is?"

Fisher's dull expression returned to Tacha. "I ask a question, I don't need a question back."

"She's in there," Tacha said.

"I thought I saw a convict come in here."

"He's in there with her."

"Doing what?"

"Doing *it*," Tacha said. "What do you think?"

Bob Fisher took time to give her a look before he walked over to the stock room. Then he didn't hesitate: he pushed the door and let it bang wide open and stood looking at them on the flat bolts of striped prison material they had spread on the floor, at the two of them lying close and pulling apart, at their upturned faces that were momentarily startled.

"You through?" Fisher said.

Shelby started to grin and shake his head. "I guess you caught us, boss."

Tacha could see Norma's skirt pulled up and her bare thighs. She saw Shelby, behind Fisher, getting to his feet. He was buttoning the top of his pants now. Norma was sitting up, slowly buttoning her blouse, then touching her hair, brushing it away from her face.

Tacha and the tailor began working again as Fisher looked around at them. He motioned Norma to get up. "You go on to your cell till I'm ready for you."

Shelby waited, while Norma gave Fisher a look and a shrug and walked out. He said then, "Were me and her doing something wrong? Against regulations?"

"You come with me," Fisher said.

Once outside, they moved off across the yard, toward the far end of the mess hall. Fisher held his set expression as his gaze moved about the yard. Shelby couldn't figure him out.

"Where we going?"

"I want to tell the new superintendent what you were doing."

"I didn't know of any law against it."

Fisher kept walking.

"What's going on?" Shelby said. Christ, the man was actually taking him in. Before they got to the latrine adobe Shelby said, "Well, I wanted to talk to him anyway." He paused. "About this guard that watches the girls take their bath. Pulls loose a brick and peeks in at them."

Fisher took six strides before saying, "She know who this guard is?"

"You bet," Shelby said.

"Then tell the sup'rintendent."

Son of a bitch. He was bluffing. Shelby glanced at him, but couldn't tell a thing from the man's expression.

Just past the latrine Shelby said, "I imagine this guard has got a real eyeful, oh man, but looking ain't near anything like doing, I'll tell you, 'cause I've done both. That Norma has got a natural-born instinct for pleasing a man. You know what she does?"

Fisher didn't answer.

Shelby waited, but not too long. "She knows secret things I bet there ain't ten women in the world can do. I been to Memphis, I been to Tulsa, to Nogales, I know what I'm talking about. You feel her mouth brushing your face and whispering dirty things in your ear—you know something? Once a man's had some of that woman—I mean somebody outside—he'd allow himself to be locked up in this place the rest of his life if he thought he could get some every other night. Get her right after she comes out of the bath."

Shelby paused to let Fisher think about it. As they were nearing the outside stairs he said, "Man, I tell you, anybody seen her bare-ass naked knows that's got to be a woman built for pleasure."

"Upstairs," Fisher said.

Shelby went up two steps and paused, looking around over his shoulder. "The thing is, though. She don't give it out to nobody but me. Less I say it's all right." Shelby looked right at his eyes. "You understand me, boss?"

Mr. Manly heard them coming down the hall. He swiveled around from the window and moved the two file folders to one side of the desk, covering the Bible. He picked up a pencil. On his note pad were written the names *Harold Jackson* and *Raymond San Carlos*. both underlined, and the notations: *Ten days will be Feb. 23, 1909. Talk to both at same time. Ref. to St. Paul to the Corinthians 11:19–33 and 12:1–9.*

When the knock came he said, "Come in" at once, but didn't look up until he knew they were in the room, close to the desk, and he had written on the note paper: *See Ephesians* 4: 1–6.

Bob Fisher came right out with it. "He wants to tell you something."

In that moment Shelby had no idea what he would say; because Fisher wasn't bluffing and wasn't afraid of him; because Fisher stood up and was a tough son of a bitch and wasn't going to lie and lose face in front of any con. Maybe Fisher would deny the accusation, say prove it. Shelby didn't know what Fisher would do. He needed time to think. The next moment Mr. Manly was smiling up at him.

"I'm sorry I don't know everybody's name yet."

"This is Frank Shelby," Fisher said. "He wants to tell you something."

Shelby watched the little man rise and offer his hand and say, "I'm Everett Manly, your new superintendent." He watched Mr. Manly sit down again and look off somewhere.

"Frank Shelby . . . Shelby . . . forty-five years for armed robbery. Is that right?"

Shelby nodded.

"Forty-five years," Mr. Manly said. "That's a long time. Are you working to get some time off for good behavior?"

"I sure am," Shelby said. He didn't know if the man was serious or not, but he said it.

"How long have you been here at Yuma?"

"Little over a year."

"Have you got a good record here? Keep out of fights and trouble?"

"Yes, *sir*."

"Ever been in the snake den?"

"No, sir."

"Got two boys in there now for fighting, you know."

Shelby smiled a little and shook his head. "It's funny you should mention them," he said. "Those two boys are what I wanted to talk to you about."

Bob Fisher turned to look at him but didn't say a word.

"I was wondering," Shelby went on, "what you'd think of us staging a prize fight between those two boys?"

" A prize fight?" Mr. Manly frowned. "Don't you think they've done enough fighting? Lord, it seems all they like to do is fight."

"They keep fighting," Shelby said, "because they never get it settled. But, I figure, once they have it out there'll be peace between them. You see what I mean?"

Mr. Manly began to nod, slowly. "Maybe."

"We could get them some boxing gloves in town. I don't mean the prison pay for them. We could take us up a collection among the convicts."

"I sure never thought of fighting as a way to achieve peace. Bob, have you?"

Fisher said quietly, "No, I haven't."

Shelby shrugged. "Well, peace always seems to follow a war."

"You got a point there, Frank."

"I know the convicts would enjoy it. I mean it would keep their minds occupied a while. They don't get much entertainment here."

"That's another good point," Mr. Manly said.

Shelby waited as Mr. Manly nodded, looking as if he was falling asleep. "Well, that's all I had to say. I sure hope you give it some thought, if just for the sake of those two boys. So they can get it settled."

"I promise you I will," Mr. Manly said. "Bob, what do you think about it? Off-hand."

"I been in prison work a long time," Fisher said. "I never heard of anything like this."

"I'll tell you what, boys. Let me think on it." Mr. Manly got up out of the chair, extending a hand to Shelby. "It's nice meeting you, Frank. You keep up the good work and you'll be out of here before you know it."

"Sir," Shelby said, "I surely hope so."

■   ■   ■

Bob Fisher didn't say a word until they were down the stairs and Shelby was heading off along the side of the building, in the shade.

"Where you going?"

Shelby turned, a few steps away. "See about some chow."

"You can lose your privileges," Fisher said. "All of them inside one minute."

Go easy, Shelby thought, and said, "It's up to you."

"I can give it all to somebody else. The stuff you sell, the booze, the soft jobs. I pick somebody, the tough boys will side with him and once it's done he's the man inside and you're another con on the rock pile."

"I'm not arguing with you," Shelby said. "I used my head and put together what I got. You allow it because I keep the cons in line and it makes your job easier. You didn't give me a thing when I started."

"Maybe not, but I can sure take it all away from you."

"I know that."

"I will, less you stay clear of Norma Davis."

Shelby started to smile—he couldn't help it—even with Fisher's grim, serious face staring at him.

"Watch yourself," Fisher said. "You say the wrong thing, it's done. I'm telling you to keep away from the women. You don't, you lose everything you got."

That was all Bob Fisher had to say. He turned and went back up the stairs. Shelby watched him, feeling better than he'd felt in days. He sure would keep away from the women. He'd give Norma all the room she needed. The state Bob Fisher was in, Norma would have his pants off him before the week was out.

SIX

"**B**oys, I tell you the Lord loves us all as His children; but you cross Him and He can be mean as a roaring lion. Not mean because he hates you boys, no-sir; mean because he hates sin and evil so much. You don't believe me, read your Psalms, fifty, twenty-two, where it says, 'Now consider this, ye that forget God, lest I tear you in pieces'—you hear that?—'tear you in *pieces* and there be none to deliver. . . .' None to deliver means there ain't nothing left of you."

Mr. Manly couldn't tell a thing from their expressions. Sometimes they were looking at him, sometimes they weren't. Their heads didn't move much. Their eyes did. Raymond's eyes would go to the window and stay there a while. Harold would stare at the wall or the bookcase, and look as if he was asleep with his eyes open.

Mr. Manly flipped back a few pages in his Bible. When he looked up again his glasses gleamed in the overhead light. He had brought the two boys out of the snake den after only three days this time. Bob Fisher hadn't said a word. He'd marched them over, got them fed and cleaned up, and here they were. Here, but somewhere else in their minds. Standing across the desk fifteen, twenty minutes now, and Mr. Manly wondered if either of them had listened to a word he'd said.

"Again in the Psalms, boys, chapter eleven, sixth verse, it says, 'Upon the wicked shall rain snares, fire and brimstone and a horrible tempest'—that's like a storm—'and this shall be the portion of their cup.'

"Raymond, look at me. 'He that keepeth the commandments keepeth his own soul'—Proverbs, chapter nineteen, verse sixteen—'but he that despiseth His way shall die.'

"Harold Jackson of Fort Valley, Georgia, 'There shall be no reward for the evil man.' That's Proverbs again, twenty-four, twenty. 'The candle of the wicked shall be put out.' Harold, you understand that?"

"Yes-suh, captain."

"What does it mean?"

"It mean they put out your candle."

"It means God will put *you* out. You're the candle, Harold. If you're evil you get no reward and the Lord God will snuff out your life. You want that to happen?"

"No-suh, captain."

"Raymond, you want to have your life snuffed out?"

"No, sir, I don't want no part of that."

"It will happen as sure as it is written in the Book. Harold, you believe in the Book?"

"What Book is that, captain?"

"The Holy Bible."

"Yes-suh, I believe it."

"Raymond, you believe it?"

"What is that again?"

"Do you believe in the Holy Bible as being the inspired word of Almighty God as told by Him directly into the ears of the boys that wrote it?"

"I guess so," Raymond said.

"Raymond, you don't guess about your salvation. You believe in Holy Scripture and its truths, or you don't."

"I believe it," Raymond said.

"Have you ever been to church?"

"I think so. When I was little."

"Harold, you ever attend services?"

"You mean was I in the arm service, captain?"

"I mean have you ever been to church."

"Yes, I been there, captain."

"When was the last time?"

"Let's see," Harold said. "I think I went in Cuba one time."

"You *think* you went to church?"

"They talk in this language I don't know what they saying, captain."

"That was ten years ago," Mr. Manly said, "and you don't know if it was a church service or not."

"I think it was."

"Raymond, what about you?"

"Yes, sir, when I was little, all the time."

"What do you remember?"

"About Jesus and all. You know, how they nail him to this cross."

"Do you know the Ten Commandments?"

"I think I know some of them," Raymond said. "Thou shall not steal. Thou shall not commit adultery."

"Thou shalt not kill," Mr. Manly prompted.

"Thou shall not kill. That's one of them."

"The one that sent you here. Both of you. And now you're disobeying that commandment again by fighting. Did you know that? When you fight you break the Lord's commandment against killing?"

"What if you only hit him?" Raymond asked. "Beat him up good, but he don't die."

"It's the same thing. Look, when you hit somebody you hurt him a little bit or your hurt him a lot. When you kill somebody you hurt him for good. So hitting is the same as killing without going all the way. You understand that, Harold?"

"What was that, captain?"

Mr. Manly swiveled around slowly to look out the window, toward the convicts standing by the main cellblock. Close to a hundred men here, and only a handful of them, at the most, understood the Divine Word. Mr. Manly was sixty years old and knew he would never have time to teach them all. He only had a few months here before the place was closed. Then what? He had to do what he could, that's all. He had to begin somewhere, even if his work was never finished.

He came around again to face them and said, "Boys, the Lord has put it on the line to us. He says you got to keep His commandments. He says you don't keep them, you die. That doesn't mean you die and they put in a grave—no-sir. It means you die and go straight down to hell to suffer the fires of the damned. Raymond, you ever burn yourself?"

"Yes, sir, my hand one time."

"Boys, imagine getting burned all over for the rest of your life by the hottest fire you ever saw, hotter'n a blast furnace."

"You'd die," Raymond said.

"Only it doesn't kill you," Mr. Manly said quickly. "See, it's a special kind of fire that hurts terrible but never burns you up."

They looked at him, or seemed to be looking at him; he wasn't sure.

He tried again. "Like just your head is sticking out of the fire. You understand? So it don't suffocate you. But, boy, these flames are licking at your body and it's so hot you're a-screaming your lungs out, 'Water, water, somebody give me just a drop of water—please!' But it's too late, because far as you're concerned the Lord is fresh out of mercy."

Raymond was looking at the window again and Harold was studying the wall.

"Hell—" Mr. Manly began. He was silent for a while before he said, "It's a terrible place to be and I'm glad you boys are determined not to go there."

Harold said, "Where's that, captain?"

After they were gone Mr. Manly could still see them standing there. He got up and walked around them, picturing them from the back now, seeing the Negro's heavy, sloping shoulders, the Indian standing with a slight cock to his hip, hands loose at his sides. He'd like to stick a pin in them to see if they jumped. He'd like to holler in their ears. What's the matter with you? Don't you understand plain English? Are you too ignorant, or are you too full of evil? Answer me!

If they didn't understand the Holy Word, how was he ever going to preach it to them? He raised his eyes to the high ceiling and said, "Lord, if You're going to send me sinners, send me some with schooling, will you, please?"

He hadn't meant to say it out loud. In the silence that followed he hurried around the desk to sit down again.

Maybe that was the answer, though, and saying it out loud was the sign. Save somebody else, somebody who'd understand him, instead of two boys who couldn't even read and write. Sixty years old, he didn't have time to start saving illiterates. Somebody like Frank Shelby. Save him.

No, Frank was already trying. It was pretty clear he'd seen the error of his past life and was trying to correct it.

Norma Davis.

Get Norma in here and ask her if she was ready to accept the Lord Jesus Christ as her saviour. If she hadn't already.

No, something told Mr. Manly she hadn't yet. She was in for

robbery, had shot a man, and had been arrested for prostitution in Wichita, Kansas. It wasn't likely she'd had time to be saved. She looked smart though.

Sit her down there, Mr. Manly thought.

He wasn't sure how he'd begin, but he'd get around to picking some whores out of the Bible to tell her about—like that woman at the well. Jesus knew she was a whore, but He was still friendly and talked to her. See, He wasn't uppity about whores, they were just sinners to him like any other sinners. Take the time they're stoning the whore and He stops them, saying, Wait, only whoever of ye is without sin may cast a stone. And they had to quit doing it. See, Norma, we are all of us sinners in one way or another.

He kept looking at the way her top buttons were undone and the blouse was pulled open so he could see part of the valley between her breasts.

Where the soap had run down and over her belly.

She was sitting there trying to tempt him. Sure, she'd try to tempt him, try to show him up as a hypocrite.

She would undo a couple more buttons and he'd watch her calmly. He would say quietly, shaking his head slowly, "Norma, Norma."

She'd pull that blouse wide open and her eyes and her breasts would be staring right smack at him.

Sit back in the swivel chair then; show her he was at ease. Keep the expression very calm. And kindly.

She'd get up and lean over the desk then so they'd hang down. Great big round things with big reddish-brown tips. Then she'd jiggle them a little and he'd say in his quiet voice, "Norma, what are you doing that for? Don't you feel silly?"

Maybe he wouldn't ask her if she felt silly, but he'd say something.

She'd see she wasn't getting him, so then she'd take off her belt and slowly undo her skirt, watching him all the time, and let it fall. She'd back off a little bit and put her hands on her hips so he could see her good.

"Norma, child, cover your nakedness."

No, sir, that wasn't going to stop her. She was coming around the desk now. She'd stepped out of the skirt and was taking off the blouse, all the way off, coming toward him now without a stitch on.

He had better stand up, or it would be hard to talk to her.

Mr. Manly rose from the chair. He reached out to place his

hands on Norma's bare shoulders and, smiling gently, said, "Child, 'If ye live after the flesh ye shall die'—Romans, eight, thirteen— 'but if ye mortify the deeds of the body, ye shall live.' "

From the doorway Bob Fisher said, "Excuse me."

Mr. Manly came around, seeing the open door that had been left open when the two went out; he dropped his hands awkwardly to the edge of the desk.

Bob Fisher kept staring at him.

"I was just seeing if I could remember a particular verse from Romans," Mr. Manly said.

"How'd you do with Harold and Raymond?"

"It's too early to tell. I want to see them again in the morning."

"They got work to do."

"In the morning," Mr. Manly said.

Bob Fisher thought it over, then nodded and left the office. Walking down the hall, he was thinking that the little preacher may have been trying to remember a verse, but he sure looked like a man about to get laid.

Lord, give me these two, Mr. Manly said to the window and to the yard below. Give me a sign that they understand and are will- ing to receive the Lord Jesus Christ into their hearts.

He didn't mean a tongue of fire had to appear over the two boys' heads, or they had to get knocked to the ground the way St. Paul did. All they had to do was show some interest, a willingness to ac- cept their salvation.

Lord, I need these two to prove my worthiness and devotion as a preacher of your Holy Writ. I need them to show for thirty years service in your ministry. Lord, I need them for my record, and I ex- pect You know it.

Sit them down this time. Maybe that would help. Mr. Manly turned from the window and told them to take chairs. "Over there," he said. "Bring them up close to the desk."

They hesitated, looking around. It seemed to take them for- ever to carry the chairs over, their leg chains clinking on the wooden floor. He waited until they were settled, both of them look- ing past him, seeing what there was to see at this lower angle than yesterday.

"I'm going to tell you something. I know you both had humble beginnings. You were poor, you've been hungry, you've experi- enced all kinds of hardships and you've spent time in jail. Well,

I never been to jail before I got sent here by the Bureau"—Mr. Manly paused as he grinned; neither of them noticing it—"I'll tell you though, I'll bet you I didn't begin any better off than you boys did. I was born in Clayburn County, Tennessee—either of you been there?"

Raymond shook his head. Harold said nothing.

"Well, it's in the mountains. I didn't visit Knoxville till I was fifteen years old, and it wasn't forty miles from home. I could've stayed there and farmed, or I could have run off and got into trouble. But you know what I did? I joined the Holy Word Pentacostal Youth Crusade and pledged myself to the service of the Lord Jesus. I preached over twenty years in Tennessee and Kentucky before coming out here to devote the rest of my life to mission work— the rest of it, five years, ten years. You know when your time is up and the Lord's going to call you?"

Harold Jackson's eyes were closed.

"Harold"—the eyes came open—"you don't know when you're going to die, do you?"

"No-suh, captain."

"Are you ready to die?"

"No-suh, captain. I don't think I ever be ready."

"St. Paul was ready."

"Yes-suh."

"Not at first he wasn't. Not until the Lord knocked him smack off his horse with a bolt of lightning and said, 'Saul, Saul, why do you persecuteth me?' Paul was a Jew-boy at that time and he was persecuting the Christians. Did you know that, Raymond?"

"No, I never knew that."

"Yes, sir, before he became Paul he was a Jew-boy name of Saul, used to put Christians to death, kill them in terrible ways. But once he become a Christian himself he made up for all the bad things he'd done by his own suffering. Raymond, you ever been stoned?"

"Like with rocks?"

"Hit with big rocks."

"I don't think so."

"Harold, you ever been shipwrecked?"

"I don't recall, captain."

Mr. Manly opened his Bible. "You boys think you've experienced hardships, listen, I'm going to read you something. From two Corinthians. 'Brethren, gladly you put up with fools, because you are wise . . .' Let me skip down. 'But whereas any man is bold . . . Are they ministers of Christ?' Here it is. '. . . in many more labors, in lashes above measure, often exposed to death. From the Jews'— listen to this—'five times I received forty lashes less one. Thrice I was scourged, once I was stoned, thrice I suffered shipwreck, a night and a day I was adrift on the sea; on journeyings often, in perils from floods, in perils from robbers, in perils from my own nation . . . in labor and hardships, in many sleepless nights, in hunger and thirst, in fastings often, in cold and nakedness.' "

Mr. Manly looked up. "Here's the thing, boys. St. Paul asked God three times to let him up from all these hardships. And you know what God said to him?" Mr. Manly's gaze dropped to the book. "He said, 'My grace is sufficient for thee, for strength is made perfect in weakness.' "

Now Mr. Manly sat back, just barely smiling, looking expectantly from Raymond to Harold, waiting for one of them to speak. Either one, he didn't care.

He didn't even care what they said, as long as one of them spoke.

Raymond was looking down at his hands, fooling with one of his fingernails. Harold was looking down too, his head bent low, and his eyes could have been open or closed.

"Strength—did you hear that, boys?—is made perfect in weakness."

He waited.

He could ask them what it meant.

He began thinking about the words. If you're weak the Lord helps you. Or strength stands out more in a weak person. Like it's more perfect, more complete, when a weak person gets strong.

No, that wasn't what it meant.

It meant no matter how weak you were you could get strong if you wanted.

Maybe. Or else it was the part just before which was the important part. God saying My grace is sufficient for thee. That's right, no matter what the temptaion was.

Norma Davis could come in here and show herself and do all kinds of terrible things—God's grace would be sufficient. That was good to know.

It wasn't helping those two boys any, though. He had to watch that, thinking of himself more than them. They were the ones had to be saved. They had wandered from the truth and it was up to him to bring them back. For . . . 'whoever brings back a sinner from the error of his ways will save his own soul from death'—James, five-something—'and it will cover a multitude of sins.' "

That was the whole thing. If he could save these two boys he'd have nothing to worry about the rest of his life. He could maybe even slip once in a while—give in to temptation—without fear of his soul getting sent to hell. He wouldn't give in on purpose. You couldn't do that. But if somebody dragged you in and you went in scrapping, that was different.

"Boys," Mr. Manly said, "whoever brings back a sinner saves his own soul from death and it will cover a multitude of sins. Now do you want your souls to be saved, or don't you?"

Mr. Manly spent two days reading and studying before he called Raymond and Harold into the office again.

While they were standing by the desk he asked them how they were getting along. Neither of them wanted to answer that. He asked if there had been any trouble between them since the last time they were here. They both said no, sir. He asked if there had been any mean words between them. They said no, sir. Then it looked like they were getting somewhere, Mr. Manly said, and told them to bring the chairs over and sit down.

" 'We know,' " he said to Raymond, " 'that we have passed from death unto life because we love the brethren. He that loveth not his brethren abideth in death.' " Mr. Manly looked at Harold Jackson. " 'Whoever hateth his brother is a murderer, and ye know that no murderer hath eternal life abiding in him.' James, chapter three, the fourteenth and fifteenth verses."

They were looking at him. That was good. They weren't squinting or frowning, as if they were trying to figure out the words, or nodding agreement; but by golly they were looking at him and not out the window.

"Brethren means brother," he said. "You know that. It doesn't mean just your real brother, if you happen to have any brothers. It means everybody's your brethren. You two are brethren and I'm your brethren, everybody here at Yuma and everybody in the whole world, we are all brethren of Jesus Christ and sons of Almighty God. Even women. What I'm talking about, even women are your brethren, but we don't have to get into that. I'm saying we are all related by blood and I'll tell you why. You listening?"

Raymond's gaze came away from the window, his eyes opening wide with interest.

Harold said, "Yes-suh, captain."

"We are all related," Mr. Manly said, watching them, "because we all come from the first two people in the world, old Adam and Eve, who started the human race. They had children and their children had children and the children's children had some more, and it kept going that way until the whole world become populated."

Harold Jackson said, "Who did the children marry?"

"They married each other."

"I mean children in the same family."

Mr. Manly nodded. "Each other. They married among theirselves."

"You mean a boy did it with his sister?"

"Oh," Mr. Manly said. "Yes, but it was different then. God said it was all right because it was the only way to get the earth populated. See, in just a few generations you got so many people they're marrying cousins now, and second cousins, and a couple hundred years it's not even like they're kin any more."

Mr. Manly decided not to tell them about Adam living to be nine hundred and thirty and Seth and Enoch and Kenan and Methuselah, all of them getting up past nine hundred years old before they died. He had to leave out details or it might confuse them. It was enough to tell them how the population multiplied and the people gradually spread all over the world.

"If we all come from the same people," Raymond said, "where do niggers come from?"

So Mr. Manly had to tell them about Noah and his three sons, Shem, Ham, and Japheth, and how Ham made some dirty remark on seeing his daddy sleeping naked after drinking too much wine. For that Noah banished Ham and made his son a "slave of slaves." Ham and his family had most likely gone on down to Africa and that was where niggers came from, descendents of Ham.

Harold Jackson said, "Where does it say Indins come from?"

Mr. Manly shook his head. "It don't say and it don't matter. People moved all over the world, and those living in a certain place got to look alike on account of the climate. So now you got your white race, your yellow race, and your black race."

"What's an Indin?" Harold said. "What race?"

"They're not sure," Mr. Manly answered. "Probably somewhere

in between. Like yellow with a little nigger thrown in. You can call it the Indian race if you want. The colored race is the only one mentioned in the Bible, on account of the story of Noah and Ham."

Harold said, "How do they know everybody was white before that?"

Mr. Manly frowned. What kind of a question was that? "They just know it. I guess because Adam and Eve was white." He said then, "There's nothing wrong with being a nigger. God made you a nigger for a reason. I mean some people have to be niggers and some have to be Indians. Some have to be white. But we are all still brethren."

Harold's eyes remained on Mr. Manly. "It say in the Bible this man went to Africa?"

"It wasn't called Africa then, but they're pretty sure that's where he went. His people multiplied and before you know it they're living all over Africa and that's how you got your different tribes. Your Zulus. Your Pygmies. You got your—oh, all different ones with those African names."

"Zulus," Harold Jackson said. "I heard something about Zulus one time."

Mr. Manly leaned forward on the edge of the desk. "What did you hear about them?"

"I don't know. I remember somebody talking about Zulus. Somebody saying the word."

"Harold, you know something? For all you know you might be a Zulu yourself."

Harold gave him a funny look. "I was born in Fort Valley, Georgia."

"Where was your mama and daddy born?"

"Fort Valley."

"Where was your granddaddy born?"

"I don't know."

"Or your great granddaddy. You know, he might have been born in Africa and brought over here as a slave. Maybe not him, but somebody before him, a kin of yours, was brought over. All your kin before him lived in Africa, and if they lived in a certain part of Africa then, by golly, they were Zulus."

Mr. Manly had a book about Africa in his collection. He remembered a drawing of a Zulu warrior, a tall Negro standing with a spear and a slender black and white cowhide shield.

He said, "Harold, your people are fine hunters and warriors. Oh, they're heathen, they paint theirselves up red and yellow and wear beads made out of lion's claws; but, Harold, they got to kill the lion first, with spears, and you don't go out and kill a lion unless you got plenty of nerve."

"With a spear, huh?" Harold said.

"Long spear they use, and this shield made out of cowhide. Some of them grow little beards and cut holes in the lobes of their ears and stick in these big hunks of dried sugar cane, if I remember correctly."

"They have sugar cane?"

"That's what it said in the book."

"They had a lot of sugar cane in Cuba. I never see anybody put it in their ear."

"Like earrings," Mr. Manly said. "I imagine they use all kinds of things. Gold, silver, if they got it."

"What do they wear?"

"Oh, just a little skimpy outfit. Some kind of cloth or animal skin around their middle. Nothing up here. Wait a second," Mr. Manly said. He went over to his bookcase. He found the book right away, but had to skim through it twice before he found the picture and laid the book open in front of Harold. "There. That's your Zulu warrior."

Harold hunched over the book. As he studied the picture Mr. Manly said, "Something else I remember. It says in there these Zulus can run. I mean *run*. The boys training to be warriors, they'd run twenty miles, take a little rest and run some more. Run thirty-forty miles a day isn't anything for a Zulu. Then go out and kill a lion. Or a elephant."

Mr. Manly noticed Raymond San Carlos glancing over at the book and he said quickly, "Same with your Indians; especially your desert tribes, like the Apaches. They can run all day long, I understand, and not take a drink of water till sundown. They know where to find water, too, way out in the middle of the desert. Man told me once, when Apaches are going where they know there isn't any water they take a horse's intestine and fill it full of water and wrap it around their bodies. He said he'd match an Apache Indian against a camel for traveling across the desert without any water."

"There's plenty of water," Raymond said, "if you know where to look."

"That's what I understand."

"Some of the older men at San Carlos, they'd take us boys and make us go up in the mountains and stay there two, three days without food or water."

"You did that?"

"Plenty of times."

"You'd find water?"

"Sure, and something to eat. Not much, but enough to hold us."

"Say, I just read in the paper," Mr. Manly said. "You know who died the other day? Geronimo."

"Is that right?"

"Fort Sill, Oklahoma. Died of pneumonia."

"That's too bad," Raymond said. "I mean I think he would rather have got killed fighting."

"You ever seen him? No, you would have been too young."

"Sure, I seen him. Listen, I'll tell you something I never told anybody. My father was in his band. Geronimo's."

"Is that a fact?"

"He was killed in Mexico when the soldiers went down there."

"My goodness," Mr. Manly said, "we're talking about warriors, you're the son of an Apache warrior."

"I never told anybody that."

"Why not? I'd think you'd be proud to tell it."

"It doesn't do me any good."

"But if it's true—"

"You think I'm lying?"

"I mean since it's a fact, why not tell it?"

"It don't make any difference to me. I could be Apache, I could be Mexican, I'm in Yuma the rest of my life."

"But you're living that life," Mr. Manly said. "If a person's an Indian then he should look at himself as an Indian. Like I told Harold, God made him a nigger for a reason. All right, God made you an Indian. There's nothing wrong with being an Indian. Why, do you know that about half our states have Indian names? Mississippi. The state I come from, Tennessee. Arizona. The Colorado River out yonder. Yuma."

"I don't know," Harold said, "that spear looks like it could break easy."

Mr. Manly looked over at him and at the book. "They know how to make 'em."

"They fight other people?"

"Sure they did. Beat 'em, too. What I understand, your Zulus owned most of the southern part of Africa, took it from other tribes and ruled over them."

"Never got beat, uh?"

"Not that I ever heard of. No, sir, they're the greatest warriors in Africa."

"Nobody ever beat the Apache," Raymond said, "till the U. S. Army come with all their goddamn guns."

"Raymond, don't ever take the Lord's name in vain like that."

"Apaches beat the Pimas, the Papagoes, Maricopas—took anything we wanted from them."

"Well, I don't hold with raiding and killing," Mr. Manly said, "but I'll tell you there is something noble about your uneducated savage that you don't see in a lot of white men. I mean just the way your warrior stands, up straight with his shoulders back and never says too much, doesn't talk just to hear himself, like a lot of white people I know. I'll tell you something else, boys. Savage warriors have never been known to lie or go back on their word, and that's a fact. Man up at the reservation told me that Indians don't even have a word in their language for lie. Same thing with your Zulus. I reckon if a boy can run all day long and kill lions with a spear, he don't ever *have* to lie."

"I never heard of Apaches with spears," Raymond said.

"Oh, yes, they had them. And bows and arrows."

Harold was waiting. "I expect the Zulus got guns now, don't they?"

"I don't know about that," Mr. Manly answered. "Maybe they don't need guns. Figure spears are good enough." A smile touched his mouth as he looked across the desk at Raymond and Harold. "The thing that tickles me," he said, "I'm liable to have a couple of real honest-to-goodness Apache and Zulu warriors sitting right here in my office and I didn't even know it."

That evening, when Bob Fisher got back after supper, the guard at the sally port told him Mr. Manly wanted to see him right away. Fisher asked him what for, and the guard said how was he supposed to know. Fisher told the man to watch his mouth, and headed across the compound to see what the little squirt wanted.

Fisher paused by the stairs and looked over toward the cook shack. The women would be starting their bath about now.

Mr. Manly was writing something, but put it aside as Fisher came in. He said, "Pull up a chair," and seemed anxious to talk.

"There's a couple of things I got to do yet tonight."

"I wanted to talk to you about our Apache and our Zulu."

"How's that?"

"Raymond and Harold. I've been thinking about Frank Shelby's idea—he seems like a pretty sensible young man, doesn't he?"

Jesus Christ, Bob Fisher thought. He said, "I guess he's smart enough."

Mr. Manly smiled. "Though not smart enough to stay out of jail. Well, I've been thinking about this boxing-match idea. I want you to know I've given it a lot of thought."

Fisher waited.

"I want Frank Shelby to understand it too—you might mention it to him if you see him before I do."

"I'll tell him," Fisher said. He started to go.

"Hey, I haven't told you what I decided."

Fisher turned to the desk again.

"I've been thinking—a boxing match wouldn't be too good. We want them to stop fighting and we tell them to go ahead and fight. That doesn't sound right, does it?"

"I'll tell him that."

"You're sure in a hurry this evening, Bob."

"It's time I made the rounds is all."

"Well, I could walk around with you if you want and we could talk."

"That's all right," Fisher said, "go ahead."

"Well, as I said, we won't have the boxing match. You know what we're going to have instead?"

"What?"

"We're going to have a race. I mean Harold and Raymond are going to have a race."

"A race," Fisher said.

"A foot race. The faster man wins and gets some kind of a prize, but I haven't figured that part of it out yet."

"They're going to run a race," Fisher said.

"Out in the exercise yard. Down to the far end and back, maybe a couple of times."

"When do you want this race held?"

"Tomorrow I guess, during free time."

"You figure it'll stop them fighting, uh?"

"We don't have anything to lose," Mr. Manly said. "A good race might just do the trick."

Get out of here, Bob Fisher thought. He said, "Well, I'll tell them."

"I've already done that."

"I'll tell Frank Shelby then." Fisher edged toward the door and got his hand on the knob.

"You know what it is?" Mr. Manly was leaning back in his chair with a peaceful, thoughtful expression. "It's sort of a race of races," he said. "You know what I mean? The Negro against the Indian, black man against red man. I don't mean to prove that one's better than the other. I mean as a way to stir up their pride and get them interested in doing something with theirselves. You know what I mean?"

Bob Fisher stared at him.

"See, the way I figure them—" Mr. Manly motioned to the chair again. "Sit down, Bob, I'll tell you how I see these two boys, and why I believe we can help them."

By the time Fisher got down to the yard, the women had taken their bath. They were back in their cellblock and he had to find R. E. Baylis for the keys.

"I already locked everybody in," the guard said.

"I know you did. That's why I need the keys."

"Is there something wrong somewhere?"

Bob Fisher had never wanted to look at that woman as bad as he did this evening. God, he felt like he *had* to look at her, but everybody was getting in his way, wasting time. His wife at supper nagging at him again about moving to Florence. The little squirt preacher who believed he could save a couple of bad convicts. Now a slow-witted guard asking him questions.

"Just give me the keys," Fisher said.

He didn't go over there directly. He walked past the TB cellblock first and looked in at the empty yard, at the lantern light showing in most of the cells and the dark ovals of the cells that were not occupied. The nigger and the Indian were in separate cells. They were doing a fair job on the wall; but, Jesus, they'd get it done a lot sooner if the little squirt would let them work instead of wasting time preaching to them. Now foot races. God Almighty.

Once you were through the gate of the women's cellblock, the area was more like a room than a yard—a little closed-in courtyard and two cells carved into the granite wall.

There was lantern light in both cells. Fisher looked in at Tacha first and asked her what she was doing. Tacha was sitting on a stool in the smoky dimness of the cell. She said, "I'm reading," and looked down at the book again. Bob Fisher told himself to take it easy now and not to be impatient. He looked in Tacha's cell almost a minute longer before moving on to Norma's.

She was stretched out in her bunk, staring right at him when he looked through the iron strips of the door. A blanket covered her, but one bare arm and shoulder were out of the blanket and, Jesus, it didn't look like she had any clothes on. His gaze moved around the cell to show he wasn't too interested in her.

"Everything all right?"

"That's a funny thing to ask," Norma said. "Like this is a hotel."

"I haven't looked in here in a while."

"I know you haven't."

"You need another blanket or anything?"

"What's anything?"

"I mean like kerosene for the lantern."

"I think there's enough. The light's awful low though."

"Turn it up."

"I can't. I think the wick's stuck. Or else it's burned down."

"You want me to take a look at it?"

"Would you? I'd appreciate it."

Bob Fisher brought the ring of keys out of his coat pocket with the key to Norma's cell in his hand. As he opened the door and came in, Norma raised up on one elbow, holding the blanket in front of her. He didn't look at her; he went right to the lamp and peered in through the smoky glass. As he turned the wick up slowly, the light grew brighter, then dimmed again as he turned it down.

"It seems all right now." Fisher glanced at her, twisted bare back. He tried the lantern a few more times, twisting the wick up and down and knowing her bare back—and that meant her bare front too—wasn't four feet away from him. "It must've been stuck," he said.

"I guess it was. Will you turn it down now? Just so there's a nice glow."

"How's that?"

"That's perfect."

"I think you got enough wick in there."

"I think so. Do you want to get in bed with me?"

"Jesus Christ," Bob Fisher said.

"Well, do you?"

"You're a nervy thing, aren't you?"

Norma twisted around a little more and let the blanket fall. "I can't help it."

"You can't help what?"

"If I want you to do it to me."

"Jesus," Bob Fisher said. He looked at the cell door and then at Norma again, cleared his throat and said in a lower tone, "I never heard a girl asking for it before."

"Well," Norma said, throwing the blanket aside as she got up from the bunk and moved toward him, "you're hearing it now, daddy."

"Listen, Tacha's right next door."

"She can't see us."

"She can hear."

"Then we'll whisper." Norma began unbuttoning his coat.

"We can't do nothing here."

"Why not?"

"One of the guards might come by."

"Now you're teasing me. Nobody's allowed in here at night, and you know it."

"Boy, you got big ones."

"There, now slip your coat off."

"I can't stay here more'n a few minutes."

"Then quit talking," Norma said.

SEVEN

Frank Shelby said, "A race, what do you mean, a race?"

"I mean a foot race," Fisher told him. "The nigger and the Indin are going to run a race from one end of the yard to the other and back again, and you and every convict in this place are going to be out here to watch it."

"A race," Shelby said again. "Nobody cares about any foot race."

"You don't have to care," Fisher said. "I'm not asking you to care. I'm telling you to close your store and get everybody's ass out of the cellblock. They can stand here or over along the south wall. Ten minutes, I want everybody out."

"This is supposed to be our free time."

"I'll tell you when you get free time."

"What if we want to make some bets?"

"I don't care, long as you keep it quiet. I don't want any arguments, or have to hit anybody over the head."

"Ten minutes, it doesn't give us much time to figure out how to bet."

"You don't know who's going to win," Fisher said. "What's the difference?"

About half the convicts were already in the yard. Fisher waited for the rest of them to file out: the card players and the convicts who could afford Frank Shelby's whiskey and the ones who were always in their bunks between working and eating. They came out of the cellblock and stood around waiting for something to happen. The guards up on the wall came out of the towers and looked around too, as if they didn't know what was going on. Bob Fisher hadn't told any of them about the race. It wouldn't take more than a couple of minutes. He told the convicts to keep the middle area of the yard clear. They started asking him what was going on, but he walked away from them toward the mess hall. It was good that he did. When Mr. Manly appeared on the stairway at the end of the building Fisher was able to get to him before he reached the yard.

"You better stay up on the stairs."

Mr. Manly looked surprised. "I was going over there with the convicts."

"It's happened a sup'rintendent's been grabbed and a knife put at his throat till the gate was opened."

"You go among the convicts; all the guards do."

"But if any of us are grabbed the gate stays closed. They know that. They don't know about you."

"I just wanted to mingle a little," Mr. Manly said. He looked out toward the yard. "Are they ready?"

"Soon as they get their leg-irons off."

A few minutes later, Raymond and Harold were brought down the length of the yard. The convicts watched them, and a few called out to them. Mr. Manly didn't hear what they said, but he noticed neither Raymond nor Harold looked over that way. When they reached the stairs he said. "Well, boys, are you ready?"

"You want us to run," Raymond said. "You wasn't kidding, uh?"

"Course I wasn't."

"I don't know. We just got the irons off. My legs feel funny."

"You want to warm up first?"

Harold Jackson said, "I'm ready any time he is."

Raymond shrugged. "Let's run the race."

Mr. Manly made sure they understood—down to the end of the yard, touch the wall between the snake den and the women's cellblock, and come back past the stairs, a distance Mr. Manly figured to be about a hundred and twenty yards or so. He and Mr. Fisher would be at the top of the stairs in the judge's stand. Mr. Fisher would fire off a revolver as the starting signal. "So," Mr. Manly said, "if you boys are ready—"

There was some noise from the convicts as Raymond and Harold took off as the shot was fired and passed the main cellblock in a dead heat. Raymond hit the far wall and came off in one motion. Harold stumbled and dug hard on the way back but was five or six yards behind Raymond going across the finish.

They stood with their hands on their hips breathing in and out while Mr. Manly leaned over the rail of the stair landing, smiling down at them. He said, "Hey, boys, you sure gave it the old try. Rest a few minutes and we'll run it again."

Raymond looked over at Harold. They got down again and went off with the sound of the revolver, Raymond letting Harold set the pace this time, staying with him and not kicking out ahead until they were almost to the finish line. This time he took it by two strides, with the convicts yelling at them to *run*.

Raymond could feel his chest burning now. He walked around breathing with his mouth open, looking up at the sky that was fading to gray with the sun below the west wall, walking around in little circles and seeing Mr. Manly up there now. As Raymond turned away he heard Harold say, "Let's do it again," and he had to go along.

Harold dug all the way this time; he felt his thighs knotting and pushed it some more, down and back and, with the convicts yelling, came in a good seven strides ahead of the Indian. Right away Harold said, "Let's do it again."

In the fourth race he was again six or seven strides faster than Raymond.

In the fifth race, neither of them looked as if he was going to make it back to the finish. They ran pumping their arms and gasping for air, and Harold might have been ahead by a half-stride past the stairs; but Raymond stumbled and fell forward trying to catch himself, and it was hard to tell who won. There wasn't a sound from the convicts this time. Some of them weren't even looking this way. They were milling around, smoking cigarettes, talking among themselves.

Mr. Manly wasn't watching the convicts. He was leaning over the railing looking down at his two boys: at Raymond lying stretched out on his back and at Harold sitting, leaning back on his hands with his face raised to the sky.

"Hey, boys," Mr. Manly called, "you know what I want you to do now? First I want you to get up. Come on, boys, get up on your feet. Raymond, you hear me?"

"He looks like he's out," Fisher said.

"No, he's all right. See?"

Mr. Manly leaned closer over the rail. "Now I want you two to walk up to each other. Go on, do as I say. It won't hurt you. Now I want you both to reach out and shake hands. . . .

"Don't look up here. Look at each other and shake hands."

Mr. Manly started to grin and, by golly, he really felt good. "Bob, look at that."

"I see it," Fisher said.

Mr. Manly called out now, "Boys, by the time you get done running together you're going to be good friends. You wait and see."

The next day, while they were working on the face wall in the TB cellblock, Raymond was squatting down mixing mortar in a bucket and groaned as he got to his feet. "Goddamn legs," he said.

"I know what you mean," Harold said. He was laying a brick, tapping it into place with the handle of his trowel, and hesitated as he heard his own voice and realized he had spoken to Raymond. He didn't look over at him; he picked up another brick and laid it in place. It was quiet in the yard. The tubercular convicts were in their cells, out of the heat and the sun. Harold could hear a switch-engine working, way down the hill in the Southern Pacific yard; he could hear the freight cars banging together as they were coupled.

After a minute or so Raymond said, "I can't hardly walk today."

"From running," Harold said.

"They don't put the leg-irons back on, uh?"

"I wondered if they forgot to."

"I think so. They wouldn't leave them off unless they forgot."

There was silence again until Harold said, "They can leave them off, it's all right with me."

"Sure," Raymond said, "I don't care they leave them off."

"Place in Florida, this prison farm, you got to wear them all the time."

"Yeah? I hope I never get sent there."

"You ever been to Cuba?"

"No, I never have."

"That's a fine place. I believe I like to go back there sometime."

"Live there?"

"Maybe. I don't know."

"Look like we need some more bricks," Raymond said.

The convicts mixing the adobe mud straightened up with their shovels in front of them as Raymond and Harold came across the yard pushing their wheelbarrows. Joe Dean stepped around to the other side of the mud so he could keep an eye on the south-wall tower guard. He waited until the two boys were close, heading for the brick pile.

"Well, now," Joe Dean said, "I believe it's the two sweethearts."

"If they come back for some more," another convict said, "I'm going to cut somebody this time."

Joe Dean watched them begin loading the wheelbarrows. "See, what they do," he said. "they start a ruckus so they'll get sent to the snake den. Sure, they get in there, just the two of them. Man, they hug and kiss, do all kinds of things to each other."

"That is Mr. Joe Dean talking," Harold said. "I believe he wants to get hit in the mouth with a 'dobe brick."

"I want to see you try that," Joe Dean said.

"Sometime when the guard ain't looking," Harold said. "Maybe when you ain't looking either."

They finished loading their wheelbarrows and left.

In the mess hall at supper they sat across one end of a table. No one else sat with them. Raymond looked around at the convicts hunched over eating. No one seemed aware of them. They were all talking or concentrating on their food. He said to Harold, "God-damn beans, they always got to burn them."

"I've had worse beans," Harold said. "Worse everything. What I like is some chicken, that's what I miss. Chicken's good."

"I like a beefsteak. With peppers and catsup."

"Beefsteak's good too. You like fried fish?"

"I never had it."

"You never had fish?"

"I don't think so."

"Man, where you been you never had fish?"

"I don't know, I never had it."

"We got a big river right outside."

"I never seen anybody fishing."

"How long it take you to swim across?"

"Maybe five minutes."

"That's a long time to swim."

"Too long. They get a boat out quick."

"Anybody try to dig out of here?"

"I never heard of it," Raymond said. "The ones that go they al-ways run from a work detail, outside."

"Anybody make it?"

"Not since I been here."

"Man start running he got to know where he's going. He got to have a place to go to." Harold looked up from his plate. "How long you here for?"

"Life."

"That's a long time, ain't it?"

They were back at work on the cell wall the next day when a guard came and got them. It was about mid-afternoon. Neither of them asked where they were going; they figured they were going to hear another sermon from the man. They marched in front of the guard down the length of the yard and past the brick detail. When they got near the mess hall they veered a little toward the stairway and the guard said, "Keep going, straight ahead."

Raymond and Harold couldn't believe it. The guard marched them through the gates of the sally port and right up to Mr. Rynning's twenty-horsepower Ford Touring Car.

"Let me try to explain it to you again," Mr. Manly said to Bob Fisher. "I believe these boys have got to develop some pride in theirselves. I don't mean they're supposed to get uppity with us. I mean they got to look at theirselves as man in the sight of men, and children in the eyes of God."

"Well, I don't know anything about that part," Bob Fisher said. "To me they are a couple of bad cons, and if you want my advice based on years of dealing with these people, we put their leg-irons back on."

"They can't run in leg-irons."

"I know they can't. They need to work and they need to get knocked down a few times. A convict stands up to you, you better knock him down quick."

"Have they stood up to you, Bob?"

"One of them served time in Leavenworth, the other one tried to swim the river and they're both trying to kill one another. I call that standing up to me."

"You say they're hard cases, Bob, and I say they're like little children, because they're just now beginning to learn about living with their fellowman, which to them means living with white men and getting along with white men."

"Long as they're here," Fisher said, "they damn well better. We only got one set of rules."

Mr. Manly shook his head. "I don't mean to change the rules for them." It was harder to explain than he thought it would be. He couldn't look right at Fisher; the man's solemn expression, across the desk, distracted him. He would glance at Fisher and then look down at the sheet of paper that was partly covered with oval shapes that were like shields, and long thin lines that curved awkwardly into spear heads. "I don't mean to treat them as privileged characters either. But we're not going to turn them into white men, are we?"

"We sure aren't."

"We're not going to tell them they're just as good as white men, are we?"

"I don't see how we could do that," Fisher said.

"So we tell them what an Indian is good at and what a nigger is good at."

"Niggers lie and Indians steal."

"Bob, we tell them what they're good at as members of their race. We already got it started. We tell them Indians and niggers are the best runners in the world."

"I guess if they're scared enough."

"We train them hard and, by golly, they begin to believe it."

"Yeah?"

"Once they begin to believe in something, they begin to believe in themselves."

"Yeah?"

"That's all there is to it."

"Well, maybe you ought to get some white boys to run against them."

"Bob, I'm not interested in them running *races*. This has got to do with distance and endurance. Being able to do something no one else in this prison can do. That race out in the yard was all wrong, more I think about it."

"Frank Shelby said he figured the men wouldn't mind seeing different kinds of races instead of just back and forth. He said run them all over and have them jump things—like climb up the wall on ropes, see who can get to the top first. He said he thought the men would get a kick out of that."

"Bob, this is a show. It doesn't prove nothing. I'm talking about these boys running *miles*."

"Miles, uh?"

"Like their granddaddies used to do."

"How's that?"

"Like Harold Jackson's people back in Africa. Bob, they kill lions with *spears*."

"Harold killed a man with a lead pipe."

"There," Mr. Manly said. "That's the difference. That's what he's become because he's forgot what it's like to be a Zulu nigger warrior."

Jesus Christ, Bob Fisher said to himself. The little squirt shouldn't be sitting behind the desk, he should be over in the goddamn crazy hole. He said, "You want them to run miles, uh?"

"Start them out a few miles a day. Work up to ten miles, twenty miles. We'll see how they do."

"Well, it will be something to see, all right, them running back and forth across the yard. I imagine the convicts will make a few remarks to them. The two boys get riled up and lose their temper, they're back in the snake den and I don't see you've made any progress at all."

"I've already thought of that," Mr. Manly said. "They're not going to run in the yard. They're going to run outside."

The convicts putting up the adobe wall out at the cemetery were the first ones to see them. A man raised up to stretch the kinks out of his back and said, "Look-it up there!"

They heard the Ford Touring Car as they looked around and saw it up on the slope, moving along the north wall with the two boys running behind it. Nobody could figure it out. Somebody asked what were they chasing the car for. Another convict said they weren't chasing the car, they were being taken somewhere. See, there was a guard in the back seat with a rifle. They could see him good against the pale wall of the prison. Nobody had ever seen convicts taken somewhere like that. Any time the car went out it went down to Yuma, but no convicts were ever in the car or behind it or anywhere near it. One of the convicts asked the work-detail guard where he supposed they were going. The guard said it beat him. That motor car belonged to Mr. Rynning and was only used for official business.

It was the stone-quarry gang that saw them next. They looked squinting up through the white dust and saw the Ford Touring Car and the two boys running to keep up with it, about twenty feet behind the car and just barely visible in all the dust the car was raising. The stone-quarry gang watched until the car was past the open rim and the only thing left to see was the dust hanging in the sunlight. Somebody said they certainly had it ass-backwards; the car was supposed to be chasing the cons. They tried to figure it out, but nobody had an answer that made much sense.

Two guards and two convicts, including Joe Dean, coming back in the wagon from delivering a load of adobe bricks in town, saw them next—saw them pass right by on the road—and Joe Dean and the other convict and the two guards turned around and watched them until the car crossed the railroad tracks and passed behind some depot sheds. Joe Dean said he could understand why the guards didn't want the spook and the Indian riding with them, but he still had never seen anything like it in all the time he'd been here. The guards said they had never seen anything like it either. There was funny things going on. Those two had raced each other, maybe they were racing the car now. Joe Dean said Goddamn, this was the craziest prison he had ever been in.

That first day, the best they could run in one stretch was a little over a mile. They did that once: down prison hill and along the railroad tracks and out back of town, out into the country. Most of the time, in the three hours they were out, they would run as far as they could, seldom more than a quarter of a mile—then have to quit and walk for a while, breathing hard with their mouths open and their lungs on fire. They would drop thirty to forty feet back of the car and the guard with the Winchester would yell at them to come on, get the lead out of their feet.

Harold said to Raymond, "I had any lead in my feet I'd take and hit that man in the mouth with it."

"We tell him we got to rest," Raymond said.

They did that twice, sat down at the side of the road in the meadow grass and watched the guard coming with the rifle and the car backing up through its own dust. The first time the guard pointed the rifle and yelled for them to get on their feet. Harold told him they couldn't move and asked him if he was going to shoot them for being tired.

"Captain, we *want* to run, but our legs won't mind what we tell them."

So the guard gave them five minutes and they sat back in the grass to let their muscles relax and stared at the distant mountains while the guards sat in the car smoking their cigarettes.

Harold said to Raymond, "What are we doing this for?"

Raymond gave him a funny look. "Because we're tired, what do you think?"

"I mean running. What are we running for?"

"They say to run, we run."

"It's that little preacher."

"Sure it is. What do you think, these guards thought of it?"

"That little man's crazy, ain't he?"

"I don't know," Raymond said. "Most of the time I don't understand him. He's got something in his head about running."

"Running's all right if you in a hurry and you know where you going."

"That road don't go anywhere."

"What's up ahead?"

"The desert," Raymond said. "Maybe after a while you come to a town."

"You know how to drive that thing?"

"A car? I never even been in one."

Harold was chewing on a weed stem, looking at the car. "It would be nice to have a ride home, wouldn't it?"

"It might be worth the running," Raymond said.

The guard got them up and they ran some more. They ran and walked and ran again for almost another mile, and this time when they went down they stretched out full length: Harold on his stomach, head down and his arms propping him up; Raymond on his back with his chest rising and falling.

After ten minutes the guard said all right, they were starting back now. Neither of them moved as the car turned around and rolled past them. The guard asked if they heard him. He said goddamn-it, they better get up quick. Harold said captain, their legs hurt so bad it didn't look like they could make it. The guard levered a cartridge into the chamber of the Winchester and said their legs would hurt one hell of a lot more with a .44 slug shot through them. They got up and fell in behind the car. Once they tried to run and had to stop within a dozen yards. It wasn't any use, Harold said. The legs wouldn't do what they was told. They could walk though. All right, the guard said, then walk. But god*damn*, they were so slow, poking along, he had to keep yelling at them to come on. After a while, still not in sight of the railroad tracks, the guard driving said to the other guard, if they didn't hurry they were going to miss supper call. The guard with the Winchester said well, what was he supposed to do about it? The guard driving said it looked like there was only one thing they *could* do.

Raymond liked it when the car stopped and the guard with the rifle, looking like he wanted to kill them, said all right, goddamn-it, get in.

Harold liked it when they drove past the cemetery work detail filing back to prison. The convicts had moved off the road and were looking back, waiting for the car. As they went by Harold raised one hand and waved. He said to Raymond, "Look at them poor boys. I believe they convicts."

EIGHT

"You know why they won't try to escape?" Mr. Manly said.

Bob Fisher stood at the desk and didn't say anything, because the answer was going to come from the little preacher anyway.

"Because they see the good in this. They realize this is their chance to become something."

"Running across a pasture field."

"You know what I mean."

"Take a man outside enough times," Fisher said, "he'll run for the hills."

"Not these two boys."

"Any two. They been outside every day for a week and they're smelling fresh air."

"Two weeks, and they can run three miles without stopping," Mr. Manly said. "Another couple of weeks I want to see them running five miles, maybe six."

"They'll run as long as it's easier than working."

Mr. Manly smiled a little. "I see you don't know them very well."

"I have known them all my life," Bob Fisher said. "When running becomes harder than working, they'll figure a way to get out of it. They'll break each other's legs if they have to."

"All right, then I'll talk to them again. You can be present, Bob, and I'll prove to you you're wrong."

"I understand you write a weekly report to Mr. Rynning," Fisher said. "Have you told him what you're doing?"

"As a matter of fact, I have."

"You told him you got them running outside?"

"I told him I'm trying something out on two boys considered

incorrigible, a program that combines spiritual teaching and physical exercise. He's made no mention to me what he thinks. But if you want to write to him, Bob, go right ahead."

"If it's all the same to you," Fisher said, "I want it on the record I didn't have nothing to do with this in any way at all."

Three miles wasn't so bad and it was easier to breathe at the end of the stretch. It didn't feel as if their lungs were burning any more. They would walk for a few minutes and run another mile and then walk again. Maybe they could do it again, run another mile before resting. But why do it if they didn't have to, if the guards didn't expect it? They would run a little way and when Raymond or Harold would call out they had to rest the car would stop and wait for them.

"I think we could do it," Raymond said.

"Sure we could."

"Maybe run four, five miles at the start."

"We could do that too," Harold said, "but why would we want to?"

"I mean to see if we could do it."

"Man, we could run five miles right now if we wanted."

"I don't know."

"If we had something to run for. All I see it doing is getting us tired."

"It's better than laying adobes, or working on the rock pile."

"I believe you're right there," Harold said.

"Well," Raymond said, "we can try four miles, five miles at any time we want. What's the hurry?"

"What's the hurry," Harold said. "I wish that son of a bitch would give us a cigarette. Look at him sucking on it and blowing the smoke out. Man."

They were getting along all right with the guards, because the guards were finding out this was pretty good duty, driving around the countryside in a Ford Touring Car. Ride around for a few hours. Smoke any time they wanted. Put the canvas top up if it got too hot in the sun. The guards weren't dumb, though. They stayed away from trees and the river bank, keeping to open range country once they had followed the railroad tracks out beyond town.

The idea of a train going by interested Harold. He pictured them running along the road where it was close to the tracks and the train coming up behind them out of the depot, not moving too fast. As the guards watched the train, Harold saw himself and Raymond break through the weeds to the gravel roadbed, run with the train and swing up on one of those iron-rung ladders they had on boxcars. Then the good part. The guards are watching the train and all of a sudden the guards see them on the boxcar—*waving to them.*

"Waving good-bye," Harold said to Raymond when they were resting one time and he told him about it.

Raymond was grinning. "They see the train going away, they don't know what to do."

"Oh, they take a couple of shots," Harold said. "But they so excited, man, they can't even hit the train."

"We're waving bye-bye."

"Yeah, while they shooting at us."

"It would be something, all right." Raymond had to wipe his eyes.

After a minute Harold said, "Where does the train go to?"

"I don't know. I guess different places."

"That's the trouble," Harold said. "You got to know where you going. You can't stay on the train. Sooner or later you got to get off and start running again."

"You think we could run five miles, uh?"

"If we wanted to," Harold said.

It was about a week later that Mr. Manly woke up in the middle of the night and said out loud in the bedroom, "All right, if you're going to keep worrying about it, why don't you see for yourself what they're doing?"

That's what he did the next day: hopped in the front seat of the Ford Touring Car and went along to watch the two boys do their road work.

It didn't bother the guard driving too much. He had less to say was all. But the guard with the Winchester yelled at Raymond and Harold more than he ever did before to come on, pick 'em up, keep closer to the car. Mr. Manly said the dust was probably bothering them. The guard said it was bothering him too, because he had to see them before he could watch them. He said you get a con outside you watch him every second.

Raymond and Harold ran three miles and saw Mr. Manly

looking at his watch. Later on, when they were resting, he came over and squatted down in the grass with them.

"Three miles in twenty-five minutes," he said. "That's pretty good. You reckon you could cover five miles in an hour?"

"I don't think so," Raymond said. "It's not us, we want to do it. It's our legs."

"Well, wanting something is half of getting it," Mr. Manly said. "I mean if you want something bad enough."

"Sure, we want to do it."

"Why?"

"Why? Well, I guess because we got to do it."

"You just said you wanted to."

"Yeah, we like to run."

"And I'm asking you why." Mr. Manly waited a moment. "Somebody told me all you fellas want to do is get out of work."

"Who tole you that?"

"It doesn't matter who it was. You know what I told him? I told him he didn't know you boys very well. I told him you were working harder now, running, than you ever worked in your life."

"That's right," Raymond said.

"Because you see a chance of doing something nobody else in the prison can do. Run twenty miles in a day."

Raymond said, "You want us to run twenty miles?"

"*You* want to run twenty miles. You're an Apache Indian, aren't you? And Harold's a Zulu. Well, by golly, an Apache Indian and a Zulu can run twenty miles, thirty miles a day, and there ain't a white man in this territory can say that."

"You want us to run twenty miles?" Raymond said again.

"I want you to start thinking of who you are, that's what I want. I want you to start thinking like warriors for a change instead of like convicts."

Raymond was watching him, nodding as he listened. He said, "Do these waryers think different than other people?"

"They think of who they are." An angry little edge came into Mr. Manly's tone. "They got pride in their tribe and their job, and everything they do is to make them better warriors—the way they live, the way they dress, the way they train to harden theirselves, the way they go without food or water to show their bodies their will power is in charge here and, by golly, their bodies better do what they're told. Raymond, you say you're Apache Indian?"

"Yes, sir, that's right."

"Harold, you believe you're a Zulu?"

"Yes-suh, captain, a Zulu."

"Then prove it to me, both of you. Let me see how good you are."

As Mr. Manly got to his feet he glanced over at the guards, feeling a little funny now in the silence and wondering if they had been listening. Well, so what if they had? He was superintendent, wasn't he? And he answered right back, You're darn right.

"You boys get ready for some real training," he said now. "I'm taking you at your word."

Raymond waited until he walked away and had reached the car. "Who do you think tole him we're doing this to get out of work?"

"I don't know," Harold said. "Who do you think?"

"I think that son of a bitch Frank Shelby."

"Yeah," Harold said, "he'd do it, wouldn't he?"

On Visiting Day the mess-hall tables were placed in a single line, dividing the room down the middle. The visitors remained on one side and the convicts on the other. Friends and relatives could sit down facing each other if they found a place at the tables; but they couldn't touch, not even hands, and a visitor was not allowed to pass anything to a convict.

Frank Shelby always got a place at the tables and his visitor was always his brother, a slightly older and heavier brother, but used to taking orders from Frank.

Virgil Shelby said, "By May for sure."

"I don't want a month," Frank said. "I want a day."

"I'm telling you what I know. They're done building the place, they're doing something inside the walls now and they won't let anybody in."

"You can talk to a workman."

"I talked to plenty of workmen. They don't know anything."

"What about the railroad?"

"Same thing. Old boys in the saloon talk about moving the convicts, but they don't know when."

"Somebody knows."

"Maybe they don't. Frank, what are you worried about? Whatever the day is we're going to be ready. I've been over and across that rail line eight times—nine times now—and I know just where I'm going to take you off that train."

"You're talking too loud."

Virgil took time to look down the table both ways, at the convicts hunched over the tables shoulder to shoulder and their visitors crowded in on this side, everyone trying to talk naturally without being overheard. When Virgil looked at his brother again, he said, "What I want to know is how many?"

"Me. Junior, Soonzy, Joe Dean. Norma." Frank Shelby paused. "No, we don't need to take Norma."

"It's up to you."

"No, we don't need her."

"That's four. I want to know you're together, all in the same place, because once we hit that train there's going to be striped suits running all over the countryside."

"That might be all right."

"It could be. Give them some people to chase after. But it could mess things up too."

"Well, right now all I hear is you wondering what's going to happen. You come with more than that, or I live the next forty years in Florence, Arizona."

"I'm going to stay in Yuma a while, see what I can find out about the train. You need any money?" Virgil asked.

"If I have to buy some guards. I don't know, get me three, four hundred."

"I'll send it in with the stores. Anything else?"

"A good idea, buddy."

"Don't worry, Frank, we're going to get you out. I'll swear to it."

"Yeah, well, I'll see you."

"Next month," Virgil said. He turned to swing a leg over the bench, then looked at his brother again. "Something funny I seen coming here—these two convicts running behind a Ford automobile. What do you suppose they was doing, Frank?"

Shelby had to tear his pants nearly off to see Norma again. He ripped them down the in-seam from crotch to ankle and told the warehouse guard he'd caught them on some bailing wire and, man, it had almost fixed him good. The guard said to get another pair out of stores. Shelby said all right, and he'd leave his ripped pants at the tailor's on the way back. The guard knew what Shelby was up to; he accepted the sack of Bull Durham Shelby offered and played the game with him. It wasn't hurting anybody.

So he got his new pants and headed for the tailor shop. As soon as he was inside, Norma Davis came off the work table, where she was sitting smoking a cigarette, and went into the stock room. Shelby threw the ripped pants at the tailor, told Tacha to watch out the window for Bob Fisher, and followed Norma into the back room, closing the door behind him.

"He's not as sure of himself as he used to be," Tacha said. "He's worried."

The tailor was studying the ripped seam closely.

Tacha was looking out the window, at the colorless tone of the yard in sunlight: adobe and granite and black shadow lines in the glare. The brick detail was at work across the yard, but she couldn't hear them. She listened for sounds, out in the yard and in the room behind her, but there were none.

"They're quiet in there, uh?"

The tailor said nothing.

"You expect them to make sounds like animals, those two. That old turnkey makes sounds. God, like he's dying. Like somebody stuck a knife—" Tacha stopped.

"I don't know what you're talking about," the tailor said.

"I'm talking about Mr. Fisher, the turnkey, the sounds he makes when he's in her cell."

"And I don't want to know." The tailor kept his head low over his sewing machine.

"He sneaks in at night—"

"I said I don't want to hear about it."

"He hasn't been coming very long. Just the past few weeks. Not every night either. He makes some excuse to go in there, like to fix the lantern or search the place for I don't know what. One time she say, 'Oh, I think there is a tarantula in here,' and the turnkey hurries in there to kill it. I want to say to him, knowing he's taking off his pants then, 'Hey, mister, that's a funny thing to kill a tarantula with.'"

"I'm not listening to you," the tailor said. "Not a word."

In the closeness of the stock room Shelby stepped back to rest his arm on one of the shelves. Watching Norma, he loosened his hat, setting it lightly on his forehead. "Goodness," he said, "I didn't even take off my hat, did I?"

Norma let her skirt fall. She smoothed it over her hips and began buttoning her blouse. "I feel like a mare, standing like that."

"Honey, you don't look like a mare. I believe you are about the trickiest thing I ever met."

"I know a few more ways."

"I bet you do, for a fact."

"That old man, he breathes through his nose right in your ear. Real loud, like he's having heart failure."

Shelby grinned. "That would be something. He has a stroke while he's in there with you."

"I'll tell you, he isn't any fun at all."

"You ain't loving him for the pleasure, sweetheart. You're supposed to be finding out things."

"He doesn't know yet when we're going."

"You asked him?"

"I said to him, 'I will sure be glad to get out of this place.' He said it wouldn't be much longer and I said, 'Oh, when are we leaving here?' He said he didn't know for sure, probably in a couple of months."

"We got to know the day," Shelby said.

"Well, if he don't know it he can't hardly tell me, can he?"

"Maybe he can find it out."

"From who?"

"I don't know. The superintendent, somebody."

"That little fella, he walks around, he looks like he's lost, can't find his mama."

"Well, mama, maybe you should talk to him."

"Get him to come to my cell."

"Jesus, you'd eat him up."

Norma giggled. "You say terrible things."

"I mean by the time you're through there wouldn't be nothing left of him."

"If *you're* through, you better get out of here."

"I talked to Virgil. He doesn't know anything either."

"Don't worry," Norma said. "One of us'll find out. I just want to be sure you take me along when the time comes."

Shelby gave her a nice little sad smile and shook his head slowly. "Sweetheart," he said, "how could I go anywhere without you?"

Good timing, Norma Davis believed, was one of the most important things in life. You had to think of the other person. You had to know his moods and reactions and know the right moment to spring little surprises. You didn't want the person getting too excited and ruining everything before it was time.

That's why she brought Bob Fisher along for almost two months before she told him her secret.

It was strange; like instinct. One night, as she heard the key turning in the iron door of the cellblock, she knew it was Bob and, for some reason, she also knew she was going to tell him tonight. Though not right away.

First he had to go through his act. He had to look in at Tacha and ask her what was she doing, reading? Then he had to come over and see Norma in the bunk and look around the cell for a minute and ask if everything was all right. Norma was ready. She told him she had a terrible sore ankle and would he look at it and see if it was sprained or anything. She got him in there and then had to slow down and be patient while he actually, honest to God, looked at her ankle and said in a loud voice it looked all right to him. He whispered after that, getting out of his coat and into the bunk with her, but raising up every once in a while to look at the cell door.

Norma said, "What's the matter?"

"Tacha, she can hear everything."

"If she bothers you, why don't you put her some place else?"

"This is the woman's block. There isn't any place else."

Norma got her hand inside his shirt and started fooling with the hair on his chest. "How does Tacha look to you?"

"Cut it out, it tickles," Fisher said. "What do you mean, how does she look?"

"I don't know, I don' think she looks so good. I hear her coughing at night."

"Listen, I only got a few minutes."

Norma handled the next part of it, making him believe he was driving her wild, and as he lay on the edge of the bunk breathing out of his nose, she told him her secret.

She said, "Guess what? I know somebody who's planning to escape."

That got him up and leaning over her again.

"Who?"

"I heard once," Norma said, "if you help the authorities here they'll help you."

"Who is it?"

"I heard of convicts who helped stop men trying to escape and got pardoned. Is that right?"

"It's happened."

"They were freed?"

"That's right."

"You think it might happen again?"

"It could. Who's going out?"

"Not out of here. From the train. You think if I found out all about it and told you I'd get a pardon?"

"I think you might," Fisher said. "I can't promise, but you'd have a good chance."

"It's Frank Shelby."

"That's what I thought."

"His brother Virgil's going to help him."

"Where do they jump the train?"

"Frank doesn't know yet, but soon as I find out I'll tell you."

"You promise?"

"Cross my heart."

"You're a sweet girl, Norma. You know that?"

She smiled at him in the dim glow of the lantern and said, "I try to be."

Another week passed before Bob Fisher thought of something else Norma had said.

He was in the tailor shop that day, just checking, not for any special reason. Tacha looked up at him and said, "Norma's not here."

"I can see that."

"She's at the toilet—if you're looking for her."

"I'm not looking for her," Fisher said.

He wasn't sure if Tacha was smiling then or not—like telling him she knew all about him. Little Mexican bitch, she had better not try to get smart with him.

It was then he thought of what Norma had said. About Tacha not looking so good. Coughing at night.

Hell, yes, Bob Fisher said to himself and wondered why he hadn't thought of it before. There was only one place around here to put anybody who was coughing sick. Over in the TB cellblock.

NINE

The guard, R. E. Baylis, was instructed to move the Mexican girl to the TB area after work, right before supper. It sounded easy enough.

But when he told Tacha she held back and didn't want to go. What for? Look at her. Did she look like she had TB? She wasn't even sick. R. E. Baylis told her to get her things, she was going over there and that's all there was to it. She asked him if Mr. Fisher had given the order, and when he said sure, Tacha said she thought so; she should have known he would do something like this. Goddamn-it, R. E. Baylis thought, he didn't have to explain anything to her. He did though. He said it must be they were sending her over there to help out—bring the lungers their food, get them their medicine. He said there were two boys in there supposed to be looking after the lungers, but nobody had seen much of them the past couple of months or so, what with all the running they were doing. They would go out early in the morning, just about the time it was getting light, and generally not get back until the afternoon. He said some of the guards were talking about them, how they had changed; but he hadn't seen them in a while. Tacha only half listened to him. She wasn't interested in the two convicts, she was thinking about the TB cellblock and wondering what it would be like to live there. She remembered the two he was talking about; she knew them by sight. Though when she walked into the TB yard and saw them again, she did not recognize them immediately as the same two men.

R. E. Baylis got a close look at them and went to find Bob Fisher.

"She give you any trouble?" Fisher asked.

He sat at a table in the empty mess hall with a cup of coffee in front of him. The cooks were bringing in the serving pans and setting up for supper.

"No trouble once I got her there," R. E. Baylis said. "What I want to know is what the Indin and the nigger are doing?"

"I don't know anything about them and don't want to know. They're Mr. Manly's private convicts." Fisher held his cup close to his face and would lean in to sip at it.

"Haven't you seen them lately?"

"I see them go by once in a while, going out the gate."

"But you haven't been over there? You haven't seen them close?"

"Whatever he's got them doing isn't any of my business. I told him I don't want no part of it."

"You don't care what they're doing?"

"I got an inventory of equipment and stores have to be tallied before we ship out of here and that ain't very long away."

"You don't care if they made spears," R. E. Baylis said, "and they're throwing them at a board stuck in the ground?"

Bob Fisher started coughing and spilled some of his coffee down the front of his uniform.

Mr. Manly said, "Yes, I know they got spears. Made of bamboo fishing poles and brick-laying trowels stuck into one end for the point. If a man can use a trowel to work with all day, why can't he use one for exercise?"

"Because a spear is a weapon," Fisher said. "You can kill a man with it."

"Bob, you got some kind of stain there on your uniform."

"What I mean is you don't let convicts make *spears*."

"Why not, if they're for a good purpose?"

No, Bob Fisher said to himself—with R. E. Baylis standing next to him, listening to it all—this time, goddamn-it, don't let him mix you up. He said, "Mr. Manly, for some reason I seem to have trouble understanding you."

"What is it you don't understand, Bob?"

"Every time I come up here, it's like you and me are talking about two different things. I come in, I know what the rules are here and I know what I want to say. Then you begin talking and it's like we get onto something else."

"We look at a question from different points of view," Mr. Manly said. "That's all it is."

"All right, R. E. Baylis here says they got spears. I haven't been over to see for myself. We was downstairs—I don't know, something told me I should see you about it first."

"I'm glad you did."

"How long have they had 'em?"

"About two weeks. Bob, they run fourteen miles yesterday. Only stopped three times to rest."

"I don't see what that's got to do with the spears."

"Well, you said you wanted it to show in the record you're not having anything to do with this business. Isn't that right?"

"I want it to show I'm against their being taken outside."

"I haven't told you anything what's going on, have I?"

"I haven't asked neither."

"That's right. This is the first time you've mentioned those boys in over two months. You don't know what I'm teaching them, but you come in here and tell me they can't have spears."

"It's in the rules."

"It says in the rules they can't have spears for any purpose whatsoever?"

"It say a man found with a weapon is to be put under maximum security for no less than ten days."

"You mean put in the snake den."

"I sure do."

"You believe those two boys have been found with weapons?"

"When you make a spear out of a trowel, it becomes a weapon."

"But what if I was the one told them to make the spears?"

"I was afraid you might say that."

"As a matter of fact, I got them the fishing poles myself. Bought them in town."

"Bought them in town," Bob Fisher said. His head seemed to nod a little as he stared at Mr. Manly. "This here is what I meant before about not understanding some things. I would sure like to know why you want them to have spears?"

"Bob," Mr. Manly said, "that's the only way to learn, isn't it? Ask questions." He looked up past Fisher then, at the wall clock. "Say, it's about supper time already."

"Mr. Manly, I'll wait on supper if you'll explain them spears to me."

"I'll do better than that," Mr. Manly said, "I'll show you. First though we got to get us a pitcher of ice water."

"I'll even pass on that," Fisher said. "I'm not thirsty *or* hungry."

Mr. Manly gave him a patient, understanding grin. "The ice water isn't for us, Bob."

"No sir," Fisher said. He was nodding again, very slowly, solemnly. "I should've known better, shouldn't I?"

Tacha remembered them from months before wearing leg-irons and pushing the wheelbarrows. She remembered the Negro working without a shirt on and remembered thinking the other one tall for an Indian. She had never spoken to them or watched them for a definite reason. She had probably not been closer than fifty feet to either of them. But she was aware now of the striking change in their appearance and at first it gave her a strange, tense feeling. She was afraid of them.

The guard had looked as if he was afraid of them too, and maybe that was part of the strange feeling. He didn't tell her which cell was to be hers. He stared at the Indian and the Negro, who were across the sixty-foot yard by the wall, and then hurried away, leaving her here.

As soon as he was gone the tubercular convicts began talking to her. One of them asked if she had come to live with them. When she nodded he said she could bunk with him if she wanted. They laughed and another one said no, come on in his cell, he would show her a fine old time. She didn't like the way they stared at her. They sat in front of their cells on stools and a wooden bunk frame and looked as if they had been there a long time and seldom shaved or washed themselves.

She wasn't sure if the Indian and the Negro were watching her. The Indian was holding something that looked like a fishing pole. The Negro was standing by an upright board that was as tall as he was and seemed to be nailed to a post. Another of the poles was sticking out of the board. Neither of them was wearing a shirt; that was the first thing she noticed about them from across the yard.

They came over when she turned to look at the cells and one of the tubercular convicts told her again to come on, put her blanket and stuff in with his. Now, when she looked around, not knowing what to do, she saw them approaching.

She saw the Indian's hair, how long it was, covering his ears, and the striped red and black cloth he wore as a headband. She saw the Negro's mustache that curved around his mouth into a short beard and the cuts on his face, like knife scars, that slanted down from both of his cheekbones. This was when she was afraid of them, as they walked up to her.

"The cell on the end," Raymond said. "Why don't you take that one?"

She made herself hold his gaze. "Who else is in there, you?"

"Nobody else."

Harold said, "You got the TB?"

"I don't have it yet."

"You do something to Frank Shelby?"

"Maybe I did," she said, "I don't know."

"If you don't have the TB," Harold said, "you did something to somebody."

She began to feel less afraid already, talking to them, and yet she knew there was something different about their faces and the way they looked at her. "I think the turnkey, Mr. Fisher, did it," Tacha said, "so I wouldn't see him going in with Norma."

"I guess there are all kinds of things going on," Harold said. "They put you in here, it's not so bad. It was cold at night when we first come, colder than the big cellblock, but now it's all right." He glanced toward the tubercular convicts. "Don't worry about the scarecrows. They won't hurt you."

"They lock everybody in at night," Raymond said. "During the day one of them tries something, you can run."

That was a strange thing too: being afraid of them at first because of the way they looked, then hearing them say not to worry and feeling at ease with them, believing them.

Raymond said, "We fixed up that cell for you. It's like a new one."

She was inside unrolling her bedding when the guard returned with the superintendent and the turnkey, Mr. Fisher. She heard one of them say, "Harold, come out here," and she looked up to see them through the open doorway: the little man in the dark suit and two in guard uniforms, one of them, R. E. Baylis, holding a dented tin pitcher. The Indian was still in the yard, not far from them, but she didn't see the Negro. The superintendent was looking toward her cell now, squinting into the dim interior.

Mr. Manly wanted to keep an eye on Bob Fisher and watch his reactions, but seeing the woman distracted him.

"Who's that in there, Norma Davis?"

"The other one," Fisher said, "the Mexican."

"I didn't see any report on her being sick."

"She's working here. Your two boys run off, there's nobody to fetch things for the lungers."

Mr. Manly didn't like to look at the tubercular convicts; they gave him a creepy feeling, the way they sat there all day like lizzards and never seemed to move. He gave them a glance and called again, "Harold, come on out here."

The Negro was buttoning a prison shirt as he appeared in the doorway. "You want me, captain?"

"Come over here, will you?"

Mr. Manly was watching Fisher now. The man's flat open-eyed expression tickled him: old Bob Fisher staring at Harold, then looking over at Raymond, then back at Harold again, trying to figure out the change that had come over them. The change was something more than just their appearance. It was something Mr. Manly felt, and he was pretty sure now Bob Fisher was feeling it too.

"What's the matter, Bob, ain't you ever seen an Apache or a Zulu before?"

"I seen Apaches."

"Then what're you staring at?"

Fisher looked over at Harold again. "What're them cuts on his face?"

"Tell him, Harold."

"They tribal marks, captain."

Fisher said, "What the hell tribe's a field nigger belong to?"

Harold touched his face, feeling the welts of scar tissue that were not yet completely healed. He said, "My tribe, captain."

"He cut his own face like that?"

Fisher kept staring at the Negro as Mr. Manly said, "He saw it in a Africa book I got—picture of a native with these marks like tatoos on his face. I didn't tell him to do it, you understand. He just figured it would be all right, I guess. Isn't that so, Harold?"

"Yes-suh, captain."

"Same with Raymond. He figured if he's a full-blooded Apache Indian then he should let his hair grow and wear one of them bands."

"We come over here to look at spears," Fisher said.

Mr. Manly frowned, shaking his head. "Don't you see the connection yet? A spear is part of a warrior's get-up, like a tool is to a working man. Listen, I told you, didn't I, these boys can run fifteen miles in a day now and only stop a couple of times to rest."

"I thought it was fourteen miles," Fisher said.

"Fourteen, fifteen—here's the thing. They can run that far *and* go from morning to supper time without a drink of water, any time they want."

"A man will do that in the snake den if I make him." Bob Fisher wasn't backing off this time.

Mr. Manly wasn't letting go. "Inside," he said, "is different than running out in the hot sun. Listen, they each pour theirselves a cup of water in the morning and you know what they do? They see who can go all day without taking a drink or more than a couple of sips." He held his hand out to R. E. Baylis and said, "Let me have the pitcher." Then he looked at Raymond and Harold again. "Which of you won today?"

"I did," Raymond said.

"Let's see your cups."

Raymond went into his cell and was back in a moment with a tin cup in each hand. "He drank his. See, I got some left."

"Then you get the pitcher of ice water," Mr. Manly said. "And, Harold, you get to watch him drink it."

Raymond raised the pitcher and drank out of the side of it, not taking very much before lowering it again and holding it in front of him.

"See that?" Mr. Manly said. "He knows better than to gulp it down. One day Raymond wins, the next day Harold gets the ice water. I mean they can both do it any time they want."

"I would sure like to see them spears," Fisher said.

Mr. Manly asked Harold where they were and he said, "Over yonder by the wall, captain."

Tacha watched them cross the yard. The Negro waited for the Indian to put the pitcher on the ground and she noticed they gave each other a look as they fell in behind the little man in the dark suit and the two guards. They were over by the wall a few minutes talking while Mr. Fisher hefted one of the bamboo spears and felt the point of it with his finger. Then the superintendent took the spear from him and gave it to the Indian. The Negro picked up the other spear from against the wall and they came back this way, toward the cells, at least a dozen paces before turning around. Beyond them, the group moved away from the upright board. The Indian and the Negro faced the target for a moment, then stepped back several more feet, noticing Tacha now in the doorway of her cell.

She said, "You're going to hit that, way down there?"

"Not today," Raymond answered.

Everyone in the yard was watching them now. They raised the spears shoulder high, took aim with their outstretched left arms pointing, and threw them hard in a low arc, almost at the same moment. Both spears fell short and skidded along the ground past the board to stop at the base of the wall.

Raymond and Harold waited. In the group across the yard Mr. Manly seemed to be doing the talking, gesturing with his hands. He was facing Bob Fisher and did not look over this way. After a few minutes they left the yard, and now Mr. Manly, as he went through the gate last, looked over and waved.

"Well," Raymond said—he stooped to pick up the tin pitcher—"who wants some ice water?"

Within a few days Tacha realized that, since moving to the TB cellblock, she felt better—whether it made sense or not. Maybe part of the feeling was being outside most of the day and not bent over a sewing machine listening to Norma or trying to talk to the old man. Already that seemed like a long time ago. She was happier now. She even enjoyed being with the tubercular convicts and didn't mind the way they talked to her sometimes, saying she was a pretty good nurse though they would sure rather have her be something else. They needed to talk like men so she smiled and didn't take anything they said as an offense.

In the afternoon the Apache and the Zulu would come in through the gate, walking slowly, carrying their shirts. One of the tubercular convicts would yell over, asking how far they had run and one or the other would tell them twelve, fifteen, sixteen miles. They would drink the water in their cups. One of the convicts would fill the cups again from the bucket they kept in the shade. After drinking the second cup they would decide who the winner would be that day and pour just a little more water into his cup, leaving the other one empty. The TB convicts got a kick out of this and always laughed. Every day it was the same. They drank the water and then went into the cell to lie on their bunks. In less than an hour the TB convicts would be yelling for them to come out and start throwing their spears. They would get out their money or rolled cigarettes when the Apache and the Zulu appeared and, after letting them warm up a few minutes, at least two of the convicts would bet on every throw. Later on, after the work crews were in for the day, there would be convicts over from the main yard watching through the gate. None of them ever came into the TB yard. They were betting too and would yell at the Apache and the Zulu—calling them by those names—to hit the board, cut the son of a bitch dead center. Frank Shelby appeared at the gate only once. After that the convicts had to pay to watch and make bets. Soonzy, Junior, and Joe Dean were at the grillwork every day during free time.

Harold Jackson, the Zulu, walked over to the gate one time. He said, "How come we do all the work, you make all the money?"

Junior told him to get back over there and start throwing his goddamn spear or whatever it was.

Harold let the convicts get a good look at his face scars before he walked away. After the next throw, when he and Raymond were pulling their spears out of the board, Harold said, "Somebody always telling you what to do, huh?"

"Every place you go," Raymond said.

They were good with the spears. Though when the convicts from the outside yard were at the gate watching they never threw from farther than thirty-five feet away, or tried to place the spears in a particular part of the board. If they wanted to, they could hit the board high or low at the same time.

It was Tacha who noticed their work shoes coming apart from the running and made moccasins for them, sewing them by hand— calf-high Apache moccasins she fashioned out of old leather water bags and feed sacks.

And it was Tacha who told Raymond he should put war paint on his face. He wasn't scarey enough looking.

"Where do you get war paint?" Raymond asked her, "At the store?"

"I think from berries."

"Well, I don't see no berries around here."

The next day she got iodine and a can of white enamel from the sick ward and, after supper, sat Raymond on a stool and painted a white streak across the bridge of his nose from cheekbone to cheekbone, and orange-red iodine stripes along the jawline to his chin.

Harold Jackson liked it, so Tacha painted a white stripe across his forehead and another one down between his eyes to the tip of his nose.

"Hey, we waryers now," Raymond said.

They looked at themselves in Tacha's hand mirror and both of them grinned. They were pretty mean-looking boys. Harold said, "Lady, what else do these waryers put on?"

Tacha said she guessed anything they wanted. She opened a little sack and gave Raymond two strands of turquoise beads, a string for around his neck and another string, doubled, for around his right arm, up high.

She asked Harold if he wanted a ring for his nose, He said no, thank you, lady, but remembered Mr. Manly talking about the Zulus putting chunks of sugar cane in their ear lobes and he let Tacha pierce one of his ears and attach a single gold earring. It looked good with the tribal scars and the mustache that curved into a short beard. "All I need me is a lion to spear," Harold said. He was Harold Jackson the Zulu, and he could feel it without looking in the mirror.

He didn't talk to Raymond about the feeling because he knew Raymond, in a way of his own, Raymond the Apache, had the same feeling. In front of the convicts who watched them throw spears or in front of the two guards who took them out to run, Harold could look at Raymond, their eyes would meet for a moment and each knew what the other was thinking. They didn't talk very much, even to each other. They walked slowly and seemed to expend no extra effort in their movements. They knew they could do something no other men in the prison could do—they could run all day and go without water—and it was part of the good feeling.

They began to put fresh paint on their faces almost every day, in the afternoon before they threw the spears.

TEN

The evening Junior and Joe Dean came for them they were sitting out in front of the cells with Tacha. It was after supper, just beginning to get dark. For a little while Tacha had been pretending to tell them their fortunes, using an old deck of cards and turning them up one at a time in the fading light. She told Harold she saw him sleeping under a banana tree with a big smile on his face. Sure, Cuba, Harold said. With the next card she saw him killing a lion with his spear and Harold was saying they didn't have no lions in Cuba, when Junior came up to them. Joe Dean stood over a little way with his hands in his pockets, watching.

"Frank wants to see you," Junior said. "Both of you." He took time to look at Tacha while he waited for them to get up. When neither of them moved he said, "You hear me? Frank wants you."

"What's he want?" Harold said.

"He's going to want me to kick your ass you don't get moving."

Raymond looked at Harold, and Harold looked at Raymond. Finally they got up and followed them across the yard, though they moved so goddamn slow Worley Lewis, Jr. had to keep waiting for them with his hands on his hips, telling them to come on, *move*. They looked back once and saw Joe Dean still over by the cells. He seemed to be waiting for them to leave.

Soonzy was in the passageway of the main cellblock, standing in the light that was coming from No. 14. He motioned them inside.

They went into the cell, then stopped short. Frank Shelby was sitting on his throne reading a newspaper, hunched over before his own shadow on the back wall. He didn't look up; he made them wait several minutes before he finally rose, pulled up his pants and buckled his belt. Junior and Soonzy crowded the doorway behind them.

"Come closer to the light," Shelby said. He waited for them to move into the space between the bunks, to where the electric overhead light, with its tin shield, was almost directly above them.

"I want to ask you two something. I want to know how come you got your faces painted up like that."

They kept looking at him, but neither of them spoke.

"You going to tell me?"

"I don't know," Raymond said. "I guess it's hard to explain."

"Did anybody tell you to put it on?"

"No, we done it ourselves."

"Has this Mr. Manly seen it?"

"Yeah, but he didn't say nothing."

"You just figured it would be a good idea, uh?"

"I don't know," Raymond said. "We just done it, I guess."

"You want to look like a couple of circus clowns, is that it?"

"No, we didn't think of that."

"Maybe you want to look like a wild Indin," Shelby said, "and him, he wants to look like some kind of boogey-man native. Maybe that's it."

Raymond shrugged. "Maybe something like that. It's hard to explain."

"What does Mr. Jackson say about it?"

"If you know why we put it on," Harold said, "what are you asking us for?"

"Because it bothers me," Shelby answered. "I can't believe anybody would want to look like a nigger native. Even a nigger. Same as I can't believe anybody would want to look like a Wild West Show Indin 'less he was paid to do it. Somebody paying you, Raymond?"

"Nobody's paying us."

"See, Raymond, what bothers me—how can we learn people like you to act like white men if you're going to play you're savages? You see what I mean? You want to move back in this cell block, but who do you think would want to live with you?"

"We're not white men," Raymond said.

"Jesus Christ, I know that. I'm saying if you want to live with white men then you got to try to act like white men. You start playing you're an Apache and a goddamn Zulu or something, that's the same as saying you don't want to be a white man, and that's what bothers me something awful, when I see that going on."

There was a little space of silence before Harold said, "What do you want us to do?"

"We'll do it," Shelby said. "We're going to remind you how you're supposed to act."

Soonzy took Harold from behind with a fist in his hair and a forearm around his neck. He dragged Harold backward and as Raymond turned, Junior stepped in and hit Raymond with a belt wrapped around his fist. He had to hit Raymond again before he could get a good hold on him and pull him out of the cell. Joe Dean and a half-dozen convicts were waiting in the passageway. They got Raymond and Harold down on their backs on the cement. They sat on their legs and a convict stood on each of their outstretched hands and arms while another man got down and pulled their hair tight to keep them from moving their heads. Then Joe Dean took a brush and the can of enamel Tacha had got from the sick ward and painted both of their faces pure white.

When R. E. Baylis came through to lock up, Shelby told him to look at the goddamn mess out there, white paint all over the cement and dirty words painted on the wall. He said that nigger and his red nigger friend sneaked over and started messing up the place, but they caught the two and painted them as a lesson. Shelby said to R. E. Baylis goddamn-it, why didn't he throw them in the snake den so they would quit bothering people. R. E. Baylis said he would tell Bob Fisher.

The next morning after breakfast, Shelby came out of the mess hall frowning in the sunlight and looking over the work details forming in the yard. He was walking toward the supply group when somebody called his name from behind. Bob Fisher was standing by the mess hall door: grim-looking tough old son of a bitch in his gray sack guard uniform. Shelby sure didn't want to, but he walked back to where the turnkey was standing.

"They don't know how to write even their names," Fisher said.

"Well"—Shelby took a moment to think—"maybe they got the paint for somebody else do to it."

"Joe Dean got the paint."

"Joe did that?"

"Him and Soonzy and Junior are going to clean it up before they go to work."

"Well, if they did it—"

"You're going to help them."

"Me? I'm on the supply detail. You know that."

"Or you can go with the quarry gang," Fisher said. "It don't make any difference to me."

"Quarry gang?" Shelby grinned to show Fisher he thought he was kidding. "I don't believe I ever done that kind of work."

"You'll do it if I say so."

"Listen, just because we painted those two boys up. We were teaching them a lesson, that's all. Christ, they go around here thinking they're something the way they fixed theirselves up—somebody had to teach them."

"I do the teaching here," Fisher said. "I'm teaching that to you right now."

Dumb, stone-face guard son of a bitch. Shelby said, "Well," half-turning to look off thoughtfully toward the work groups waiting in the yard. "I hope those people don't get sore about this. You know how it is, how they listen to me and trust me. If they figure I'm getting treated unfair, they're liable to sit right down and not move from the yard, every one of them."

"If you believe that," Fisher said, "you better tell them I'll shoot the first man that sits down, and if they all sit down at once I'll shoot you."

Shelby waited. He didn't look at Bob Fisher; he kept his gaze on the convicts. After a moment he said, "You're kneeling on me for a reason, aren't you? You're waiting to see me make a terrible mistake."

"I believe you've already made it," Fisher said. He turned and went into the mess hall.

Scraping paint off cement was better than working in the quarry. It was hot in the passageway, but there was no sun beating down on them and they weren't breathing chalk dust. Shelby sat in his cell and let Junior, Soonzy, and Joe Dean do the work, until Bob Fisher came by. Fisher didn't say anything; he looked in at him and Shelby came out and picked up a trowel and started scraping. When Fisher was gone, Shelby sat back on his heels and said, "I'm going to bust me a guard, I'll tell you, if that man's anywhere near us when we leave."

The scraping stopped as he spoke, as Junior and Soonzy and Joe Dean waited to hear whatever he had to say.

"There is something bothering him," Shelby said. "He wants to nail me down. He could do it any time he feels like it, couldn't he? He could put me in the quarry or the snake den—that man could chain me to the wall. But he's waiting on something."

Joe Dean said, "Waiting on what?"

"I don't know. Unless he's telling me he knows what's going on. He could be saying, 'I got my eye on you, buddy. I'm waiting for you to make the wrong move.'"

"What could he know?" Joe Dean said, "We don't know anything ourselves."

"He could know we're thinking about it."

"He could be guessing."

"I mean," Shelby said, "he could *know*. Norma could have told him. She's the only other person who could."

Junior was frowning. "What would Norma want to tell him for?"

"Jesus Christ," Shelby said, "because she's Norma. She don't need a reason, she does what she feels like doing. Listen, she needs money she gets herself a forty-four and pours liquor into some crazy boy and they try and rob a goddamn *bank*. She's seeing Bob Fisher, and she's the only one could have told him anything."

"I say he's guessing," Joe Dean said. "The time's coming to move all these convicts, he's nervous at the thought of it, and starts guessing we're up to something."

"That could be right," Shelby said. "But the only way I can find out for sure is to talk to Norma." He was silent a moment. "I don't know. With old Bob watching every move I got to stay clear of the tailor shop."

"Why don't we bring her over here?" Junior said. "Right after supper everybody's in the yard. Shoot, we can get her in here, anywhere you want, no trouble."

"Hey, boy," Shelby grinned, "now you're talking."

Jesus, yes, what was he worrying about that old man turnkey for? He had to watch that and never worry out loud or raise his voice or lose his temper. He had to watch when little pissy-ant started to bother him. The Indin and the nigger had bothered him. It wasn't even important; but goddamn-it, it had bothered him and he had done something about it. See—but because of it Bob

Fisher had come down on him and this was not anytime to get Bob Fisher nervous and watchful. Never trust a nervous person unless you've got a gun on him. That was a rule. And when you've got the gun on him shoot him or hit him with it, quick, but don't let him starting crying and begging for his life and spilling the goddamn payroll all over the floor—the way it had happened in the paymaster's office at the Cornelia Mine near Ajo. They would have been out of there before the security guards arrived if he hadn't spilled the money. The paymaster would be alive if he hadn't spilled the money, and they wouldn't be in Yuma. There was such a thing as bad luck. Anything could happen during a holdup. But there had been five payroll and bank robberies before the Cornelia Mine job where no one had spilled the money or reached for a gun or walked in unexpectedly. They had been successful because they had kept calm and in control, and that was the way they had to do it again, to get out of here.

It had surely bothered him though—the way the Indin and the nigger had painted their faces.

Junior pushed through the mess-hall door behind Norma as she went out, and told her to go visit Tacha. That's how easy it was. When Norma got to the TB yard Joe Dean, standing by the gate, nodded toward the first cell. She saw Tacha sitting over a ways with the Indian and the Negro, and noticed there was something strange about them: they looked sick, with a gray pallor to their skin, even the Negro. Norma looked at Joe Dean and again he nodded toward the first cell.

Soonzy stepped out and walked past her as she approached the doorway. Shelby was waiting inside, standing with an arm on the upper bunk. He didn't grin or reach for her, he said, "How're you getting along with your boy friend?"

"He still hasn't told me anything, if that's what you mean."

"I'm more interested in what you might have told him."

Norma smiled and seemed to relax. "You know, as I walked in here I thought you were a little tense about something."

"You haven't answered my question."

"What is it I might have told him?"

"Come on, Norma."

"I mean what's there to tell him? You don't have any plan you've told me about."

"I don't know," Shelby said, "it looks to me like you got your own plan."

"I ask him. Every time he comes in I bring it up. 'Honey, when are we going to get out of this awful place?' But he won't tell me anything."

"You were pretty sure one time you could squeeze it out of him."

"I don't believe he knows any more than we do."

"I'll tell you what," Shelby said. "I'll give you three more days to find out. You don't know anything by then, I don't see any reason to take you with us."

Norma took her time. She kept her eyes on Shelby, holding him and waiting a little, then stepped in close so that she was almost touching him with her body. She waited again before saying, quietly, "What're you being so mean for?"

Shelby said, "Man." He said, "Come on, Norma, if I want to put you on the bunk I'll put you on the bunk. Don't give me no sweetheart talk, all right? I want you to tell me if you're working something with that old man. Now hold on—I want you to keep looking right at me and tell me to my face yes or no—yes, 'I have told him,' or no, 'I have not told him.' "

Norma put on a frown now that brought her eyebrows together and gave her a nice hurt look.

"Frank, what do you want me to tell you?" She spaced the words to show how honest and truthful she was being, knowing that her upturned, frowning face was pretty nice and that her breasts were about an inch away from the upcurve of his belly.

She looked good all right, and if he put her down on the bunk she'd be something. But Frank Shelby was looking at a train and keeping calm, keeping his voice down, and he said, "Norma, if you don't find out anything in three days you don't leave this place."

It was Sunday, Visiting Day, that Mr. Manly decided he would make an announcement. He called Bob Fisher into his office to tell him, then thought better of it—Fisher would only object and argue—so he began talking about Raymond and Harold instead of his announcement.

"I'll tell you," Mr. Manly said, "I'm not so much interested in who did it as I am in *why* they did it. They got paint in their eyes, in their nose. They had to wash theirselves in gasoline and then they didn't get it all off."

"Well, there's no way of finding out now," Fisher said. "You ask them, there isn't anybody knows a thing."

"The men who did it know."

"Well, sure, the ones that did it."

"I'd like to know what a man thinks like would paint another person."

"They were painting theirselves before."

"I believe you see the difference, Bob."

"These are convicts," Fisher said. "They get mean they don't need a reason. It's the way they are."

"I'm thinking I better talk to them."

"But we don't know who done it."

"I mean talk to all of them. I want to talk to them about something else any way."

"About what?"

"Maybe I can make the person who did it come forward and admit it."

"Mister, if you believe that you don't know anything a-tall about convicts. You talked to Raymond and Harold, didn't you?"

"Yes, I did."

"And they won't even tell you who done it, will they?"

"I can't understand that."

"Because they're convicts. They know if they ever told you they'd get their heads beat against a cell wall. This is between them and the other convicts. If the convicts don't want them to paint up like savages then I believe we should stay out of it and let them settle it theirselves."

"But they've got rights—the two boys. What about them?"

"I don't know. I'm not talking about justice," Fisher said. "I'm talking about running a prison. If the convicts want these two to act a certain way or not act a certain way, we should keep out of it. It keeps them quiet and it don't cost us a cent. When you push against the whole convict body it had better to be important and you had better be ready to shoot and kill people if they push back."

"I told them they could put on their paint if they wanted."

"Well, that's up to you," Fisher said. "Or it's up to them. I notice they been keeping their faces clean."

When Mr. Manly didn't speak right away, Fisher said, "If it's all right with you I want to get downstairs and keep an eye on things. It's Visiting Day."

Mr. Manly looked up. "That's right, it is. You know, I didn't tell you I been wanting to make an announcement. I believe I'll do it right now—sure, while some of them have their relatives here visiting." Mr. Manly's expression was bright and cheerful, as if he thought this was sure a swell idea.

"I don't know what you're doing," Shelby said, "but so far it isn't worth a rat's ass, is it?" He sat facing his brother, Virgil, who was leaning in against the table and looking directly at Frank to show he was sincere and doing everything he could to find out when the goddamn train was leaving. There were convicts and their visitors all the way down the line of tables that divided the mess hall: hunched over talking, filling the room with a low hum of voices.

"It ain't like looking up a schedule," Virgil said. "I believe this would be a special train, two or three cars probably. All right, I ask a lot of questions over at the railroad yard they begin wondering who I am, and somebody says hey, that's Virgil Shelby. His brother's up on the hill."

"That's Virgil Shelby," Frank said. "Jesus, do you believe people know who you are? You could be a mine engineer. You could be interested in hauling in equipment and you ask how they handle special trains. 'You ever put on a special run? You do? Like what kind?' Jesus, I mean you got to use your head and think for a change."

"Frank, I'm ready. I don't need to know more than a day ahead when you leave. I got me some good boys and, I'm telling you, we're going to *do* it."

"You're going to do what?"

"Get you off that train."

"How?"

"Stop it if we have to."

"How, Virgil?"

"Dynamite the track."

"Then what?"

"Then climb aboard."

"With the guards shooting at you?"

"You got to be doing something too," Virgil said. "Inside the train."

"I'm doing something right now. I'm seeing you don't know

what you're talking about. And unless we know when the train leaves and where it stops, we're not going to be able to work out a plan. Do you see that, Virgil?"

"The train goes to Florence. We know that."

"Do we know if it stops anywhere? If it stops, Virgil, wouldn't that be the place to get on?"

"If it stops."

"That's right. That's what you got to find out. Because how are you going to know where to wait and when to wait if you don't know when the train's leaving here? Virgil, are you listening to me?"

His brother was looking past him at something. Shelby glanced over his shoulder. He turned then and kept looking as Mr. Manly, with Bob Fisher on the stairs at the far end of the mess hall, said, "May I have your attention a moment, please?"

Mr. Manly waited until the hum of voices trailed off and he saw the faces down the line of tables looking toward him: upturned, solemn faces, like people in church waiting for the sermon. Mr. Manly grinned. He always liked to open with a light touch.

He said, "I'm not going to make a speech, if any of you are worried about that. I just want to make a brief announcement while your relatives and loved ones are here. It will save the boys writing to tell you and I know some of them don't write as often as they should. By the way, I'm Everett Manly, the acting superintendent here in Mr. Rynning's absence." He paused to clear his throat.

"Now then—I am very pleased to announce that this will be the last Visiting Day at Yuma Territorial Prison. A week from tomorrow the first group of men will leave on the Southern Pacific for the new penitentiary at Florence, a fine new place I think you all are going to be very pleased with. Now you won't be able to tell your relatives or loved ones what day exactly you'll be leaving, but I promise you in three weeks everybody will be out of here and this place will open its doors forever and become a page in history. That's about all I can tell you right now for the present. However, if any of you have questions I will be glad to try and answer them."

Frank Shelby kept looking at the little man on the stairway. He said to himself, It's a trick. But the longer he stared at him—the lit-

tle fellow standing up there waiting for questions—he knew Mr.
Manly was telling the truth.

Virgil said, "Well, I guess that answers the question, doesn't it?"

Shelby didn't look at his brother. He was afraid he might lose
his temper and hit Virgil in the mouth.

ELEVEN

For three sacks of Mail Pouch, R. E. Baylis told Shelby the convicts would be sent out in groups of about forty at a time, going over every other day, it looked like, on the regular morning run.

R. E. Baylis even got Shelby a Southern Pacific schedule. Leave Yuma at 6:15 A.M. Pass through Sentinel at 8:56; no stop unless they needed coal or water. They'd stop at Gila at 9:51, where they'd be fed on the train; no one allowed off. They'd arrive in Phoenix at 2:40 P.M., switch the cars over to a Phoenix & Eastern train and arrive at Florence about 5:30 P.M. Bob Fisher planned to make the first run and the last one, the first one to see what the trip was like and the last one so he could lock up and officially hand over the keys.

Shelby asked R. E. Baylis if he would put him and his friends down for the first run, because they were sure anxious to get out of here. R. E. Baylis said he didn't know if it could be done, but maybe he could try to arrange it. Shelby gave him fifty dollars to try as hard as he could.

The guard told Bob Fisher about Shelby's request, since Fisher would see the list anyway. Why the first train? Fisher wanted to know. What was the difference? R. E. Baylis asked. All the trains were going to the penitentiary. Fisher put himself in Shelby's place and thought about it a while. Maybe Shelby was anxious to leave, that could be a fact. But it wasn't the reason he wanted to be on the first train. It was so he would know exactly which train he'd be on, so he could tell somebody outside.

Fisher said all right, tell him he could go on the first train. But then, when the time came, they'd pull Shelby out of line and hold him for the last train. "I want him riding with me," Fisher said, "But not before I look over the route."

It bothered R. E. Baylis because Shelby had always treated him square and given him tobacco and things. He stopped by Shelby's cell that evening and said Lord, he could sure use that fifty dollars, but he would give it back. Bob Fisher was making them go on the last train. Shelby looked pretty disappointed. By God, he was big about it though. He let R. E. Baylis keep the fifty dollars anyway.

The next morning when he saw Junior and Soonzy and Joe Dean, Shelby grinned and said, "Boys, always trust a son of a bitch to be a son of a bitch. We're taking the last train."

All he had to do now was to get a letter of instructions to Virgil at the railroad hotel in Yuma. For a couple more sacks of Mail Pouch R. E. Baylis would probably deliver it personally.

Virgil Shelby and his three men arrived at Stout's Hotel in Gila on a Wednesday afternoon. Mr. Stout and a couple of Southern Pacific division men in the lobby got a kick out of these dudes who said they were heading south into the Saucedas to do some prospecting. All they had were bedrolls and rifles and a pack mule loaded with suitcases. The dudes were as serious about it though as they were ignorant. They bought four remount horses at the livery and two 50-pound cases of No. 1 dynamite at Tom Child's trading store, and on Thursday morning they rode out of Gila. They rode south two miles before turning west and doubling back to follow the train tracks.

They arrived in sight of the Southern Pacific water stop at Sentinel that evening and from a grove of trees studied the wooden buildings and frame structure that stood silently against a dark line of palo verdes. A water tank, a coaling shed, a section house and a little one-room station with a light showing in the window, that's all there was here.

As soon as Virgil saw the place he knew Frank was right again. Sometimes it made him mad when he sounded dumb in front of his brother. He had finished the sixth grade and Frank had gone on to the seventh or eighth. Maybe when Frank was looking at him, waiting, he would say the wrong thing or sound dumb; but Jesus, he had gone into places with a gun and put the gun in a man's face and got what he wanted. Frank didn't have to worry about him going in with a gun. He had not found out the important facts of the matter talking to the railroad people. He had not thought up the plan in all the time he'd had to do it. But he could sure do what Frank said in his letter. He had three good boys who would go with him for two hundred and fifty dollars each and bring the guns and know how to use them. These boys drank too much and got in fights, but they were the captains for this kind of work. Try and pick them. Try and get three fellows who had the nerve to stop a prison train and take off the people you wanted and do it right, without a lot of shooting and getting nervous and running off into the desert and hiding in a cave. He wished he had more like them, but these three said they could do the job and would put their guns on anybody for two hundred and fifty dollars.

He had a man named Howard Crowder who had worked for railroad lines in both the United States and Mexico, before he turned to holding up trains and spent ten years in Yuma.

He had an old hand named Dancey who had ridden with him and Frank before, and had been with them at the Cornelia Mine payroll robbery and had got away.

He had a third one named Billy Santos who had smuggled across the border whatever could be carried and was worth anything and knew all the trails and water holes south of here.

Five o'clock the next morning it still looked good and still looked easy as they walked into the little station at Sentinel with their suitcases and asked the S.P. man when the next eastbound train was coming through.

The S.P. man said 8:56 this morning, but that train was not due to stop on account of it was carrying convicts some place.

Virgil asked him if there was anybody over in the section house. The S.P. man said no, he was alone. A crew had gone out on the 8:45 to Gila the night before and another crew was coming from Yuma sometime today.

Virgil looked over at Billy Santos. Billy went outside. Howard Crowder and Dancey remained sitting on the bench. The suitcases and bedrolls and rifles and two cases of dynamite were on the floor by them. No, the S.P. man behind the counter said, they couldn't take the 8:56, though they could get on the 8:48 this evening if they wanted to hang around all day. But what will you do with your horses? he said then. You rode in here, didn't you?

Virgil was at the counter now. He nodded to the telegrapher's key on the desk behind the S.P. man and said, "I hope you can work that thing, mister."

The S.P. man said, "Sure, I can work it. Else I wouldn't be here."

"That's good," Virgil said. "It's better if they hear a touch they are used to hearing."

The S.P. man gave Virgil a funny look, then let his gaze shift over to the two men on the bench with all the gear in front of them. They looked back at him; they didn't move or say anything. The S.P. man was wondering if he should send a message to the division office at Gila; tell them there were three dudes hanging around here with rifles and dynamite and ask if they had been seen in Gila the day before. He could probably get away with it. How would these people know what he was saying? Just then the Mexican-looking one came back in, his eyes on the one standing by the counter, and shook his head.

Virgil said, "You all might as well get dressed."

The S.P. man watched them open the suitcases and take out gray and white convict suits. He watched them pull the pants and coats on over the clothes they were wearing and shove revolvers down into the pants and button the coats. One of them brought a double-barrel shotgun out of a suitcase in two pieces and sat down to fit the stock to the barrels. Watching them, the S.P. man said to Virgil Shelby, "Hey, what's going on? What is this?"

"This is how you stop a train," Virgil told him. "These are prisoners that escaped off the train that come through the day before yesterday."

"Nobody escaped," the S.P. man said.

Virgil nodded up and down. "Yes, they did, mister, and I'm the deputy sheriff of Maricopa County who's going to put them back on the train for Florence."

"If you're a deputy of this county," the S.P. man said, "then you're a new one."

"All right," Virgil said, "I'm a new one."

"If you're one at all."

Virgil pulled a .44 revolver from inside his coat and pointed it in the S.P. man's face. He said, "All you got to do is telegraph the Yuma depot at exactly six A.M. with a message for the prison superintendent, Mr. Everett Manly. You're going to say three escaped convicts are being held here at Sentinel and you request the train to stop and take them aboard. You also request an immediate answer and, mister," Virgil said, "I don't want you to send it one word different than I tell it to you. You understand?"

The S.P. man nodded. "I understand, but it ain't going to work. If three were missing at the head-count when they got to Florence, they would have already told Yuma about it."

"That's a fact," Virgil said. "That's why we had somebody wire the prison from Phoenix Wednesday night and report three missing." Virgil looked around then and said, "Howard?"

The one named Howard Crowder had a silver dollar in his hand. He began tapping the coin rapidly on the wooden bench next to him in sharp longs and shorts that were loud in the closed room. Virgil watched the expression on the S.P. man's face, the mouth come open a little.

"You understand that too?" Virgil asked him.

The S.P. man nodded.

"What did he say?"

"He said, 'Send correct message or you are a dead man.' "

"I'm happy you understand it," Virgil said.

The S.P. man watched the one named Dancey pry open a wooden case that was marked *High Explosives—Dangerous* and take out a paraffin-coated packet of dynamite sticks. He watched Dancey get out a coil of copper wire and detonator caps and work the wire gently into the open end of the cap and then crimp the end closed with his teeth. The Mexican-looking one was taking a box plunger out of a canvas bag. The S.P. man said to himself, My God, somebody is going to get killed and I am going to see it.

At six A.M. he sent the message to the depot at Yuma, where they would then be loading the convicts onto the train.

The Southern Pacific equipment that left Yuma that Friday morning was made up of a 4-4-0 locomotive, a baggage car, two day coaches for regular passengers (though only eleven people were aboard), another baggage car, and an old wooden coach from the Cannanea-Rio Yaqui-El Pacifico line. The last twenty-seven convicts to leave the prison were locked inside this coach along with Bob Fisher and three armed guards. Behind, bringing up the rear, was a caboose that carried Mr. Manly and three more guards.

Bob Fisher had personally made up the list of prisoners for this last run to Florence: only twenty-seven, including Frank Shelby and his bunch. Most of the others were short-term prisoners and trusties who wouldn't be expected to make trouble. A small, semi-harmless group which, Bob Fisher believed, would make it easy for him to keep an eye on Shelby. Also aboard were the TB convicts, the two women and Harold Jackson and Raymond San Carlos.

Harold and Raymond were near the rear of the coach. The only ones behind them were Bob Fisher and the guards. Ahead of them

were the TB convicts, then two rows of empty seats, then the rest
of the prisoners scattered along both sides of the aisle in the back-
to-back straw seats. The two women were in the front of the coach.
The doors at both ends were padlocked. The windows were glass,
but they were not made to open.

Before the train was five minutes out of Yuma every convict in
the coach knew they were going to stop in Sentinel to pick up three
men who had escaped on Wednesday and had been recaptured the
next day. There was a lot of talk about who the three were.

Bob Fisher didn't say a word. He sat patiently waiting for the
train to reach Sentinel, thinking about the message they had
received Wednesday evening: *Three convicts missing on arrival
Phoenix. Local and county authorities alerted.* Signed, *Sheriff,
Maricopa County.* What bothered Fisher, there had been no information sent from Florence, nothing from Mr. Rynning, no further
word from anybody until the wire was received at the depot this
morning. Mr. Manly had wired back they would stop for the prisoners and Bob Fisher had not said a word to anybody since. Something wasn't right and he had to think it through.

About 7:30 A.M., halfway to Sentinel, Fisher said to the guard
sitting next to him, "Put your gun on Frank Shelby and don't move
it till we get to Florence."

Harold Jackson, next to the window, looked out at the flat desert
country that stretched to distant dark mounds, mountains that would
take a day to reach on foot, maybe half a day if a man was to run.
But a mountain was nothing to run to. There was nothing out there
but sky and rocks and desert growth that looked as if it would
never die, but offered a man no hope of life. It was the same land
he had looked at a few months before, going in the other direction,
sitting in the same upright straw seat handcuffed to a sheriff's man.
The Indian sitting next to him now nudged his arm and Harold
looked up.

The Davis woman was coming down the aisle from the front of
the coach. She passed them and a moment later Harold heard the
door to the toilet open and close. Looking out the window again,
Harold said, 'What's out there, that way?"

"Mexico," Raymond answered. "Across the desert and the mountain, and if you can find water, Mexico."

"You know where the water is?"

"First twenty-five, thirty miles there isn't any."

"What about after that?"

"I know some places."

"You could find them?"

"I'm not going through the window if that's what you're thinking about."

"The train's going to stop in Sentinel".

"They open the door to put people on," Raymond said. "They ain't letting anybody off."

"We don't know what they going to do," Harold said, "till we get there." He heard the woman come out of the toilet compartment and waited for her to walk past.

She didn't appear. Harold turned to look out the window across the aisle. Over his shoulder he could see the Davis woman standing by Bob Fisher's seat. She was saying something but keeping her voice down and he couldn't make out the words. He heard Fisher though.

Fisher said, "Is that right?" The woman said something else and Fisher said, "If you don't know where what's the good of telling me? How are you helping? Anybody could say what you're saying and if it turns out right try to get credit. But you haven't told me nothing yet."

"All right," Norma Davis said. "It's going to be at Sentinel."

"You could be guessing, for all I know."

"Take my word," the woman said.

Bob Fisher didn't say anything for a while. The train swayed and clicked along the tracks and there was no sound behind Harold Jackson. He glanced over his shoulder. Fisher was getting up, handing his revolver to the guard sitting across the aisle. Then he was past Harold, walking up the aisle and holding the woman by the arm to move her along ahead of him.

Frank Shelby looked up as they stopped at his seat. He was sitting with Junior; Soonzy and Joe Dean were facing them.

"This lady says you're going to try to escape," Fisher said to Shelby. "What do you think about that?"

Shelby's shoulders and head swayed slightly with the motion of the train. He looked up at Fisher and Norma, looking from one to the other before he said, "If I haven't told her any such thing, how would she know?"

"She says you're getting off at Sentinel."

"Well, if she tells me how I'm going to do it and it sounds good, I might try it." Shelby grinned a little. "Do you believe her?"

"I believe she might be telling a story," Fisher said, "but I also believe it might be true. That's why I've got a gun pointed at your head till we get to Florence. Do you understand me?"

"I sure do." Shelby nodded, looking straight up at Bob Fisher. He said then, "Do you mind if I have a talk with Norma? I'd like to know why she's making up stories."

"She's all yours," Fisher said.

Harold nudged Raymond. They watched Fisher coming back down the aisle. Beyond him they saw Junior get up to give the Davis woman his seat. Tacha was turned around watching. She moved over close to the window as Junior approached her and sat down.

Behind Harold and Raymond one of the guards said, "You letting the woman sit with the men?"

"They're all the same as far as I can see," Fisher answered. "All convicts."

Virgil Shelby, holding a shotgun across his arm, was out on the platform when the train came into sight. He heard it and saw its smoke first, then spotted the locomotive way down the tracks. This was the worst part, right now, seeing the train getting bigger and bigger and seeing the steam blowing out with the screeching sound of the brakes. The locomotive was rolling slowly as it came past the coaling shed and the water tower, easing into the station, rolling past the platform now hissing steam, the engine and the baggage cars and the two coaches with the half-dozen faces in the windows looking out at him. He could feel those people staring at him, wondering who he was. Virgil didn't look back at them. He kept his eyes on the last coach and caboose and saw them jerk to a stop before reaching the platform—out on open ground just this side of the water tower.

"Come on out," Virgil said to the station house.

Howard Crowder and Dancey and Billy Santos came out into the sunlight through the open door. Their hands were behind their backs, as though they might have been tied. Virgil moved them out of the doorway, down to the end of the platform and stood them against the wall of the building: three convicts waiting to be put aboard a prison train, tired-looking, beaten, their hat brims pulled down against the bright morning glare.

Virgil watched Bob Fisher, followed by another guard with a rifle come down the step-rungs at the far end of the prison coach. Two more guards with rifles were coming along the side of the caboose and somebody else was in the caboose window: a man wearing glasses who was sticking his head out and saying something to the two guards who had come out of the prison coach.

Bob Fisher didn't look around at Mr. Manly in the caboose window. He kept his gaze on the three convicts and the man with the shotgun. He called out, "What're the names of those men you got?"

"I'm just delivering these people," Virgil called back. "I wasn't introduced to them."

Bob Fisher and the guard with him and the two guards from the caboose came on past the prison coach but stopped before they reached the platform.

"You the only one guarding them?" Fisher asked.

"Yes, sir, I'm the one found them, I'm the one brought them in."

"I've seen you some place," Fisher said.

"Sure, delivering a prisoner. About a year ago."

"Where's the station man at?"

"He's inside."

"Call him out."

"I reckon he heard you." Virgil looked over his shoulder as the S.P. man appeared in the doorway. "There he is. Hey, listen, you want these three boys or don't you? I been watching them all night, I'm tired."

"I want to know who they are," Fisher said. "If you're not going to tell me, I want them to call out their names."

There was silence. Virgil knew the time had come and he had to put the shotgun on Fisher and fill up the silence and get this thing done right now, or else drop the gun and forget the whole thing. No more than eight seconds passed in the silence, though it seemed like eight minutes to Virgil. Bob Fisher's hand went inside his coat and Virgil didn't have to think about it any more. He heard glass shatter as somebody kicked through a window in the prison coach. Bob Fisher drew a revolver, half turning toward the prison coach at the same time, but not turning quickly enough as Virgil put the shotgun on him and gave him a load point-blank in the side of the chest. And as the guards saw Fisher go down and were raising their rifles the three men in convict clothes brought their revolvers from behind their backs and fired as fast as they could swing their guns from one gray suit to another. All three guards were dropped where they stood, though one of them, on his knees, shot Billy Santos through the head before Virgil could get his shotgun on the man and finish him with the second load.

A rifle came out the caboose window and a barrel smashed the glass of a window in the prison coach, but it was too late. Virgil was pressed close to the side of the baggage car, out of the line of fire, and the two men in prison clothes had the S.P. man and were using him for a shield as they backed into the station house.

Virgil could look directly across the platform to the open doorway. He took time to reload the shotgun. He looked up and down the length of the train, then over at the doorway again.

"Hey, Dancey," Virgil called over, "send that train man out with the dynamite."

He had to wait a little bit before the S.P. man appeared in the doorway, straining to hold the fifty-pound case in his arms, having trouble with the dead weight, or else terrified of what he was holding.

"Walk down to the end of the platform with it," Virgil told him, "so they can see what you got. When you come back, walk up by that first passenger coach. Where everybody's looking out the window."

Jesus, the man could hardly take a step he was so scared of dropping the case. When he was down at the end of the platform, the copper wire trailing behind him and leading into the station. Virgil stepped away from the baggage car and called out, "Hey, you guards! You hear me? Throw out your guns and come out with your hands in the air, or we're going to put dynamite under a passenger coach and blow everybody clear to hell. You hear me?"

They heard him.

Mr. Manly and the three guards who were left came out to stand by the caboose. The prisoners began to yell and break the windows on both sides of the coach, but they quieted down when Frank Shelby and his three boys walked off the train and wouldn't let anybody else follow.

They are going to shoot us, Mr. Manly said to himself. He saw Frank Shelby looking toward them. Then Frank was looking at the dead guards and at Bob Fisher in particular. "I wish you hadn't of killed him," he heard Shelby say.

"I had to," the man with the shotgun said.

And then Shelby said, "I wanted to do it."

Junior said that if he hadn't kicked out the window they might still be in there. That was all they said for a while that Mr. Manly heard. Shelby and his three convict friends went into the station house. They came out a few minutes later wearing work clothes and might have been ranch hands for all anybody would know to look at them.

Mr. Manly didn't see who it was that placed the case of dynamite at the front end of the train, under the cowcatcher, but saw one of them playing out the wire back along the platform and around the off side of the station house. Standing on the platform, Frank Shelby and the one with the shotgun seemed to be in a serious conversation. Then Frank said something to Junior, who boarded the train again and brought out Norma Davis. Mr. Manly could see she was frightened, as if afraid they were going to shoot her or do something to her. Junior and Joe Dean took her into the station house. Frank Shelby came over then. Mr. Manly expected him to draw a gun.

"Four of us are leaving," Shelby said. "You can have the rest."

"What about the woman?"

"I mean five of us. Norma's going along."

"You're not going to harm her, are you?" Shelby kept staring at him, and Mr. Manly couldn't think straight. All he could say was, "I hope you know that what you're doing is wrong, an offence against Almighty God as well as your fellowman."

"Jesus Christ," Shelby said, and walked away.

Lord, help me, Mr. Manly said, and called out, "Frank, listen to me."

But Shelby didn't look back. The platform was deserted now except for the Mexican-looking man who lay dead with his arm hanging over the edge. They were mounting horses on the other side of the station. Mr. Manly could hear the horses. Then, from where he stood, he could see several of the horses past the corner of the building. He saw Junior stand in his stirrups to reach the telegraph wire at the edge of the roof and cut it with a knife. Another man was on the ground, stooped over a wooden box. Shelby nodded to him and kicked his horse, heading out into the open desert, away from the station. As the rest of them followed, raising a thin dust cloud, the man on the ground pushed down on the box.

The dynamite charge raised the front end of the locomotive off the track, derailed the first baggage car and sent the coaches slamming back against each other, twisting the couplings and tearing loose the end car, rolling it a hundred feet down the track. Mr. Manly dropped flat with the awful, ear-splitting sound of the explosion. He wasn't sure if he threw himself down or was knocked down by the concussion. When he opened his eyes there was dirt in his mouth, his head throbbed as if he had been hit with a hammer, and for a minute or so he could see nothing but smoke or dust or steam from the engine, a cloud that enveloped the station and lay heavily over the platform.

He heard men's voices. He was aware of one of the guards lying close to him and looked to see if the man was hurt. The guard was pushing himself up, shaking his head. Mr. Manly got quickly to his feet and looked around. The caboose was no longer behind him; it was down the track and the prison coach was only a few feet away where the convicts were coming out, coughing and waving at the smoke with their hands. Mr. Manly called out, "Is anybody hurt?"

No one answered him directly. The convicts were standing around; they seemed dazed. No one was attempting to run away. He saw one of the guards with a rifle now on the platform, holding the gun on the prisoners, who were paying no attention to him. At the other end of the platform there were a few people from the passenger coach. They stood looking at the locomotive that was shooting white steam and stood leaning awkwardly toward the platform, as if it might fall over any minute.

He wanted to be doing something. He had to be doing something. Five prisoners gone, four guards dead, a train blown up, telegraph line cut, no idea when help would come or where to go from here. He could hear Mr. Rynning saying, "You let them do all that? Man, this is your responsibility and you'll answer for it."

"Captain, you want us to follow them?"

Mr. Manly turned, not recognizing the voice at first. Harold Jackson, the Zulu, was standing next to him.

"What? I'm sorry, I didn't hear you."

"I said, you want us to follow them? Me and Raymond."

Mr. Manly perked up. "There are horses here?"

"No-suh, man say the nearest horses are at Gila. That's most of a day's ride."

"Then how would you expect to follow them?"

"We run, captain."

"There are eight of them—on horses."

"We don't mean to fight them, captain. We mean maybe we can follow them and see which way they go. Then when you get some help, you know, maybe we can tell this help where they went."

"They'll be thirty miles away before dark."

"So will we, captain."

"Follow them on foot—"

"Yes-suh, only we would have to go right now. Captain, they going to run those horses at first to get some distance and we would have to run the first five, six miles, no stopping, to keep their dust in sight. Raymond say it's all flat and open, no water. Just some little bushes. We don't have to follow them all day. We see where they going and get back here at dark."

Mr. Manly was frowning, looking around because, Lord, there was too much to think about at one time. He said, "I can't send convicts to chase after convicts. My God."

"They do it in Florida, captain. Trusties handle the dogs. I seen it."

"I have to get the telegraph wire fixed, that's the main thing."

"I hear the train man say they busted his key, he don't know if he can fix it," Harold Jackson said. "You going to sit here till tonight before anybody come—while Frank Shelby and them are making distance. But if me and the Apache follow them we can leave signs."

Mr. Manly noticed Raymond San Carlos now behind Harold. Raymond was nodding. "Sure," he said, "we can leave pieces of our clothes for them to follow if you give us something else to wear. Maybe you should give us some guns too, in case we get close to them, or for firing signals."

"I can't do that," Mr. Manly said. "No, I can't give you guns."

"How about our spears then?" Raymond said. "We get hungry we could use the spears maybe to stick something."

"The spears might be all right." Mr. Manly nodded.

"Spears and two canteens of water," Raymond said. "And the other clothes. Some people see us they won't think we're convicts running away."

"Pair of pants and a shirt," Mr. Manly said.

"And a couple of blankets. In case we don't get back before dark and we got to sleep outside. We can get our bedrolls and the spears," Raymond said. "They're with all the baggage in that car we loaded."

"You'd try to be back before dark?"

"Yes, sir, we don't like to sleep outside if we don't have to."

"Well," Mr. Manly said. He paused. He was trying to think of an alternative. He didn't believe that sending these two out would do any good. He pictured them coming back at dusk and sinking to the ground exhausted. But at least it would be doing something—now. Mr. Rynning or somebody would ask him, What did you do?

And he'd say, I sent trackers out after them. I got these two boys that are runners. He said, "Well, find your stuff and get started. I'll tell the guards."

They left the water stop at Sentinel running almost due south. They ran several hundred yards before looking back to see the smoke still hanging in a dull cloud over the buildings and the palo verde trees. They ran for another half-mile or so, loping easily and not speaking, carrying their spears and their new guard-gray pants and shirts wrapped in their blanket rolls. They ran until they reached a gradual rise and ran down the other side to find themselves in a shallow wash, out of sight of the water stop.

They looked at each other now. Harold grinned and Raymond grinned. They sat down on the bank of the wash and began laughing, until soon both of them had tears in their eyes.

TWELVE

Harold said, "What way do we go?"

Raymond got up on the bank of the dry wash and stood looking out at the desert that was a flat burned-out waste as far as they could see. There were patches of dusty scrub growth, but no cactus or trees from here to the dark rise of the mountains to the south.

"That way," Raymond said. "To the Crater Mountains and down to the Little Ajos. Two days we come to Ajo, the town, steal some horses, go on south to Bates Well. The next day we come to Quitobaquito, a little water-hole village, and cross the border. After that, I don't know."

"Three days, uh?"

"Without horses."

"Frank Shelby, he going the same way?"

"He could go to Clarkstown instead of Ajo. They near each other. One the white man's town, the other the Mexican town."

"But he's going the same way we are."

"There isn't no other way south from here."

"I'd like to get him in front of me one minute," Harold said.

"Man," Raymond said, "you would have to move fast to get him first."

"Maybe we run into him sometime."

"Only if we run," Raymond said.

Harold was silent a moment. "If we did, we'd get out of here quicker, wouldn't we? If we run."

"Sure, maybe save a day. If we're any good."

"You think we couldn't run to those mountains?"

"Sure we could, we wanted to."

"Is there water?"

"There used to be."

"Then that's probably where he's heading to camp tonight, uh? What do you think?"

"He's got to go that way. He might as well."

"We was to get there tonight," Harold said, "we might run into him."

"We might run into all of them."

"Not if we saw them first. Waited for him to get alone."

Raymond grinned. "Play with him a little."

"Man, that would be good, wouldn't it?" Harold said. "Scare him some."

"Scare hell out of him."

"Paint his face," Harold said. He began to smile thinking about it.

"Take his clothes. Paint him all over."

"Now you talking. You got any?"

"I brought some iodine and a little bottle of white. Listen," Raymond said, "we're going that way. Why don't we take a little run and see how Frank's doing?"

Harold stood up. When they had tied their blanket rolls across one shoulder and picked up their spears, the Apache and the Zulu began their run across the southern Arizona desert.

They ran ten miles in the furnace heat of sand and rock and dry, white-crusted playas and didn't break their stride until the sun was directly over head. They walked a mile and ran another mile before they stopped to rest and allowed themselves a drink of water from the canteens, a short drink and then a mouthful they held in their mouths while they screwed closed the canteens and hung them over their shoulders again. They rested fifteen minutes and before the tiredness could creep in to stiffen their legs they stood up without a word and started off again toward the mountains.

For a mile or so they would be aware of their running. Then, in time, they would become lost in the monotonous stride of their pace, running, but each somewhere else in his mind, seeing cool mountain pastures or palm trees or thinking of nothing at all, running and hearing themselves sucking the heated air in and letting it out, but not feeling the agony of running. They had learned to do this in the past months, to detach themselves and be inside or outside the running man but not part of him for long minutes at a time. When they broke stride they would always walk and sometimes run again before resting. At times they felt they were getting no closer to the mountains, though finally the slopes began to take shape, changing from a dark mass to dun-colored slopes and shadowed contours. At mid-afternoon they saw the first trace of dust rising in the distance. Both of them saw it and they kept their eyes on the wispy, moving cloud that would rise and vanish against the sky. The dust was something good to watch and seeing it was better than stretching out in the grass and going to sleep. It meant Frank Shelby was only a few miles ahead of them.

They came to the arroyo in the shadowed foothills of the Crater Mountains a little after five o'clock. There was good brush cover here and a natural road that would take them up into high country. They would camp above Shelby if they could and watch him, Raymond said, but first he had to go out and find the son of a bitch. You rest, he told Harold, and the Zulu gave him a dead-pan look and stared at him until he was gone. Harold sat back against the cool, shaded wall of the gulley. He wouldn't let himself go to sleep though. He kept his eyes open and waited for the Apache, listening and not moving, letting the tight weariness ease out of his body. By the time Raymond returned the arroyo was dark. The only light they could see were sun reflections on the high peaks above them.

"They're in some trees," Raymond said, "about a half-mile from here. Taking it easy, they even got a fire."

"All of them there?"

"I count eight, eight horses."

"Can we get close?"

"Right above them. Frank's put two men up in the rocks—they can see all around the camp."

"What do you think?" Harold said.

"I think we should take the two in the rocks. See what Frank does in the morning when nobody's there."

The grin spread over Harold's face. That sounded pretty good.

They slept for a few hours and when they woke up it was night. Harold touched Raymond. The Indian sat up without making a sound. He opened a canvas bag and took out the small bottles of iodine and white paint and they began to get ready.

There was no sun yet on this side of the mountain, still cold dark in the early morning when Virgil Shelby came down out of the rocks and crossed the open slope to the trees. He could make out his brother and the woman by the fire. He could hear the horses and knew Frank's men were saddling them and gathering up their gear.

Frank and the woman looked up as Virgil approached, and Frank said, "They coming?"

"I don't know. I didn't see them."

"What do you mean you didn't see them?"

"They weren't up there."

Frank Shelby got up off the ground. He dumped his coffee as he walked to the edge of the trees to look up at the tumbled rocks and the escarpment that rose steeply against the sky.

"They're asleep somewhere," he said. "You must've looked the wrong places."

"I looked all over up there."

"They're asleep," Shelby said. "Go on up there and look again."

When Virgil came back the second time Frank said, Jesus Christ, what good are you? And sent Junior and Joe Dean up into the rocks. When they came down he went up himself to have a look and was still up there as the sunlight began to spread over the slope and they could feel the heat of day coming down on them.

"There's no sign of anything," Virgil said. "There's no sign they were even here."

"I put them here," Frank Shelby said. "One right where you're standing, Dancey over about a hundred feet. I put them here myself."

"Well, they're not here now," Virgil said.

"Jesus Christ, I know that." Frank looked over at Junior and Soonzy. "You counted the horses?"

"We'd a-heard them taking horses."

"I asked if you counted them!"

"Christ, we got them saddled. I don't have to count them."

"Then they walked away," Frank Shelby said, his tone quieter now.

Virgil shook his head. "I hadn't paid them yet."

"They walked away," Shelby said again. "I don't know why, but they did."

"Can you see Dancey walking off into the mountains?" Virgil said. "I'm telling you I hadn't *paid* them."

"There's nothing up there could have carried them off. No animal, no man. There is no sign they did anything but walk away," Shelby said, "and that's the way we're going to leave it."

He said no more until they were down in the trees again, ready to ride out. Nobody said anything.

Then Frank told Joe Dean he was to ride ahead of them like a point man. Virgil, he said, was to stay closer in the hills and ride swing, though he would also be ahead of them looking for natural trails.

"Looking for trails," Virgil said. "If you believe those two men walked off, then what is it that's tightening up your hind end?"

"You're older than me," Frank said, "but no bigger, and I will sure close your mouth if you want it done."

"Jesus, can't you take some kidding?"

"Not from you," his brother said.

They were in a high meadow that had taken more than an hour to reach, at least a thousand feet above Shelby's camp. Dancey and Howard Crowder sat on the ground close to each other. The Apache and the Zulu stood off from them leaning on their spears, their blankets laid over their shoulders as they waited for the sun to spread across the field. They would be leaving in a few minutes. They planned to get out ahead of Shelby and be waiting for him. These two, Dancey and Crowder, they would leave here. They had taken their revolvers and gun belts, the only things they wanted from them.

"They're going to kill us," Dancey whispered.

Howard Crowder told him for God sake to keep quiet, they'd hear him.

They had been in the meadow most of the night, brought here after each had been sitting in the rocks, drowsing, and had felt the spear point at the back of his neck. They hadn't got a good look at the two yet. They believed both were Indians—even though there were no Indians around here, and no Indians had carried spears in fifty years. Then they would have to be loco Indians escaped from an asylum or kicked out of their village. That's what they were. That's why Dancey believed they were going to kill him and Howard.

Finally, in the morning light, when the Zulu walked over to them and Dancey got a close look at his face—God Almighty, with the paint and the scars and the short pointed beard and the earring—he closed his eyes and expected to feel the spear in his chest any second.

Harold said, "You two wait here till after we're gone."

Dancey opened his eyes and Howard Crowder said "What?"

"We're going to leave, then you can find your way out of here."

Howard Crowder said, "But we don't know where we are."

"You up on a mountain."

"How do we get down?"

"You look around for a while you find a trail. By that time your friends will be gone without you, so you might as well go home." Howard started to turn away.

"Wait a minute," Howard Crowder said. "We don't have horses, we don't have any food or water. How are we supposed to get across the desert?"

"It's up to you," Harold said. "Walk if you want or stay here and die, it's up to you."

"We didn't do nothing to you," Dancey said.

Harold looked at him. "That's why we haven't killed you."

"Then what do you want us for?"

"We don't want you," Harold said. "We want Frank Shelby."

Virgil rejoined the group at noon to report he hadn't seen a thing, not any natural trail either that would save them time. They were into the foothills of the Little Ajos and he sure wished Billy Santos had not got shot in the head in the train station, because Billy would have had them to Clarkstown by now. They would be sitting at a table with cold beer and fried meat instead of squatting on the ground eating hash out of a can. He asked if he should stay with the group now. Norma Davis looked pretty good even if she was kind of sweaty and dirty; she was built and had nice long hair. He wouldn't mind riding with her a while and maybe arranging something for that night.

Frank, it looked like, was still not talking. Virgil asked him again if he should stay with the group and this time Frank said no and told him to finish his grub and ride out. He said, "Find the road to Clarkstown or don't bother coming back, because there would be no use of having you around."

So Virgil and Joe Dean rode out about fifteen minutes ahead of the others. When they split up Virgil worked his way deeper into the foothills to look for some kind of a road. He crossed brush slopes and arroyos, holding to a south-southeast course, but he didn't see anything that resembled even a foot path. It was a few hours after leaving the group, about three o'clock in the afternoon, that Virgil came across the Indian and it was the damnedest thing he'd ever seen in his life.

There he was out in the middle of nowhere sitting at the shady edge of a mesquite thicket wrapped in an army blanket. A real Apache Indian, red headband and all and even with some paint on

his face and a staff or something that was sticking out of the
bushes. It looked like a fishing pole. That was the first thing Virgil
thought of: an Apache Indian out in the desert fishing in a mesquite patch—the damnedest thing he'd ever seen.

Virgil said, "Hey, Indin, you sabe English any?"

Raymond San Carlos remained squatted on the ground. He nodded once.

"I'm looking for the road to Clarkstown."

Raymond shook his head now. "I don't know."

"You speak pretty good. Tell me something, what're you doing
out here?"

"I'm not doing nothing."

"You live around here?"

Raymond pointed off to the side. "Not far."

"How come you got that paint on your face?"

"I just put it there."

"How come if you live around here you don't know where
Clarkstown is?"

"I don't know."

"Jesus, you must be a dumb Indin. Have you seen anybody else
come through here today?"

"Nobody."

"You haven't seen me, have you?"

"What?"

"You haven't seen nobody and you haven't seen me either."

Raymond said nothing.

"I don't know," Virgil said now. "Some sheriff's people ask you
you're liable to tell them, aren't you? You got family around here?"

"Nobody else."

"Just you all alone. Nobody would miss you then, would they?
Listen, buddy, I don't mean anything personal, but I'm afraid you
seeing me isn't a good idea. I'm going to have to shoot you."

Raymond stood up now, slowly.

"You can run if you want," Virgil said, "or you can stand there
and take it, I don't care; but don't start hollering and carrying on.
All right?"

Virgil was wearing a shoulder rig under his coat. He looked
down as he unbuttoned the one button, drew a .44 Colt and looked
up to see something coming at him and gasped as if the wind was
knocked out of him as he grabbed hold of the fishing pole sticking

out of his chest and saw the Indian standing there watching him and saw the sky and the sun, and that was all.

Raymond dragged Virgil's body into the mesquite. He left his spear in there too. He had two revolvers, a Winchester rifle and a horse. He didn't need a spear any more.

Joe Dean's horse smelled water. He was sure of it, so he let the animal have its head and Joe Dean went along for the ride—down into a wide canyon that was green and yellow with spring growth. When he saw the cottonwoods and then the round soft shape of the willows against the canyon slope, Joe Dean patted the horse's neck and guided him with the reins again.

It was a still pool, but not stagnant, undercutting a shelf of rock and mirroring the cliffs and canyon walls. Joe Dean dismounted. He led his horse down a bank of shale to the pool, then went belly-down at the edge and drank with his face in the water. He drank all he wanted before emptying the little bit left in his canteen and filling it to the top. Then he stretched out and drank again. He wished he had time to strip off his clothes and dive in. But he had better get the others first or Frank would see he'd bathed and start kicking and screaming again. Once he got them here they would probably all want to take a bath. That would be something, Norma in there with them, grabbing some of her under the water when Frank wasn't looking. Then she'd get out and lie up there on the bank to dry off in the sun. Nice soft white body—

Joe Dean was pushing himself up, looking at the pool and aware now of the reflections in the still water: the slope of the canyon wall high above, the shelf of rock behind him, sandy brown, and something else, something dark that resembled a man's shape, and he felt that cold prickly feeling up between his shouder blades to his neck.

It was probably a crevice, shadowed inside. It couldn't be a man. Joe Dean got to his feet, then turned around and looked up.

Harold Jackson—bare to the waist, and a blanket over one shoulder, with his beard and tribal scars and streak of white paint—stood looking down at him from the rock shelf.

"How you doing?" Harold said. "You get enough water?"

Joe Dean stared at him. He didn't answer right away. God, no. He was thinking and trying to decide quickly if it was a good thing or a bad thing to be looking up at Harold Jackson at a water hole in the Little Ajo Mountains.

He said finally, "How'd you get here?"

"Same way you did."

"You got away after we left?"

"Looks like it, don't it?"

"Well, that must've been something. Just you?"

"No, Raymond come with me."

"I don't see him. Where is he?"

"He's around some place."

"If there wasn't any horses left, how'd you get here?"

"How you think?"

"I'm asking you, Sambo."

"We run, Joe."

"You're saying you run here all the way from Sentinel?"

"Well, we stop last night," Harold said, and kept watching him. "Up in the Crater Mountains."

"Is that right? We camped up there too."

"I know you did," Harold said.

Joe Dean was silent for a long moment before he said, "You killed Howard and Dancey, didn't you?"

"No, we never killed them. We let them go."

"What do you want?"

"Not you, Joe. Unless you want to take part."

Joe Dean's revolver was in his belt. He didn't see a gun or a knife or anything on Harold, just the blanket over his shoulder and covering his arm. It looked like it would be pretty easy. So he drew his revolver.

As he did, though, Harold pulled the blanket across his body with his left hand. His right hand came up holding Howard Crowder's .44 and he shot Joe Dean with it three times in the chest. And now Harold had two revolvers, a rifle, and a horse. He left Joe Dean lying next to the pool for Shelby to find.

They had passed Clarkstown, Shelby decided. Missed it. Which meant they were still in the Little Ajo Mountains, past the chance of having a sit-down hot meal today, but that much closer to the border. That part was all right. What bothered him, they had not seen Virgil or Joe Dean since noon.

It was almost four o'clock now. Junior and Soonzy were riding ahead about thirty yards. Norma was keeping up with Shelby, staying close, afraid of him but more afraid of falling behind and finding herself alone. If Shelby didn't know where they were, Norma knew that she, by herself, would never find her way out. She had no idea why Shelby had brought her, other than at Virgil's request to have a woman along. No one had approached her in the camp last night. She knew, though, once they were across the border and the men relaxed and quit looking behind them, one of them, probably Virgil, would come to her with that fixed expression on his face and she would take him on and be nice to him as long as she had no other choice.

"We were through here one time," Shelby said. "We went up through Copper Canyon to Clarkstown the morning we went after the Cornelia Mine payroll. I don't see any familiar sights, though. It all looks the same."

She knew he wasn't speaking to her directly. He was thinking out loud, or stoking his confidence with the sound of his own voice.

"From here what we want to hit is Growler Pass," Shelby said. "Top the pass and we're at Bates Well. Then we got two ways to go. Southeast to Dripping Springs and on down to Sonoyta. Or a shorter trail to the border through Quitobaquito. I haven't decided yet which way we'll go. When Virgil comes in I'll ask him if Billy Santos said anything about which trail's best this time of the year."

"What happened to the two men last night?" Norma asked him.

Shelby didn't answer. She wasn't sure if she should ask him again. Before she could decide, Junior was riding back toward them and Shelby had reined in to wait for him.

Junior was grinning. "I believe Joe Dean's found us some water. His tracks lead into that canyon yonder and it's chock full of green brush and willow trees."

"There's a tank somewhere in these hills," Shelby said.

"Well, I believe we've found it," Junior said.

They found the natural tank at the end of the canyon. They found Joe Dean lying with his head and outstretched arms in the still water. And they found planted in the sand next to him, sticking straight up, a spear made of a bamboo fishing pole and a mortar trowel.

THIRTEEN

They camped on high ground south of Bates Well and in the morning came down through giant saguaro country, down through a hollow in the hills to within sight of Quitobaquito.

There it was, a row of weathered adobes and stock pens beyond a water hole that resembled a shallow, stagnant lake—a worn-out village on the bank of a dying pool that was rimmed with rushes and weeds and a few stunted trees.

Shelby didn't like it.

He had pictured a green oasis and found a dusty, desert water hole. He had imagined a village where they could trade for food and fresh horses, a gateway to Mexico with the border lying not far beyond the village, across the Rio Sonoyta.

He didn't like the look of the place. He didn't like not seeing any people over there. He didn't like the open fifty yards between here and the water hole.

He waited in a cover of rocks and brush with Norma and Junior and Soonzy behind him, and Mexico waiting less than a mile away. They could go around Quitobaquito. But if they did, where was the next water? The Sonoyta could be dried up, for all he knew. They could head for Santo Domingo, a fair-sized town that shouldn't be too far away. But what if they missed it? There was water right in front of them and, goddamn-it, they were going to have some, all they wanted. But he hesitated, studying the village, waiting for some sign of life other than a dog barking, and remembering Joe Dean with the three bullets in his chest.

Junior said, "Jesus, are we gong to sit here in the sun all day?"

"I'll let you know," Shelby said.

"You want me to get the water?"

"I did, I would have told you."

"Well, then tell me, goddamn-it. You think I'm scared to?"

Soonzy settled it. He said, "I think maybe everybody's off some place to a wedding or something. That's probably what it is. These people, somebody dies or gets married, they come from all over."

"Maybe," Shelby said.

"I don't see no other way but for me to go in there and find out. What do you say, Frank?"

After a moment Shelby nodded. "All right, go take a look."

"If it's the nigger and the Indin," Soonzy said, "if they're in there, I'll bring 'em out."

Raymond held the wooden shutter open an inch, enough so he could watch Soonzy coming in from the east end of the village, mounted, a rifle across his lap. Riding right in, Raymond thought. Dumb, or sure of himself, or maybe both. He could stick a .44 out the window and shoot him as he went by. Except that it would be a risk. He couldn't afford to miss and have Soonzy shooting in here. Raymond let the shutter close.

He pressed a finger to his lips and turned to the fourteen people, the men and women and children who were huddled in the dim room, sitting on the floor and looking up at him now, watching silently, even the two smallest children. The people were Mexican and Papago. They wore white cotton and cast-off clothes. They had lived here all their lives and they were used to armed men riding through Quitobaquito. Raymond had told them these were bad men coming who might steal from them and harm them. They believed him and they waited in silence. Now they could hear the horse's hoofs on the hard-packed street. Raymond stood by the door with a revolver in his had. The sound of the horse passed. Raymond waited, then opened the door a crack and looked out. Soonzy was nowhere in sight.

If anybody was going to shoot at anybody going for water, Soonzy decided, it would have to be from one of the adobes facing the water hole. There was a tree in the backyard of the first one that would block a clear shot across the hole. So that left him only two places to search—two low-roofed, crumbling adobes that stood bare in the sunlight, showing their worn bricks and looking like part of the land.

Soonzy stayed close to the walls on the front side of the street. When he came to the first adobe facing the water hole, he reached down to push the door open, ducked his head, and walked his horse inside.

He came out into the backyard on foot, holding a revolver now, and seeing just one end of the water hole because the tree was in the way. From the next adobe, though, a person would have a clear shot. There weren't any side windows, which was good. It let Soonzy walk right up to the place. He edged around the corner, following his revolver to the back door and got right up against the boards so he could listen. He gave himself time; there was no hurry. Then he was glad he did when the sound came from inside, a little creaking sound, like a door or a window being opened.

Harold eased open the front door a little more. He still couldn't see anything. The man had been down at the end of the street, coming this way on his horse big as anything, and now he was gone. He looked down half a block and across the street, at the adobe, where Raymond was waiting with the people, keeping them quiet and out of the way. He saw Raymond coming out; Harold wanted to wave to him to get inside. What was he doing?

The back door banged open and Soonzy was standing in the room covering him with a Colt revolver.

"Got you," Soonzy said. "Throw the gun outside and turn this way. Where's that red nigger at?"

"You mean Raymond?" Harold said. "He left. I don't know where he went."

"Which one of you shot Joe Dean, you or him?"

"I did. I haven't seen Raymond since before that."

"What'd you do with Virgil?"

"I don't think I know any Virgil."

"Frank's brother. He took us off the train."

"I haven't seen him."

"You want me to pull the trigger?"

"I guess you'll pull it whether I tell or not." Harold felt the door behind him touch the heel of his right foot. He had not moved the foot, but now he felt the door push gently against it.

"I'll tell Frank Shelby," Harold said then. "How'll that be? You take me to Frank I'll tell him where his brother is and them other two boys. But if you shoot me he won't ever know where his brother's at, will he? He's liable to get mad at somebody."

Soonzy had to think about that. He wasn't going to be talked into anything he didn't want to do. He said, "Whether I shoot you now or later you're still going to be dead."

"It's up to you," Harold said.

"All right, turn around and open the door."

"Yes-suh, captain," Harold said.

He opened the door and stepped aside and Raymond, in the doorway, fired twice and hit Soonzy dead center both times.

Shelby and Junior and Norma Davis heard the shots. They sounded far off, but the reports were thin and clear and unmistakable. Soonzy had gone into the village. Two shots were fired and Soonzy had not come out. They crouched fifty yards from water with empty canteens and the border less than a mile away.

Norma said they should go back to Bates Well. They could be there by evening, get water, and take the other trail south.

And run into a posse coming down from Gila, Shelby said. They didn't have time enough even to wait here till dark. They had to go with water or go without it, but they had to go, now.

So Junior said Jesus, give me the goddamn canteens or we will be here all day. He said maybe those two could paint theirselves up and bushwack a man, but he would bet ten dollars gold they couldn't shoot worth a damn for any distance. He'd get the water and be back in a minute. Shelby told Junior he would return fire and cover him if they started shooting, and Junior said that was mighty big of him.

"There," Raymond said. "You see him?"

Harold looked out past the door frame to the water hole. "Whereabouts?"

Raymond was at the window of the adobe. "He worked his way over to the right, coming in on the other side of the tree. You'll see him in a minute."

"Which one?"

"It looked like Junior."

"He can't sit still, can he?"

"I guess he's thirsty," Raymond said. "There he is. He thinks that tree's hiding him."

Harold could see him now, over to the right a little, approaching the bank of the water hole, running across the open in a hunch-shouldered crouch, keeping his head down behind nothing.

"How far do you think?" Raymond said.

Harold raised his Winchester and put the front sight on Junior. "Hundred yards, a little more."

"Can you hit him?"

Harold watched Junior slide down the sandy bank and begin filling the canteens, four of them, kneeling in the water and filling them one at a time. "Yeah, I can hit him," Harold said, and he was thinking, He's taking too long. He should fill them all at once, push them under and hold them down.

"What do you think?" Raymond said.

"I don't know."

"He ever do anything to you?"

"He done enough."

"I don't know either," Raymond said.

"He'd kill you. He wouldn't have to think about it."

"I guess he would."

"He'd enjoy it."

"I don't know," Raymond said. "It's different, seeing him when he don't see us."

"Well," Harold said, "if he gets the water we might not see him again. We might not see Frank Shelby again either. You want Frank?"

"I guess so."

"I do too," Harold said.

They let Junior come up the bank with the canteens, up to the rim before they shot him. Both fired at once and Junior slid back down to the edge of the still pool.

Norma looked at it this way: they would either give up, or they would be killed. Giving up would be taking a chance. But it would be less chancey if she gave up on her own, without Shelby. After all, Shelby had forced her to come along and that was a fact, whether the Indian and the Negro realized it or not. She had never been really unkind to them in prison; she had had nothing to do with them. So there was no reason for them to harm her now— once she explained she was more on their side than on Frank's. If they were feeling mean and had rape on their mind, well, she could handle that easily enough.

There was one canteen left, Joe Dean's. Norma picked it up and waited for Shelby's reaction.

"They'll shoot you too," he said.

"I don't think so."

"Why, because you're a woman?"

"That might help."

"God Almighty, you don't know them, do you?"

"I know they've got nothing against me. They're mad at you, Frank, not me."

"They've killed six people we know of. You just watched them gun Junior—and you're going to walk out there in the open?"

"Do you believe I might have a chance?"

Shelby paused. "A skinny one."

"Skinny or not, it's the only one we have, isn't it?"

"You'd put your life up to help me?"

"I'm just as thirsty as you are."

"Norma, I don't know—two days ago you were trying to turn me in."

"That's a long story, and if we get out of here we can talk about it sometime, Frank."

"You really believe you can do it."

"I want to so bad."

Boy, she was something. She was a tough, good-looking woman, and by God, maybe she could pull it. Frank said, "It might work. You know it?"

"I'm going way around to the side," Norma said, "where those bushes are. Honey, if they start shooting—"

"You're going to make it, Norma, I know you are. I got a feeling about this and I *know* it's going to work." He gave her a hug and rubbed his hand gently up and down her back, which was damp with perspiration. He said, "You hurry back now."

Norma said, "I will, sweetheart."

Watching her cross the open ground, Shelby got his rifle up between a notch in the rocks and put it on the middle adobe across the water hole. Norma was approaching from the left, the same way Junior had gone in, but circling wider than Junior had, going way around and now approaching the pool where tall rushes grew along the bank. Duck down in there, Shelby said. But Norma kept going, circling the water hole, following the bank as it curved around toward the far side. Jesus, she had nerve; she was heading for the bushes almost to the other side. But then she was past the bushes. She was running. She was into the yard where the big tree stood before Shelby said, "Goddamn you!" out loud, and swung his Winchester on the moving figure in the striped skirt. He fired and levered and fired two more before they opened up from the house and he had to go down behind the rocks. By the time he looked again she was inside.

Frank Shelby gave up an hour later. He waved a flour sack at them for a while, then brought the three horses down out of the brush and led them around the water hole toward the row of adobes. He had figured out most of what he was going to say. The tone was the important thing. Take them by surprise. Bluff them. Push them off balance. They'd expect him to run and hide, but instead he was walking up to them. He could talk to them. Christ, a dumb nigger and an Indin who'd been taking orders and saying yes-sir all their lives. They had run scared from the train and had been scared into killing. That's what happened. They were scared to death of being caught and taken back to prison. So he would have to be gentle with them at first and calm them down, the way you'd calm a green horse that was nervous and skittish. There, there, boys, what's all this commotion about? Show them he wasn't afraid, and gradually take charge. Take care of Norma also. God, he was dying to get his hands on Norma.

Harold and Raymond came out of the adobe first, with rifles, though not pointing them at him. Norma came out behind them and moved over to the side, grinning at him, goddamn her. It made Shelby mad, though it didn't hold his attention. Harold and Raymond did that with their painted faces staring at him; no expression, just staring, waiting for him.

As he reached the yard Shelby grinned and said, "Boys, I believe it's about time we cut out this foolishness. What do you say?"

Harold and Raymond waited.

Shelby said, "I mean what are we doing shooting at each other for? We're on the same side. We spent months together in that hell hole on the bluff and, by Jesus, we jumped the train together, didn't we?"

Harold and Raymond waited.

Shelby said, "If there was some misunderstanding you had with my men we can talk about it later because, boys, right now I believe we should get over that border before we do any more standing around talking."

And Harold and Raymond waited.

Shelby did too, a moment. He said then, "Have I done anything to you? Outside of a little pissy-ass difference we had, haven't I al-

ways treated you boys fair? What do you want from me? You want
me to pay you something? I'll tell you what, I'll pay you both to
hire on and ride with me. What do you say?"

Harold Jackson said, "You're going to ride with us, man. Free."

"To where?"

"Back to Sentinel."

Norma started laughing as Shelby said, "Jesus, are you crazy?
What are you talking about, back to Sentinel? You mean back to
prison?"

"That's right," Harold said. "Me and Raymond decide that's the
thing you'd like the worst."

She stopped laughing altogether as Raymond said, "You're going too, lady."

"Why?" Norma looked dazed, taken completely by surprise.
"I'm not with him. What have I ever done to you?"

"Nobody has ever done anything to us," Raymond said to Harold.
"Did you know that?"

The section gang that arrived from Gila told Mr. Manly no, they
had not heard any news yet. There were posses out from the Sand
Tank Mountains to the Little Ajos, but nobody had reported seeing
anything. At least it had not been reported to the railroad.

They asked Mr. Manly how long he had been here at Sentinel
and he told them five days, since the escape. He didn't tell them
Mr. Rynning had wired and instructed him to stay. "You have five
days," Mr. Rynning said. "If convict pair you released do not return, report same to sheriff, Maricopa. Report in person to me."

Mr. Manly took that to mean he was to wait here five full days
and leave the morning of the sixth. The first two days there had
been a mob here. Railroad people with equipment, a half-dozen
guards that had been sent over from Florence, and the Maricopa
sheriff, who had been here getting statements and the descriptions
of the escaped convicts. He had told the Maricopa sheriff about
sending out the two trackers and the man had said, trackers?
Where did you get trackers? He told him and the man had stared at
him with a funny look. It was the sheriff who must have told Mr.
Rynning about Harold and Raymond.

The railroad had sent an engine with a crane to lift the locomotive and the baggage car onto the track. Then the train had to be
pulled all the way to the yard at Gila, where a new locomotive was
hooked up and the prisoners were taken on to Florence. There had

certainly been a lot of excitement those two days. Since then the place had been deserted except for the telegrapher and the section gang. They were usually busy and it gave Mr. Manly time to think of what he would tell Mr. Rynning.

It wasn't an easy thing to explain: trusting two convicts enough to let them go off alone. Two murderers, Mr. Rynning would say. Yes, that was true; but he had still trusted them. And until this morning he had expected to see them again. That was the sad part. He sincerely believed he had made progress with Harold and Raymond. He believed he had taught them something worthwhile about life, about living with their fellowman. But evidently he had been wrong. Or, to look at it honestly, he had failed. Another failure after forty years of failures.

He was in the station house late in the afternoon of the fifth day, talking to the telegrapher, passing time. Neither had spoken for a while when the telegrapher said, "You hear something?" He went to the window and said, "Riders coming in." After a pause he said, "Lord in heaven!" And Mr. Manly knew.

He was off the bench and outside, standing there waiting for them, grinning, beaming, as they rode up: his Apache and his Zulu—thank you, God, just look at them!—bringing in Frank Shelby and the woman with ropes around their necks, bringing them in tied fast and making Mr. Manly, at this moment, the happiest man on earth.

Mr. Manly said, "I don't believe it. Boys, I am looking at it and I don't believe it. Do you know there are posses all over the country looking for these people?"

"We passed some of them," Raymond said.

"They still after the others?"

"I guess they are," Raymond said.

"Boys, I'll tell you, I've been waiting here for days, worried sick about you. I even began to wonder—I hate to say it but it's true—I even began to wonder if you were coming back. Now listen, I want to hear all about it, but first I want to say this. For what you've done here, for your loyalty and courage, risking your lives to bring these people back—which you didn't even have to do—I am going to personally see that you're treated like white men at Florence and are given decent work to do."

The Apache and the Zulu sat easily in their saddles watching Mr. Manly, their painted faces staring at him without expression.

"I'll tell you something else," Mr. Manly said. "You keep your record clean at Florence, I'll go before the prison board myself and make a formal request that your sentences be commuted, which means cut way down." Mr. Manly was beaming. He said, "Fellas, what do you think of that?"

They continued to watch him until Harold Jackson the Zulu, leaning on his saddle horn, said to Mr. Manly, "Fuck you, captain."

They let go of the ropes that led to Frank Shelby and the woman. They turned their horses in tight circles and rode out, leaving a mist of fine dust hanging in the air.

GUNSIGHTS

ONE

The gentleman from *Harper's Weekly*, who didn't know mesquite beans from goat shit, looked up from his reference collection of back issues and said, "I've got it!" Very pleased with himself. "We'll call this affair . . . are you ready? The Early-Moon Feud."

The news reporters in the Gold Dollar shrugged and thought some more, though most of them went on calling it the Rincon Mountains War, which seemed to have enough ring to it.

Somebody said, "What's the matter with the Sweetmary War?" Sweetmary being the name of the mining town where all the gawkers and news reporters had gathered to watch the show. The man from the *St. Louis Globe-Democrat* wanted to call it the Last of The Great Indian Wars. Or—he also mentioned to see how it would sound—the Great Apache Uprising of 1893. Or the Bloody Apache Uprising, etc.

The man from the St. Louis newspaper was reminded that, first, it wasn't an uprising and, second, there weren't just Apache Indians up in the mountains; there were also some niggers. The man from St. Louis, being funny, said, "Well, what if we call it the Last of the Great Indian-Nigger Wars?" A man from Florence said, "Well, you have got the chili-pickers in it also. What about them?" Yes, there were some Mexican settlers too, who had been farming up there a hundred years; they were also involved.

What it was, it was a land war.

The LaSalle Mining Company of New Jersey wanted the land. And the Indians from the White Tanks agency, the colored and the Mexicans—all of them actually living up there—wanted it also.

Dana Moon was the Indian Agent at White Tanks, originally established as a reservation for Warm Springs Apaches, or Mimbreños, and a few Lipan and Tonto-Mojave family groups. The agency was located sixteen miles north of Sweetmary and about the same distance west of the San Pedro River. The reservation land was not in dispute. The problem was, many of Moon's Apaches had wandered away from White Tanks—a bleak, young-desert area—to set up rancherías in the mountains. No one, until now, had complained about it.

Brendan Early worked for LaSalle Mining, sort of, with the title Coordinating Manager, Southwest Region, and was living in Sweetmary at the time.

It was said that he and Dana Moon had been up and down the trail together, had shared dry camps and hot corners, and that was why the *Harper's Weekly* man wanted to call it the Early-Moon Feud; which, as you see, had nothing to do with the heavens or astrology.

Nor was there any personal bitterness between them. The question was: What would happen to their bond of friendship, which had tied them together as though on two ends of a short riata, one not venturing too far without running into the other? Would their friendship endure? Or would they now, holding to opposite principles, cut the riata clean and try to kill one another?

Bringing the land question down to personalities, it presented these two as the star attractions: two well-known, soon-to-be-legendary figures about to butt heads. It brought the crowds to Sweetmary to fill up both hotels, the Congress and the Alamosa, a dozen boarding houses, the seven restaurants and thirteen saloons in town. For several weeks this throng swelled the normal population of about four hundred souls, which included the locals, those engaged in commerce, nearby farmers and ranchers and the miners at the Sweetmary Works. Now there were curiosity seekers, gawkers, from all over the Territory and parts of New Mexico.

(Not here yet were the hundred or more gunmen eventually hired by the company to "protect its leases" and quartered at the mine works. These men were paid, it was said, twenty dollars a week.)

There were newspaper representatives from the *Phoenix Republican, Phoenix Gazette, Yuma Sentinel, Safford Arizonian, Tucson Star, Florence Enterprise, Prescott Courier, Cococino Sun, Clifton Copper Era, Graham County Bulletin, Tombstone Prospector, St. Louis Globe-Democrat, Chicago Times* and the *New York Tribune.*

Harper's Weekly had hired the renowned photographer C.S. Fly of Tombstone to cover the war with his camera, the way he had pictorially recorded Crook's campaign against Geronimo and his renegade Apaches.

C.S. Fly set up a studio on LaSalle Street and there presented "showings" of many of his celebrated photographs of Indians, hangings, memorial parades and well-known personages, including Geronimo, former president Garfield and several of Brendan Early and Dana Moon. The two photos that were perhaps best known showed them at Fort Huachuca, June 16, 1887, with a prisoner they had brought in that day.

There they were, six years ago:

Brendan Early, in his hip-cocked cavalry pose. First Lieutenant of the 10th at Huachuca but wearing civilian dress, a very tight-fitting light-colored suit of clothes; bare-headed to show his brown wavy hair; a silky-looking kerchief at his throat; a matched pair of Smith and Wesson .44 Russians, butt-forward in Army holsters, each with the flap cut off; cavalry boots wiped clean for the pose; Brendan holding his Spencer carbine like a walking cane, palm resting on the upraised barrel. He seems to be trying to look down his nose like an Eastern dandy while suppressing a grin that shows clearly in his eyes.

In contrast:

Dana Moon with his dark, drooping mustache that makes him appear sad; hat brim straight and low over his eyes, a bulge in his bony countenance indicating the ever-present plug of tobacco; dark suit of clothes and a polka-dot neckerchief. Dana's .44 Colt's revolver is in a shoulder rig, a glint of it showing. He grips a Big-fifty Sharps in one hand, a sawed-off 12-gauge Greener in the other. All those guns for a man who looks so mild, so solemn.

Between the two:

Half a head shorter is a one-eyed Mimbreño Apache named Loco. What a funny-looking little man, huh? Black eyepatch, black stringy hair hanging from the bandana covering his head, he looks like a pirate of some kind, wearing an old dirty suitcoat and a loincloth. But don't laugh at him. Loco has killed many people and went to Washington to meet Grover Cleveland when times were better.

The caption beneath the photo, which appeared that year in *Harper's Weekly*, reads:

Lt. Brendan Early   Loco   Dana Moon
Two Famous Heroes of the West with a Captive
Red Devil

There was also a photo of the Two Famous Heroes standing on either side of an attractive fair-haired young lady in a torn and dirty cotton dress; she is wearing a man's shirt over her quite filthy attire, the shirt unbuttoned, hanging free. The young lady does not seem happy to be posing for her picture that day at Fort Huachuca. She looks as though she might walk up to the camera and kick it over.

The caption beneath this one reads:

Lt. Brendan Early   Katherine McKean   Dana Moon
Following Her Ordeal, Katy McKean
Gratefully Thanks Her Rescuers

In the *Harper's Weekly* article there was mention of a 10th Cavalry sergeant by the name of Bo Catlett, a Negro. Though he did not appear in either of the photographs, Sergeant Catlett had accompanied the Two Famous Heroes in their quest to apprehend the Apache warchief, Loco, and shared credit for bringing him in and rescuing the McKean girl. In the article, Sergeant Catlett was asked where he had gotten the name Bo. "I believe it short for 'Boy,' suh," was his reply.

Not many days before the photographs were taken by C.S. Fly, the five principals involved—Early, Moon, the McKean girl, Loco and Bo Catlett—were down in Old Mexico taking part in an adventure that would dramatically change their lives and, subsequently, lead to the Big Shootout known by most as The Rincon Mountain War.

TWO

1

St. Helen and Points South: June, 1887

Dana Moon had come down from Whiteriver to guide for Lieutenant Early and his company of 10th Cavalry out of Huachuca. They met at St. Helen, a stage stop on the Hatch & Hodges Central Mail Section route, where the "massacre" had take place: the massacre being one dead swamper, shot several times and his head shoved into his bucket of axel grease; the driver of the stage, his shotgun rider and one passenger, a Mr. R. Holmes of St. David. Four were dead; two passengers caught in the gunfire and wounded superficially; and one passenger abducted, Miss Katherine McKean of Benson, on her way home from visiting kin in Tucson.

Loco was recognized as the leader of the raiding party (How many one-eyed Apaches were there between San Carlos and Fort Huachuca?) and was last seen trailing due south toward the Whetstone Mountains, though more likely was heading for the San Pedro and open country: Loco, the McKean girl and about twenty others in the band that had jumped the reservation a few days before.

"Or about ten," Dana Moon said. "Those people"—meaning Apaches—"can cause you to piss your britches and see double."

Brendan Early, in his dusty blues, looked at the situation, staring south into the sun haze and heat waves, looking at nothing. But Brendan Early was in charge here and had to give a command.

What did they have? In the past month close to 150 Warm Springs people had jumped the San Carlos reservation, women and children as well as bucks, and made a beeline down the San Pedro

Valley to Old Mexico and the fortress heights of the Sierra
Madres. Loco's bunch was the rear guard, gathering fresh mounts
and firearms along the way. Maybe Bren Early's troopers could
ride like wild men a day and a night, killing some horses and
maybe, just maybe, cut Loco off at the crossing.

Or, a lieutenant in the U.S. Cavalry might ride through the scrub
and say, "What border?" even after ten years on frontier station,
cross leisurely with extra mounts and do the job.

Dana Moon—sent down here by Al Sieber, Chief of Scouts at
San Carlos—waited, not giving the lieutenant any help. He sat his
chestnut gelding, looking down from there with the tobacco wad
in his jaw. He didn't spit; he didn't do a thing.

While Lieutenant Early was thinking, Then what? Track the
renegades, run 'em to ground? Except his troop of U.S. Cavalry
would be an invading army, wouldn't it? having crossed an inter-
national boundary contrary to treaty agreement and the mutual respect of foreign soil, customs, emigration, all that bullshit.

"Lord Jehovah protect us from dumb-ass officialdom," said the
lieutenant out loud to no one in particular.

All soil west of the Pecos looked the same to Bren Early—
born and raised in Monroe, Michigan (adopted home of George
Armstrong Custer), before matriculating at West Point, somehow getting through, one hundred seventy-ninth in a class of one
ninety-two—and there was no glory standing around a wagon yard
watching civilians bleed.

Dana Moon read sign—grain shucks in horse shit, and could
tell you where the rider had come from how long ago—and sometimes he could read Bren Early's mind. He said, "You're gonna
hurt your head thinking. You want to do it, I'll take you four and a
half days' ride southeast, yes, across the line toward Morelos, and
on the sixth day Loco and his fellas will ride up to our camp. But
not with all your troopers. You and me and Bo Catlett to handle the
cavvy if he wants to come, six mounts on the string, grain and water. If you don't want to do it I think I'll quit government work; I'm
tired looking over the fence and watching dust settle."

"On the sixth day," Bren Early said, nodding. "And on the seventh day we'll rest, huh?"

He bought the tight-fitting suit of clothes off the St. Helen station agent for seven dollars, and for three more got Bo Catlett a
coat, vest and derby hat. Hey, boy, they were going to Old Mexico
like three dude tourists:

Rode southeast and crossed into Sonora at dusk, guided by the faint lights of a border town, against the full-dark moonside of the sky.

2

Dana Moon's plan: ride straight for a well he knew would be on Loco's route; get down there in the neighborhood, scout the rascal and his band to make sure they were coming; then, when they arrived, parley with the thirsty renegades, keeping their guns between the Apaches and a drink of water. Talk them out of the McKean girl first—if she was still alive—then talk about the weather or whatever they wanted, gradually getting the discussion around to a return trip to San Carlso for everybody, all expenses paid.

Or commence firing when they draw within range, Bren Early thought, seeing it written up as a major skirmish or, better yet, the Battle of . . . whatever the name of this rancho used to be, sitting in the scrub oak foothills: three weathered adobes in a row like a small garrison, mesquite-pole outbuilding and corral, part of an adobe wall enclosing the yard.

Out fifty yards of worn-out pasture was a windmill rigged to a stock tank of scummy water. From the end house or the wall, three men could cover the tank and a thirsty traveler would have to get permission to drink if the three men didn't want him to.

The Battle of Rancho Diablo. Give it a hellfire exciting name. Who'd know the difference?

On the sixth day Dana Moon rode in from his early-morning scout, field glasses hanging on his chest. He said, "What ever happens the way you expect it to?" He did spit right then.

Bren Early saw it. He said, "Duty at Huachuca."

"They split up," Dana Moon told him and Bo Catlett. "It looks to be Loco and the young lady coming ahead. They'll be here by noon, the ones with the herd maybe an hour behind. And some more dust coming out of the west."

"Federales," Bo Catlett said.

"Not enough of 'em," Moon said. "Some other party; maybe eight or ten."

They brought the spare horses and feed into the middle adobe, three saddled horses into the building closest to the stock-tank end of the yard, and went inside to wait.

Hoofprints out there meant nothing; people came through here all times of the year traveling between Morelos and Bavispe and points beyond, this being the gateway to the Sierra Madres.

Still, when Loco came, leading the second horse and rider they took to be the girl, he hung back 300 yards—the horses straining toward the smell of water—and began to circle as he approached the rancho again, coming around through the pasture now, keeping the wall between him and the adobes.

"We'll have to wing him," Bren Early said, flat against the wall with his Spencer, next to a front window.

Moon watched through the slit opening in the wooden door. He said to Bo Catlett, "Mount up."

Bo Catlett did and had to remain hunched over in the McClellan, his derby hat grazing the low roof.

"That one-eyed Indian is a little speck of a target, isn't he?" Bren Early said.

"Tired and thirsty," Moon said. "I'm going out." He looked up at Bo Catlett. "He flushes when he sees me, run him down. There won't be any need to shoot."

Bren Early, dropping the stock of his Spencer to the dirt floor, said, "Shit. And parley awhile." He didn't like it; then thought of something and squinted out past the window frame again.

"I wonder what that girl looks like," he said. "I wonder what the one-eyed son of a bitch's been doing to her."

Moon said, "Probably looks at her and thinks the same thing you would." He glanced up to see Bo Catlett showing his yellow-white teeth, grinning at him, and Moon thought of his mother telling him a long time ago why colored people had good, strong teeth: because they ate cold leftovers in the kitchen and couldn't afford to buy candy and things that weren't good for you.

Outside, Moon raised his arm. He saw Loco stop about a hundred yards off: the Apache deciding how much he wanted water or if he could win a race if he turned and ran. He saw the roan horse behind coming up next to Loco—yes, blond hair stirring, the McKean girl. Then saw something he didn't expect: the girl twisting in her saddle and shoving the Apache hard with both hands, sending him off his horse to land hard and lie there a moment while the girl reached to unhitch the lead line for the Indian's saddle; and now she was kicking her roan out of there, not bothering to look back as Moon yelled at her, "Wait! . . . Hey, come on back!" Then turning, getting out of the way as he called to Bo, "Get her!"

Bo Catlett came out of the door chute, chin pressed into the horse's mane, rose up in the yard and pressed down again as the horse cleared the four-foot adobe wall—Loco standing now, watching for a moment, then gathering his reins and coming on, not interested in the two horses racing across the pasture toward a haze of mountains.

3

They sat inside the doorway of the house with no furniture: Dana Moon and Loco with cups of sweet black coffee, the square of outside light between them on the earth floor. Bren Early came over from the fireplace where the coffee pot sat on a sheet of tin over the smoldering mesquite sticks. He stood looking out the window that was behind the Apache.

Loco said in Spanish, "Tell him I don't like him there."

Moon looked up at Bren. "He asks you to join us."

"Tell him he smells."

Moon motioned to him. "Come on, be sociable." To Loco he said in Spanish, "So, here we are."

Squatting down, Bren Early said, "Ask him, for Christ sake, what he did to the girl."

The Apache's one eye shifted. "Did to her? Did what?" he said in English.

"Is she all right?" asked Moon.

"She needs to be beaten," the Apache said. "Maybe cut off the end of her nose."

"Jesus Christ," Bren Early said. He got up and stepped to the window again.

"He speaks of Hey-soo Cristo." The Apache paused and said, using Spanish again, "What is the matter he can't sit down?"

"He wants to do battle," Moon said.

The Apache stretched open his one eye, raising his brow as if to shrug. "Wouldn't it be good if we could have what we want? I take all the mountains sunrise of the river San Pedro. You take all your people and go back to Washington"—pronouncing it Wasi-tona—"be by your big chief, Grover Cleveland. Man, he was very fat, do you know it?"

"He eats good," Moon said.

"Yes, but he gave us nothing. We sat in a room in chairs. He didn't seem to know why we were there."

"You liked Washington?" asked Moon.

"Good water there," Loco said, "but no country or mountains that I saw. Now they are sending our people to Fort Sill in Oklahoma. Is it like Washington?"

"I don't know," Moon said. "*He* served there one time," looking up at Bren Early.

"I believe it," the Apache said.

"It's like San Carlos, but with more people and houses."

"With mountains?"

"I don't think so," Moon said. "I've never been there. I've never been to Washington either. I've been to Sonora . . . Santa Fe, in the New Mexico Territory."

"The buildings in Washington are white," Loco said. "There are men made of iron on horses also made of iron. Many buildings and good water. You should go there and live if that's what your people like."

"I like mountains, as you do," Moon said. "I was born here, up on Oak Creek. I want to stay here, the same as you do. But there's a difference. They say, 'Put Loco and his people on the train to Fort Sill.' I can say, 'Put him on yourself, I won't do it.' And somebody puts you on the train. It's too bad, but what can I do about it?"

"Jesus Christ," Bren Early said, listening to them talking so seriously and understanding the drift but not the essence of what they were saying and feeling.

Moon raised his eyes, "We're looking at the situation."

Bren Early made a gun out of his right index finger, aimed it at the back of Loco's head and said, "Pow. That's how you solve it. You two're chatting—last week he shot four people dead. So we send him to Oklahoma for a vacation."

"It's the high part of his life to raid and steal horses, since the first Spaniard came up this valley," Moon said. "What else does he know? What's right and what's wrong on his side of the fence?'"

"My life is to meet the hostile enemy and destroy him," Bren said. "That's what I know."

"Listen to yourself," Moon said. "You want a war, go find one." He began gathering Spanish words again and said to Loco, "When your men arrive, tell them to get all of your people here in the mountains and bring them back to San Carlos. You go with us. It's the way it has to be for right now."

"Maybe it won't be so easy," Loco said. "There are others coming too."

Yes, the dust from the west, eight or ten riders. "Who are they?" Moon asked.

Loco touched the dirty red pirate bandana covering his head. "The ones who take hair."

"You're sure of it?"

"If they're not of you, or not the soldiers of Mexico, who are they?" the Apache said.

4

Bo Catlett came back with Katy McKean, the girl eyeing them with suspicion as she rode into the yard, sitting her roan like they'd have to pull her off it. Then sitting up there feeling left out, because they didn't have time for her those first moments. Bo Catlett began telling them about the riders coming. He said it looked like they had scattered the Indian herd and the two sides had exchanged gunfire, Bo Catlett hearing the reports in the distance. Now some of them for sure, if not all, were coming this way and it wouldn't be too long before they'd see the dust.

Bren Early studied the girl as he listened, thinking to himself, My, my, my, the poor sweet young thing all dirty and tattered, like the savages had rolled her on the ground and torn at her dress to get it off.

He said, "Miss," helping her down, taking her by the arm, "come on inside out of the hot sun." She pulled her arm away, giving him a mean look, and Bren said, "What're you mad at *me* for? I just want to give you some coffee."

"I ain't going in there with him," the McKean girl said, looking at Loco standing in the doorway. "Less you want to loan me one of your guns."

"Don't worry," Bren said. "He gets familiar with you again, I'll make the little heathen marry you. But how are you, all things being equal?"

The girl said, "What do you mean *again*?"

"I was just teasing," Bren said, "showing you there's nothing to worry about."

"He tried things," the McKean girl said. "I hit him in his good eye and kicked him up under his skirt where it'd do the most good. But I ain't going in that room with him. I still got his smell in my nose."

Dana Moon took her gently by the arm. She looked at him but didn't resist as he said in his quiet tone, "You been through something, lady, I know; and we're going to watch over you."

"Thank you," the girl said, subdued.

"But you got to do what I tell you for the time being, you understand? You can kick and scream when you get home, but right now try and act nice."

5

Who were they?, was the question: Watching from the windows as they had waited for the Indian, Moon and Bren Early with their glasses on the riders raising dust across the old pasture.

"Seven, eight," Bren Early said. "Like cowpunchers heading for town."

"Starting to hang back, sniff the air," Dana Moon said. What did those people out there know, looking this way? First, trailing Apaches with a horse herd and a white woman. Then, seeing a man in a derby hat riding off with her. They would have to be confused.

"They traded shots," Bren Early said and paused, thinking, Then what? "If they wanted the horses, why didn't they take 'em?"

Which was about where Moon was in his own mind. "Say they did, and left somebody with the herd. How many you count, Bo?"

"Ten," Bo Catlett said. "Coulda been another one."

"And they saw you for sure."

"Couldn't miss us—time I got the lady turned around."

"They're cowhands," the McKean girl said, with that edge to her tone again, not feeling very rescued crowded into this adobe room with four men and animals. She had moved up by Moon's window and stood close to him, seeing the hard bump in his jaw, wondering if he would ever spit; then would look over at Bren Early, maybe admiring his long wavy hair, or the tight, shrunk-looking suit molded to his tall frame. Squinting out the window, she said, "You can tell by the look of them, the way they ride."

Still, the McKean girl had to admit—without saying it aloud—

it was a bunch of riders for not having any cows, and moving south at that, not like they were heading home from a drive.

"There was a man used to sell us beef at San Carlos," Moon said. "I believe the name was Sundeen." Still watching through his glasses, seeing the riders at four hundred yards now, spreading out more as they came at a choppy walk, not a sound from them yet.

"I used to know him," the McKean girl said, a little surprised.

Maybe they didn't hear her. Bo Catlett said, "The same man supplied meat to Huachuca. Look in his war-bag you see a running iron, it's Phil Sundeen. Used to bring his beef in vented every which way; cows look like somebody was learning to write on 'em."

Moon said, "If I remember—hired vaqueros he paid twenty a month and feed. And we see some Mexican hats, don't we?"

"Which one's Sundeen?" Bren Early asked.

As Moon studied the bunch through his glasses, the McKean girl, squinting, said, "That stringy one on the sorrel—I bet he's got a hatband made of silver conchas."

"Something there's catching the light," Moon said.

"And forty-fours in crossed belts with silver buckles?"

"You got him," Moon said.

"Don't anybody listen to me," the McKean girl said. "I used to know him when his dad was still running things, before they sent Phil Sundeen to Yuma prison."

"That's the one," Moon said. "You knew him, huh?"

"I was ac*quaint*ed with him," the McKean girl said. "I wasn't to have nothing to do with him and that was fine with me. He was cheeky, loud and had ugly ways about him."

Bren Early said, "What was he in prison for?"

"As this colored man said, for using his running iron freely," the McKean girl answered. "It might be he run a herd down here to the Mexicans. On the way home he sees One-Eye here and decides to go for the bounty trade. Ask the Indin. He wouldn't have given himself up otherwise, would he?"

The men in the adobe room looked at this girl who seemed to know what she was talking about. How old? Still in her twenties, a healthy-looking girl, though dirty and sunburned at the moment. Yes, she knew a few hard facts of life.

Bren Early, leaning against the wall by his window, looked from the girl to Loco. "You must be worth plenty, all these people coming to see you."

"Make 'em bid high," the McKean girl said, "and look at the scrip before you hand him over, or that son of a bitch Sundeen will try and cheat you."

The men in the room had to look at that girl again.

Moon saw the waiting expression in Loco's eye and said, "He ain't going with them, he's going home."

"I know he's going home," Bren Early said. "I didn't come six days for the ride."

"If it means an argument, what difference does it make who takes him?" the McKean girl asked. She was serious.

Bren Early said, "Because he belongs to me, that's why."

And Moon said to her, going over to his horse, "I'll try and explain it to you sometime."

Bren Early was watching the riders, two hundred yards now, still coming spread out. "We got blind sides in here," he said. "Let's get out to the wall."

Moon was bringing a spare revolver out of his saddle bag, a Smith & Wesson .38 double-action model. He said, "You don't mean everybody."

Bren Early looked at him. "I'm referring to you and me only. Shouldn't that do the job?"

Moon pulled his sawed-off Greener from inside his blanket roll. Coming back to the window he handed the .38 to the McKean girl, saying, "You don't have to cock it, just keep pulling on the trigger's the way it works. But let me tell you something." Moon paused, looking at the Apache only a few feet away. "He's with us, you understand? He's ours. Nobody else's." Moon looked at Bo Catlett then and said, "Bo, give him his gun. Soon as it's over, take it back."

Walking out to the adobe wall, carrying their firearms, they watched the riders coming on, the riders looking this way but cutting an angle toward the stock tank.

"We'll let 'em water," Bren Early said.

"You give 'em too much they'll camp there," Moon said.

"We got no choice but have a talk first, do we?"

"No," Moon said.

"So they'll water and stretch first, take a pee and look the situation over. I hope they don't use dirty language and offend the girl's ears."

"Don't worry about *her*," Moon said.

He laid his Greener on the chest-high crumbling wall, leaned the Sharps against it, cocked, in front of him, lossened the Colt's in his shoulder rig, then decided to take his coat off: folded it neatly and laid it on the wall a few feet away.

"They're watching us," he said.

"I hope so," Bren Early said.

Bren had leaned his Spencer against the adobe wall. Now he drew his big .44 S & W Russians, broke each one open to slide a bullet into the empty sixth chamber and reholstered his guns.

Sundeen's bunch was at the stock tank now, fifty yards off, stepping down from the saddles.

Bren Early said, "At Chancellorsville, a Major Peter Keenan took his Eighth Pennsylvania Cavalry, four hundred men and— buying time for the artillery to set up—charged them full against ten thousand Confederate infantry. Talk about odds."

Moon turned his head a little. "What happened to 'em?"

"They all got killed."

6

The Mexican in the straw Chihuahua hat who came over to talk looked at first like he was out for a stroll, squinting up at the sky and off at the haze of mountains, inspecting a cholla bush, looking everywhere but at Moon and Early until he was about thirty feet from the adobe wall, then giving them a surprised look: like, what're you doing here?

The riders back of him, small figures, stood around while their horses watered in the corrugated tank and in the slough that had formed from seepage. One of the figures—it looked to be Sundeen—had his peter out and was taking a leak facing this way: telling them what he thought of the situation.

The Mexican touched his hat, loosening it and setting it again. Even with the revolver on his leg and the cartridge belt across his chest he seemed friendly standing there.

He said, "Good afternoon. How are you today?"

Moon and Bren Early watched him, Bren murmuring, "Jesus Christ," under his breath.

"It's good to reach water on a hot day," the Mexican said. "Have you been here very long?"

Moon and Bren Early seemed patient, waiting for him to get to it.

"We looking for friends of ours," the Mexican said. "We wonder if you see anybody ride by here the past hour."

Bren Early said, "Haven't seen a soul."

The Mexican took time to look past them and study the adobes, seeing the white smoke rising from the first chimney and vanishing in the glare.

"Where your horses?"

"Out of the sun," Bren Early said.

"You good to them," the Mexican said. "What else you got in there?"

"Troop of cavalry," Bren Early said and called out, "Sergeant!"

Bo Catlett, with a Spencer, appeared in the doorway of the first adobe, calling back, "Suh!"

The Mexican began to shake his head very slowly. "You got the Uninah States Army in there? Man, I like to see that." His gaze returned to Bren Early and Moon. "Soldiers . . . but you don't have no uniforms on." He paused. "You don't want nobody to know you here, huh? Listen, we won't tell nobody."

"You don't know what you've seen, what you haven't seen," Bren Early said. "Leave it at that."

The Mexican said, "You don't want to invite me in there?"

Moon drew his Colt from the shoulder rig and put it on the Mexican. "You got a count of three to move out of here," he said. "One . . . two . . . three—"

"Espere," the Mexican said. "Wait. It's all right with me." He began to back away, his gaze holding on Moon's revolver. "You don't want to be friends, all right, maybe some other time. Good afternoon to you."

7

The Mexican, whose name was Ruben Vega, forty-four years of age, something like seven to ten years older than the two men at the wall, said to himself, Never again. Going there like that and acting a fool. Good afternoon. How are you today? They knew, those two. They knew what was going on and weren't buying any of that foolish shit today. Never again, Ruben Vega said to himself again, walking back to the stock tank . . . Sundeen waiting for him.

Sundeen with his eyes creased in the sun glare, pulling the funneled brim of his hat down lower.

"He was bluffing you. Don't you know when a man's bluffing?"
Like the joke was on Ruben Vega and Sundeen had seen through it
right away.

"Sometimes I don't see the bluff if the man's good at it," Ruben
Vega said. "These two mean it. Why is it worth it to them?, I don't
know. But they mean it."

"Eight to three," Sundeen said. "What difference is it what they
mean?, the Indin's ours."

"I don't know," Ruben Vega said, shaking his head. "You better
talk to them yourself."

Sundeen wasn't listening now. He was squinting past the Mexican and touching his two-week's growth of beard, fondling it, ca-
ressing himself, as he studied the pair of figures at the wall. One of
them had yelled, "Sergeant," and the booger had stuck his head out.
Soldiers—chased after the Apache and now had him in there. That
part was clear enough. The girl, she must be in there, too. But eight
guns against three was what it came to. So what was the problem?
Ask for the Apache. Ask at gunpoint if need be. Those people
would have no choice but to hand him over and be happy to do it.

He said to the Mexican, "Send two around back to make 'em
nervous. The rest of us'll walk in." The Mexican didn't say anything and Sundeen looked at him. "What's the matter?"

"It isn't the way to do it."

Sundeen looked at the Mexican's old-leather face, at the thick,
tobacco-stained mustache covering his mouth and the tiny blood
lines in his tired-looking eyes.

"You're getting old, you know it?"

"I think that's it," Ruben Vega said. "I'm getting old because
I'm still alive."

Sundeen wanted to push him and say, Goddamn it, quit kicking dirt and come on; there's nothing to this. But he knew Ruben
Vega pretty well. He paid him fifty dollars a month because Ruben Vega was good with men, even white men, and was one trail-
wise first-class segundo to have riding point with a herd of rustled
stock, or tracking after a loose Apache with a Mexican price on his
head. Like the one-eyed Mimbre, Loco: 2,000 pesos, dead or alive.

When Ruben Vega spoke, Sundeen generally paid attention.
But this time—Ruben had been bluffed out, was all, and was trying to save his face, sound wise, like he knew something as fact;

whereas it was just an off-day for him and his back ached or his piles were bothering him.

Sundeen looked over at his riders, part of them hunkered down in the stingy shade of the stock tank: four Americans and two skinny Mexicans with their heavy criss-crossed gunbelts. He said to Ruben Vega, "I'll show you how white men do it," grinning a little. "I'll send your two boys around back where it's safe, and march in with the rest of these ugly bronc stompers myself."

"I'll watch you," Ruben Vega said.

Sundeen looked over at the riders again, saying, "Who wants to earn a month's wages this fine afternoon?"

8

"Now we're getting to it," Bren Early said, seeing the five men assembling, starting to come out from the tank, spreading out in a line. "I don't see a rifle amongst them; so they intend to come close, don't they?" And told himself not to talk so much, or else Dana would think he was nervous.

"The other two," Dana Moon said. "Leaving or what?"

Two with Mexican hats, mounted, were moving away from the tank, off to the right, heading out into the scrub.

"Do we want them behind us?"

"Uh-unh," Bren Early said. He picked up his Spencer as Moon hefted his Sharps, watching the two Mexican riders swinging wide, going out to nearly two hundred yards as they began to circle at a gallop.

"The horses first," said Moon, "if that's agreeable."

"I suppose," the cavalryman answered, "but it's a shame."

"If they keep coming, you finish it. I'll tend to the others."

Moon stole a look at the five on foot coming out from the tank, taking their time, one remaining back there with the horses.

He said, "When you're ready."

They pressed Spencer and Sharps to their shoulders and almost instantly the hard, heavy reports came BAM-BAM in the stillness and the two running horses two hundred yards out stumbled and went down with their riders in sudden burts of dust, the tiny figures flying, tumbling.

Moon turned his empty Sharps on the line of five, saw them stop dead.

Bren Early called, "Sergeant!"

Moon didn't look around. He heard off behind him, "Suh!" And Bren Early calmly, "Two on the flank. Keep 'em there. They move, shoot 'em." And the black voice saying, "Suh!" and that was done.

The five had broken line and were looking out that way, losing some of their starch maybe. But the one with crossed gunbelts and silver buckles was saying something, getting them back in business and they were coming again, the line of men about fifteen feet wide—Sundeen in the middle—every one of them shaggy and scruffy, rannies with hard squints trying to look mean, and they did.

The last exchange made between Moon and Bren Early was Moon saying, "If it comes to it, work from the ends," and Bren Early saying, "And meet at the silver buckles."

Now the floor was Sundeen's, bringing his line to a halt at a distance Moon's eyes measured as a long stride short of forty feet. A good working range: close enough for a sawed-off, far enough you'd have to aim a revolver if you had nerve enough to take the time. Who were these brush poppers? Were they any good? Moon and Bren Early were about to find out.

Sundeen said to the two at the wall, "Are you nervous or something? We come to talk to you is all."

He waited a moment, but they didn't say anything. Then looked off into the distance at the two dead horses and the riders stranded out there before bringing his gaze back to the wall.

"Like shooting a buck, that range. I guess you've done it in your time. But here looking at it close to earth is different, huh? You see what you got on your hands? Now then," Sundeen said, "you also got that red nigger in there by the name of Loco we want you to hand over to us. Do you see a reason to discuss it any?"

"He's mine," Bren Early said. "He goes home with me."

"Oh, are you the gent in charge?" asked Sundeen. "Then tell me something. What difference does it make who takes this Indin, long as we rid the earth of him?"

"I was sent to get him," Bren Early said, "and I did."

"A long piece from home without your uniform on, soldier boy. I bet you shouldn't even be 'cross the border here. What I'm saying, it looks like I got more right to the red nigger than you have. I got the law on my side."

"But I've got the Indian," Bren Early said. "What remains is how dearly you want to pay for him."

"Turn it around," Sundeen said. "Why would you put up your life to keep him? I'm gonna ride out with him, one way or the other."

Moon said then, "You ever mount up again you'll do it bleeding to death."

Sundeen shook his head. What was the matter with these two?— and had to make himself calm down. He said, "Listen to us grown men arguing over a little one-eyed Indin."

"What's he worth," asked Moon, "couple thousand pesos?"

"Sure, there's something in it, or we wouldn't be talking," Sundeen answered. "But you can't hand him in and collect the bounty, not if you're U.S. Army. They find out back home, they'll cut your buttons off, won't they? Drum you out. It may be duty with you, if you say it is; but it's pure business with me. Way to make a living." Sundeen paused. He said then, "It gives me an idea. What we might do is divvy him up. You give me his hair and his eye patch, something to identify him to the Mex gover'ment, and you take the rest of him back where you came from. And if that ain't a deal I never heard one."

Sundeen glanced both ways at the pair of riders on either side of him, then looked at the two behind the low wall again, pleased with himself, his display of wisdom and generosity.

Bren Early did stop and think a moment. Yes, if they'd had to shoot the Indian they'd be bringing him back dead anyway. But how would they explain his tonsured head, the scalplock ripped from his skull? Then realized, No, that wasn't the point at all. It was a question of principle, beyond reason or even good sense. A question of standing at the drawn line and never backing off.

Bren Early said to Moon, but for all to hear, "Do you want to tell him to stick it in his horse, or should I?"

Sundeen was a grunt away from giving in to his violent nature; but knew his men had to look at him or hear him and all of them pull at the same time to do the job right. Put the two off guard and then hit. It wasn't gong the way he thought it would—that goddamn Ruben Vega telling him, knowing something. With the hook still in his belly but holding on to good judgment, Sundeen said, "I'm gonna go talk to my partner a minute. See if we can think of a way to satisfy us."

Moon and Bren Early watched him turn away from them, his rannies looking at him like, What's going on? Sundeen dropping a word as he glanced left and right, all of them moving off now.

Bren said, "He's used to having his way."

Moon said, "But he didn't come prepared, did he?"

"I'll give them three more steps," Bren said and pulled his matched Smith & Wesson .44s. Moon drew his Colt's, gathered the sawed-off Greener from the wall in his left hand.

Three more strides—that was it.

The five came around with weapons in their hands, Sundeen hollering something, and his two men on the ends fell dead in the first sudden explosion from the wall, before they were full around, Bren Early and Moon with revolvers extended, aiming, firing at the scattering, snap-shooting line, Bren holding both the big .44 Russians out in front of him and moving his head right and left to look down the barrels and fire; Moon holding the Greener low against its hard buck and letting go a Double-O charge at a half-kneeling figure and seeing the man's arm fly up with the big-bore report, swinging the Greener on Sundeen and raking his boots with a charge as Sundeen stumbled and Bren Early fired, shooting his hat off, firing again and seeing the man let go of his revolvers and grab his face with both hands as he sank to the ground.

They went over the wall and walked out to where the five lay without moving.

"Four dead," Bren Early said.

Moon nodded. "For no reason. This one looks to be right behind."

Sundeen was still alive, lying in the sun as his life drained from shotgun wounds in both legs, bullet wounds in his neck, through his left cheek and where part of his left ear had been shot away.

Ruben Vega came out to them, looking at the men on the ground. He said, "Well, I tried to tell him."

The Mexican began to think of how he would get Sundeen to Morelos, or if he should try; and if he should take the others over their horses or leave them here. He walked around them, nudging one and then another with his boot, making sure they were dead; then began to recite the names of these men, as though saying last words over them:

Lonnie Baker.

Clement Hurd.

Dick Maddox.

Jack McWilliams.

Moon and Bren Early heard him, but they were looking toward the adobe now, seeing the girl and the sergeant and the Indian in the yard, and they didn't listen to the names carefully and store them away. It could have helped them later if they did.

THREE

1

When the news reporters first came here to cover the War they had to look for the "angle." The Big Company trying to run off the little homesteaders was good stuff; they could write it as factually as need be from both sides. But it would be far better if Personalities were involved: names of newsworthy individuals that readers would recognize, or, feel dumb if they didn't after the news articles described their colorful and exciting past histories.

What could you do with William A. Vandozen, the LaSalle Mining vice-president who was completely lacking in color, appeared in town once in awhile but would not talk to anyone when he did?

What kind of story would you get from an Apache Indian homesteader named Iskay-mon-ti-zah who didn't speak English anyway?

This was, in part, the reason Dana Moon and Brendan Early were elected to be the principal antagonists, bound to come together sooner or later, which would be the climax, the Big Story: two living legends in a fight to the finish.

Fine, the editors of the newspapers would wire back to their reporters. But who are they? What did they do? GET TO WORK AND DIG UP SOME BACKGROUND! was the tone of the wires if not the actual words.

The news reporters hanging out at the Gold Dollar would shake their heads. Just like a goddamn editor—like asking what Wild Bill Hickok did for a living. (What *did* he do? No one asked.) They all nodded their heads in agreement as to editors.

All right, they'd go talk to the principals involved.

But try to get a straight answer from Brendan Early, who was stuck-up, high-and-mighty, vain and rude when interviewed. They would ask him questions such as: "What is it like to kill a man?" He would stare back at them and not answer. "Do you think you will die by the gun?" Answer: "If you don't leave, somebody will." Or they would ask a question in a group none would dare ask alone: "What turned you against humanity?" The famous Bren Early: "Pains in the ass like you people." They would see him drinking whiskey and playing faro, then not see him for days while he remained holed-up in his room in the Congress Hotel or visited the mysterious Mrs. Pierson who lived in a house on Mill Street without any visible means of support.

Or try to locate Dana Moon, having to go all the way up into the mountains on a two-day pack. Finally, there he was. Ask him a list of shrewd questions and have him say, "You people don't know what you're talking about, do you?"

So the reporters filed embroidered stories based on heresay and sketchy information they accepted as fact. They wrote that Bren Early had been court-martialed following the Sonora Incident and cashiered out of the Army. Since then he had been:

A hunting guide.

Road agent.

Convict in a work gang.

Gold prospector.

Had shot and killed anywhere from ten to twenty men.

All this before selling his claim to LaSalle Mining and joining the company. Great stuff, plenty of material here to work with.

Dana Moon's background wasn't as colorful, though it was solid ground to build on. After Sonora he had been fired from his position as Assistant Supervisor, San Carlos Indian Reservation, and had entered the business of mustanging: supplying remounts to Fort Huachuca and stage horses to Hatch & Hodges, before they shut down their lines. He was known to be a rough customer who had shot and killed a few men himself. Now, and for the past few years, Dana Moon was in charge of the Apache sub-agency at White Tanks.

Yes, Moon and Early had crossed paths several times since the Sonora Incident, which is what made the "angle" of these two eventually tearing into each other a natural. Headlines, with facts slightly bent, practically wrote themselves.

PERSONAL FEUD SETS STAGE FOR LAND FIGHT
MOON AND EARLY FACTIONS LINE UP FOR BATTLE

Great stuff.

While all the "color" was being written, a young *Chicago Times* journalist by the name of Maurice Dumas, who had not yet mastered a pose of cynicism or world-weariness, did talk to both Bren Early and Dana Moon. Young Maurice Dumas asked straight questions and didn't know any better when he got direct answers.

Beginner's luck, the other news reporters said.

2

Was it luck? Or the fact Maurice Dumas had trained himself to jump out of bed each day at 6:30 A.M. and immediately check his list of THINGS TO DO. At seven he walked into the Congress Hotel dining room and there was Brendan Early, alone: the first time Maurice Dumas had ever seen the man without a crowd around him.

"Excuse me, but would you mind if I interviewed you?" Nervous as hell.

Brendan Early looked up from his T-bone steak, tomatoes and scrambled eggs. He looked different than he did in the C.S. Fly photos: his face was thinner and he now wore a heavy mustache that curved down around his mouth and was darker than his hair.

"Let me hear your first question."

"Well—were you chucked out of the Army or did you retire?"

"You mean you are asking instead of telling me?" Brendan Early said. "Sit down."

Both surprised and encouraged, Maurice Dumas took off his cap and did as he was told. He couldn't believe it.

"I quit, resigned my commission," Bren Early said.

"What did you do right after that?"

"I rested."

"Thought of what you would do next?"

"Thought of staying alive. I thought quite a lot about it."

"Meaning you had to make a living?"

"I thought of ladies somewhat. But most often I thought of staying alive."

"I believe you advertised your services to lead western hunting expeditions. In Chicago and other eastern papers?"

"It's true. The advertisement said, 'Ladies welcome . . . Your dear lady will be well protected and taken care of.' "

"How long were you a hunting guide?"

"I wasn't a guide, I *hired* guides to do the work while I led the expeditions."

"How long did you do that?"

"Till I got tired of smiling."

The news reporter wasn't sure he understood that; but he preferred to cover ground rather than clear up minor points. He watched Mr. Early take a silver flask from inside his dark suit-coat and pour a good slug into his coffee.

"Is that whiskey?"

"Cognac. I don't drink whiskey in the morning."

"May I continue?"

"Please do."

"It's said you've killed between ten and twenty men. How many exactly did you?"

"That's not the question to ask."

Maurice Dumas thought a moment. "Did you know their names?"

And saw Mr. Early pause over his breakfast and look at him with interest.

"That's the question. How did you know to ask it?"

"It seemed like a good one," the reporter said.

Brendan Early nodded, saying, "It's interesting that some of them—I don't mean the back-shooters, of course—would announce themselves with the sound of death in their tone. 'Mr. Early . . . I am R.J. Baker.' Then stare with a hard, solemn look, like I was supposed to faint or piss my britches."

"Really? What happened that time? The one said his name was Baker."

"Don't you want some breakfast?"

"I'll just have some of this coffee, if I may."

Eating his steak, watching the young reporter pour himself a cup from the silver pot on the table, Brendan Early said, "Are you sure you're from a newspaper? You aren't like the rest of that snotty bunch at all."

"Chicago Times," Maurice Dumas said. "There are so many things I want to ask you about." Including the mysterious Mrs. Pier-son, who lived over on Mill Street. Was she just a friend or what?

"Don't be nervous." Brendan Early looked through the doors to the railroad clock in the hall. "We got till I get tired of talking or you decide you know more than I do. This morning I'm going shooting."

"You mean—up there?"

"No, I'm gonna step out into the desert and limber up my revolvers and test my eyesight."

"Getting ready for the showdown," Maurice Dumas said, squirming in his chair a little.

"You're starting to sound like the others," Brendan Early said. "Don't tell me things. Ask me."

"I'm sorry. How come you're going out to limber up your revolvers?"

"Today and tomorrow. I intend to shoot off several boxes of forty-fours. Because sometime soon, I've been told, an acquaintance from long ago will arrive in Benson by train, get here somehow or other, and I don't know his present frame of mind."

"You mean somebody who wants to kill you?"

"Ask him that one. Fella by the name of Phil Sundeen, come back from the dead."

Maurice Dumas frowned. What was going on? He said, "Sundeen. I don't believe I've heard that name before."

"Well, write it down. It could be an item for your paper."

FOUR

1

Dragoon Mountains: April, 1888

The smell of the mares was on the wind, but the stud did not seem to like this graze as a place to breed. He lowered his head, giving the signal, and the mares and the stallions skitting around them followed after as the lead mare moved off.

Seven days Dana Moon had been tracking this herd, gradually, patiently moving the wild horses toward a barranca they'd fenced off with brush; a week of watching, getting to know them, Moon thinking on and off: If you were the stud, which one would you pick to mount first?

It would be hard. There were some good-looking mares in that bunch. But each time he wondered about it Moon found his gaze cutting out the palomino, the golden-haired girl, from the rest of the mares. She attracted the most overtures from the stallions who'd come sniffing her flanks. Moon would watch the palomino jump gracefully and give the boys a ladylike kick in the muzzle—saving it for the stud.

Out here a week tracking with his six Mimbre riders, former members of the Apache Police at San Carlos, now mustangers working for the Dana Moon Remount & Stage Team Supply Company—if anyone were to ask who he was and what he did.

Though it was not the answer he gave the fool who came riding upwind out of the sun haze. There he was, a speck of sound and smell and the herd was *gone*, like it would run forever, the Mimbres gathering and chasing off through the dust to keep them located. The fool, two black specks now, came clopping across the scrub waste, *clop clop clop clop,* leading a pack animal, not even knowing what a goddamn fool he was.

Yet he appeared to be a rider himself, sweat-dirty Stetson down on his eyes, someone who should know better.

A little bell rang inside Moon's head.

Pay attention.

"Are you Dana Moon?"

An official tone. A policeman verifying the name before saying you're under arrest. Or a messenger boy from somewhere.

"You just wiped out a week of tracking," Moon said. "You know it?"

"I guess it ain't your day," the man said and drew a pistol and immediately began firing at Moon, shooting him in the thigh, just above his right knee, shooting his horse through the neck and withers, the horse screaming and throwing its head as Moon drew his Colt's and shot the man twice through the chest.

He was a fool after all, not as real as he appeared. But who was he?

One of Moon's Mimbre riders, who was called Red, came back to find his boss sitting on the ground twisting his polka-dot scarf around his leg. The leg looked a mess, the entire thigh bleeding where the bullet had dug its way through Moon's flesh to come out just below his hip bone.

"I never even saw him before," Moon said. "See if he's got a wallet or something." He knew the man lying by his horse was dead; he didn't have to ask that.

There were seventeen dollars in a wallet and a folded soiled letter addressed to Asa Maddox, c/o Maricopa Cattle Company, Bisbee, Arizona Territory. The tablet-paper letter said:

Asa Maddox:

That was good news you sent that you have finally got him located. If you do not want to wait for us I cannot stop you, but then we will not wait for you either and will proceed with our plan to get the other one. I think you are wrong in doing this alone instead of with us, but as I have mentioned I cannot stop you nor do I blame you much for your eagerness.

Good luck.

(Signed)

J. A. McWilliams

Moon said, "Who is Asa Maddox? Who in the hell is J. A. McWilliams?"

Red, hunkered down next to Moon, looked at him but did not say anything.

"Well, shit," Moon said. "I guess I'm going to Benson a week early."

2

Florence: May, 1888

The cowboy standing at the end of the Grayback Hotel bar said, "Are you Captain Early?"

From his midpoint position, Bren Early's gaze moved from his glass of cold beer down in that direction.

"I am."

"There is a man here looking for you."

The man who stepped out from behind the rangy cowboy, a large-framed man himself, wore a dark business suit, a gold watch chain across the vest, a gray Stetson that looked like it had just come out of the box.

"Are you Mr. Johnson?" Bren Early asked. It was the name of the party he was supposed to meet here in Florence.

Instead of answering, the man walked over to a Douglas chair against the back wall where a maroon felt traveling bag sat waiting.

Bren Early liked businessmen hunters who were conscientious about the clause "Fee in Advance" and handed it over before they shook hands and said how much they'd been looking forward to this expedition. Raising his cold beer, Bren Early looked up at the clock on the wall between the back-bar mirrors. It was 11:48 in the morning. He liked the idea of putting five hundred dollars in his pocket before noon. He liked the quiet of a morning barroom—the heat and heavy work left outside with Bo Catlett and the light-blue hunting wagon. He'd bring Bo out a glass of beer after.

The cowboy was still sideways to the bar, facing this way. Like making sure he wasn't going to leave. Or so that he'd see the pistol stuck in the cowboy's belt. Why was this cowboy staring at him?

The man in the business suit was bending over his open traveling bag, taking a lot of time. Why wasn't the money on his person?

Bren Early put down his glass of beer. He heard the man in the business suit say, as the man came around, finally, with the pistol:

"This is for Jack McWilliams, you Indin-loving son of a bitch—"

(Though, the bartender testified at the Pinal County Sheriff's Inquest, the gentleman never got to say the last word.)

Bren Early shot the man with a .44 Smith & Wesson, the slug exploding from the barrel, obliterating the word and taking the man cleanly through the brisket . . . shot the cowboy dead through the heart, heard him drop his weapon and fall heavily as he put the Smith on the man in the business suit again, not 100 percent sure about this one.

The man was slumped awkwardly in a pole-axed daze, half-lying-sitting on the maroon travel bag, bewildered, wondering how his plan had suddenly gone to hell, staring up at Bren Early with maybe ten minutes of life remaining in him.

"You rehearsed that, didn't you?" Bren Early said. "I'll bet it sounded good when you said it to a mirror."

Blood seeped out between the man's fingers pressed to his rib cage, trying to hold himself together, breathing and hearing the wound bubble and breathe back at him, sucking air, the man then breathing quicker, harder, to draw air up into his mouth before the wound got it all.

"You should not have begun that speech," Bren Early said. "But a lot of good it does advising you now, huh? . . . Has anybody an idea who this man is?"

J. A. McWilliams of Prescott, a supplier of drilling equipment and high explosives, according to identifying papers. The cowboy with him remained nameless—at least to Bren Early, who left Florence with Bo Catlett and their blue hunting wagon as soon as he was cleared of any willful intent to do harm.

McWilliams. It was a somewhat familiar name, but did not stir any clear recollections from the past.

3

Benson: May, 1888

For nearly a month Dana Moon lived in Room 107 of the Charles Crooker Hotel, waiting for his wound to heal. With the windows facing east it was a hot room mornings, but he liked it because it gave him a view of country and cottonwoods along the river. In the evening he listened to train whistles and the banging-clanging activity over in the switch yard.

He had planned to come to Benson a week later to visit the whorehouse and maybe call on Katy McKean and see if there was a future respectable possibility there.

Now Katy McKean was calling on him. The first time she came he wondered: Will she leave the hotel room door open?

No, she didn't. She sat in the big chair between the windows, and Moon, sitting upright in bed, had to squint to see her face with the sun glare on the windows. He couldn't ask her to pull the shades. After her second visit he got up and struggled one-legged with the horsehide chair, moving it all the way around the bed and after that, when she came, the good view was to the west.

Well, how have you been? . . . Fine . . . I hardly recognize Benson the way it's grown . . . Has it? . . . You live with your folks? . . . Yes, and three young brothers; a place down the river a few miles . . . Bren ever come by to see you? . . . Now and then.

It required three visits from her before he asked, "How come you aren't married with a place of your own?"

"Why aren't you?"

"It hasn't been something I've thought about," Moon said. "Up till now." (Why was he saying this? He had come to town to visit the whorehouse and look at possibilities only.)

"Well, I haven't met the man yet," the McKean girl said. "They come out, my dad looks them over. The best he gives is a shrug. The drag riders he won't even speak to."

"Your dad," Moon said. "Whose choice is it, yours or his?"

"He knows a few things I haven't learned yet," the McKean girl said. She wore boots under her cotton skirt, the toes hooked on the sideboard of Moon's bed, her knees raised and a little apart. He couldn't see anything, but he was aware of her limbs and imagined them being very white and smooth, white thighs—Jesus—and a patch of soft hair.

Moon sat up straight in bed, the comforter pulled up to his waist over his clean longjohns, his hair and mustache combed, bay rum rubbed into his face and wearing his polka-dot scarf loosely for her visit. He was seasoned and weathered for his thirty-four years, looking closer to forty. The McKean girl was about twenty-three, a good-looking woman who could have her pick but was in no hurry; knew her own mind, or her dad's. Bren Early was thirty one or thirty two, closer to her age, liked the ladies and they liked him. Why, Moon wondered, did he always think of Bren when the McKean girl was here? Hell, ask her.

"Are you interested in Bren?"

"*In*terested? You mean to marry?"

"Yes."

"What's he got to offer? A wagon painted blue to look like a Conestoga, a string of horses . . . What else?"

"I wasn't thinking of what he owns."

"He's full of himself."

"He's got potential."

"Who hasn't?"

"What's your dad think of him?"

"My dad says time's passed him by."

"What's your dad do, whittle and say wise things?"

"He runs a cattle outfit and drives here twice a year," the McKean girl said. "When I got home from Old Mexico he rode up to San Carlos to shoot that one-eyed Apache dead, but they'd already shipped him off to Indian Territory."

"You have a deep fondness and respect for your old dad, haven't you?"

"He's the only one I got and he isn't that old."

"Man that marries you has to measure up to him?"

"I'd be a fool to choose less, wouldn't I?"

"I got to meet this dad of yours," Moon said.

"I'll fetch you in a buckboard," the McKean girl said.

During his third week Moon went downriver to a cluster of adobes, the McKean homestead, and sat out under the ramada in the early evening with her dad. They discussed gunshot wounds, reservation Indians, cattle, graze and wild horses. After a little while McKean invited Moon to share some corn whiskey with little specks of charcoal in it.

"You want to marry my daughter?"

Maybe important decisions were made like any other. Without thinking too much. "Yes, I do."

"I don't see what in the hell you got to give her."

"Me," Moon said.

"Well, you present more in person than any I've seen, including General Early; but what does she do, camp with your Mimbres and eat mule?"

"I'll think of a way," Moon said.

The next day when the McKean girl came to visit, and before she could sit down, Moon pulled her to him, felt her hold back till he got her down on the bed, lying across it, felt a terrible pain in his wounded thigh from the exertion and sweat break out on his forehead.

She said, "How're you going to do it?"

He thought she meant perform the act of love. "Don't worry, it can be done."

"You're gonna leave mustanging?"

"Oh," Moon said.

"And settle someplace?"

Moon nodded solemnly and said, "I love you," the first time in his life hearing the actual statement out loud.

"I hope so," the McKean girl said. "We can kiss and you can touch me up here if you want, but that's all till I see what my future is."

"It's a deal," Moon said.

He never did make it to the whorehouse. In fact, he swore he would never visit one again as long as he lived.

4

Apache Pass Station: September, 1888

This trip Bren Early had taken a party from Chicago, three men and the wife of one of them, south of the Pass into the Chiricahua Mountains for mule deer and a look at some authentic Apache Indians. The eastern hunters remained in camp while Bren and Bo Catlett drove the blue wagon to Apache Pass to pick up whiskey and supplies shipped down in the stage from Willcox. Bren was happy to get away from his five-hundred-dollar party.

He was in the back of the wagon, yawning and stretching, waking up from a nap, as Bo Catlett pulled the team into the station yard, Bo yelling at the agent's three kids to get out of the way. There were riding horses in the corral and, on the bench in front of the adobe, three saddles where they usually kept the wash basins. An olla of water hung from the mesquite-pole awning. Going inside, Bo Catlett noticed the saddles.

Three men who looked to have been sleeping as well as traveling in their suits of clothes were playing cards at the near end of the long passenger table. Edgar Watson, the station agent, said, "Where's the Captain?"

Bo Catlett didn't answer him. One of the men at the table stood up and moved to the door to look out. Edgar Watson was at the window now. He said, "There he is."

Looking past the man in the door, Bo Catlett could see Captain Early coming out of the wagon, climbing over the tailgate. The man in the doorway said to Edgar Watson, "Tell your kids to come inside." The other two were also standing now, both holding rifles. A shotgun lay on the table.

Pretending not to notice anything, Bo Catlett said, "Mr. Watson, draw a glass of beer if you will, please."

Edgar Watson, seeming bewildered, said a strange thing, considering what was going on in this close, low-ceilinged room. He said, "You know I can't serve you in here."

Bo Catlett believed he was born in Arkansas or Missouri. He was liberated by Jayhawkers and, at age fifteen, joined the 1st Kansas Colored Volunteers at Camp Jim Lane in February, 1863; saw immediate combat against Rebel irregulars and Missouri bushwhackers and was wounded at Honey Springs in June of '63. He guarded Confederate prisoners at Rock Island; served with the Occupation at Galveston and saw picket duty on the Rio Grande before transferring to the Department of Arizona where he drew the 10th Cavalry, Fort Huachuca, as his last regimental home in a twenty-four-year Army career. Some white officer—before Bren Early's time—dubbed Benjamin Catlett the *beau sabruer* of the nigger outfit and that was how he'd gotten his nickname. Bo Catlett was mustered out not long after the Sonora Incident—which did not affect his record—and had been working for Captain Early Hunting Expeditions, Inc. almost a year now. He liked to hear Bren Early talk about the war because the Captain was like a history book, full of information about battles and who did what. It didn't matter the Captain was still a little seven-year old boy when fifteen-year-old Bo Catlett was getting shot through the hip at Honey Springs, or that the Captain didn't get his commission till something like ten years after Appomattox Court House. The Captain knew his war. He told Bo Catlett that he had never objected to colored boys being in the Army or killing white men during the war. But he would admit with candor his disappointment at being assigned to the Colored 10th rather than the "Dandy 5th," George

Rosebud Crook's fighting outfit. No, the Captain had nothing against colored people.

There were sure some who did, though.

And there were some who had it in for the Captain, too.

Bren Early, standing by the tailgate of the wagon, wasn't wearing his revolvers. But as soon as he saw the three saddles on the wash bench and heard Edgar Watson call to his kids, Bren reached over the wagon gate, pulled his gunbelt toward him and was in that position, left arm inside, his fingers touching one of his revolvers, when the man's voice said, "We didn't expect you for a couple more days."

Bren looked over his right shoulder at the three coming out from the adobe, two rifles, a shotgun in the middle, and said to himself, Shit. There wasn't any way to mistake their intention.

The man with the shotgun, wearing a hat, an old suit and no collar or tie, said, "I'm R. J. Baker."

Bren Early waited. Yes? Why was that supposed to tell him anything? He said, "How do you do?" seeing Bo Catlett coming out of the adobe behind them: his dear friend and fellow cavalryman, the twenty-four-year seasoned campaigner he hoped to hell was at this moment armed to his teeth.

The man with the shotgun said, "It's time to even a score, you wavy-haired son of a bitch."

Wavy-haired, Bren Early thought and said, "If you intend to try it, you better look around behind you."

"God Almighty, you think I'm dumb!" the man named Baker said, as though it was the final insult. He jammed the shotgun to his shoulder; the barrels of the two rifles came up, metal flashing in the afternoon sunlight, and there was no way to stop them.

Edgar Watson, the station agent, had told his wife and children to stay in the kitchen. He heard the gunfire all at once, at least four or five shots exploding almost simultaneously. Edgar Watson rushed to the window by the bar and looked out to see the three cardplayers lying on the hardpack, Bren Early standing out by his wagon with a smoking revolver; then the colored man, Bo, who must have been just outside the house, walking out to look at the three on the ground.

When they came in, Edgar Watson drew a beer and placed it on the bar for Bren Early. He was surprised then when the colored man, Bo, raised an old Navy Colt's—exactly like the one kept under the bar—and laid it on the shiny oak surface. The colored man said, "Thank you for the use," before Edgar Watson realized it *was* his own gun. Bren Early told him to draw a beer for his friend Bo and Edgar Watson did so. Upon examining the Colt's, he found two rounds had been fired from the gun. Still, when Edgar Watson told the story later—and as many times as he told it—it was Bren Early who had shot the three cardplayers when they tried to kill him.

5

McKean's Ranch on the San Pedro: October, 1888

Moon rode up in the cool of early evening leading the palomino on a hackamore. He dropped the rope and the good-looking young mare stood right where she was, not flicking a muscle.

"She reminded me of you," Moon said to the McKean girl, who replied:

"I hope not her hind end."

"Her hair and her eyes," Moon said. "She answers to Goldie."

The McKean girl's mother and dad and three brothers came out to look at the palomino, the horse shying a little as they put their hands on her. Mr. McKean said the horse was still pretty green, huh? Moon said no, it was the horse had not seen so many people before at one time and felt crowded. They kidded him that he was bringing horses now, courting like an Indian.

Moon told them at supper he had been offered a government job as agent at White Tanks, working for the Bureau of Indian Affairs. He would be paid $1,500 a year and given a house and land for farming.

All the McKeans looked at Katy who was across the table from him, the mother saying it sounded wonderful.

Moon did not feel natural sitting there waiting for approval. He said, "But I don't care for flat land, no matter if it has good water and will grow anything you plant. I'm not a grain farmer. I told them I want high graze and would pick my own homesite or else they could keep their wonderful offer."

The McKeans all looked at Katy again.

"They're thinking about it," Moon said. "Meanwhile I got horse contracts to deliver."

"When'll you be back?" Mr. McKean asked.

"Not before Christmas."

"You wait too long," McKean said, "this girl might not be here."

"It's up to me when I get back and up to her if she wants to wait." Moon felt better as soon as he said it.

6

St. Helen: February, 1889

Bren Early said hadn't they met here one time before? Moon said it was a small world, wasn't it?

Moon here delivering a string of horses to the Hatch & Hodges relay station. Bren Early here to make a stage connection, out of the hunting expedition business and going to Tucson to sleep in a feather bed with a woman and make all the noise he wanted.

He said, "Do you know what it's like to make love to a woman dying for it and have to be quiet as a snake lest you wake up her husband?"

"No I don't," Moon said, "but I'm willing to hear about it."

There was snow up in the Rincons, a wind moaning outside, a dismal, depressing kind of day. But snug inside the relay station. They stood at the bar and had whiskey before Bren shed his buffalo overcoat and Moon peeled off his sheepskin and wornout chaps. Then sat at the plank table with a bottle of whiskey and mugs of coffee, smelling meat frying; next to them were giant shadows on the plaster wall, dark twin images in a glow of coal-oil light. Like two old pards drinking and catching up on each other's life, wondering how they could have spent a whole year and a half apart. Neither one of them mentioned the McKean girl.

The main topic: Was somebody shooting at you? Yeah—you too? And getting that business finally cleared up. Bren saying he had come out here to be an Indian Fighter and so far had killed nine white men, counting the first two from the bunch in Sonora (the two Bo Catlett had shot), and two he would tell Moon about presently. Moon, not digging up any bodies from the past, said, Well, you're ahead of me there.

But what about this loving a woman and not making any noise?

"Something happens to those women when they come out here," Bren said. "Or it's the type of woman to begin with, like to put a Winchester to her shoulder and feel it kick."

"Or the wavy-haired guide giving her his U.S. Cavalry look," Moon said. "You wear your saber?"

Bren straightened a little as if to argue, then shrugged, admitting yes, there was a point in that he was a man of this western country; and the woman's husband, out here with his gold-plated Henry in a crocodile case, was still a real-estate man from Chicago or a home builder from Pittsburgh.

"Get to the good part," Moon said.

Bren told him about the party he took up into the Chiricahuas: the man named Bert Grumbach, millionaire president of Prudential Realty in Chicago; his colored valet; a young assistant in Grumbach's company who wore a stiff collar and necktie, as the man did; and the man's wife Greta, yes indeed, who was even rounder and better-looking than that French actress Sarah Bernhardt.

As soon as he met them at Willcox with the wagon and saddle horses, Bren said he could see what kind of trip it was going to be: the man, Bert Grumbach, one of those know-it-all talkers, who'd been everywhere hunting and had a game room full of trophies to prove it, considered this trip not much more than going out back to shoot rabbits. The wife, Greta, was quiet, not at all critical like other wives. ("How many times you gonna tell that tiger story?" Or; "You think drinking all that whiskey proves you're a man?") No, Bert Grumbach would be talking away and Bren would feel Greta's eyes on him. He'd glance over and sure enough, she'd be staring, giving him a calm, steady look with her eyes. Christ, Bren said, you knew exactly what she wanted.

She did not try to outdo her husband either, though she was a fair shot for a woman, dropping a mule-deer buck at two hundred yards with a clean hit through the shoulders.

Moon asked if they left deer laying all over the mountain and Bren said no, the guides took most of the meat to the fort Indians at Bowie.

It wasn't all hunting. Time was spent sitting around camp drinking, eating venison steaks, talking and drinking some more, Grumbach belittling the setup and the fare. Bren said he would perform a routine with his .44 Russians, blowing up a row of dead whiskey bottles, which the Eastern hunters usually ate up. Except Grumbach wasn't impressed. He had a matched pair of Merwin & Hulbert six-shooters, beauties he took out of a rosewood box, nickle-plated with carved ivory grips. He'd aim, left hand on his hip, and fire and hit bottles, cans, pine cones at twenty paces, chipmunks, ground squirrels, ospreys and horned owls. He was a regular killer, Bren said.

"And he caught you with his wife," Moon said.

"Not outright," Bren said. "I believe he only suspected, but it was enough."

What happened, Greta began coming to Bren's tent late at night. The first time, he tried in a nice way to get her to leave; but as she took her robe off and stood bare-ass, she said unless he did likewise she would scream. There was no choice but to give in to her, Bren said. But it was ticklish business, her moaning and him saying shhh, be quiet, his nerves alive as another part of him did the job at hand. Five or six nights, that was the drill.

The morning of the final day of the hunt, Bert Grumbach walked up to Bren, slapped his face with a glove and said, "I assume you will choose pistols. May I suggest twenty paces?"

Moon had an idea what happened next, since Bren was sitting here telling it; but he did not interrupt or even pick up his whiskey glass as Bren continued.

Bren said to the man, Now wait a minute. You know what you're doing? The man said he demanded satisfaction, his honor being abused. Bren said, But is it worth it? You might die. Grumbach gave him a superior look and had his assistant draw up a paper stating this was a duel of honor and if one of the participants was killed or injured, the other would not be legally culpable, hereby and so on, attesting with their signatures they were entering into it willingly and pledging to exonerate the other of blame whatever the outcome.

Bren said they stood about sixty feet apart, each with a revolver held at his side. Bo Catlett would fire his own weapon, the assistant holding a rifle on Bo to see he fired up in the air, and that would be the signal.

"Yeah?" Moon said, hunching over the plank table.

"Aiming at a man and seeing him drawing a bead on you isn't the same as shooting chipmunks," Bren said, "or even wilder animals."

"No, it isn't," Moon said. "He hurried, didn't he?"

"He dropped his hand from his off hip, stood straddle-legged and began firing as fast as he could. Having to protect myself, I shot him once, dead center."

"What did Greta do?"

"Nothing. We rolled Grumbach up in a piece of canvas, had a

coffin made in Willcox and shipped him home with his legal papers. Greta said thank you very much for a wonderful and exciting time."

"Well," Moon said, "you have come to be a shooter, haven't you?"

"Not by choice," Bren said. "There was another fella at Bowie tried his luck when I sold my wagon and string. Announced he was an old compadre of one Clement Hurd. How come they all tracked after me and only one of them tried for you as a prize?"

"You advertise," Moon said. "Captain Early, the great hunter and lover. When did you get promoted?"

"I thought it sounded like a proper rank to have," Bren said. "Well, I've bid farewell to the world of commerce and won't be advertising any more. It's a good business if you have an agreeable nature and can stand grinning at people who don't know hotcakes from horseshit."

"I'm leaving my business, too," Moon said. "Gonna try working for the government one more time."

Bren Early was off somewhere in his mind. He sighed, turning in his chair to sit back against his shadow on the plaster wall.

"Down in Sonora that time, we stood at the line, didn't we?"

"I guess it's something you make up your mind to," Bren Early said, "if you don't care to kiss ass. But my, it can complicate your life."

FIVE

1

Young Maurice Dumas of the *Chicago Times* looked at his list of THINGS TO DO:

Interview W. A. Vandozen, LaSalle Mining v.p. staying at Congress.

How? The only chance would be to run into the man accidentally, as he did with Early, and show the man he was courteous (took his cap off), industrious and did not ask personal or embarrassing questions or make brash assumptions.

And then kiss his hinie, why don't you? Maurice Dumas thought.

It had been pure luck with Brendan Early, the timing, catching him in a talkative mood. Then being invited out to the desert to watch him shoot: amazing, studying the man as he calmly blazed away with two different sets of matched revolvers: one pair, Smith & Wesson, big and mean-looking; the other, ivory-handled, nickle-plated Merwin & Hulberts that Early said were given to him by a wealthy and grateful lady from Chicago. Not saying why she had been grateful. At first—out there shooting at saguaro and barrel cactus that were about the girth of a man—Early seemed troubled about the accuracy of his weapons. But within an hour his confidence was restored and as they rode back to Sweetmary Early told about the Sonora Incident and what he knew of Phil Sundeen. Which covered the next item on Maurice Dumas' THINGS TO DO.

Find out about this Sundeen.

Early said he had assumed the man was buried beneath Mexican soil and was surprised to learn he was alive and kicking. Different other LaSalle Mining people said that Sundeen had been hired by the company as Supervisor in Charge of Protection and Public Safety and was to see that no one infringed on company leases, destroyed company property or exposed themselves to harm or injury in areas related to company mining operations.

What?

The news reporters in the Gold Dollar said what it meant in plain English: Phil Sundeen had been hired to bust heads, shoot trespassers and run them off company land. And that included all the Indians, niggers and Mexicans living up in the Rincons. For months the two sides had been threatening and calling each other names. Finally, as soon as Sundeen arrived, there would be some action to write about. Yes, the company had called him in, a spokesman said, as an expert in restoring order and maintaining peace.

Good, the newsmen said, because it certainly wasn't much of a war without any shooting.

"I said restore peace," the company spokesman said. And a reporter said, "We know what you mean."

But wait a minute. Why hire Sundeen? Why not let Bren Early, known to be a shooter, restore order and maintain peace?

Because Mr. Early had his own responsibilities as Coordinating Manager of the Southwest Region, the company spokesman said.

According to the journalists that was a pile of horse shit. Not one of them, including Maurice Dumas, had yet to see Bren Early sitting at a desk or coordinating much other than a draw poker hand. Bren Early had been hired as part of the deal when the company bought his claims, and his executive title had been made up out of thin air. They *could* put him to work if they wanted. Otherwise Early was to keep himself available to show visiting dignitaries and politicians the Works: which meant the local whorehouses and gambling parlors and—if the visitors were inclined—take them out hunting or to look at some live Indians. It was said the company was paying Early a guaranteed $100,000 over ten years, plus a one-percent royalty on all the milled copper sent to market. He was a rich man.

O.K., but now Early and Sundeen were on the same side. What about the bitterness between them—as reported by Maurice Dumas? How would it affect the Early-Moon Feud? Would it be like a preliminary event, winner getting to go against Dana Moon?

The journalists sat down to have a few drinks and think about that one, see if they could develop a side issue cross-plot to lay over the main action. They fooled with possible headline themes such as:

Prospect of Preliminary Showdown Delays War
Will New Man Live to Take Command?
Shoot-Out Expected on LaSalle Street

All this even before Phil Sundeen arrived in town. If he had the least intention of gunning for Bren Early he would find the atmosphere most conducive.

Meanwhile, Maurice Dumas was working on the third item on his list of THINGS TO DO.

Interview Dana Moon.

2

When Maurice Dumas arrived at White Tanks he didn't know what was going on: all these Apaches, about a hundred of them out in the pasture near the agency buildings and stock pens, sitting around campfires, roasting chunks of beef while others were chanting and a line of women were doing some kind of shuffle dance. Like it was an Indian Fourth of July picnic or some kind of tribal pow-wow. Some of the men wore hats and parts of white men's clothes, a pair of trousers, a vest; though most of them still wore skirts and high moccasins and thick headbands wrapped around their coarse hair.

Maurice Dumas found out it was Meat Day. When the beef allotment provided by the government was delivered, the Apaches always butchered a few head on the spot and had a feast. They would stuff themselves with meat, eating it straight, drink some corn beer, or tulapai, as it was called, spend the night here in the agency pasture and, in the morning, drive their skimpy herd up into the mountains to their rancherías. Maurice Dumas remembered being told that Apaches always camped high and wouldn't be caught dead living down in the flats. It was part of the problem in this land dispute which he wanted to discuss with Dana Moon—if he could find him.

Well, it seemed he was getting luckier all the time—just by chance arriving on Meat Day—dismounting his hired horse in front of the Indian Agency office, a one-story adobe building with a wooden front porch, and there was Moon himself sitting in a straight chair tilted back, his boots up on the porch rail, at rest. Perfect, Maurice Dumas thought. The Indian agent in his seat of governmental authority, while his charges performed their tribal rites.

Moon looked exactly as he did in the C. S. Fly photos, though not as buttoned up and strapped together. He did not appear to be armed. His belt buckle was undone and he was smoking a cigar. When Maurice Dumas introduced himself, Moon asked if he would like something to eat. The news reporter said no thanks. He handed Moon a paper bag saying, "A little something for you," and watched as Moon took out the bottle of Green River bourbon whiskey and read the label unhurriedly before placing the quart on the plank floor next to him. "Thank you," he said.

"I just wanted to talk to you a little," Maurice Dumas said. "Ask your opinion of a few things."

"Ask," Moon said.

"I didn't think you lived here at the agency."

"I don't. I'm a few miles up that barranca," lowering his head and looking west, beyond the pasture and the gathering of feasting Indians. "I'm here for Meat Day and will leave soon as I'm able to." He seemed full but not too uncomfortable.

"Do you live up there alone?"

"My wife and I."

"Oh, I didn't know you were married."

"Why would you?"

"I mean nobody's mentioned it."

"Does it make a difference in how you see me?"

"I mean I'm just surprised," Maurice Dumas said. "If there's gonna be trouble and all—I was thinking, having your wife there could make it harder for you."

Moon said, "Do you know how many wives are up there? How many families?"

"I guess I hadn't thought of it."

"You call it a war, you like to keep it simple," Moon said. "These men against those men. Line 'em up, let's see who wins. Well, to do that we'd have to get rid of the women and children. Where should we send them?"

"As I said, I hadn't thought about it."

"What do you think about?" Moon asked. The front legs of the chair hit the plank floor as Moon got up and went into the agency office.

Now what? Was he offended by something? No, Moon came

out again with two glasses, sat down and poured them a couple of drinks.

Maurice Dumas pulled a chair over next to Moon's. "I'm only an observer," he said, sitting down and carefully tilting back. "I don't take sides, I remain objective."

"You're on a side whether you like it or not," Moon said. "You're on the side of commerce and, I imagine, you believe in progress and good government."

"What's wrong with that?"

"Copper is progress and the land has been leased to the mine company by the government."

Maurice Dumas didn't like the insinuation. "That doesn't mean I'm on the side of the company. But if we're talking about legal rights, I'd have to say *they*, the legal right, are. The company owns mineral rights to the land for a hundred years."

"You feel that's long enough?"

"I don't know how long it takes."

Moon took a sip of whiskey and drew on his cigar. "You happen to know what the mine company's doing up there?"

"Right now they're surveying," Maurice Dumas said, "trying to locate veins and ore loads that look promising."

"And how are they doing that?"

"As I understand, they set off dynamite, then pick around, see what they've got."

Moon waited.

"So far, I guess they haven't found anything worth sinking a shaft in."

"But they spook the herds, scatter 'em all over, kill what they want for meat," Moon said. "They've blown up stock tanks, ruined the natural watershed, wiped out crops and some homes in rock slides. They tear up a man's land, clean him out, and leave it."

"It's theirs to tear up," the news reporter said.

"No, it isn't," Moon said, in a quiet but ominous tone.

The whiskey made Maurice Dumas feel confident and knowledgeable. He said, "I'd like to say you're right. Good for you. But the fact remains your Indians are off the White Tanks reservation by several miles. And the other people up there, whoever they are, are living on land without deed or title. So LaSalle Mining, legally, has every right to make them leave."

"You asked my opinion," Moon said. "Are you gonna print it in the paper?"

"I hope to, yes."

"You're not writing anything down."

"I have a good memory," Maurice Dumas said.

"Well, remember this," Moon said. "The Mimbre Apaches were hunting up there before Christopher Columbus came over in his boat, and till now nobody's said a word about it, not even the Indian Bureau. There's a settlement of colored people, colored soldiers who've taken Indian wives, all of them at one time in the United States Tenth Cavalry. You would think the government owed them at least a friendly nod, wouldn't you? The Mexicans living up there have claims that go back a hundred years or more to Spanish land grants. The Mexicans went to Federal Claims Court to try to protect their property. They got thrown out. I wrote to the Indian Bureau about the Apaches up there—it's *their* land, let 'em live on it. No, they said, get your people back to White Tanks or you're fired. You see the influence the company has? Generations they've hunted, roamed through those mountains. Government doesn't say a word till the big company kneels on 'em for a favor. Yes sir, we'll see to it right away, Mr. LaSalle—"

"Is there a Mr. LaSalle?" Maurice didn't think so.

"I went to Federal District Court to get an injunction. I wanted to restrict the mine company to certain areas—they find ore, O.K., they pay a royalty on it to any people that have to move. They don't find any ore, they clean up their mess and get out. The judge held up my injunction—cost me fifty dollars to have written—like it was paper you keep in the privy and threw it out of court."

"Legal affairs get complicated," the news reporter offered.

"Do you want to tell me how it is," Moon said, "or you want to listen."

"I'm sorry. Go on."

"All these people I've mentioned number only about two hundred and sixty, counting old ones, women and young children. Fewer than fifty able-bodied men. And they're spread all over. By that, I mean they don't present any kind of unified force. The mine company can send a pack of armed men up there with guns and dynamite to take the land, and you know what will happen?"

"Well, eventually—" the reporter began.

"Before eventually," Moon said. "You know what will happen? Do you want to go ask the people what they'll do if armed men come?"

"Will they tell me?"

"They'll tell you it's their land. If the company wants it, the company will have to take it."

"Well," the news reporter said, a little surprised, "that's exactly what the company will do, take it."

"When you write your article for the paper," Moon said, "don't write the end till it happens."

SIX

1

White Tanks: May, 1889

Moon and four Mimbre Apaches were whitewashing the agency office when the McKean girl rode up on her palomino. They appeared to have the job almost done—the adobe walls clean and shining white—and were now slapping the wash on a front porch made of new lumber that looked to be a recent addition.

The McKean girl wore a blue bandana over her hair and a blue skirt that was bunched in front of her on the saddle and hung down on the sides just past the top of her boots.

Sitting her horse, watching, she thought of India: pictures she had seen of whitewashed mud buildings on barren land and little brown men in white breechclouts and turbans—though the headpieces the Apaches wore were rusty red or brown, dark colors, and their black hair hung in strands past their shoulders. It was strange she thought of India Indians and not American Indians. Or not so strange, because this place did not seem to belong in the mountains of Arizona. Other times looking at Apaches, when she saw them close, she thought of gypsies: dark men wearing regular clothes, but in strange, colorful combinations of shirts made from dresses beneath checkered vests, striped pants tucked into high moccasins and wearing jewelry, men wearing beads and metal trinkets. The Mexicans called them barbarians. People the McKean girl knew called them red niggers and heathens.

Moon—he was saying something in a strange tongue and the Apaches, with whitewash smeared over their bare skin, were laughing. She had never heard an Apache laugh, nor had even thought of them laughing before this. Coming here was like visiting a strange land.

One of the Apaches saw her and said something to Moon. He turned from his painting and came down from the porch as the Apaches watched. He looked strange himself: suspenders over his bare, hairy chest, his body pure white but his forearms weathered brown, like he was wearing long gloves. He was looking at her leg, her thigh beneath the skirt, as he approached.

She expected him to pat the mare and pretend to be interested in her, saying how's Goldie. But he didn't. He looked from her leg up to her face, squinting in the sun, and said, "You getting anxious?"

"It's been seven months," Katy McKean said. "If you've changed your mind I want to know."

"I've been building our house," Moon said.

The McKean girl looked at the whitewashed adobe, and the stock pens, the outpost on the barren flats, dressed with a flagpole flying the stars and stripes. Like a model post office.

"That?" she said.

"Christ, no," Moon said. "That's not a house, that's a symbol. Our house is seven miles up the draw, made of 'dobe plaster and stone. Front porch is finished and a mud fence is being put up now."

"You like front porches," the McKean girl said. "Well, they must've given you what you wanted. What do you do in return?"

"Keep the peace. Count heads. I'm a high-paid tally hand is what I am."

"Tell them jokes, like you were doing?"

"See eye to eye," Moon said. "A man catches his wife in the bushes with some other fella—you know what he does? He cuts the end of her nose off. The wife's mother gets upset and tells the police to arrest the husband and punish him and the police dump it in my lap."

"And what do you do?"

"Tell the woman she looks better with a short nose—I don't know what I do," Moon said. "I live near them—not with them— and try not to change their customs too much."

"Like moving to a strange heathen land," the McKean girl said, unconsciously touching her nose.

"Well, Christian people, they caught a woman in adultery they used to stone her to death. Customs change in time."

"But they never do anything to the man," the McKean girl said.

"Ask your dad, the old philosopher, about that one," Moon said. "Ask him if it's all right for you to come live among the heathens."

"When?"

"Next fall sometime," Moon said. "October."

"Next month," the McKean girl said, "the third Saturday in June at St. John the Apostle's, ten A.M. Who's gonna be your best man, one of these little dark fellas?"

The wedding took place the fourth Saturday in June and the best man was Brendan Early: Bren looking at the bride in church, looking at her in the dining room of the Charles Crooker Hotel where the reception was held, still not believing she had chosen quiet Dana Moon. It wasn't that Bren had sought her hand and been rejected. He had not gotten around to asking her; though it had always been in the back of his mind he might easily marry her someday. Right now, as Dana's wife, she was the best-looking girl he had ever seen, and the cleanest-looking, dressed in white with her blonde hair showing. And now it was too late. Amazing. Like he'd blinked his eyes and two years had passed. They asked him what he was doing these days and he said, well (not about to tell these industrious people he was making a living as a mine-camp cardplayer), he was looking into a mining deal at the present time—saying it because he had in his pocket the title to a staked-out claim he'd won in a $2,000-call poker game. Yes, he was in mining now.

And told others on the Helvetia stage—pushed by a nagging conscience or some curious urge, having seen his old chum settling down with a wife he thought *he* would someday have. Time was passing him by and it wasn't the ticket for a gentleman graduate of the U.S. Military Academy to be making a living dealing faro or peaking at hole cards. Why *not* look into this claim he now owned? He had title and a signed assay report that indicated a pocket of high-yield gold ore if not a lode.

Starting out on that return trip to nowhere he was in mining. Before the stage had reached its destination Bren Early was in an altogether different situation.

2

The Benson-Helvetia Stage: June, 1889

Three very plain-looking ladies who had got off the train from an Eastern trip had so much baggage, inside and out, there was only room for Bren Early and one other passenger: a fifty-year-old dandy who wore a cavalry mustache, his hat brim curved up on one side, and carried a cane with a silver knob.

Bren Early and the Dandy sat next to each other facing the plain-looking, chattering ladies who seemed excitable and nervous and were probably sweating to death in their buttoned-up velvet travel outfits. Facing them wasn't so bad; Bren could look out the window at the countryside moving past in the rickety, rattling pounding of the stagecoach; but the Dandy, with his leather hatbox and travel bag, lounged in a way that took up more than half the seat, sticking his leg out at an angle and forcing Bren Early to sit against the sideboards. Bren nudged the Dandy's leg to acquire more room and the Dandy said, "If you don't mind, sir," sticking his leg out again.

"I do," Bren Early said, "since I paid for half this bench."

"And I paid in receiving a wound to this leg in the war," the Dandy said. "So, if you don't mind."

The ladies gave him sympathetic looks and one of them arranged her travel case so the Dandy could prop his leg on it. The Dandy had a cane, yes, but Bren Early had seen the man walk out of the Benson station to the coach without a limp or faltering gait. Then one of the ladies asked him whom he had served with.

The Dandy said, "I had the honor of serving with the Texas Brigade, Madam, attached to General Longstreet's command, and received my wound at the Battle of the Wilderness, May 6, 1864. Exactly twenty-five years ago last month."

Bren Early listened, thinking, Ask him a question, he gives you plenty of answer. One of the ladies said it must have been horrible being wounded in battle and said she was so thankful she was a woman.

"It was ill fate," the Dandy said, "to be wounded in victory while giving the enemy cold steel, routing them, putting to flight some of the most highly regarded regiments in Yankeedom. But I have no regrets. The fortunes of war sent a minié ball through my leg and an Army wagon delivered me to the hospital at Belle Plain."

"Whose wagon?" Bren Early said.

The Dandy gave him a superior look and said, "Sir?"

"You are only half right in what you tell these ladies," Bren Early said. "You did meet six of the most respected regiments in the Union Army: the Second, Sixth and Seventh Wisconsin, the Nineteenth Indiana and the Twenty-fourth Michigan. You met the men of the Iron Brigade and if you ever meet one again, take off your hat and buy him a drink, for you're lucky to be alive."

"You couldn't have been there," the Dandy said, still with the superior look.

"No," Bren Early said, "but I've studied the action up and down the Orange Plank Road and through the woods set afire by artillery. The Iron Brigade, outnumbered, fought Longstreet to a standstill and *you*, if you were taken to Belle Plain then you went as a prisoner because the Confederate line never reached that far east."

The Dandy looked at the ladies and shrugged with a weary sigh. See what a wounded veteran has to put up with?

Bren Early had to hold on from grabbing the mincing son of a bitch and throwing him out the window. With the ladies giving him cold-fish looks he pulled his new Stetson down over his eyes and made up his mind to sleep.

Lulled by the rumbling racket of the coach he saw himself high on a shelf of rock against a glorious blue sky, a gentle breeze blowing. There he was on the narrow ledge, ignoring the thousand-foot drop directly behind him, swinging his pick effortlessly, dislodging a tremendous boulder and seeing in the exposed seam the glitter of gold particles imbedded in rock, chunks of gold he flicked out with his penknife, nuggets he scooped up from the ground and dropped into canvas sacks. He saw a pile of sacks in a cavern and saw himself hefting them, estimating the weight of his fortune at $35 an ounce . . . $560 a pound . . . $56,000 a hundred pounds . . . He slept and awoke to feel the coach swaying, slowing down, coming to a stop, the three ladies and the Dandy leaning over to look out the windows. The driver, or somebody up above them, was saying, "Everybody do what they say. Don't anybody try to be brave."

The ladies were now even more excitable and nervous and began to make sounds like they were going to cry. The Dandy gathered his hatbox and travel bag against him and slipped his right hand inside his waistcoat.

The voice up top said, "We're not carrying no mail or anything but baggage."

And another voice said, "Let's see if you can step off the boot with your hands in the air."

Shit, Bren Early thought.

His revolvers were in his war-bag beneath his feet, stowed away so as not to upset the homely, twittery ladies, and, for the sake of comfort. What would anybody hope to get robbing this chicken coop? The only important stop between Benson and points west was Sweetmary, a mining town; and he doubted a tacky outfit like this stage line would be entrusted to deliver a payroll. No—he was sure of it, because there was just the driver on top, no armed guard with him, not even a helper. Cheap goddamn outfit.

A rider on a sorrel came up to the side of the coach, Bren seeing his pistol extended, a young cowboy face beneath an old curled-brim hat.

"You, mister," the young rider said to the Dandy, "let me see your paws. All of you keep your paws out in plain sight."

Another one, Bren Early was thinking. Practiced it and it sounded good. Times must be bad.

Looking past the sorrel Bren could see two more riders beyond the road in the scrub, and the driver standing by the front wheel now, a shotgun on the ground. The rider on the sorrel was squinting up at the baggage, nudging his horse closer. He dismounted then and opened the coach door to look in at the petrified ladies in velvet and the two gentlemen across from them. Someone behind the young rider yelled, "Pull that gear offa there!"

Making him do all the work while they sit back, Bren thought. Dumb kid. In bad company.

The young rider stepped up on the rung and into the door opening, reaching up to the baggage rack with both hands. His leather chaps, his gunbelt, his skinny trunk in a dirty cotton skirt were right there, filling the doorway. Bren thinking, He's too dumb to live long at his trade. Hoping the kid wasn't excitable. Let him get out of here with some of the ladies' trinkets and the Dandy's silver cane and think he's made a haul. Bren had three twenty-dollar gold pieces and some change he'd contribute to the cause. Get it done so they could get on with the ride.

Sitting back resigned, letting it happen, Bren wasn't prepared—

he couldn't believe it—when the fifty-year-old Dandy made his move, hunching forward as he drew a nickle-plated pistol from inside his coat and shoved the gun at the exposed shirtfront in the doorway, pointing the barrel right where the young rider's shirttail was coming out of his pants as he reached above him.

Bren said, "No!" grabbing at the Dandy's left arm, the man wrenching away and coming back to swat him across the face with his silver-tipped cane—the son of a bitch, if that was the way he wanted it . . . Bren cocked his forearm and backhanded his fist and arm across the man's upper body. But too late. The nickle-plate jabbed into the shirtfront and went off with a report that rang loud in the wooden coach. The young rider cried out, hands in the air, and was gone. The women were screaming now and the Dandy was firing again—the little dude son of a bitch, maybe he *had* raised hell at the Wilderness with his Texas Brigade. He was raising hell now, snapping shots at the two riders until Bren Early backhanded him again, hard, giving himself room to get out of the coach.

He saw the young rider lying on the ground, the sorrel skitting away. He saw the driver kneeling, raising the shotgun and the two mounted men whipping their horses out of there with the twin sounds of the double-barrel reports, the riders streaking dust across the scrub waste, gone, leaving the young rider behind.

Kneeling over him, Bren knew the boy was dead before he touched his throat for a pulse. Dead in an old blood-stained shirt hanging out of his belt; converted Navy cap-and-ball lying in the dust next to him. Poor dumb kid, gone before he could learn anything. He heard the Dandy saying something.

"He's one of them."

Bren Early looked up, seeing the driver coming over, reloading the shotgun.

"I had a feeling about him and, goddamn it, I was right," the Dandy said. "He's the inside man. Tried to stop me."

Bren said, "You idiot. You killed this boy for no reason."

The driver was pointing his shotgun at him, saying, "Put your hands in the air."

3

Sweetmary: June, 1889

Mr. and Mrs. Dana Moon got out of the Charles Crooker Hotel in Benson after two honeymoon nights in the bridal suite and coming down to breakfast to feel everybody in the dining room looking at them and the waitress grinning and saying, "Well, how are we this morning, just fine?" They loaded a buckboard with their gear, saddles, two trunks of linen, china and household goods, and took the old stage road west, trailing their horses. Why stay cooped up in somebody else's room when they had a new home in the mountains with an inside water pump and a view of practically the entire San Pedro Valley?

In late afternoon they came to Sweetmary, a town named for a copper mine, a town growing out of the mine works and crushing mill high up on the grade: the town beginning from company buildings and reaching down to flatland to form streets, rows of houses and business establishments—Moon remembering it as a settlement of tents and huts, shebangs made of scrap lumber, only a year before—the town growing out of the mine just as the hump ridges of ore tailings came down the grade from the mine shafts. LaSalle was the main street and the good hotel was in Congress. One more night in somebody else's bed. In the morning they'd buy a few provisions at the company store and head due north for home.

During this trip Moon said to his wife, "You're a Katy a lot of ways; I think you'll always look young. But you're not a bashful girl, are you? I think you're more of a Kate than a Katy, and that's meant as a compliment."

In the morning, lying in the Congress Hotel bed with the sun hot on the windows, he said, "I thought people only did it at night. I mean married people."

"Who says you have to wait till dark?" She grinned at him and said then, "You mean if you're not married you can do it any time?"

"You do it when you see the chance. I guess that's it," Moon said. "Married people are busy all day, so it's become the custom to do it at night."

"Custom," Kate said. "What's the custom among the Indians? I bet whenever they feel the urge, right? You ever do it outside?"

Moon pretended he had to think to recall and Kate said, "I want to do it outside when we get home."

"I built us a *bed*."

"We'll use the bed. But I want to do it different places. Try different other ways."

Moon looked at this girl lying next to him, amazed. "What other way is there?"

"I don't know if we can do them in the daylight, but I got some ideas." She smiled at him and said, "Being married is fun, you know it?"

Moon was getting dressed, buttoning his shirt and looking out the window, when he saw Brendan Early. He said, "Jesus Christ." Kate came over in her bloomers to look too.

There he was, Moon's best man, walking along the street in a file of jail prisoners carrying shovels and picks, the group dressed in washed-out denim uniforms—the letter "P" stenciled in white on the shirts and pants—being herded along by several armed men on horseback.

"Jesus Christ," Moon said again, with awe. "What's he done now?"

When Moon found them, the work detail was clearing a drainage ditch about two miles from town, up in the hills back of the mine works. Mounted, he circled and came down from above them to approach Bren Early working with a shovel, in his jail uniform, his new Stetson dirty and sweat-stained. There were four guards with shotguns. The one on the high side, dismounted and sitting about ten yards off in the shade of a cedar stand, heard Moon first and raised his shotgun as he got to his feet.

"Don't come no closer!"

Now Bren Early straightened and was looking this way, leaning on the high end of his shovel. He watched Moon nudging his buckskin down toward them—not knowing Moon's game, so not calling out or saying anything.

"I said don't come no closer!"

This man with the shotgun was the Cochise County Deputy Sheriff for Sweetmary. His name—Moon had learned in town—was R.J. Bruckner. Moon said it now, inquiringly.

"Mr. Bruckner?"

"What do you want?"

There did not appear to be any warmth or cordiality in the man.

He was heavy-set and mean-looking with a big nose and a florid complexion to go with his ugly disposition. Moon would try sounding patient and respectful and see what happened.

He said, "My, it's a hot day to be working, isn't it?"

"You got business with me, state it," Bruckner said, "or else get your nosey ass out of here."

My oh my, Moon thought, taking off his hat and resetting it low against the sun, giving himself a little time to adjust and remain calm. The plug of tobacco in his jaw felt dry and he sucked on it a little.

"I wonder if I could have a word with one of your prisoners."

"God Almighty," Bruckner said, "get the hell away from here."

"That good-looking fella there, name of Early. His mama's worried about him," Moon said, "and sent me out looking."

"Tell his mama she can visit him at Yuma. That boy's going away for twenty years."

"Can I ask what he's done?"

"Held up the Benson stage and was caught at it."

Bren Early, standing in the drainage ditch, was shaking his head slowly, meaning no, he didn't, or just weary of it all.

"Has he been tried already?"

"Hasn't come up yet."

"Then how do you know he's getting twenty years?"

"It's what I'll recommend to the Circuit Court in Tombstone."

"Oh," Moon nodded, showing how agreeable he was. "When is the trial going to be?"

"When I take him down there," Bruckner said.

"Pretty soon now?"

"When I decide," Bruckner said, irritated now. "Get the hell away from here 'fore I put you in the ditch with him."

R.J. Bruckner did not know at that moment—as Moon's hand went to his shirtfront but stopped before going inside the coat—how close he was to being shot.

Back at the Congress Hotel Moon said to his wife, "I have never had the urge like I did right then. It's not good, to be armed and feel like that."

"But understandable," Kate said. "What are we gonna do?"

"Stay here another night, if it's all right."

"Whatever you decide," his wife said. She loved this man very much, but sometimes his calmness frightened her. She watched him wash and change his shirt and slip on the shoulder holster that held the big Colt's revolver—hidden once his coat was on, but she knew it was there and she knew the man, seeing him again standing at the adobe wall in Sonora.

After supper Mr. and Mrs. Moon sat in rocking chairs on the porch of the Congress Hotel—Kate saying, "This is what you like to do, huh?"—until the Mexican boy came up to them and said in Spanish, "He left." Moon gave the boy two bits and walked down LaSalle Street to the building with the sign that said DEPUTY SHERIFF—COCHISE COUNTY.

Inside the office he told the assistant deputy on duty he was here to see a prisoner, one Brendan Early and, before the deputy could say anything, laid a five-dollar piece on the man's desk.

"Open your coat," the deputy said.

Moon handed the man his Colt's, then followed him through a locked door, down an aisle of cells and up a back stairway to a row of cells on the second floor. Moon had never seen a jail this size, able to hold thirty or more prisoners, in a dinky mining town.

"You know *why*," Bren Early said, talking to Moon through the bars—the deputy standing back a few paces watching them—"because the son of a bitch is making money off us. The mine company pays him fifty cents a day per man to work on roads and drainage and this horse fart Bruckner puts it in his pocket."

"You talk to a lawyer?"

"Shit no, not till I go to trial. Listen, there're rummies in here for drunk and disorderly been working *months*. He thinks I'm a road agent, I could be in here a *year* before I ever see a courtroom. And then I got to face this other idiot who's gonna point to me and say I tried to rob the stage."

"Did you?"

"Jesus Christ, I'm telling you, I don't get out of here I'm gonna take my shovel and bust it over that horse fart's head."

"You're looking pretty good though," Moon said. "Better'n you did at the wedding trying to drink up all the whiskey."

Close to the bars Bren Early said, "You gonna get me out of here or I have to do it myself?"

"I have to take my wife home," Moon said. "Then, after that."

"After that, what? I'm not gonna last any time in this place. You know it, too."

"Don't get him mad at you," Moon said. "Say please and thank you or else keep your mouth shut till I get back."

"When—goddamn it."

"You might see it coming," Moon said, "but I doubt it."

■ ■ ■

This jail was hard time with no relief. Chop rocks and clear ditches or sweat to death in that second-floor, tin-roof cell. (The Fourth of July they sat up there listening to fools shooting their guns off in the street, expecting any moment bullets to come flying in the barred windows.) Bren Early could think of reports he'd read describing Confederate prisons, like Belle Isle in the James River and Libby's warehouse in Richmond, where Union soldiers rotted away and died by the thousands. Compared to those places the Sweetmary lockup was a resort hotel. But Bren would put R.J. Bruckner up with any of the sadistic guards he'd read about, including the infamous Captain Wirz of Andersonville.

One day after work Bruckner marched Bren Early down to the basement of the jail and took him into a room that was like a root cellar. Bren hoped for a moment he would be alone with Bruckner, but two other deputies stood by with pick handles while Bruckner questioned him about the stage holdup.

"One of your accomplices, now deceased, was named Pierson. What are the names of the other two?"

They stood with the lantern hanging behind them by the locked door.

"I wasn't part of it, so I don't know," Bren Early said.

Bruckner stepped forward and hooked a fist into Bren's stomach and Bren hit him hard in the face, jolting him; but that was his only punch before the two deputies stepped in, swinging their pick handles, and beat him to the dirt floor.

Bruckner said, "What's the names of your other two chums?"

Bren said, "I never saw 'em before."

"Once more," Bruckner said.

"I'll tell you one thing," Bren said.

"What is that?"

"When I get out I'm gonna tear your nose off, you ugly shit-face son of a bitch."

As with J.A. McWilliams, killed in Florence a year before while calling Bren Early some other kind of son of a bitch, did he say it all or not? Bren did not quite finish before Bruckner hit him with his fists and the deputies waded in to beat him senseless with the pick handles. Dumb, wavy-haired know-it-all; they fixed him. And they'd see he never let up a minute out on the work detail . . . where

Bren would look up at the high crests and at the brushy ravines and pray for Moon to appear as his redeemer.

"You might see it coming, but I doubt it," Moon had said.

Moon brought six Mimbre Apaches with him: the one named Red and five other stalkers who had chased wild horses with him, had served on the Apache Police at San Carlos and had raised plenty of hell before that.

They scouted Bruckner's work detail for three days, studying the man's moves and habits. The man seemed reasonably alert, that was one consideration. The other: the ground was wide open on both sides of the drainage ditch where the twenty or more prisoners had been laboring these past few days. Clearing a ditch that went where? Moon wasn't sure, unless it diverted water from the mine shafts. A slit trench came down out of a wash from the bald crest of a ridge. There were patches of owl clover on the slope, brittlebush and stubby clumps of mesquite and greasewood, but no cover to speak of.

Moon and his Mimbres talked it over in their dry camp and decided there was only one way to do the job.

Seven A.M., the seventeenth morning of Bren Early's incarceration, found him trudging up the grade with his shovel, second man in the file of prisoners—herded by four mounted guards, Bruckner bringing up the rear—Bren's eyes open as usual to scan the bleak terrain, now reaching the section of ditch they would be working today, moving up alongside it until Bruckner would stick two fingers in his mouth and whistle them to stop, jump in and commence digging and clearing.

Bren didn't see Moon. He didn't see the Mimbre Apaches—not until he heard that sharp whistle, the signal, turned to the trench and saw movement, a bush it looked like, a *bush* and part of the ground coming up out of the ditch, Christ, with a face made of dirt in it, seeing for the first time something he had only heard about: what it was like to stand in open terrain and, Christ, there they were all around you right *there* as you stood where there wasn't a sign of anything living a moment before. The Mimbres came out of the drainage ditch with greasewood in their hair, naked bodies smeared with dirt, and took the four deputies off their horses and had them on the ground, pointing revolvers in their struck-dumb faces before they knew what had happened. There were yells from the prisoners dancing around. Some of them raised their shovels and picks to beat the life out of Bruckner and his guards. But Moon and his stubby shotgun—Moon coming out of the ditch a few yards up the grade—would have none of it. He was not here in behalf of their freedom or revenge. They yelled some more and began to plead—Take us with you; don't leave us here—then cursed in loud voices, with the guards lying face down in the sand, calling Moon obscene names. But Moon never said a word to them or to anyone. Bren Early wanted to go over to Bruckner, but when Moon motioned, he followed. They rode out of there on the deputies' horses and never looked back.

Bren Early went home with Moon, up past the whitewashed agency buildings, up into the rugged east face of the Rincons. He saw Moon's stone house with its low adobe wall rimming the front of the property and its sweeping view of the San Pedro Valley. He saw Moon's wife in her light blue dress and white apron—no longer the McKean girl—saw the two cane chairs on the front porch and smelled the beef roast cooking.

"Well, now you have it, what do you do?" Bren said.

Moon looked at his wife and shrugged, not sure how to answer. "I don't know," he said, "get up in the morning and pull on my boots. How about you?"

"We'll see what happens," Bren said.

He rode out of there in borrowed clothes on a borrowed horse, but with visions of returning in relative splendor. Rich. At rest with himself. And with a glint in his eye that would say to Moon, "You *sure* you got what you want?"

4

Sweetmary: January, 1890

They were having their meeting in the stove-heated company office halfway up the grade, a wind blowing winter through the mine works: Bren Early, bearded, in his buffalo coat; Mr. Vandozen, looking like a banker in his velvet-lapeled Chesterfield and pinch-nose glasses; a man named Ross Selkirk, the superintendent of the Sweetmary works, who clenched a pipe in his jaw; and another company man, a geologist, by the name of Franklin Hovey.

Mr. Vandozen stood at a high table holding his glasses to his face as he looked over Bren Early's registered claims and assay reports. He said once, "There seems to be a question whether you're a miner, Mr. Early, or a speculator."

It wasn't the question he was waiting for, so Bren didn't answer. Mr. Vandozen tried again. "Have you actually mined any ore?"

"Some."

"This one, I'll bet," Mr. Vandozen said, holding up an assay report. "Test would indicate quite a promising concentrate, as high as forty ounces to the ton."

"Three thousand dollars an ore-wagon load," Bren said.

And Mr. Vandozen said, "Before it's milled. On the deficit side you have labor, machinery, supplies, shipping, payments on your note—" The LaSalle Mining vice president, who had come all the way from New Mexico to meet Bren Early, looked over at him. "What do you have left?"

Not a question that required an answer. Bren waited.

"What you have, at best, are pockets of dust," Mr. Vandozen said. "Fast calculations in your head, multiplying ounces times thirty-five, I can understand how it lights up men's eyes. But obviously you don't want to scratch for a few ounces, Mr. Early, or you wouldn't be here."

Bren waited.

"Our geological surveys of your claims are"—Mr. Vandozen shrugged—"interesting, but by no means conclusive enough to warrant sinking shafts and moving in equipment. Though I'm sure you feel you have a major strike."

"Gold fever, it's called," the geologist said. "The symptoms are your eyes popping out of your head." He laughed, but no one else did.

Mr. Vandozen waited longer than he had to, following the interruption. When the office was quiet and they could hear the stove hissing and the wind gusting outside, he said, "We could give you—you have five claims?—all right, five thousand dollars for the lot and a one half of one percent royalty on gold ore after so many tons are milled."

"How much on all the copper ore I've got?"

The shaggy-looking prospector in the buffalo coat stopped everyone cold with the magic word.

It brought Mr. Vandozen's face up from the reports and claim documents to look at this Mr. Early again in a new light.

"You're telling us you have copper?"

"If your geologist knows it, you know it."

"It was my understanding you were only interested in gold."

"I'm interested in all manner of things," Bren said. "What are you interested in, besides high-grade copper?"

Mr. Vandozen took off his pinch-nose glasses and inspected them before putting them away, somewhere beneath his Chesterfield.

"How much do you want?"

There, that was the question. Bren smiled in his beard.

"Ten thousand dollars for the five claims," Mr. Vandozen said. "A two percent royalty on all minerals."

Bren shook his head.

At the fifty-thousand-dollar offer he started for the door. At one-hundred thousand, plus royalties, plus a position with the company, the shaggy-looking miner-speculator stepped up to Mr. Vandozen and shook his hand. That part was done.

When the company superintendent, who was under Bren now in all matters except the actual operation of the mine, brought out a bottle of whiskey and said, "Mr. Early, I'll drink to your health but stay out of my way," Mr. Early looked at him and said:

"You run the works. There's only one area I plan to step into and I'm going to do it with both feet."

This shaggy-looking Bren Early entered the Gold Dollar with his buffalo coat draped over his left shoulder, covering his arm and hanging from shoulder to knee. He wore his Stetson, weathered now and shaped properly for all time, and his showy Merwin & Hulbert ivory-handled revolvers in worn-leather holsters. Business was humming for a cold and dismal afternoon, an hour before the day shift let out. The patrons, tending to their drinking and card playing, did not pay much attention to Bren at first. Not until he walked up behind the Sweetmary Deputy Sheriff who was hunched over the bar on his arms, and said to him:

"Mr. Bruckner?"

As the heavy-set man straightened and came around, Bren Early's right hand appeared from inside the buffalo coat with a pick handle, held short, and cracked it cleanly across the deputy sheriff's face.

Bruckner bellowed, fell sideways against the bar, came around with his great nose pouring blood and stopped dead, staring at Bren Early.

"Yes, you know me," Bren said, and swiped him again, hard, across the head.

Bruckner stumbled against the bar and this time came around with his right hand gripping his holstered Peacemaker. But caution stopped him in the nick of time from pulling it free. The left hand of this shaggy dude—standing like he was posing for a picture— was somewhere beneath that buffalo cape, and only the dude and God knew if he was holding a gun.

Bruckner said, "You're under arrest."

It was strange, Bren admired the remark. While the response from the Gold Dollar patrons was impromptu laughter, a short quick nervous fit of it, then silence. Bren was thinking, They don't know anything what it's like, do they?

He said to Bruckner then, "Wake up and listen to what I tell you. You're gonna pay me eight dollars and fifty cents for the seventeen days I spent on your work gang. You're gonna pay everyone else now working whatever they've earned. You will never again use prisoners to do company work. And as soon as I'm through talking you're gonna go across the street and get my Smith forty-fours and bring them to me in their U.S. Army holsters. If I see you come back in here holding them by the grips or carrying any other weapon, I'll understand your intention and kill you before you get through the door. Now if you doubt or misunderstand anything I've said, go ask Ross Selkirk who the new boss is around here and he'll set you straight."

Bruckner took several moments to say, "I'll be back."

Let him have that much, a small shred of self-respect. The son of a bitch.

As the batwings swung closed, Bren stepped to the bar, lifting his buffalo coat and laying it across the polished surface. The patrons behind him stared and nudged each other. Look—both his revolvers were holstered.

Brendan Early had come to Sweetmary.

SEVEN

1

A news reporter told how he had knocked on the door one evening and when Mrs. Pierson opened it he said, "Excuse me, is this a whorehouse?" The woman said, "No, it isn't," not fazed a bit, and closed the door.

Someone else said, "It may not be a house for whores, but she is little better than one."

"Or better than most," another news reporter at the Gold Dollar said, "or he wouldn't have set her up as he did. She is a doggone good-looking woman."

None of the reporters had known about Mrs. Pierson until Maurice Dumas turned the first stone and then the rest of them began to dig. Maurice Dumas himself, once he saw where the story was leading, backed off so as not to pry.

When the door of the house on Mill Street opened this time, the news reporter took off his hat and said, "Good afternoon, I'm William S. Wells, a journalist with the *St. Louis Globe-Democrat*. I'd like to ask you a few questions."

The good-looking dark-haired woman in the black dress stepped back to close the door. William S. Wells put his hand out, his foot already in place.

"Is it true Bren Early killed your son?"

Mrs. Pierson did not fight the door, though her hand remained on the knob. She looked at the journalist with little or no expression and said, "My son was killed while robbing the Benson stage by a passenger named Mr. DeLisle."

"If Bren Early did not kill your son," the journalist, Wells, said, "why did he buy this house for you?"

"He didn't buy this house for me."

"I understand he assumed the mortgage."

"Perhaps as an investment."

The journalist said, "Let's see now . . . the poor widow is running a boardinghouse, barely making ends meet following the death of her husband in a mill accident. Mr. Early comes along, pays off the note, gives you the deed to the house and you get rid of the boarders so you can live here alone . . . some of the time alone, huh?" The journalist produced a little smile. "And you want me to believe he bought it as an *invest*ment?"

Mrs. Pierson said, "Do you think I care what you believe?"

"Bren Early was on the stage your boy tried to hold up. The same Bren Early who owns this house."

"I rent from him," Mrs. Pierson said.

"Yet you're a widow with no means of support."

"I have money my husband left."

"Uh-huh. Well, you must keep it under your mattress since you don't have a bank account either."

The journalist put on his grin as he stared at Mrs. Pierson—yes, a very handsome lady with her dark dark hair parted in the middle and drawn back in a bun—knowing he had her in a corner; then stopped grinning as the door opened wider and he was looking at Brendan Early, the man moving toward him into the doorway. The journalist said, "Oh—" not knowing Bren was here. He backed away, went down the three front steps to the walk and said then, "I see an old friend of yours is in town."

Bren said nothing as he slammed the door closed.

"Why were you telling him all that?"

"What did I tell him? He seemed to know everything."

"You sounded like you were going to stand there and answer anything he asked."

The woman shrugged. "What difference does it make?" and watched Bren as he moved from the door to a front window in the parlor. "You said yourself, let them think what they want."

Holding the lace curtains apart, looking out at the street of frame houses, he said, "We can't stop them from thinking, but we don't have to answer their questions."

"They don't have to ask much," she said. "It's your house—the arrangement is fairly obvious. But as long as it isn't spoken of out loud then it isn't improper. Is that it?"

Bren wore a white shirt, a dark tie and vest; his suitcoat hung draped over the back of a chair where his holstered revolvers rested on the seat cushion. He had been preparing to go out this afternoon after spending last night and this morning with her: preparing, grooming himself, looking at himself in the mirror solemnly as if performing a ritual.

As he turned from the window now to look at her she waited, not knowing what he was going to say.

Then surprised her when he said, "Do I sound stuffy?"

She relaxed. "You sound grim, so serious."

"I'm not though. Not with you."

"No, the hard image you present to everyone else."

He came over to the chair where his coat was draped. "Maybe what I should do, put a notice in the paper. 'To Whom It May Concern . . . I'm the one wants to get married, she's the one wants to keep things as they are.' See what they ask you then."

"In other words," Janet Pierson said, "let them think what they want, as long as there's no doubt about your honor."

"I didn't mean it that way at all."

"But it's the way it is," the good-looking dark-haired woman said. "If you're going to spend your life standing on principle, you want to be sure everyone understands what the principle is."

He picked up his coat and pushed an arm into the sleeve. "You keep saying I worry about what people think of me, when I don't. All I said was, why tell that fella our personal business?"

"I'm sorry," she said. "You're right."

He pulled the coat down to fit smoothly as he turned to her. "I don't want you to say I'm *right*, I want to know what you're talking about."

"You get mad if I tell you what I feel."

He said, "Oh," and turned to the chair again to pick up his gunbelt and holsters.

"Are you coming back for supper?"

"I was planning on it. If we can have an evening without arguing."

"Are you pouting now?"

She shouldn't have said it—seeing his jaw tighten and hearing him say maybe he'd see her later, or maybe not—but sometimes she got tired of handling him so carefully, keeping him unruffled. Out in the street where he was going now, closing the door behind him, he was the legendary Bren Early who had shot and killed at least ten men who'd tested his nerve; a man whose posed photographs were displayed in the window of C.S. Fly's gallery on LaSalle Street and who was being written about by journalists from at least a dozen different newspapers. Bren Early: silent, deadly, absolutely true to his word.

But she could not help but think of a little boy playing guns.

He was a little boy sometimes when they were alone, unsure of himself.

He had come to her two and a half years ago, told her who he was and how he had met her son. He returned several times to visit, to sit in this parlor with her over coffee, and finally one day handed her the deed to the house—mortgage paid in full—asking nothing in return. Why?

He had not killed her son. A false rumor. He had, in fact, tried to prevent her son's death. But had failed and perhaps it was that simple: he felt responsible, owed her something because of his failure. He had said, "Don't ask questions. I like you, I want to do something for you." All right, and she liked him and it was easy enough to take the sign down and change the boardinghouse back to a residence. It seemed to happen naturally as they saw more of each other. He wanted a woman in town and she responded. Why not? She liked him enough.

Janet Pierson, at forty, was at least five years older than Bren. She was attractive, had maintained her slim figure, they enjoyed one another; so age was not a consideration. Until he said he wanted to marry her.

She asked why and felt early suspicions aroused. He said he wanted to marry her, that was why in itself; he loved her. Yes, he had said he loved her. And he had also said, many times, "You think too much," when she told him he really didn't want to marry her but felt an obligation or was afraid of what people thought. He had said over and over that people had nothing to do with it, goddamn it, *people* could think whatever they wanted; what *he* wanted was to be married to her. Then she had said the words that made him stare at her and then frown, perplexed, and finally get angry, the words he would never understand and she couldn't seem to explain.

She had said, "I think what you want to do is take the place of my son. You want to make up his loss."

And he had said, "You believe I think of you as my *mother*?"

Yes, but she would not admit that to him: the little boy who came in the house when he was finished playing his role on the street. She didn't understand it herself, she only felt it. So she referred to him being like a little boy without referring to herself as a mother or using the word.

There was risk involved, to tell the man who had been a cavalry officer and had stood his ground and shot ten men, that he was still, deep down, a little boy and wanted his own way. He would pound his fist down or storm out (See? she would say to herself), then calm down or come back in a little while and say, "How do you get ideas like that?"

And she would say, "I just know."

"Because you had a son? Listen, maybe what you're doing, you're still playing mama, Jesus Christ, and you're using *me*. I'm not doing it, *you* are."

Blaming her. Then saying he loved her and wanted to marry her and be with her always. Yet they very seldom went out of the house as a couple. Sitting together in a restaurant he was obviously self-conscious; as though being seen with her revealed a vulnerable, softer side of him. The only thing she was certain of: Bren Early didn't know what he wanted.

2

Maurice Dumas stood in the doorway of the Chinaman's place on Second Street. He had been waiting an hour and a half, watching toward Mill Street and, every once in a while, looking in at the empty restaurant wondering how the Chinaman stayed in business . . . then wondering if Mr. Early had forgot or had changed his mind. Twice he'd run back to the corner of Second and LaSalle and looked across the street toward the Congress Hotel. The news reporters were still waiting on the porch.

When finally he saw Early coming this way from Mill Street, Maurice Dumas felt almost overwhelming relief. In the time it took Early to reach him—Early looking neat and fresh though it was quite warm this afternoon in May—Maurice Dumas had time to compose himself.

He nodded and said, "Mr. Early."

"He arrive?"

"Yes sir, on the noon shuttle from Benson."

"Alone?"

"I believe there was a Mexican gentleman with him."

It was something to stand close to this man and watch him in unguarded moments, watch him think and make decisions that would become news stories—like watching history being made.

"They went up to the mine office first and then to the hotel," Maurice said, "I guess where he's staying. Everybody thinks you're there, too, I guess. Or will come there. So they expect the hotel is where it'll happen—if it's gonna."

Bren Early thought a little more before saying, "Go see him. Tell him you spoke to me." He paused. "Tell him I'll be in this quiet place out of the sun if he wants to have a word with me."

It was the Mexican, Ruben Vega, who came to the Chinaman's place. He greeted Early, nodding and smiling as he joined him at a back table, away from the sun glare on the windows. They could have been two old friends meeting here in the empty restaurant, though Bren Early said nothing at first because he was surprised. He felt it strange that he was glad to see this man who was smiling warmly and telling him he had not changed one bit since that time at the wall in Sonora. It was strange, too, Bren felt, that he recognized the man immediately and could tell that the man had changed; he was older and looked older, with a beard now that was streaked with gray.

"Man," Ruben Vega said, "the most intelligent thing I ever did in my life, I didn't walk up to the wall with them . . . You not drinking nothing?"

"Is he coming?" asked Bren.

"No, he's not coming. He sent me to tell you he isn't angry, it was too long ago." The Mexican looked around, saying then, "Don't they have nothing to drink in this place?"

They sent Maurice Dumas out to get a bottle of *mescal*, which the Mexican said he was thirsty for. Bren had beer, served by the Chinaman, and drank several glasses of it while they talked, allowing Maurice to sit with them but not paying any attention to him until he tried the *mescal* and made a terrible face and the Mexican said to Bren, "Your friend don't know what's good."

"If you like a drink that tastes like poison candy," Bren said, though he tried a short glass of it to see if it was still as bad as he remembered it was the first time he drank it in the sutler's store at Huachuca. "That could kill you," he said.

"No, but walking up to the wall where you and the other one stood, that would have," Ruben Vega said.

"You might have made the difference," Bren said.

"Maybe I would have shot one of you, I don't know. But something told me it would be my last day on earth."

"How did you keep him alive?"

The Mexican shrugged. "Tied him to a horse. He kept himself alive to Morelos. Then in the infirmary they cleaned him, sewed him together. He has a hole here," Ruben Vega said, touching his cheek, "some teeth missing"—he grinned—"part of his ear. But he's no more ugly than he was before. See, the ugliness is inside him. I say to him, 'Man, what is it like to be you? To live inside your body?' He don't know what I'm talking about. I say to him, 'Why don't you be tranquil and enjoy life more instead of rubbing against it?' He still don't know what I'm talking about, so I leave him alone . . . Well, let me think. Why didn't he die? I don't know. From Morelos I took him to my old home at Bavispe, then down to Hermosillo . . . Guaymas, we looked at the sea and ate fish . . . a long way around to come back here, but only in the beginning he was anxious to go back and saying what he's going to do to you when he finds you."

"Others tried," Bren said.

"Yes, we hear that. Then time pass, he stop talking about it. We do some work in New Mexico for a mine company, bring them beef. Then do other work for them, make more money than before." The Mexican shrugged again. "He's not so ugly inside now."

"He must've paid you pretty well," Bren said. "You stay with him."

"I'll tell you the truth, I almost left him by the wall in Sonora, but I work for his family, his father before him. Yes, Sundeen always pay me pretty well as segundo. If I'm going to be in that business, stealing cows, running them across the border, I'm not very particular who I work with, uh? But he isn't so bad now. He doesn't talk so much as he use to."

Bren said, "How's he look at this job he's got?"

"Well, we just come here. He has some men coming the company hired. I guess we go up and drive those people off. What else?" He raised his *mescal* glass, then paused. "But we hear your friend is up there too, the other one from the wall. How is it you're here and he's up there, your friend?"

"It's the way it is, that's all," Bren said. "This land situation, who owns what, is none of my business."

"You don't care then," Ruben Vega said, "we go up there and run him off."

Maurice Dumas' gaze moved from the Mexican to Bren Early and waited for the answer.

"You say run him off and make it sound easy," Bren said. "It isn't a question of whether I care or not, have an interest, it's whether you can do it and come back in one piece. I'm like Maurice here and all the rest. Just a spectator."

3

It was after five o'clock when Ruben Vega returned to the Congress Hotel. The men who had been pointed out to him as journalists and not a part of a business convention were still on the front porch and in the lobby. They stopped talking when he came in, but no one called to him or said anything.

He mentioned it to Sundeen who stood at the full-length mirror in his room, bare to the waist, turning his head slowly, studying himself as he trimmed his beard.

"They know I come with you, but they don't ask me anything. You know why?"

"Why?" Sundeen said to himself in the mirror.

"Because they think I shine your shoes, run errands for you."

"You saw him?"

"Yes, I talk to him, tell him you're not mad no more."

"Wavy-haired son of a bitch. He look down his nose at you?"

"A little, holding back, not saying much. But he's all right. Maybe the same as you are."

Sundeen trimmed carefully with the scissors, using a comb to cover the deep scar in his left cheek where hair did not grow and was like an indentation made with a finger that remained when the finger was withdrawn, the skin around the hole tight and shiny.

"Instead of what you think," Sundeen said, "tell me what he had to say."

"He say it's none of his business. He's going to watch."

"You believe it?"

"Now you want to know what I think. Make up your mind."

Sundeen halfturned to the mirror to study his profile, smoothing his beard with the back of his hand. "His partner's up there, but he's gonna keep his nose out of it, huh?"

Yes, they may be somewhat alike, Ruben Vega thought. He said, "The company pay him to work here, whatever he does, not to go up there and help his friend. So maybe he doesn't have the choice to make."

"What does he say about Moon?"

"Nothing. I ask, do you see him? No. I say, why don't they leave instead of causing this trouble? He say, ask them. I say well, he likes to live on a mountain—there plenty other mountains. He don't say anything. I say, what about the other people up there, they live with him? He say, you find out."

Sundeen looked at his body, sucking in his stomach, then picked up a shirt from the chair and put it on. "I think somebody's selling somebody a bill of goods. All we have to say to them is, look here, you people don't move out, this is what happens to you. Take one of 'em, stick a gun in his mouth and count three. They'll leave."

"Take which one?"

"It don't matter to me none. 'Cept it won't be Moon. Moon, I'm gonna settle with him. Early too. But I got time to think about that."

Ruben Vega was nodding. "Threaten them seriously—it look pretty easy, uh?"

"Not hard or easy but a fact of life," Sundeen said. "Nobody picks dying when there's a way not to."

Ruben Vega would agree to that. He could say to his boss, And it works both ways, for you as well as them. But why argue about it with a man who did not know how to get outside of himself to look at something? It had happened to him at the wall. It could happen to him again. Ruben Vega said, "Well, I hope you get enough men to do it."

Sundeen said, "Wait and see what's coming."

It was already arranged, since his meeting with Vandozen in Las Cruces, Vandozen asking how many men he'd need. Sundeen saying he'd wait and see. Vandozen then saying it was his custom to know things in advance, not wait and see. So he had already recruited some twenty men, among them several former Yuma prison guards, a few railroad bulls and a good number of strikebreakers from the coal fields of Pennsylvania: all hired at twenty dollars a week and looking forward to a tour of duty out in the fresh air and wide open spaces.

Today was Tuesday. A message waiting for Sundeen when he reported to the company stated his bunch would all arrive in Benson by rail on Friday. Fine. Let them get drunk and laid on Saturday, rest Sunday and they ride up into the mountains on Monday.

Sundeen said to the Mexican, "If that's all you got, you didn't learn much."

"He thought you were dead," Ruben Vega said. "I told him you should be, but you stayed alive and now you're much wiser."

Looking at him Sundeen said, "The fence-sitter. You gonna sit on the fence and watch this one too? Man, that time in Sonora—I swore I was gonna kill you after, if I hadn't been shot up."

"I save your life you feel you want to kill me," Ruben Vega said. "I think you still have something to learn."

4

Bren had not realized he was tense. Until walking back to the house on Mill Street he was aware of relief and was anxious to be with the woman again. He had not told her about Sundeen. He didn't like to argue with her or discuss serious matters. She was a woman and he wanted her to act like a woman, one he had selected. He did not expect continual expressions of gratitude; nor did he want her to wait on him or act as though her life was now dedicated solely to his pleasure. But she could make his life easier if she'd quit assuming she knew more about him than he did. Women were said to "know" and feel things men weren't able to because men were more blunt and practical. Bren believed that was a lot of horse shit. Women took advantage of men because they were all sitting on something men wanted. If they ever quit holding out or holding it over men's heads everybody would be a lot happier.

Not that Janet Pierson ever bargained with him that way. She seemed always willing and eager. He only wished she would quit thinking and analyzing why he did things and saying he wanted to be like a son to her.

Sometimes though he would bring it up, because it was on his mind, or to convince her she was wrong—as he did now, entering the front door and hearing her in the kitchen, coming up quietly behind her, pulling her into his arms, his hands moving over her body.

"I missed you," she said, resting against him.

"I missed you too. You think I'd do this to my mother?"

"I hope not."

"Unh-unh." Kissing her now, brushing her cheek and finding her ear with his mouth. "No . . . What you feel like to me is a young girl . . . soft and nice—"

She said, pressing against him, "That's what I feel. You make me aware of being a woman and it's a good feeling." This way acknowledging and appreciating him as a man, but knowing that what he needed now was to be comforted and held. Protected from something. The little boy come home—but not telling him this.

After they made love she would put her arms around him and hold him close to her in the silence and soon he would fall asleep. Then, as she would begin to ease her arm from beneath his shoulder, he would open his eyes for a moment, roll to his side and fall asleep again, freeing her. Though if she moved her hand over him, down over the taut muscles in his belly, they would make love again and after, this time, he would get out of bed as Bren Early: confident, the man who wore matched revolvers and loved her when it occurred to him to express it or when he felt the physical urge . . . not realizing the simple need to hold and be held and to believe in something other than himself.

Sometime soon she would talk to him and find out what he believed and what was important to him. And what was important to her also.

5

Was it luck or was it instinct? Maurice Dumas hoped the latter. There was always something going on when he set out to get a story: this time not at the White Tanks agency but several miles up the draw at Dana Moon's place.

The luck was running into the Apache at the agency office and letting him know through sign language—trying all kinds of motions before pointing to the office and then sticking his tongue in his cheek to resemble a wad of tobacco—that he was looking for the agent, Dana Moon.

They climbed switchbacks up a slope swept yellow-green with brittlebush and greasewood, through young saguaros that looked like a field of fence posts and on up into the wide, yawning trough of a barranca with steep walls of shale and wind-swept white oak and cedar. They climbed to open terrain, a bare crest against the sky but not the top, not yet. A little farther and there it was, finally, a wall . . . first the wall, and beyond it a low stone fortress of a house with a wooden porch and a yard full of people, horses and several wagons.

What was this, another Meat Day?

No, Maurice Dumas found out soon enough, it was a war council.

He felt strange riding in through the opening in the adobe wall with all eyes on him. Though there were not as many people as he originally thought—only about a dozen—they were certainly a colorful and unusual mixture: darkies, Mexicans and Indians, all standing around together and all, he observed now, armed to the teeth with revolvers, rifles and belts of cartridges. Specifically there were three hard-looking colored men; four Mexicans, one in a very large Chichuhua hat and bright yellow scarf; and the rest Apache Indians, including the one who brought him up here and who, Maurice Dumas found out, was named Red, an old compadre of Moon's.

"I hope I'm not interrupting anything," Maurice Dumas said, as Moon came down from the porch to greet him, "but there is something I think you better know about."

"Sundeen's arrival?" said Moon, who almost smiled then at the young reporter's look of surprise. "There are things we better know about if we intend to stay here. Have his men arrived yet?"

Maurice Dumas, again surprised, said, "What men?"

"You'd know if they had," Moon said. "So we still have some time. Step down and I'll introduce you to some of the main characters of the story you're gonna be writing."

The man seemed so aware and alert for someone who moved the way Moon did, hands in his pockets, in no hurry, big chew of tobacco in his jaw: just a plain country fellow among this colorful group of heavily armed neighbors.

First, Maurice Dumas met Mrs. Moon, Kate, and felt he must have appeared stupid when he looked up and saw a good-looking lady and not the washed-out, sodbuster woman he'd expected. When she learned where he was from, Mrs. Moon said, "Chicago, huh?

I'll bet you're glad to get away from the stockyards and breathe fresh air for a change."

The news reporter said he didn't live near the yards, fortunately, and noticed Moon looking at his wife with an amused expression and then shaking his head; just a faint movement. The man seemed to get a kick out of her. He said, "What do you know about Chicago stockyards?" She answered him, "I visited there with my dad when I was little and have never felt the urge to go back." Strange, having a conversation like that in front of everyone.

Moon said, "Maurice, shake hands with a veteran of the War of the Rebellion and a cavalryman twenty-four years."

This was the young reporter's introduction to Bo Catlett, whom he had already heard about and who did not disappoint him in his appearance, with his high boots and felt campaign hat low over his eyes. Bo Catlett's expression was kindly, yet he was mean and hard-looking in that he seemed the type who would never hold his hat in his hand and stand aside or give an inch, certainly not give up his horse ranch. The other two colored men wore boots also, standing the way cavalrymen seem to pose, and appeared just as fit and ready as Bo Catlett. There were three more former members of the Tenth up with their families or tending the herds.

Red, the little Mimbre Apache, said something in Spanish to Moon and Moon said, "He thought, when you rode up and commenced making signs, you were asking him how old he was, how many moons, till you stuck your tongue in your cheek."

The Apaches sat along the edge of the porch, Maurice Dumas noticed, while all the others stood around. (Did it mean Indians were lazy by nature?, Maurice wondered. Or smart enough to squat when they got the chance?)

The news reporter wouldn't have minded sitting down himself in one of those cane rocking chairs. But first he had to meet Armando Duro—and his young son Eladio who was about eighteen—and this introduction turned into something he never expected.

Maurice had a feeling Moon had saved Armando until last out of deference, for he seemed especially polite and careful as he addressed him in Spanish, nodding toward Maurice as Maurice caught the words *Chicago Times*. Was the Mexican impressed?

The young news reporter was, for he had heard the name Armando Duro before, though he had not known this fiery champion of Mexican land rights was living in these mountains.

Here he was now rattling off Spanish a mile a minute, his son and his companions nodding in agreement while Moon listened intently at first, then seemed to get tired of hanging on and shifted his weight from one foot to the other as Armando went on and on. When there was a pause Maurice said quickly, "I'd like to interview Señor Duro if I could."

Moon said, "If you can get a word in." Armando's eyes darted from the news reporter to Moon. "And if you—*si puede hablar en Español*. Can you?"

"Doesn't he speak English?"

"When he wants to," Moon said. "It depends if he's in one of his royal pain-in-the-ass moods or not."

If the Mexican could understand him, how come Moon was saying this in front of him? Evidently because Moon had only so much patience with the man and had run out.

Following Moon's less than kind remark, Armando turned to the young news reporter and said in English, "Will you print the truth for a change if I give it to you?"

What kind of question was that? Maurice Dumas said the *Times* always printed the truth.

"The twisting of truth to fit your purpose," Armando said, "is the same as a lie."

Maurice didn't know what the man was talking about because the paper had hardly ever printed anything about Armando Duro or Mexican land rights to begin with. It was an old issue, settled in court, dead and buried. But since the man did represent the Mexican community here, some eighty or ninety people living on scattered farms and sheep pastures, Maurice decided he'd better pay attention.

He said, "Well, I suppose you see this present situation as an opportunity to air your complaints once again, bring them into the open." Maurice heard Moon groan and knew he had said the wrong thing.

Sure enough.

Armando started talking, taking them back to the time of Spanish land grants and plodding on through the war with Mexico and the Gadsen Purchase to explain why their acreage, their sheep graze, their golden fields of corn and bean patches belonged to them as if by divine succession and not to a mining company from a state named for a small island in the English Channel (which Maurice Dumas had not realized before this).

Bo Catlett and the colored troopers shuffled around or leaned

against a wagon. Moon would continue to shift from one foot to
another. His wife, what she did was shake her head and go into the
house. Even Armando's son and the other Mexicans seemed ready
to fall asleep. Only the Apaches, sitting along the edge of the porch,
stared at Armando with rapt attention, not having any idea what he
was talking about, even though Armando would lapse into fiery
Spanish phrases every so often. He reminded the young news reporter of every politician he had ever heard speak, except that Armando talked in bigger circles that included God and kings.

"How am I going to write about all that?" Maurice said to
Moon, after.

Moon said, "You picked your line of work, I didn't."

Armando got a rolled-up sheet of heavy paper from his wagon
and came over to the news reporter opening it as you would a
proclamation, which is what it was.

"Here," Armando said, handing it to Maurice, "show this to the
mine company and print it in your newspaper so anyone who sees
one of these will know it marks the boundary of our land."

The notice said, in large black letters:

WARNING
**Anyone venturing onto
this land uninvited is**

TRESPASSING

**on property granted by
Royal Decree and witnessed
before God. Trespassers
are not welcome and will
be fired on if they cross this boundary.**

**Armando Duro
and the
People of the Mountain**

Later on, just before Maurice Dumas left to go back down the
switchback trail, he said to Moon, "Does that man know what he's
doing?"

"It's his idea of the way to do it," Moon said.

"But that warning's not gonna do any good. You think?"

"Warning?" Moon said. "It reads more like an invitation."

"Can't you stop him, shut him up?"

"I suppose," Moon said, "but the sooner it starts, the sooner it's over, huh?"

6

Moon, Bo Catlett and Red, the leader of the Mimbres, packed up into the high reaches to shoot some game, drink whiskey, have a talk and get away from their women for a few days. Moon said that's all they would have, three days. On the piney shoulder of the mountain where they camped, they could hear the mine company survey crew exploding dynamite as they searched out new ore veins: like artillery off to the west, an army gradually moving closer, having already wiped out several of the Mexican homesites.

Armando Duro had drawn the line and posted his trespass notices, giving himself a printed excuse to start shooting. But how did you tell a man like Armando he was a fool? Armando was not a listener, he was a talker.

Moon, in the high camp, took out a rough-sketch map he'd drawn and laid it on the pine needles for Bo Catlett and Red to look at, Moon pointing: little squares were homes and farms, though maybe he was missing some; the circles were graze. X's marked the areas where the survey crews had been working.

Here, scattered over the pastureland in the Western foothills, the Mexican homesteads. How would you defend them?

"No way to do it, considering they farmers," Bo Catlett said. "They ever see more than three coming they got to get out . . . Maybe try draw them up in the woods."

Moon shook his head. "Armando told them, don't leave your homes. Something about leaving your honor on the doorstep when you flee."

"I'm not talking about they should *flee*," Bo Catlett said. "But they start shooting from the house, that's where they gonna die. They don't have enough people in one place. Like you—" Bo Catlett looked at the map. "Where you at here?"

Moon pointed to the square on the Eastern slope, the closest one to the wavy line indicating the San Pedro River.

"You no better off 'n they are," Bot Catlett said, "all by yourself there."

"I got open ground in front of me and high rock behind," Moon said, "with Red and some of his people right here, watching my back door. Nobody gets close without my knowing. So . . . around here, both sides of the crest, the Apache rancherías. Red, that's you right there. Coming south a bit, these circles are the horse pastures . . . Here's the canyon, Bo, where you got your settlement."

"Niggerville," Bo Catlett said. "Some day they put railroad tracks up there, you can bet money we be on the wrong side."

"Here's the box canyon," Moon continued, "where you gather your mustangs. I'm thinking we might do something with that blind alley. You follow me?"

"Invite 'em in," Bo Catlett said, "and close the door."

"It'd be a way, wouldn't it? If they come up to Niggerville and you pull back, draw 'em into the box."

"If they dumb enough, think I'm a black lead mare," Bo Catlett said.

"We'll find out," Moon said. "Red's gonna be our eyes, huh, Red? *Los ojos.*" And said in Spanish, "The eyes of the mountain people."

The Apache nodded and said, also in Spanish, "It's been a long time since we used them."

Moon said, "Him and a bunch were gonna summer up at Whiteriver, visit some of their people, but Red's staying now for the war. That's what they call it in town, the Rincon Mountain War."

Bo Catlett seemed to be thinking about the name, trying it a few times in his mind. "We got any say in it?"

"We're still around when the smoke clears," Moon said, "I guess we can call it anything we want."

EIGHT

1

Phil Sundeen looked at the notice with the big word "WARNING" at the top like it was a birthday present he had always wanted. He read it slowly, came down to Armando's name at the bottom, said, "That's the one I want," and sent Ruben Vega out on a scout, see if the notices were "for true."

That Monday morning Ruben Vega rode a fifteen-mile loop through the west foothills, spotting the little adobes tucked away up on the slopes; seeing the planted fields, young corn not quite belly-high to his horse; seeing the notices stuck to saguaro and white oak and three times drawing rifle fire—Ruben Vega squinting up at the high rocks as the reports faded, then shaking his head and continuing on.

He made his way up through a mesquite thicket that followed the course of a draw to a point where he could study one of the videttes crouched high in the rocks, sky-lined for all to see, a young man in white with an old single-shot Springfield, defending his land. Ruben Vega, dismounted, circled behind the vidette to within forty feet and called out, *"Digame!"*

The young man in white came around, saw the bearded man holding a revolver and fired his Springfield too quickly, without taking time to aim.

Ruben Vega raised his revolver. "Tell me where I can find Armando Duro."

Thirty dollars a week to frighten this young farmer and others like him. It was a pity. Ruben Vega said to the man, who was terrified but trying to act brave, he only wanted to speak to Armando

Duro and needed directions to his house. That was all. He nodded,
listening to the young farmer, holstered his gun and left.

Yes, he told Sundeen, the notices were "for real."

"They shoot at you?"

"They don't know what they're doing."

"I *know* that," Sundeen said. "I want to know if they're good for
their word." When Ruben Vega told him yes, they had fired, though
not to hit him, Sundeen said, "All right, let's go."

He paraded out his security force: his prison guards, railroad
bulls and strikebreakers; most of whom wore city clothes and looked
like workingmen on Sunday, not one under thirty years of age,
Ruben Vega noticed. Very hard men with big fists, bellies full of
beer and whiskey from their first weekend in town, armed with
Winchester repeaters and revolvers stuck in their belts. Sixteen of
them: two had quit by Monday saying it was too hot and dusty, the
hell with it. One was dead of knife wounds and the one who had
killed him was in jail. Ruben Vega knew he would never be their
segundo, because these men would never do what a Mexican told
them. But that was all right. They could take orders directly from
Sundeen. Ruben Vega would scout for them, stay out of their way
and draw his thirty dollars a week—the most he had ever made in
his life—which would make these men even uglier if they knew
the Mexican was being paid more than they were. But he didn't
like this work. From the beginning he had not liked it at all.

He didn't like Sundeen waving off the few news reporters—one
of them the young one who had been with Early—who had hired
horses and wanted to follow. He didn't like it because it surprised
him—Sundeen not wanting them along to write about him.

He asked, "Why not bring them?"

"Not this trip," Sundeen said. "Get up there and show us the
way, partner."

Ruben Vega followed his orders and rode point, guiding Sundeen and his security force up into the hills where the WARNING
notices were nailed to the saguaro and white oak. There. Now Sundeen could do what he wanted.

Looking over his crew of bulls and headbusters sweating in
their Sunday suits, the crew squinting up at the high rock formations, Sundeen said, "Who wants to do the honors, chase their
pickets off that high ground? I'd say there's no more'n likely two
of 'em up there—couple of bean farmers couldn't hit shit if they

stuck their weapons up their ass. How about you, you and you?"
And said to the others, "Get ready now."

More than two, Ruben Vega thought, because they know we're
coming to see Armando. Maybe all the guns they have are up there
now. Guarding the pass to the man's house. Ruben Vega nudged
his mount up next to Sundeen's.

"They'll have plenty guns up there," he said quietly.

Sundeen turned in his saddle to look at him and smiled as he
spoke, as though he was talking about something else. "We don't
know till we see, partner. Till we draw fire, huh?" Then to the three
he had picked: "Go on up past the signs."

Another show to watch, Ruben Vega thought, seeing the three
men moving their horses at a walk up through the ocotillo and
yellow-flowering prickly pear, reaching the sign nailed to a saguaro . . . moving past the cactus . . . twenty feet perhaps, thirty,
when the gunfire poured out of the rocks a hundred yards away:
ten, a dozen rifles, Ruben Vega estimated, fired on the count, but
the eruption of sound coming raggedly with puffs of smoke and
followed by three single shots that chased the two riders still
mounted, both of them bent low in their saddles and circling back.
One man in his Sunday suit lay on the ground, out there alone now,
his riderless horse running free. The one on the ground didn't
move. Sundeen was yelling at his security force to commence firing. Then yelled at them to spread out as their horses began to shy
and bump each other with the rifles going off close. "Spread out
and rush 'em!" Sundeen yelled, pointing and then circling around
to make sure they were all moving forward . . . Ruben Vega watching, wondering if Sundeen knew what he was doing . . . Sundeen
pausing then as his men charged up the slope firing away . . .
Ruben Vega impressed now that these dressed-up shitkickers
would do what they were told and expose themselves to fire. Sundeen hung back, grinning as he looked over at Ruben Vega now sitting motionless in his saddle.

"Still riding the fence, huh?"

Ruben Vega said, "Well, you got a man killed."

"Three'd be better," Sundeen said, "but one's enough to inspire
them."

It didn't take much to push the farmers out of the rocks. They
reloaded and got off a volley, hitting nothing, then fell back from
the steady fire of the Winchester repeaters, some of them running,

others making their way back to Armando Duro's place where they would be forced to make a stand.

Sundeen and his people circled to high ground and found good cover in a fairly deep wash rimmed with brush. From here they looked down on Armando's house and yard: a whitewashed adobe with a roof of red clay tiles that had come from an old church in Tucson, a flower garden, a latticework covered with green vines, heavy shutters with round gunports over the windows. A snug cottage with thick walls up here in the lonesome.

Sundeen said, "Well, we can starve him out or maybe set the place on fire, but we'd never get home for supper, would we?" From a saddlebag he pulled out a towel with *Congress Hotel* printed on it and thew it to Ruben Vega, saying, "Hey, partner, make yourself useful."

Tied to a mesquite pole the towel was the truce flag Ruben Vega waved above the brush cover and held high in front of him as he walked down to the yard, unarmed, doing something for his thirty dollars a week.

He called to the house in Spanish, "Do I address Armando Duro? . . . Look, I have no gun. Will you come out, please, and talk like a gentleman? We have no fight with you. We come to talk and you begin shooting." He paused. "Before anyone else is injured please come talk to the man sent by the company. He has something important to explain."

"Say it now," a voice from the house said.

"I'm not the emissary of the company," Ruben Vega said. "Mr. Sundeen is the one. He wants to explain the company plan of making this a township . . . if you would honor us and agree to become the alcalde and administer the office."

"Where is he?" the voice asked.

"You come out and he'll come out," Ruben Vega said, beginning to feel relief now, knowing he was almost finished.

There was a long pause, silence, before the voice said again, "Where is he?"

"Up there," Ruben Vega said, pointing with his truce flag.

"He must come with no weapons. All of them must show themselves with no weapons," the voice said.

"Of course," Ruben Vega said, thinking, He's a child; you could offer him candy. As he saw the door open, Ruben Vega began to move away, turning to wave to Sundeen to come down, calling out, "All right . . . Come with your hands in the air, please!" Looking back at the house, still moving off to the side, he said in Spanish, "Your men come out too, please, everyone without weapons. We meet at this sign of truce and speak as gentlemen," thinking, Yes, isn't it a nice day and everybody's friends . . . Smile . . . but get your old ass out of the way as soon as you can, without hurrying, but move it.

2

Moon handed the glasses to Bo Catlett and picked up his Sharps rifle from the Y of the cliffrose branch in front of him.

"They all got *suits* on," Bo Catlett said, with the field glasses to his face. "Coming with their hands in the air. They sur*ren*dering?"

"You see the white flag?" Moon said.

"Man moving out of the way."

"I saw him do it once before," Moon said. "Something like this. What would you say's the range?"

From this position, where Moon and Bo Catlett, Red and three of his Mimbres crouched in the outcropping of rock and flowering cliffrose—high up on a slope of scrub pine—they had a long downview of the red-tile postage-stamp roof of the house and the tiny dark figures coming down to the yard, approaching the tiny figures in white coming out of the house.

Bo Catlett continued to study the scene through the field glasses, saying now, "You got . . . three hundred fifty yards 'tween us and them."

"Close," Moon said, "but more like four hundred," and sighted down the barrel of the Sharps. "It looks shorter aiming down." He lowered the big-bore rifle to adjust the rear sight and put it to his shoulder again to aim, both eyes open.

"Wearing suits," Bo Catlett was saying. "All dressed up to pay a visit, huh?"

Moon said something in slow Spanish, as though explaining carefully, and the Mimbres raised their Springfields and Spencers. He waited a moment and then said, *"Listo?"*

The Mimbres were ready. Bo Catlett continued to watch through the glasses.

"The one with the silver belt buckles," Moon said.

"His holsters empty," Bo Catlett said. "None of them appear armed."

"Come up here with their coats on," Moon said, "account of it's so cold. Only about ninety degrees out. Watch Sundeen, he'll do something. Take off his hat, something to give 'em a sign."

"Talking," Bo Catlett said. "Moving around some . . . Mexicans standing there listening to him, Armando, shit, look at him with his big hat on, arms folded, standing there . . . Sundeen looking up at the sky now, looking around . . . looking back at Armando . . . hey, yelling something . . . they drawing *guns*! He going for the Mexican!"

Moon fired.

The Mimbres fired.

The sounds hitting hard and flat in the stillness, echoing . . . the hard sounds hitting again, almost covering the popping sounds of pistol fire coming from the yard, where tiny dark figures and tiny white figures were left lying on the ground as the lines of figures began to come apart and scatter. The rifles echoed again, cracking the hot air hard, and in a moment the yard was empty but for the figures lying motionless: three dark figures, four white figures. A single white figure was being dragged, carried off by a crowd of dark figures.

Bo Catlett followed them through the glasses until they were out of sight, beyond a rise and a line of brush. He wasn't sure which one they'd dragged off until his gaze inched back to the yard, past the figures lying there, and saw the big Mexican hat on the ground.

"They got Armando," Bo Catlett said.

3

C.S. "Buck" Fly, who was a gentleman and had never been known to say an unkind word about anyone, paused and said, "I already shot that rooster."

"We went to very much trouble to get him," Ruben Vega said. "Rode all the way up there to talk to him."

"Is he coming here?" C.S. Fly asked, not wanting to give the Mexican a flat no, but not wanting to take the other Mexican's picture either. The other Mexican, Armando, was impatient and difficult to pose, because he thought he knew everything, including photography. C.S. Fly also had a lot on his mind. His wife was in Tombstone, where business was not too good; he had opened a gallery in Phoenix that wasn't doing much better; there was not much going on here in Sweetmary at the moment; and he was trying to make up his mind whether or not he should run for sheriff of Cochise County on the Republican ticket next year, as some of his friends were urging him to do. What did he want to take a picture of a pompous, officious Mexican land-granter for?

"You have to bring your picture machine to where he is. I'll show you," Ruben Vega said.

"Well, as I've mentioned, I already have Armando on file," Mr. Fly said. "One of him is plenty."

"But do you have him talking to Mr. Sundeen of the mine company, settling the difference between them, the two sides shaking hands in a picture you can sell to all the newspapers in the country?" Ruben Vega asked.

"No, I don't believe I have that one," C.S. Fly said. "Where is it they're meeting?"

Ruben Vega told him, a ranch out of town only a few miles, the J-L-Bar, owned by a man named Freels, a neutral ground between the mine and the mountains. Mr. Fly said all right, had his assistant load camera and equipment on a buckboard and they were on their way—heading out LaSalle Street, when the young news reporter Ruben Vega had met before rode up to join them, asking what was going on. Ruben Vega said come on, and asked where the other reporters were. (Sundeen had not said anything this time about keeping reporters away.) The young fellow from Chicago, Maurice Dumas, said they most always took a nap after their noon dinner and that's probably where they were. When he asked where they were going, Ruben Vega told him Mr. Fly was going to take a picture of an important occasion, a meeting between Sundeen and Armando.

Because his luck or intuition had been so keen lately, Maurice Dumas believed him, patting his pocket to make sure he had a pad and pencil. It looked like another *Chicago Times* exclusive coming up.

About three miles out of town, having come around a bend in the road that was banked close to a steep slope—with still a mile or so to go before reaching the J-L-Bar ranch—they saw something white hanging from a telegraph pole.

Was it a flag of some kind? There was no wind stirring it. As they approached, seeing it straight down the road now, maybe a hundred yards away, Maurice Dumas thought of a bag of laundry. Or, could it be a mail bag out by the Freels place? Something white—as they drew closer—tied to the pole about ten feet off the ground . . . No, not tied to the pole, hanging from a rope . . . Not a bag of laundry either. A man. Maurice Dumas heard the Mexican say something in Spanish. He heard C.S. Fly say, "Oh, my God."

It was Armando Duro, hung there by the neck, the rope reaching up and over the crossbar where the wires were attached and down to the base of the pole where the rope was lashed securely. Armando's head hung down, chin on his chest, his face so dark he looked like a Negro—which was why Maurice was not sure at first who it was. His hands were so much lighter in color, and his bare feet hanging there, toes pointing toward the ground. It looked as though someone had taken his boots.

Maurice heard Ruben Vega saying, "He told me, he said they'd bring him to the ranch," the Mexican not protesting but speaking very quietly. "He said they'd hold him there and take a picture, see, to prove he was being held and was unharmed."

C.S. Fly was busy setting up his camera in the road, tilting the box upward, then getting down behind it to look, then adjusting it a little more. C.S. Fly didn't say a word.

"That's what he told me," Ruben Vega said. "They would hold him there and threaten to kill him, yes, if his people didn't move away somewhere else. But he never said he would do this. Never."

Was he telling them something or talking to himself?, Maurice Dumas wondered.

Yes, it sounded more like he was trying to convince himself.

Was it an act, though, for their benefit?

No—listening to the Mexican's tone more than the actual words, Maurice Dumas believed the man was honestly surprised and telling the truth.

NINE

1

The news reporters hanging around the Congress Hotel and the Gold Dollar woke up in a hurry.

A man had been lynched in the middle of the afternoon and that goddamn kid from the *Chicago Times* had scooped them again. (The squirt was even wearing his cap cocked over more on the side of his head.)

Things were happening. C.S. Fly developed three pictures of Armando hanging from the pole like a sack of dirty laundry, made a "showing" of them in his gallery window, marched off to the telegraph office and wired Sheriff John Slaughter in Tombstone; notice, bypassing Deputy R.J. Bruckner.

Why? Because Bruckner was a company stooge and John Slaughter and C.S. Fly were friends, the newsmen speculated. Also to show the mine company that if he, Fly, ran for sheriff of Cochise County next year he was not going to place himself in the company's pocket.

Good stuff was developing. A lot of angles.

Item: Sweetmary was a company town. Without LaSalle Mining there would be no Sweetmary. Therefore the people of Sweetmary and its law enforcement agency would never testify against the company or do anything to put the company in legal jeopardy.

Item: John Slaughter wanted to serve out his term and return to ranching. It was said he was more than willing to use his political weight to help Fly get the Republican nomination. John Slaughter was not a company ass kisser, but he had been in office long enough to have become a realist. Since he was getting out anyway, what did he care what happened here in Sweetmary?

The reporters weren't finished writing that one when John

Slaughter arrived in town with a gripsack full of warrants and subpoenas and informed the press that a circuit court judge and county attorney were on their way.

Theory: He was going through the motions to show his friend C.S. Fly the facts of life, liberty and the pursuit of justice in a mine company town.

Well, at least they were making a pretty good show of it.

Item: A warrant was issued for the arrest of Phil Sundeen (not even in town a week) and a Mexican by the name of Ruben Vega (Who?). Sundeen was served, arrested and escorted to jail without incident.

Vandozen, the company vice president, was seen in town for a few hours, then was gone—off in a closed carriage to Benson and the Southern Pacific Railroad depot. But a lawyer who had arrived from Bisbee remained. That same day Sundeen posted a five-hundred-dollar bond and was released. The Mexican, Ruben Vega, could not be located.

Items:

C.S. Fly and the squirt from the *Chicago Times*, Maurice Dumas, were subpoenaed as witnesses.

Eladio Duro, Armando's son, appeared in town out of nowhere, riding a burro, and was taken into "protective custody" by John Slaughter.

Bruckner wandered around town and up to the mine works with sixteen John Doe warrants for the arrest of the members of Sundeen's security force. He returned with the same number of warrants saying they were nowhere to be found and that they had been discharged from the company payroll.

Bruckner did bring in four dead men, their Sunday suits tearing at the seams, their bodies were so swollen. Three had come from Armando's yard, another from not far away. But only two were identified from personal effects: a man named Wade Miller from Illinois and a man named Harry Shell from Kentucky. Holding his nose as he looked at the other two, Phil Sundeen said no, he did not know their names or was even sure now, because of their bloated condition, he had ever seen them before.

The reporters wanted to know: Well, why the hell didn't they ask Sundeen where the *rest* of his men were?

John Slaughter said he did, and Sundeen had answered: "Who, them? They did not like horseback riding and quit."

Well, did he try to get the truth out of Sundeen?

"You mean by the use of physical force?" John Slaughter asked the reporters. "That is not allowed in the interrogation of suspects. At least not in this county."

But had he used force or not?

Maurice Dumas wrapped a five-dollar bill around a bottle of Green River and put it on R.J. Bruckner's desk as he sat down in the deputy's office. Bruckner did not leave it there more than a moment, getting it into a drawer as Maurice was saying, "Civil servants, I've found, work hard and get little appreciation for their efforts."

"What do you want?" asked Bruckner.

"Haven't you used force on Sundeen to make him talk?"

"Make him talk about what?"

"Where his men are."

"What men? Who saw him with any men?"

"I did," Maurice said.

"Who saw him or any men out where the Mex was found?"

"I saw them here in town."

"So what did you see? Nothing. Get your smart-aleck ass out of here, sonny."

"Who else have you got as a witness," Maurice said, showing his tenacity, "besides Armando's son. Any of the other Mexicans?"

"What Mexicans?"

"Armando's people—the ones that live up there."

"They're gone," Bruckner said, "disappeared. It's you and Fly and the Mex's kid . . . and the Indin agent, Moon."

This surprised Maurice. "You subpoenaed Moon? How come?"

"We believe he saw things."

"Sundeen told you that?"

"We know, that's all."

"Has he come to town?"

"He had better be here tomorrow for the hearing. He's not, I'll go and get him. I may be going for him later on anyway."

"Why? For what?"

"Get your smart-aleck ass out of here," Bruckner said. "Time's up."

Item: The circuit court hearing—to determine if a murder had been committed and if there was sufficient reason to believe Sundeen did it—would be held on the second floor of the city jail. The cells up there had not been occupied in several years. Sections of iron bars had been removed and transported to the mine works to be used, it was said, in the construction of a storage facility for high explosives and blasting equipment. Chairs and benches from the Masonic hall and a funeral parlor were now being placed in the second-floor courtroom for the comfort of spectators and visiting newsmen.

Judge Miller Hough of Tombstone was occupying the LaSalle Suite at the Congress Hotel. Prosecutor Stuart "Stu" Ison, who had practiced law in Sweetmary until winning the county position three years ago, was staying with friends.

The services of a young attorney by the name of Goldwater— said to be a nephew of the owner of the well-known Goldwater & Cateñeda General Store in Bisbee—had been retained to act as counsel for Phil Sundeen.

Color item: The mine and crushing mill continued to work two shifts, business as usual, as the town of Sweetmary bustled with activity in preparation for the Hearing. The miners who came down the hill in their coarse work clothes seemed from another world. Many of them were, until recently, from Old World countries. Strange accents and foreign languages were not uncommon on the streets of this mining community.

The news reporters knew what their editors were going to say. Dandy . . . but, goddamn it, where was the Early-Moon confrontation stuff? The stage was set, the suspense built. Now a cattle rustler and ex-con by the name of Sundeen comes along and steals the spotlight. Did he lynch the Mexican or not? What did company-man Bren Early think about it? More important, what were Early and Moon up to during all this, squaring off or just looking at each other?

That was the trouble, they weren't doing anything. But how did you tell an editor Bren Early was holed up at Mrs. Pierson's, wouldn't answer the door, and Moon hadn't showed up yet? If, in fact, he ever would. The newsmen sent wires to their editors that said, in essence, "Big story to break soon," and had a few more drinks while they waited for something to happen.

2

The morning of the hearing the newsmen staying at the Congress came down to the dining room and there was Dana Moon and his wife having a breakfast of grits and ham. Moon did not understand what the newsmen were so excited about. Where had he *been*? Home. If they wanted to see him why didn't they come visit? They asked him why he had been subpoenaed and he said that's why they had come to town this morning, to find out.

Moon and his wife, news reporters trailing behind, stopped by the Fly Gallery to see the latest "showing" in the window: Armando hanging from the telegraph pole. Neither of them said anything as they continued down LaSalle Street to the jail and went upstairs to the hearing.

When the reporters who had been waiting outside Mrs. Pierson's house arrived, they said it didn't look like Bren Early was coming.

After all the excitement and suspense the hearing did not prove to be much of a show. (Which John Slaughter and others could have predicted from the beginning.) Though there was one surprise that stirred considerable interest.

Maurice Dumas, cap under his arm, took the witness stand and told the county attorney, yes, he had seen Mr. Sundeen ride out of Sweetmary with seventeen men. No, Mr. Sundeen would not let any of the reporters follow them. Five hours later he had joined Mr. C.S. Fly and a man in Mr. Sundeen's employ, one Ruben Vega, and accompanied them out to a place where they were to witness a meeting between Mr. Sundeen and Armando Duro. What they found instead was Armando hanging from a pole. Maurice Dumas began to tell about Ruben Vega being "genuinely astonished," but the county attorney, Stuart Ison, said that was all and for him to step down.

C.S. Fly supported the young newsman's testimony as to the purpose of their journey and what they found out on the road. He did not however—if he had witnessed it—mention Ruben Vega's stunned surprise.

Next, Eladio Duro took the stand. Answering the county attorney's questions he admitted, yes, his people had fired on Mr. Sundeen's group when they crossed the property line. (There were several objections by Mr. Goldwater, Sundeen's counsel, during Eladio's testimony, most of which were sustained by Judge Hough.) Eladio described men coming to their house and a Mexican convincing them it was safe to come out and speak to Mr. Sundeen. But as soon as they were outside, Sundeen's men drew pistols and began to shoot at them. Three people fell dead and another was wounded. Before his father could get back in the house Sundeen's men grabbed him and carried him off. Eladio was asked where his family and friends were now. He said they were hiding because they were afraid for their lives. (Objection: judgmental. Sustained.)

Mr. Goldwater, the defense attorney, cross-examined, asking Eladio if the Mexican who spoke to them first carried something in his hands. Yes, Eladio said, a flag of truce. He was asked if his people had fired weapons at Mr. Sundeen and his men. No. But weren't shots fired at Mr. Sundeen's men? No. From others not standing in the yard? Oh, yes; from Sundeen's men who were up on the slope above the house. But weren't three of Sundeen's men struck down by gunfire and killed? Yes, Eladio said. Shot by mistake, he assumed, by their own companions. Eladio was asked to think very carefully before answering the next question. Did the first shots come from the men in the yard or the men on the slope above the house? Eladio was silent and then said, they seemed to both come at the same time.

Mr. Goldwater then called Dana Moon to the stand and asked him if he had been present at Armando Duro's the morning of May the 19th.

"Not actually present," Moon said, already uncomfortable sitting here in this hot room full of people . . . picturing where the cells had been a few years before and where he had talked to Bren through the iron bars.

"But you observed what took place there?"

"Yes."

"You observed a man holding a white flag?"

"Yes."

"How far away were you?"

"About four hundred yards."

"Did you see any others, or another group of men, up on the slope above the house?"

"No."

"You observed the shooting?"

"Yes."

"Did you take part in the shooting?"

"Yes."

"Did you hit anyone?"

Moon hesitated. "I can't say for sure."

"Did you shoot to kill?"

"I fired to prevent Armando and his people, all of them unarmed, from being shot down in cold blood."

"Did you shoot to kill?"

"Yes."

Goldwater walked back to the table where Sundeen sat patiently listening before asking Moon, "Did anyone shoot at you?"

"I can't say."

"You mean you can't tell when someone is shooting at you?"

"If they did, they didn't come close."

"You were firing at . . . whom?"

Moon looked at Sundeen three strides away, closer than he had been the last time, in Sonora. Sundeen stared back at him as if ready to smile.

"Him," Moon said, "and his men. They were about . . . they were shooting at Armando's people."

"They were what?"

"I said they were shooting at Armando's people."

"But you fired at them first, didn't you?"

"They were drawing their weapons—at that distance . . . I would say they fired first or at the same time."

"You heard gunfire before you aimed and fired?"

Jesus Christ, Moon thought, feeling the perspiration under his shirt. He said, "I anticipated their fire. Their weapons were out. In a moment they were firing."

"You just said they were drawing their weapons."

"They were drawing—seeing it from that distance, weapons were out. In a moment they were firing."

"What does the distance have to do with it? You saw what you *thought* they intended to do and you reacted, didn't you? You began shooting."

"I knew what they were gonna do. What they *did*. They killed three of the Mexicans, didn't they?"

"I don't know," Mr. Goldwater said. "Did they? There was gunfire coming from two directions. Didn't you open fire first? . . ."

"No, they did."

"And they returned your fire?"

"That wasn't what happened."

"Well, from the facts we have, I would say there was either a grave misunderstanding—the two parties in the yard began to talk and you misinterpreted it, or . . . you deliberately fired at the yard, not caring who you hit, one group or the other. *Or* . . . and this is conjecture, though possibly worth investigating . . . you were purposely firing at the Mexican group—"

"Why would I do that?"

"You realize you admit you fired with intent to kill," the defense lawyer said. "That action is subject to interpretation, for I would dare to say the yard itself was a small target at four hundred yards, where the variance of a fraction of an inch could mean the difference in the taking of one man's life or another man's."

Moon looked at the county lawyer who was not objecting to any of these ideas the defense lawyer was planting. Moon said, "Sundeen was in the yard. Let's hear him tell what happened. It ought to be a pretty good story."

He saw Kate smile and heard sounds of approval from the audience.

But then the defense lawyer stepped in front of him, close, and said quietly, "I could ask who else was up there with you. Do you want to implicate others? Did they also shoot to kill?" The defense lawyer stared at him before adding, "Do you see where I can take this?" Moon felt relief when the dark-haired, well-dressed man from Bisbee turned to Judge Hough and said something and the judge asked Ison, the county lawyer, to approach the bench—the table next to which Moon sat in a straight chair.

Moon heard Goldwater say, "So far there is not one bit of evidence to support a murder charge against my client. No one here can place him with Armando at the scene of the hanging. However, your honor, if you are not reasonably convinced I'll put my client on the stand. He'll testify that he did, in fact, rescue Armando, not carry him off, and left him out there when he said he wanted to return to his people." The judge asked how could the court be certain that was what happened? The defense lawyer asked, who could dispute it?

Moon cleared his throat and almost said, "I can," at this point. He could tell them how he had watched from the high ground as the Mexicans put their dead over horses and rode out of there— maybe to somebody else's place or to hide in the timber—and Armando had not returned as long as they watched. But he couldn't tell them if they didn't ask, and it didn't look like that was going to happen. He tugged at the county lawyer's coat a couple of times, but Ison would not pay attention to him. Ison had his head stuck in there with the other two legal minds as they talked lawyer talk to each other and decided the outcome of these proceedings.

During the conference at the bench the people in the audience had begun to compare ideas and opinions and there was a buzz of noise in the low-ceilinged courtroom. It stopped when Judge Hough banged his gavel on the desk.

He said that based on a reasonable doubt because of a lack of substantial evidence the charge of suspicion of murder was hereby dismissed.

That was it. The judge left the courtroom and the news reporters converged on Moon and Sundeen: one group asking Moon if he had actually intended to kill Sundeen; another group asking Sundeen what he intended to do about it. Moon said, you heard my testimony. He was looking for the county lawyer, Ison, to tell the little ass-kisser a few things, but did not see him now. Moon felt himself being moved by the crowd clearing away from between them so that finally they stood facing each other.

Sundeen said, "Well, that's twice you have tried. Four hundred yards, huh?"

"Give or take a few," Moon said. "I see you got a hole in your face from the first time and a piece of ear missing."

The reporters were writing in their note pads now—the story unfolding before their eyes, better than they could have staged it, some of them not noticing Sundeen's hand going to his beard to stroke it gently as he stared at Moon.

"You hung a friend of mine and it doesn't look like the court is gonna do anything about it," Moon said.

Sundeen continued to stare at him. He said then, "Go on home. We'll get her done before too long."

"I suppose," Moon said.

One of the reporters said, "Get your guns and settle it now, why don't you? Out on the street."

Sundeen gave the man a hard stare and said, "For you, you little pissant? Who in the hell you think you are?"

Moon and Sundeen looked at each other again, each knowing something these reporters would never in their lives understand.

Maurice Dumas waited in front of the jail, watching the people coming out. When he saw Moon and his good-looking wife, Maurice had to push his way through the crowd to get close enough to hand Moon the folded piece of note paper. Moon looked at Maurice Dumas, nodded hello, then opened the note and read it while the reporters waited. Moon nodded to Maurice again and handed the note to his wife.

"From Bren," he said.

TEN

1

Janet Pierson felt left out. She was at ease with them, she liked them; but she didn't feel *with* them. Nor did she feel as close to Bren now. Bren and Dana Moon and his wife had shared something, had lived through an experience during another time that did not include her.

She was aware of the news reporters waiting outside the house, the crowd of them that had followed Moon and his wife here. She liked his wife, Kate; she felt she had known her a long time and the feeling surprised her. For some reason she could sympathize with her; though the young woman did not seem to need or want it. She could also sympathize with the news reporters and knew what they were feeling. She imagined—after Bren and Mr. and Mrs. Moon were gone—the reporters standing at the door asking her questions. What are they like? What did you talk about?

She imagined herself saying, Oh, they're very nice people. Polite, well-mannered.

But what did they talk about?

Nothing in particular. Old times mostly.

Did they get in a fight over the situation?

No, they're friends.

Come on, did they have words?

No. (Not exactly.)

Did they talk about any of the men they'd killed?

No, of course not.

Do you know how many those two have laid to rest?

They would get onto something like that and she would try to close the door.

Did Moon chew tobacco in the house?

Certainly not.

We hear his wife is a tough customer.

She's very nice.

Did she have anything to say?

Of course. She is not timid. She told me about their house.

Was there much tension between them, Early and Moon?

No, it was a very pleasant visit. Mr. Moon described his duties as an Indian agent. ("Through the office of Indian Affairs . . . handle all relations between the federal government and the Indians . . . direct the administration of tribal resources . . . supervise their 'trust' property . . . promote their health and physical welfare . . . guide their activities toward the attainment of economic self-sufficiency, self-government and the preservation of Indian cultural values." Bren said, "And what exactly does that mean?" And Moon said, "Try to keep them from doing what is most natural to them, raiding and making war.") While Mr. Early explained his responsibilities with the company. ("You get a big stockholder out here a thousand and some miles from home, what do you think is the first thing he wants to see?" "An Indian," Moon said. "That's the second thing," Bren said. "A whorehouse," Mrs. Moon said. "Correct," Bren said, and they had a good laugh over it.)

What else might be asked? Janet Pierson wondered if her name would appear in a newspaper or in *Harper's Weekly*. "In an interview with Mrs. Pierson, a close friend of the" . . . legendary, celebrated, renowned . . . famous . . . "the well-known figures who are playing important roles in the controversial land war . . ." What? "Mrs. Pierson stated they are very polite, well-mannered people."

She said, "I don't understand it at all. I don't. How can you sit there like it's just another day and completely ignore what's going on?"

Bren put on a concerned frown. "Honey, we're just visiting; catching up's what we're doing. You know it's been over three years?"

"Yes, I know it's been three years. You date everything you talk about," Janet Pierson said. "Sonora in eighty-seven. St. Helen's, some stagecoach station in eighty-nine. The wedding three years ago . . ."

There was a silence. They seemed content to let it go on, patient people, used to quiet; the Moons sitting together on the sofa could be on the porch Kate had described . . . Bren with a leg over the arm of his chair. Coffee cups on the end tables . . . News reporters outside dying of curiosity: Were they at each other's throats or plotting a way to kill Sundeen?

Bren said, you want some more coffee? The Moons said, no, thank you.

Janet Pierson, hands gripping the arms of her chair, said, "Would you like to hear about my past life, my marriage? How I came to live here? My husband, Paul, was a mining engineer. He designed and built the crushing mill up at the works that one day, when he wasn't feeling well and should have stayed in bed—I told him, in your condition you should *not* be walking around that machinery . . ."

Silence again.

Finally Kate Moon said, "Do you want them to talk about the situation? What do you want?"

"These *two*—" Janet Pierson began, almost angrily and had to calm herself. "These two, the heroic figures—some people must believe they're seven feet tall—what are they *doing*?"

"They're resting," Kate Moon said. "Ask them. Dana, what are you doing?"

"Wondering if we shouldn't be going."

"I'm sorry," Janet Pierson said. "I'm the one acting strange. I'm sincerely sorry."

Kate said, "Bren, what are you doing?"

"I don't know," Bren said. "Passing time? It does seem funny sitting here like this."

Moon looked at him. "What are you gonna do?"

Bren frowned again. "What do you mean, what am I gonna do?"

"Your man lynched my man."

"He isn't in any way *my* man."

"You both work for the same company."

"I don't work. I told you that. I draw money for my claims, that's all."

"All right, you're both paid by the same company."

"I don't have anything to do with this situation. What do you expect me to do, quit? You want me to walk out with them still owing me seventy thousand dollars?"

"I'm not your conscience," Moon said. "I'm not telling you what to do."

"You bet you're not."

There was a silence again.

Kate said to Janet Pierson, "You like it better now?"

"Please—I'm sorry," Janet Pierson said. She was; though she did not feel guilt or remorse. She had to hear what they thought, if she was going to understand them.

Bren rose from his chair. "I'm going to the latrine—if it ain't full of newspaper reporters."

"You still call it that?" Moon said.

Janet Pierson said she wanted to fix them something to eat and followed Bren out to the kitchen.

When they were alone, Moon said, "What are we doing here?"

"Be nice," Kate said.

"I am nice," he said. "That's all I'm doing, just sitting here being nice. I wonder what that son of a bitch Ison is doing. Probably having a drink and a good laugh with the judge and that other lawyer in his new suit."

"You knew what was gonna happen," Kate said. "Don't act so surprised."

He patted her hand. "I'm glad you're so sweet and understanding. I hope Ison and Hough run again next year so I can vote against them, the ass-kissers."

"Well, our old friend Sundeen would've got off anyway," Kate said. "What did they have to convict him with? Nothing."

"Let's go home."

"If she's fixing something, we should stay."

Moon looked toward the kitchen door. "Do you suppose he's living here with her?"

"It's his house," Kate said. "He either bought it for her, or so he can say he owns a bigger house than yours—"

"Jesus Christ," Moon said.

"I'm not sure which," Kate said. "But she's a nice person, so don't look down your nose at her."

"I'm not looking down my nose."

"I like her," Kate went on. "She's a feeling person, not afraid to tell you what she thinks."

"Or what other people think," Moon said. "You two should get along fine. You can tell us what's on our minds and save us the trouble of talking about it."

"She's worried about Bren; can't you see that?"

"Bren? Christ, nobody's shooting at Bren. He isn't even in it."

"That's what bothers her," Kate said. "He won't take sides." She looked up and smiled as Janet Pierson came into the sitting room. "We were just talking about you."

"I don't blame you," the woman said.

Kate made a tsk-tsk sound, overdoing it, shaking her head. "Why worry about what people think? You know what you're doing."

"Sometimes I guess I say too much."

"Sure, when you run out of patience," Kate said. "I know what you mean."

Moon's gaze moved from his wife to the woman, wondering what the hell they were talking about. Then looked toward the door at the sound of someone banging on it, three times. There was a pause. Janet Pierson didn't move. Then came three more loud banging sounds, the edge of somebody's fist pounding the wood panel hard enough to shake the door.

When Bren appeared again in the backyard, coming from the outhouse, the reporters on the other side of the fence in the vacant lot called to him, come on, just give us a minute or so. What were you talking about in there? . . . Debating the issues or what? . . . When's Moon going to meet Sundeen?

Then there was some kind of commotion. The reporters by the fence were looking away, moving off, then running from the vacant lot toward the front of the house. Bren went inside. There were onions and peppers on the wooden drain board in the kitchen, a pot of dry beans soaking. He heard the banging on the front door.

Janet Pierson was standing in the middle of the sitting room, saying, "They're not bashful at all, are they?"

Bren walked past her to the door, pulled it open and stopped, surprised, before he said, "What do you want?"

Deputy J.R. Bruckner stood at the door. Looking past Bren at Moon sitting on the sofa, Bruckner said, "Him. I got a warrant for the arrest of one Dana Moon. He can come like a nice fella or kicking and screaming, but either way he's coming."

2

In Benson, Ruben Vega had to find the right church first, St. John the Apostle, then had to lie to the priest to get him to come from the priest house to the church to hear his Confession.

Kneeling at the small window in the darkness of the confessional, Ruben Vega said, "Bless me, father, for I have sinned. It has been . . . thirty-seven years since my last confession."

The old priest groaned, head lowered, pinching the bridge of his nose with his eyes closed.

"Since then I have fornicated with many women . . . maybe eight hundred. No, not that many, considering my work. Maybe six hundred only."

"Do you mean bad women or good women?" the priest asked.

"They are all good, Father," Ruben Vega said. "Let me think, I stole about . . . I don't know, twenty-thousand head of beeves, but only in that time maybe fifty horses." He paused for perhaps a full minute.

"Go on."

"I'm thinking."

"Have you committed murder?"

"No."

"All the stealing you've done—you've never killed anyone?"

"Yes, of course, but it was not to commit murder. You understand the distinction? Not to *kill* someone, to take a life; but only to save my own."

The priest was silent, perhaps deciding it he should go further into this question of murder. Finally he said, "Have you made restitution?"

"For what?"

"For all you've stolen. I can't give you absolution unless you make an attempt to repay those you've harmed or injured."

Jesus, Ruben Vega thought. He said, "Look, that's done. I don't steal no more. But I can't pay back twenty thousand cows. How in the name of Christ can I do that? Oh—" He paused. "And I told a lie. I'm not dying. But, listen, man, somebody is going to," Ruben Vega said, his face close to the screen that covered the little window, "if I don't get absolution for my sins."

He had forgotten how difficult they could make it when you wanted to unburden yourself. But now he was a new person, aware of his spurs making a clear, clean ching-ing sound as he walked out of the empty church—leaving thirty-seven years with the old man in the confessional—going to the depot now to buy a ticket on the El Paso & Southwestern, ride to Douglas, cross the border and go home.

He hung around the yards watching the freight cars being switched to different tracks, smelling the coal smoke, hearing the harsh sound of the cars banging together and the wail of the whistle as an eastbound train headed out for Ochoa and the climb through Dragoon Pass. He wanted to remain outside tonight in the fresh air rather than go to a hotel in Benson; so he camped by the river and watched the young boys laughing and splashing each other, trying to catch minnows. With dark, mosquitoes came. They drove him crazy. Then it began to rain, a light, steady drizzle, and Ruben Vega said to himself: What are you doing here? He bought a bottle of *mescal* and for ten of the sixty dollars in his pocket he spent the night in a whorehouse with a plump, dark-haired girl named Rosa who thought he was very witty and laughed at everything he said when he wasn't being serious. Though some of the wittiest things he said seriously and they passed over her. That was all right. He gave her a dollar tip. In the morning Ruben Vega cashed in his ticket for the El Paso & Southwestern, mounted his horse and rode back toward the Rincon Mountains standing cleanly defined in the sunlight.

3

R.J. Bruckner said, "Look. They give me a warrant signed by Judge Hough for the arrest of Dana Moon. I served it over all kinds of commotion and people trying to argue with me and those newspaper men getting in the way. It took me and four deputies to clear them out and put Moon in detention. Now you got a complaint, go see the judge or the county attorney, it's out of my hands."

"Are you gonna drink that whole bottle yourself?" Sundeen asked.

He reached behind him to close the door, giving them some privacy in the deputy's little office with its coal-oil lamp hanging above the desk.

"I was having a touch before supper," Bruckner said, getting another glass out of his desk and placing it before Sundeen. "Not that it's any of your business."

"I see they all went home," Sundeen said, "the judge, the prosecutor and John Slaughter, leaving you with a mess, haven't they?"

"I'm doing my job," Bruckner said, pouring a short drink for Sundeen and setting the bottle within easy reach. "I don't see there's any mess here."

Sundeen leaned close as if to pick up the glass and swept the desk clean with his hand and arm, sending bottle, glasses and papers flying against the side wall. It brought the deputy's head up with a jerk, eyes staring open at the bearded, bullet-marked face, the man leaning over the desk on his hands, staring back at him.

"Look again," Sundeen said. "Listen when I'm talking to you and keep your hands in sight, else I'll draw iron and lay it across your head."

It was the beginning of a long night for R.J. Bruckner. First this one coming in and saying he wanted Moon released from jail. What? How was he supposed to do that? You think he just set a person free when somebody asked? Sundeen said he was not asking, he was telling him. He wanted Moon, but he was not going to stick a gun through the bars to get him. He wanted Moon out on the street. Bruckner would send him out and he would take care of it from there.

Ah, now that didn't sound too bad.

Except that Bruckner was looking forward to having Moon stay with him awhile. He owed Moon, the son of a bitch, at least a few lumps with a pick handle but had not gotten around to it yet.

Bruckner sat back thinking about it, saying, "Yeah, like he was shot down while trying to escape."

"Jesus, it doesn't take you long, does it?" Sundeen said.

Bruckner did not get that remark. He was thinking that he liked the idea of Moon being shot down even better than taking a pick handle to him . . . especially if it turned out he was the one pulled the trigger and not this company dude with the silver buckles.

"Yeah," he said, nodding, "let me think on it awhile."

Then was pulled up short again as Sundeen said, "You bag of shit, the thinking's been done. He walks out of here tonight at . . . let's say eleven o'clock, after you show him a release form."

"A release form? I don't have anything like that."

"Jesus, you show him *some*thing. A wire from the county clerk saying the charge's been dropped. Eleven o'clock, open the door for him to walk out and duck," Sundeen said. "You do anything else, like try and back-shoot him, you'll see fireworks go off in your face."

First Sundeen—

Then Bren Early walking into the office, looking at the mess on the floor where the bottle had knocked over the spittoon and the papers lying there were stained with tobacco juice and whiskey.

"Come to see your old partner?"

"In a minute," Early said, looking down at Bruckner from where Sundeen had stood a little while before. "You owe me a favor."

"For what?"

"Not killing you three years ago. That would be reason enough to do what I ask, but I'm gonna give you another one." Early brought paper scrip from his inside coat pocket and dropped it on the desk. "Being practical—why was he arrested in the first place?" Early watched Bruckner pick up the money and begin to count it. "Because he admitted in court trying to shoot somebody. But how're they gonna convict him if he stands mute at his trial? Moon being an agent of the federal government and all—"

"Five hundred," Bruckner said, looking up.

"Since he'd get off anyway—all you'd be doing is cutting a corner, wouldn't you?"

Bruckner folded the money into his shirt pocket and sat back, getting comfortable, big nose glistening in the coal-oil light. "I would need to do a little preparing, make it look real, you understand."

"I was thinking, in a few days when you take him to the county seat," Early said. "Out on the road someplace—"

"No, it's got to be tonight," Bruckner said.

"Why is that?"

"Because I'm on duty tonight and if I'm gonna do this I want to get it done, over with." Bruckner paused. He had to think, picture it, without taking too much time. If Sundeen and Early were both waiting outside . . . If they saw each other as Moon came out . . . If they went for each other, there'd be guns going off, wouldn't there, and he could maybe have a clear shot at Moon going out and then, what if he put the gun on Early, if Early was still standing up? . . . Shoot the accomplice . . . Jesus Christ, shoot Sundeen if he had to, if he saw the chance . . . Shoot all three of them during the confusion . . . Shoot those big names in the newspapers, God Almighty, gun them down, all three of them shot dead by Deputy Sheriff R.J. Bruckner . . . Oh yes, that's Bruckner, he's the one that gunned down Moon, Bren Early and Phil Sundeen, the Yuma terror, during a daring jailbreak . . . Wiped them out, all three of them. Jesus.

"What're you nervous about?" Early asked him.

Bruckner pulled out a handkerchief to wipe his forehead and down over his nose and mouth. "Goddamn dinky office is like a hotbox. I'm gonna get out of here pretty soon, run for the job in

Tombstone next year. Shit, if I can't beat Fly, with my experience in law enforcement—"

"Let's get this done first," Early said.

Bruckner nodded, mind made up. "Tonight, eleven o'clock . . . No, five minutes before eleven. You come, leave a horse for him in front. Step inside and give me a nod. I'll go back and get your partner, lock myself up in his cell."

"Why not the back door?" Early said. "In the alley."

"That door don't open. It's bolted shut."

"All right, let me talk to him now."

"Tell him five minutes before eleven," Bruckner said.

This time it was Moon in the cell and Early looking through the bars.

He said, "I talked to John Slaughter before they moved their show out of here. John says they didn't have a choice, you shot three men in that yard. They'll hold your trial at the county seat. Now, considering everything, the company'll turn on the pressure to get a conviction. See if they can send you to Yuma."

"It's a lot of country from here to there," Moon said. "Kate visits tomorrow, I'll talk to her about it. You don't have to get involved in this."

"I already am," Early said. "Sundeen was here about a half-hour ago. The way I see it, he doesn't want you in here either. He's been keeping quiet, but that business in Sonora's still eating him."

"I know that," Moon said.

"I talked to Bruckner and he was already there waiting. Had the time set and everything."

"What'd you pay him?"

"Not much. He owes me a favor. But wouldn't it make his heart glad to shoot you going out the door and me standing there? Or Sundeen. He paid a visit—something's already been arranged here, I can feel it."

"I can smell it," Moon said. "But this isn't any of your business. If he's gonna open the door, I'll take my own chances."

"What was it you said the time I was in there and you were out here?" Early paused before reciting the words from three years ago. " 'You might see it coming, but I doubt it.' Well, you'll probably hear me three blocks away."

"Drawing your sword and yelling, 'Charge,' " Moon said. "It should be something to watch."

4

The parlor was semi-dark with only one lamp lit, turned low. When Kate came down the stairs, Janet Pierson turned from the front window.

"Did you rest?"

"A little. I didn't sleep though."

Kate walked over to the hall tree and took down her husband's suitcoat and holstered revolver. (They had taken him out of the house in his shirtsleeves, hurrying to get him past the throng of newsmen.)

Watching her, Janet said, "I envy you. I'm not sure why, but I do."

Kate draped the coat over the back of a chair. Holding the shoulder holster, she slipped the Colt's revolver in and out of the smooth leather groove, then drew the gun and looked at the loads in the chambers as she said, "You don't have to envy anyone. You can do whatever you want with your life."

"But you *know* what you want."

"This minute I do," Kate said. "I want my husband. If I have to shoot somebody to get him, I will. It's not something I have to think about and decide." She looked toward the kitchen, at the sound of the back door opening and closing, then at Janet again. "This doesn't mean anything to you personally. Why get mixed up in something just for the sake of taking sides?"

The question was left unanswered. Bren Early came in from the kitchen with saddlebags over one shoulder.

"I haven't seen a soul in front," Janet said to him.

"Tired of waiting around," Bren said. "They're in the saloon telling each other stories." He took the holstered revolver from Kate and slipped it into the saddlebag that hung in front of him. "I still think it'd be better if you waited here."

Kate shook her head. "I'll be out on the road. If you won't let me any closer—"

"You might hear shooting," Bren said. "This man wants to make it look real. Stay where you are till Moon gets there. But for some reason he doesn't—he gets delayed or has to ride out the other way, you come back here."

"What do you mean, gets delayed? I thought it was all arranged."

"It is. I'm talking about if something happens to change the plan . . . somebody comes along doesn't know about it. That's all."

"You're not telling me everything," Kate said. "What is it?"

"Believe me," Bren said, "Dana's gonna walk out. But you have to be patient and not spook if you hear a lot of noise. All right? Wait'll I'm gone a few minutes before you leave."

"I'll be out there before eleven," Kate said. "By the first bend."

Janet watched Bren pick up Moon's coat, then lean toward Kate and kiss her on the cheek. Turning he looked at Janet. "I'll be back in a little while." And went out through the kitchen.

The room was quiet again.

"I don't know what to say to him." Janet turned to the window to watch for him. He'd ride past the front of the house leading Moon's horse.

"Then don't say anything," Kate said, walking over to her, her gaze going out the window to the dark street.

"I feel—I don't feel part of him or what any of you are doing."

"Well, you can come up the mountain for a visit, except I don't think it's a very good time." Kate paused and put her hand on Janet's shoulder. "Why don't you just marry him and quit thinking about it?"

"You sound like Bren now."

"If you have to be absolutely sure before you make a move," Kate said, "then forget it. Else you're gonna be sitting here with cobwebs all over you."

5

LaSalle Street was quiet: first-shift miners in bed for the night, the second shift still up at the works where dots of lantern light marked the shaft scaffolding and company buildings; the crushing mill was dark, the ore tailings black humps running down the slope.

Sundeen, mounted, came down out of that darkness into the main street, holding his horse to a walk past the store fronts and evenly spaced young trees planted to grow along the sidewalk. The porch of the Congress Hotel was deserted. Lights showed in the lobby and in saloons and upstairs windows down the street. It was quarter to eleven. At the sound of gunfire they'd pour out of the saloons—most of them who were sober or not betting against a pot—the news reporters coming out of their hangout, the Gold Dollar, which was on the northeast corner of LaSalle and Fourth streets. The jail was on the southwest corner, the cellblock extending along Fourth toward Mill Street. On the corner across Fourth from the jail was the Maricopa State Bank. On the corner across LaSalle—where Sundeen now dropped his reins and stepped down from his horse—was the I.S. Weiss Mercantile Store.

Sundeen, looking at the jail and its two lighted windows—the one to the left of the door Bruckner's office—did not see the dark figure sitting on the steps of the bank, catty-corner from him.

When the figure got to its feet Sundeen caught the movement and knew who it was: yes, crossing Fourth Street toward the jail with something dark draped over his shoulder and carrying a short club or something in his left hand. No, not a club. The object gave off a glint and took shape in the light from the jail window and Sundeen saw it was a stubby little shotgun.

Early stopped. He half turned to look across toward the Mercantile Store.

"It isn't gonna be as easy as you thought."

"What is?" Sundeen said. Shit.

"Where's all your men at?"

"I didn't think I'd need them this evening."

"Well," Early said, "you better decide if you're gonna be there when we come out."

"God damn Bruckner," Sundeen said. "I think he has got cow shit for brains."

"No, he's not one to put your money on," Early said. "Well, I'll see you if you're still gonna be there." He moved past the jail window toward the front door.

There was nobody to trust, Bruckner had decided. Not a friend, not one of his four deputies. Not in something like this. The chance, if it came, would be there for him alone and he would have to do it himself if he wanted to reap the benefits. And, oh my Lord, the benefits. Both at hand and in the near future, with a saloon-full of news reporters across the street to begin the spread of his fame which would lead to his fortune. All he had to do, at the exact moment when he saw the chance, was pull the trigger three times—at least two times—and in the coming year he would be the Fighting Sheriff of Cochise County . . . working angles the mine company and the taxpayers never knew existed. Being ready was the key. Here is how he would do it:

Early sticks his head in the door, gives him the nod.

Unarmed, he goes back to the lockup, thanking the Lord he had put Moon in a cell by himself.

He steps in, Moon steps out, locks him in. As soon as Moon is through the door, into the front part of the jail . . .

He unlocks the cell with a spare key, goes through to the front, gets the loaded shotgun and Peacemaker from under the cabinet . . .

Runs to the door—maybe hearing Sundeen's gunfire about then—and opens up on them with the shotgun, close behind, while they're busy with Sundeen.

Then, as Sundeen comes across the street—and before anybody is out of the Gold Dollar—blow out Sundeen's lights.

If Sundeen's fire turns them back in the jail, which was possible, he'd bust them as they came through the door. Then step out and shoot Sundeen with the Peacemaker, saying later the man had fired at him after he'd told him to drop his gun, so he'd had no choice but to return fire. (He could hear himself telling it, saying something about being sworn to enforce the law, by God, no matter who the armed men were he had to face.) Killing the two should buy him the ticket to the county seat; but he would like to notch up Sundeen also, long as he was at it.

In case of an unexpected turn—if he somehow lost his weapons and found himself at close quarters, he had a two-shot bellygun under his vest, pressing into his vitals.

At a quarter to eleven Bruckner stopped pacing around the front room of the jail, moving from the railing that divided the room to the front window and back, went into his office and sat down, wishing he had just a couple swallows of that Green River drying on the floor.

At five to eleven he thought he heard voices outside. He turned to the window, but came around again as he heard the door open and close. Bren Early appeared in the doorway to his office wearing his .44's, saddlebags over his shoulder and carrying a sawed-off shotgun. At this moment Bruckner's plan began to go all to hell.

"O.K.," Bruckner said, getting up and coming out to the front room as Early stepped back. "You got his horse?"

Early nodded.

"I'll fetch him. Go on outside."

Early looked at Bruckner's empty holster, then over at the gun rack, locked with two vertical iron bars. "Where the keys?"

"Don't worry—go on outside." Bruckner took a ring of keys from the desk in the front room, walked to the metal-ribbed door leading to the cell block and unlocked it before looking back at Early.

"What're you waiting on?"

Early moved toward him, making a motion with the sawed-off shotgun.

Early coming back with him wasn't in the plan. But maybe it wouldn't hurt anything. It could even make it easier, having the two right together.

Bruckner glanced over his shoulder walking down the row of cells. He raised his hands as one of the prisoners, then another, saw them and pushed up from their bunks. A voice behind Early said, "Hey, partner, open this one. Let me out of this shit hole."

Moon stood at his cell door. He stepped aside as Bruckner entered, made a half-turn and came around to slam a fist into the side of Bruckner's face. The deputy hit the adobe wall and slid to the floor. Moon stood over him a moment, seeing blood coming out of the man's nose. He said, "Don't ever put your hands on me again," and gave him a parting boot in the ribs, drawing a sharp gasp from Bruckner.

Early held the lockup door open as Moon came through, then slammed it closed, cutting off the voices of the prisoners yelling to be let out.

"Sundeen was out in front. Just him I could see, but it doesn't mean he's alone," Early said.

From the saddlebags Moon took his folded-up coat and shoulder rig and slipped them on, saying, "How far you going in this?"

"See you get out of here, that's all. But Sundeen's a different matter. I mean if he wants to try." Early paused. "If he doesn't, maybe we should go find him, get the matter settled."

Moon was smoothing his coat, adjusting the fit of the holster beneath his left arm. He took the sawed-off from Early. "I ain't lost any sleep over him. Least I haven't yet."

"No, but he's gonna bother you now, he gets the chance. I'd just as soon finish it."

Moon seemed to study him, forming words in his mind. "Is it you've been sitting around too long, you're itchy? Or you just wanted to shoot somebody?"

"I can go home and leave it up to you," Early said, a cold edge there.

"Yes, you can. And I'd probably handle him one way or the other."

Early stared at Moon a moment, turned and walked toward the door.

Moon said, "You understand what I mean? I want to be sure about him."

Early pulled the door wide open and stepped aside. "Go on and find out then." Still with the cold edge.

Shit, Moon thought. He said, "Get over your touchiness. You sound like a woman." And walked out the door past him—the hell with it—out into the middle of the street, looking around, before he saw his horse over by the side of the bank. He didn't see any sign of Sundeen and didn't expect to; the man wasn't going to shoot out of the dark and not get stand-up credit for his kill.

Early came out to the board sidewalk, pulling the door partly closed behind him. He said, "Go on home, sit on your porch. Kate's waiting up by the bend."

"Thanks," Moon said, glancing over, already moving toward Fourth Street.

"You don't have to thank me for anything," Early said. "We're even now, right? Don't owe each other a thing."

Jesus, Moon thought. He should hear himself.

He saw the light in the half-closed doorway behind Early widen. He saw a figure, Bruckner, and yelled, "Bren!" and had to drop the sawed-off with Bren in the way and the door too far; he had to drop it to pull the goddamn saddlebags off his shoulder and come out with the Colt's, seeing Early throwing himself out of the way as Bruckner's shotgun exploded and Moon's revolver kicked in his hand and he saw Bruckner punched off his feet as the .44 took him somewhere in the middle of his body. Bren was up then, yelling at him to go on, get out of here, waving his arm.

You better, Moon thought, picking up the sawed-off. He could see Bruckner's feet in the doorway, beyond Early. And sounds now from across the street, people starting to come out of the Gold Dollar, standing there, looking this way. Moon reached his horse and stepped up; he pointed toward Mill Street and was gone in the darkness.

ELEVEN

1

Moon stopped at White Tanks on the way home "to put in an appearance," he told Kate, say hello to the reservation Apaches he hadn't seen in weeks and sort through his mail—any directives, bulletins or other bull shit he might have received from Washington.

Kate said she was glad she didn't have to read it. She would go home and light the fire. He watched her take off across the pasture toward the brushy slope and start up the switchback trail that climbed through the field of saguaro, watching her until she was a tiny speck, his little wife up there on the mountain, and said to himself, "You know how lucky you are?" He was anxious to get home to her. Maybe he'd look at the mail but check on the reservation people tomorrow.

He sat down at his desk though, to read the letter from the Bureau of Indian Affairs, Interior Department, Washington, D.C. It took him about a quarter of an hour to find out all the two and a half pages of official language actually said was, he was fired . . . would be relieved of his duties for disregarding such and such, as of a date three months from now. Fired because he hadn't brought his Indians down off the mountain, failing to comply with directive number . . . some long number. The fools. They could have said it in two words.

He'd go home and tell Kate and watch her eyes open—Kate poised there, not knowing whether to show relief or rail at the imbeciles in the bureau, pausing and then asking, "Well, how do you feel about it?"

How did he feel?

Relief, yes, able to wade out of the official muck, walk off. Or would he be walking *out*, leaving the reservation people when they needed him? Well, they may need *some*body, but he wasn't doing them a hell of a lot of good, was he? And what difference did it make now, since he didn't have a choice but to leave? Thinking about all that at once, blaming himself for not having thought of an answer sooner . . . and hearing the bootsteps on the porch, the ching-ing sound, without first hearing a horse approach—

The Mexican stood in the open doorway. The one from Sonora. The one from Duro's yard with the white flag. Hesitant. Raising his hands from his sides.

"You didn't walk here," Moon said.

"I didn't want to startle you. Maybe you come out shooting you hear me," Ruben Vega said. "Listen to me and believe it, all right? I don't work for Sundeen no more, but he's up on the mountain."

"Where?" Moon came out of his swivel chair.

"Going to your house."

"When was this?"

"Last night, very late."

Moon came around his desk and Ruben Vega had to get out of his way. He followed Moon out to the porch.

"Wait. I want to tell you something. I didn't *see* him up there, I heard it, where he's going."

Moon, at his horse gathering the reins, looked up at the Mexican. "Tell it quick."

"See, I quit him. I went to Benson. I was going to go home, but I decide after all the years, after all the bad things I done—"

Moon stepped up into his saddle.

"I came back here to do some good, be on the good side for a change—whether you believe me or not." He saw Moon's look. "Listen to me, all right? I came back, I stop by this place where I believe his men have been waiting, the J-L-Bar, an old, worn-out place. Yes, there they are. They say, where you been? Listen—"

Moon was reining, moving out.

"They say to me Sundeen comes tonight and we go up the mountain to get the man name Moon. You hear me?" Shouting it.

Ruben Vega ran to his horse ground-tied in the pasture. Maybe he would catch up to Moon already racing for the brush slope, maybe he wouldn't.

■ ■ ■

She'd say to him, "Come on to bed." He'd say, "It's daytime." She'd say, "I mean to *sleep*," after riding most the night—God, she had been glad to see him coming out the road with the lights of Sweetmary behind him. She wanted at least to hug and kiss him awhile, touch him, make sure he was here.

Kate built a fire in the stove and put on a pot of coffee before going outside again to tend Goldie. She led the palomino around the house to the corral that was made of upright mesquite poles wired together. This pen was attached to a timber and thatched-roof structure open at both ends that served as a horse barn. Kate heard the sound—a horse hoof on gravel . . . a soft whinny . . . then silence—as she was leading Goldie across the corral.

She looked through the barn to the back of the property where open graze reached to a brush thicket and a tumble of boulders. There the ground began to climb again. An Apache could be passing by. Even when Moon said they were close she rarely saw one, unless they were coming out and wanted to be seen. They kept to themselves. Red, the little bow-legged chief, was the only one she had ever spoken to; the women just grinned when she tried talking to them in Spanish learned from Moon. Yes, it could be an Apache going by. Her gaze raised to the escarpment of seamed rock standing against the sky. Or they might be up there watching over her.

But she had the feeling someone else was much closer. She turned to Goldie, patting her as she moved back to the saddlebags, raised the leather flap close to her face and drew the .38 double-action revolver Moon had given her that time in Sonora and had given to her again in the past month.

Someone was watching her. Not Apaches, someone else.

Kate led Goldie back to the mesquite-pole gate, dragged it open enough to let them through. As she prepared to mount—looking over the saddle and through the open-ended barn again, she saw the four riders coming out of the brush thicket, walking their horses, looking right at her. Kate stepped into the saddle kicking, turned the corner to the front of the house and reined in, not knowing what to do, Goldie sidestepping, nervous, feeling Kate's heels and the reins and, between the two, Kate's indecision.

Sundeen sat his mount with two riders near. A bunch more were by the abode wall and coming through the gate on foot, all of them holding rifles.

"Well, it's been a long time," Kate said, resigned.

"What?" Sundeen studied her, not knowing what she meant.

"You don't remember, do you?"

Sundeen, squinting now, shook his head.

"One time, I was twelve years old playing by the river," Kate said. "You come along, tried to pull my britches down and I smacked you with a rock."

"Jesus Christ," Sundeen said, "down Lanoria."

"You were grown then, too, you dirty pervert."

"Yeah, I believe I recall that—hit me with a big goddamn rock." He looked at one of his riders who was wearing a vest and derby hat. "Thing musta weighed five pounds. Hit me square on the forehead with it." Sundeen nudged his horse forward. "So you're the one, huh? You should've give in that time and seen the elephant at an early age." Still coming toward her. "Or I could give you another chance while we're waiting around." He pulled in then. "Hey now—but you better throw that gun down first."

Kate raised the .38 from her lap. "Or I could put a hole in the other side of your face, match the one you already got."

"Sweetheart," Sundeen said, "before you could aim that parlor gun I'd have sent you off to the angels. Now let it fall."

Of course, the man was thinking of his wife. Ruben Vega realized this. He should have realized also—knowing something about Moon—the man would control his emotion and not ride blindly up the ravine to be shot from his saddle. So Ruben Vega was able to catch up with the man once they were in the high rocks, somewhere north of the ravine, perhaps on an approach to the side or back of the house; Ruben Vega wasn't exactly sure where they were when he reached Moon. Or when the Apache appeared ahead of them, waiting in the trail. One moment the steep terrain ahead empty, the next moment the dark little half-naked man standing there with a carbine and a cartridge belt around his skirt. A headband of dark wool, as dark as his dark-leather face; he could be an old man, or any age.

The Apache, Red, motioned and went off through the towering outcropping of rocks, through a seam that became a trail when they dismounted and followed, winding, climbing through the rock and brush until the trail opened and the entire sky seemed to be close above them, a very clear soft blue. A beautiful day to feel good and be alive, the Mexican was thinking. Except for the situation, the man's wife—Moon and the Apache, and now three more Apaches who had appeared from nowhere, were looking down the wall of rock . . . as though from the top of a church steeple, the Mexican thought, seeing the stone side of the house below, the thatched roof of a barn, a corral, riders in the front yard . . . the glint of the woman's blonde hair in the sunlight close to Sundeen . . . Yes, it was Sundeen and two others . . . four more coming from the corral side of the house . . . the rest of them out by the abode wall, watching the approach from the ravine.

A good day, the Mexican thought, feeling alive and yet calm inside. A day he would mark in his mind, whatever the date was. He would find it out later.

He said to Moon, "Is there a way down from here?"

Moon looked at him. The man could skip all the questions in his mind and trust him or not.

Moon said, "You go down . . . then what?"

The man was open. He had nothing to lose by listening.

"You stay behind me, out of sight," Ruben Vega said. "Come in close as you can when I talk to him."

"Tell him what?"

"I don't know. What comes in my mind. He'll be curious a few minutes—where have you been, partner? All that. Then you have to be close. I can talk to him some more, but it comes out the same in the end, uh? He isn't going to say to your wife, go on, stay out of the way. So—" the Mexican shrugged.

"Thirteen of them," Moon said.

"More than that last night at the J-L-Bar. He hired some more maybe he send someplace else, I don't know." Moon was staring at him again and Ruben Vega said, "I never done this before, but it's a good day to begin. Now, how do you get down from here?"

There were ten at the abode wall now, dismounted. One with a derby hat sat his horse in the middle of the yard, a Winchester across his lap, squinting up at the high rocks. One on the porch was holding a coffee pot. Sundeen, still mounted, was gazing about, looking up at the rocks trying to see something, nervous or not sure with that high ground above him. Moon's wife was still on the palomino: as though Sundeen hadn't made up his mind yet, keep her here or take her somewhere, or trying to think of a way to use her.

Good, Ruben Vega thought, approaching the yard from the corral side of the house, almost to the yard before they saw him. Very good.

"I think you need me," the Mexican said, "for eyes. Man, I ride up, you don't even see me."

Sundeen gave him a patient look, shaking his head. "Where the hell you been?"

"I went to Benson to go to church," Ruben Vega said.

"Yeah, I know, piss all your money away and come back for some more, haven't you? Well, make yourself useful, partner. Ride on down a ways and see if he's coming."

"I already did," Ruben Vega said. "He's coming up pretty soon, over there," pointing to the wall where the shooters were waiting with their rifles, not wearing their suitcoats now, several of them with straw hats pulled down low.

The one in the derby hat rode over that way and Sundeen sat for some moments twisted around in his saddle, looking toward the wall.

Now, the Mexican thought, right hand on his thigh, inches from his revolver.

But he couldn't do it and the next moment it was too late. Sundeen was turning back to him.

Ruben Vega looked away. He saw the revolver on the ground next to the palomino. Moon's wife sat still, though her eyes moved and she listened. Of course, she listened. He wished he could tell her something: Be ready. Be watching me.

"Alone?"

"What?" the Mexican said.

"Was he alone?"

"Yes. Maybe they can see him now," the Mexican said and looked toward the wall again.

But Sundeen didn't turn this time and the Mexican had a strange feeling of relief, not having to decide in that moment to pull his gun . . . not wanting to shoot the man from a blind side, but not wanting to die either. So how was he supposed to do it? Thirty-seven years doing this, carrying a gun since he was fourteen years old, not worrying before about killing a man if he believed the man might kill him first. Why was he thinking about it now? Because he was getting old. Sundeen would say to him, you're getting old; and he would say, yes, because I'm still alive. It was a beautiful day and if it was going to be the one he'd remember he'd better do it now. Without thinking anymore.

But he thought of one more thing.

He said, "I'm taking the woman."

Alerting her with his words.

But alerting Sundeen also—seeing his expression only for a moment puzzled.

His hand going to his holster, to the hard grip of the .44, the Mexican saw Sundeen's hand moving, and knew he shouldn't have said anything and now was going to lose . . . But the woman was moving, kicking her palomino around . . . as Sundeen's revolver cleared and he was firing and firing again . . . and, Christ, it was like being punched hard, hearing himself grunt with the wind going out of him and the .44 in his hand, trying to put it on Sundeen . . . *ughhh,* grunting again in the noise of something hard socking him in the chest . . . firing as he saw the blue sky and felt himself going back, falling—

Sundeen had several thoughts in the next moments:

That was a good horse, Ruben's, not to have moved under all that commotion, the horse standing there, his old segundo gone crazy and now dead on the ground.

Everybody back there see it? It was time he showed them something.

Three snap shots dead center. Any *one* would have killed the crazy Mexican.

Three shots. Two left in his Peacemaker—that thought hitting him all at once as he saw the movement, as he saw the Apaches first, *Apaches,* a bunch of them off in the scrub, and Moon appearing at the corner of the house, Moon yelling his wife's name. Moon blocked out for a moment as the palomino shot past him— the woman's blonde hair in the horse's blond mane. Sundeen extended his Peacemaker and fired, saw Moon again, there he was, and tried to concentrate his aim on Moon with one load left—and the heavy fire came all at once from the scrub. Sundeen fired at Moon suddenly moving—shit—yanked his reins to get out of there, yelling, "Get 'em, goddamn it . . . get 'em!"

Moon wanted him so bad, putting his Colt's gun on the man tight-reining, kicking his horse, at the same time, seeing the ones way over by the wall raising their rifles, opening fire, and thinking, *Kate,* looking to see where she was—there, past him, still low in her saddle and cutting through the scrub to come around by the corral behind him. In that moment of concern letting Sundeen get the jump he needed, Sundeen beating his mount toward the shooters by the wall. Moon aimed stiff-armed, ignoring the shooters, pulled the trigger five times, holding the sawed-off in his left hand and wishing he had the Sharps for just one, take his time and *right then*, blow out Sundeen's soul as his horse cleared the wall and there he was for a split moment against the sky. But not today.

Now it was Moon's turn to get out of there.

They withdrew to high ground, Moon, his wife and his Apaches, and took careful shots at the figures crouched on the other side of the wall now. The figures would return fire, shooting at puffs of smoke. Ruben Vega's body lay in the yard, his chestnut horse nuzzling him as though it were grazing.

"Keep 'em away from the house," Moon said.

Kate remembered the one on the porch with the coffee pot, the fresh coffee she'd made for her husband, and said there was one already in there.

After awhile heavy black smoke began to pour out of the stone chimney.

"He's burning the place," Kate said. "He's burning our home."

Moon waited in the high rocks with his Sharps rifle, seeing, from this angle, the side and back of the house, the clay-tile roof and most of the yard, but not the porch, the front of the house. The thick smoke billowed up from the chimney.

When the smoke began to seep out across the yard from the front, Moon judging it was coming out of the door and windows, he raised the Sharps and pressed his cheek to the smooth stock, the big curled hammer eased back in front of his eyes, the barrel pointing into the yard, and waited.

Finally Kate said, "There he is."

Moon saw the figure appear beyond his front sight, running for the wall. There was a faint sound, the men down there yelling, cheering him on. The figure reached the wall and bounded up to go over it in one motion. Moon paused, seeing the man stop and draw himself up to stand on the wall with hands on his hips and look around at his work . . . the smoke pouring out of the house.

Another fool, Moon thought. He shot the fool cleanly off the wall, the man dying as the heavy sound boomed out into the distance. It was not much satisfaction. After awhile Sundeen and his shooters pulled out.

Moon and Kate went down to their house, beat at the smoldering pockets of fire with blankets and dragged out the charred furniture that had been piled in the middle of the room. When this was done, Moon put the Mexican over his horse. They took him down to the White Tanks cemetery, buried him and recited a prayer over his grave. If they ever learned his name they would put up a marker.

2

R.J. Bruckner showed the news reporters and anyone interested the little derringer that had saved his life. The gun, lying on the deputy's desk, looked like it had been hit with a hammer. Patting his belly, Bruckner said he kept the little pea-shooter right here, see, exactly where Moon's bullet had caught him. The bullet struck the derringer and embedded parts of it into his flesh the doctor had to pull out with tweezers.

Where had Moon got a gun to shoot with?, the newsmen wanted to know.

When his wife had visited, Bruckner said. He had taken Mrs. Moon's word she had no weapons on her person, so had not searched her.

Maurice Dumas, who was present, asked himself when Moon's wife had visited him in the eight hours Moon was in jail. Maurice thought about it and shook his head. She hadn't.

Bruckner said Moon had pulled the gun and locked him in the cell, not knowing—Bruckner patting his pocket now—he always carried a spare key. He had then grabbed his six-shooter, run out to the street and would have shot Moon dead had not Bren Early gotten in the way, Early having come just then to visit Moon.

The news reporters gave Bruckner narrow looks while some of them laughed out loud, which was a mistake. It shut off Bruckner's trust of them and willingness to talk. After that it was like pulling teeth to get information from him.

Grimly he stuck to his story that it was Moon's wife who'd given him the gun and had brought the horse some of the newsmen had actually seen running down Fourth Street toward Mill with Moon aboard. Yes, in fact Moon had sneered at him and actually *told* him, when he was being locked in the cell, that it was his wife had brought it. Also, he knew for a fact Moon's wife had left Mrs. Pierson's house about the time of Moon's escape. She was no longer in town, was she? "Now get your asses out of my office." Bruckner didn't have any need for these grinning, smart-aleck out-of-towners. He had work to do. First thing, post the wanted dodger on Dana Moon. It showed Moon's face, taken from a C.S. Fly photo, and said:

$5,000
REWARD

(Dead or Alive)

for information leading to
the arrest or seizure of

DANA MOON
Escaped Fugitive

37 years of age, dark hair, dark-
complected. Former United States
Government Indian Agent at White
Tanks Sub-agency. Approach with
caution. If whereabouts known,
notify Deputy Sheriff R.J. Bruckner,
Sweetmary, Arizona Territory.

Bruckner hung the dodger outside the jail on a bulletin board for all to see. On the same board were:

A LaSalle Mining Company notice warning hunters and prospectors to avoid posted areas where survey crews were working with dynamite.

And, a recruiting poster—"HIGH PAY—INTERESTING WORK"—calling for individuals who were experienced in the handling of firearms and owned their own horse to apply for a position with the LaSalle Mining Security Division. "$20 A WEEK TO START. SEE P. SUNDEEN."

Maurice Dumas looked at the board for several minutes, the thought striking him, wasn't it strange the company posters were right there with the Moon "wanted" dodger? Like the company was footing the bill for all three enterprises. They surely looked alike in appearance. He could write an article about that, posing the question: Was the company paying for Dana Moon's arrest . . . or death? (Bruckner had refused to answer that directly, saying it was county business.)

But first, locate Early, if possible, and see if he was willing to chat about things in general. Maurice Dumas was still feeling intuitive as well as pretty lucky.

Was it because he had not yet been pushy, but had politely given his name and said he was sorry to have disturbed her? Maurice couldn't believe it when she said come in. Look at that. The first news reporter to be invited into the house of the mysterious Mrs. Pierson. He entered hesitantly, cap in hand, looking around with an expression of awe, for this place could some day be of historical interest.

She did not invite him to sit down, but immediately said, "You're the one he talks to, aren't you?"

"Well, we have spoken privately several times, yes," Maurice said. "I mean he's told me things he hasn't told the other journalists, that I know of."

"Like what?"

"Well . . . how he feels about things."

"He does? He tells you that, how he feels?"

"I don't mean to imply I have his complete confidence, no, ma'am." He didn't realize until now that she was upset. Judging from her tone, more than a little angry.

"Well, the next time you see him," Janet Pierson said, "tell him to quit acting like a spoiled brat and grow up."

"Mr. *Early*?"

"Like he got out of bed on the wrong side every morning. Tell him to make up his mind what he's mad at. If it's me, if I'm to blame, I'll gladly move out. Ask him if that's what he wants. Because I'm not taking any more of his pouting."

"Bren *Early*?"

"Or his silence. All day he sat here, he didn't say a word. 'Can I get you something? . . . Would you like your dinner now?' Like walking on eggs, being so careful not to bother him too much. He'd grunt something. Did that mean yes or no? He'd grunt something else. Finally I said, 'Well, if you're gonna act as if I'm not here, one of us might as well leave.' No answer. Can you imagine living with someone like that?"

She did not seem too mysterious now.

"Bren Early?" Maurice said, puzzled. "No, I can't imagine him like that. He's so . . . calm. Are you sure he wasn't just being calm?"

"God," Janet Pierson said, "you *don't* know him, do you? You believe the one in the photograph with the revolvers is the real person."

"Well, what I do know about him is certainly real and impressive enough to me," Maurice said.

"It is, huh?" Mrs. Pierson said something then that Maurice thought about for a long time after. She said, "That C.S. Fly, he should take all pictures of famous people in their underwear, and when they're not looking."

He found Bren Early where he should have looked first, the Chinaman's: Early sitting in the quiet room, though near the front this time, by one of the windows. He was sipping whiskey. On the table in front of him was a handwritten menu, in ink, and one of the Dana Moon "wanted" dodgers, Moon's face in the photo looking up at Bren Early.

Maurice Dumas left his cap on and pulled up a chair. "The Chicago Kid," some of the others were calling him now. Or "Lucky Maurice." Luck, hell, it was sensing a story and digging for it, letting nothing discourage or deter. Go after it.

"Moon's wife didn't bring him the gun," Maurice said. He was going to add, flatly, "You did," but softened it at the last second. "I have a feeling it might have been you."

Bren Early was looking at the menu. He said, "Did you know this place is called The Oriental?"

"No, I didn't think it had a name."

"The Oriental," Early said.

Maurice waited a moment. "I also believe the company put up the five-thousand reward. Because I don't think the county would spend that kind of money on something that's—when you get right down to it—company business. Am I right or wrong?"

Early said, "Are you gonna have something to eat?"

"No, I don't think so."

"Well, if you aren't gonna eat, why don't you leave?"

Maurice felt a chill go up the back of his neck. He managed to say, "I just thought we might talk."

"There's nothing to talk about," Early said.

"Well, maybe I will have something to eat, if it's all right."

Maurice ate some kind of pork dish, sitting there self-conscious, feeling he should have left and tried the man at a better time. Though Early did say one thing as he sipped his whiskey and then picked up the Moon "wanted" poster. He said, "A man who likes his front porch hasn't any business on one of these."

"No," Maurice said, to agree.

"Sometimes they put the wrong people on these things."

Early didn't say anything after that. He finished his whiskey and walked out, leaving the young reporter sitting there with his pork dish.

TWELVE

1

Sundeen appeared in Sweetmary, picked up fresh mounts and supplies and went out again with twenty men, some eager new ones along. He'd hinted he was close to running Moon to ground, but would not give details. This time Maurice Dumas and several news reporters trailed after him, keeping well behind his dust.

There were saddle bums and gunnysackers who came up from around Charleston and Fairbank with Moon's "wanted" dodger folded in their pockets.

These men would study the pictures of Moon in Fly's gallery a long time, pretending to have keen looks in their eyes. They would drink whiskey in the saloons—all these ragtag chuck-line riders turned manhunters—talking in loud voices how they packed their .45-70's for distance or how an old Ballard could outshoot a Henry. They would go out to their campsites along the Benson road, stare up at the Rincons and talk about dogging the man's sign clear to hell for that kind of reward money, come back here and buy a saloon with a whorehouse upstairs.

Best chance, everyone agreed, squat down in a blind and wait for the shot. Moon was bound to appear somewhere, though not likely to be snared and taken alive. Yes, it was up to chance; but some lucky bird would get the shot, come back with Moon wrapped in canvas and collect the $5,000; more money than could be made in ten years of herding and fence riding.

The saddle bums and gunnysackers straggled out in pairs and small groups, those who had soldiered saying they were going on an extended campaign and would forage, live off the country. Most of them came dragging back in four or five days, hungry and thirsty, saying shit, Moon wasn't up there—like they had expected to find him sitting on a stump waiting. Wasn't anybody up there far as they could see.

How about Sundeen?

Him either.

The news reporters who had trailed out after Sundeen came back with sore legs and behinds—all of them except the Chicago Kid—to say Phil Sundeen had not found anything either. All he was doing was pushing his men up one draw and down another, finding some empty huts but not a sign of the mountain people.

Days went by. What seemed to be the last of the manhunters came limping in with the same story—nothing up there but wind and dry washes—and looked around for old chums who had gone out in other parties. A rough tally indicated some had not returned. Were they still hunting? Not likely, unless they were living on mesquite beans. Were they dead? Or had they gone home by way of Benson?

Ask Moon that one.

Ask him if you could ever find him. Or if he was still up there. Maybe he had left here for safer climes.

Like hell, said a man by the name of Asa Bailey from Contention. He had seen Moon, close enough to touch the tobacco wad in the man's jaw.

The news reporters sat him down at a table in the Gold Dollar with a full bottle, got out their note pads and said, O.K., go ahead.

Asa Bailey told them there had been three of them in the party and gave the names Wesley and Urban as the other two—last seen headed southeast, having sworn off manhunting forever.

They had come across Sundeen and his bunch at the Moon place and Sundeen had run them off, telling them to keep their nose out of company business. They had stayed close enough to watch, though, and observed Sundeen riding off with most of his men, leaving two or three at the burnt-out house. Yes, Sundeen had set a torch to the place, though the roof and walls seemed in good shape.

Asa Bailey said he had been a contract guide out of Camp Grant some years before and knew Moon and his Apaches surely weren't going to stand around nor leave directions where they went. Moon would use his Apaches as his eyes and pull tricks to decoy Sundeen out of his boots: let him see a wisp of smoke up in the high reaches and Sundeen would take half a day getting up there to a cold fire set by some Apache woman or little kid. Let them wear themselves out and go home hungry, was Moon's game, all the time watching Sundeen.

"So we would play it too," Asa Bailey said, "pretend we was Moon and hang back off Sundeen's flank and sooner or later cross Moon's sign. Sundeen'd camp, we'd camp, rigging triplines, and making a circle around us with loose rocks we'd hear if somebody tried to approach.

"We were the stalkers, huh? Like hell. Imagine you're sitting all night in what you believe is an ambush. Dawn, you're asleep as Wesley and Urban are over a ways gathering the horses. You feel something—not hear it, *feel* it. And open your eyes in the cold gray light and not dare to even grunt. The man's hunched over you with the barrel tip of his six-gun sticking in your mouth. There he was with the kindly eyes and the tobacco wad you see in the pictures."

There wasn't a sound at that table until one of the newsmen said, "Well, what did he say?"

"What did he *say*? Nothing."

"Nothing at all?"

Asa Bailey reached across an angle of the table, grabbed the newsman by the shirtfront, drew his revolver and stuck it in the man's bug-eyed face, saying, "You want me to explain things to you or do you get the picture?"

2

Franklin Hovey, the company geologist, came in with a survey crew and two ore wagons of camp gear and equipment. Noticeably shaken, he said he would quit his job before going out with another survey party. "You don't *see* them," he said, "but there they are, like they rose out of the ground."

The news reporters finally got hold of him coming out of the telegraph office and practically bums-rushed him to the Gold Dollar. "Here, Franklin, something for your nerves." The reporters having a glass also since they were here.

"Whom did you telegraph?" they asked him.

"Mr. Vandozen. He must be apprised of what's happened."

The reporters raised their eyebrows and asked, "Well, what did happen out there?"

Franklin Hovey said his crew of eight had been working across a southwest section of the range at about seven thousand feet. One morning, three days ago, a tall nigger had appeared at their camp, came walking his horse in as they were sitting at the map table having breakfast. He gave them a polite good morning, said his name was Catlett and asked if they planned to blast hereabouts.

"I told him yes, and pointed to an outcropping of ledge along the south face that looked promising. I can't give you his exact words as the darkie said them, but he took off his old hat, scratched his wooly head and said, 'If you disturbs that rock, boss, it gwine come down in de canyon where de tanks at. Is you sure you wants to do that?' "

A couple of the reporters looked at each other with helpless expressions of pain, but no one interrupted the geologist. Franklin Hovey said, "See, there was a natural water tank in the canyon where they grazed a herd of horses. I told the darkie, 'That might be; but since the canyon is part of the company lease, we can blow it clear to hell if it strikes our fancy.' The darkie said something like, 'Strike yo fancy, huh?', not understanding the figure of speech. He said, 'Boss, we sees that rock come down in there, we-uns gwine strike yo fancy clean off this mountain.' I said, 'And who is the we-uns gwine do sech a thing as that?' "

Franklin sat back, beginning to relax with some liquor in him, glancing around the table to see if everyone appreciated his dialect. There were a couple of chuckles.

"The darkie himself smiled, knowing it was meant only as good-natured parody, and said, 'If y'all be so kind, jes don't mess the graze and the water. Awright, boss?'

"Now one of our powdermen went over to the wagon where we kept the explosives, got a stick of Number One and pointed it at the darkie, saying—this was *not* good-natured, though I'll admit it was funny at the time. The powderman pointed the stick and said, 'How'd you like it if we tie this to your tail, Mr. Nig, with a lit fuse and see how fast it can send you home?' The darkie, Catlett, said, 'Yeah, boss, that would send a body home, I expects so.' He smiled again. But this time there was something different about his smile."

There was a silence. Those around the table could see by Franklin Hovey's expression he was thinking about that time again, that moment, as though realizing now it should have warned him, at least told him something.

"Did you blow the ledge?" a reporter asked.

"Yes, we did. Though we set off a small warning charge first to indicate our intention. I insisted we do that."

The reporters waited, seeing the next part coming, remembering the story Asa Bailey, the former contract guide, had told only a few days before.

"Our party was well armed," Franklin Hovey continued, "and we set a watch that night around the perimeter of the camp. As I've said, we were at about seven thousand feet on bare, open ground. With night guards on four sides and enough moonlight to see by, we were positive no one could sneak up to that camp."

"They hit you at dawn," a reporter said.

Others told him to shut up as Franklin Hovey shook his head.

"No, we arose, folded our cots, ate breakfast . . . dis*cussed* the darkie's threat while we were eating and, I remember, laughed about it, some of the others imitating him, saying, 'Yessuh, boss, ah's gwine strike yo fancy,' things like that. After breakfast we went over to the dynamite wagon to get what we'd need for the day—you might've seen it, a big ore wagon with a heavy canvas top to keep the explosives dry and out of the weather. One of the men opened the back end"—Franklin paused—"and they came out. They came out of the wagon that was in the middle of our camp, in the *middle*, our tents and the two other wagons surrounding it. They came *out* of it . . . the same colored man and another one and two Indians." Franklin shook his head, awed by the memory of it. "I don't even see how there was room in there with the fifty-pound cases, much less how they got in to begin with . . . Well, they held guns on us, took ours and threw them into the canyon . . . tied our hands in front of us and then tied the eight of us together in a line, arm to arm . . . while the one named Catlett took a dynamite cartridge, primed it with a Number Six detonator and crimped onto that about ten feet of fuse, knowing exactly how to set the blasting cap in there and gather the end of the cartridge paper around it tight and bind it up good with twine. This man, I realized, knew how to shoot dynamite. I said, 'Now wait a minute, boy, we are only doing our job here, following orders.' The darkie said, 'Thas all ah'm doing too, boss. Gwine send y'all home.' I said to him again, 'Now wait a minute,' and the other members of the crew began to get edgy and speak up, saying we were only working men out here doing a job. The darkie said, 'Y'all doing a job awright, on our houses.' "

"Was Moon there?" a reporter asked.

"I told you," Franklin Hovey said, "it was the two colored men and two Apache Indians which, I forgot to mention, had streaks of yellowish-brown paint on their faces.

"The other colored man also began to prime sticks with blasting caps; so that between the two of them they soon had eight sticks of dynamite ready to fire, though not yet with the fuses attached. The one named Catlett approached me and poked a stick down into the front of my pants. Again, as you can imagine, I began to reason with him. He shook his head, pulled the stick out and walked around the line of us tied shoulder to shoulder and now placed the dynamite stick in my back pocket, saying, 'Yeah, tha's the place.' "

Many of the reporters were grinning and had to quickly put on a serious, interested expression as Franklin Hovey looked around the table.

"Well, they were behind us for several minutes, so we couldn't see what they were doing. Then they placed a stick of Number One, which will shatter solid rock into small fragments—they placed a stick in every man's back pocket or down into his pants if he didn't have a pocket. Then came around in front of us again and began drawing the fuses out between our legs, laying each one on the ground in about a ten-foot length.

"I forgot to mention they had found a box of cigars in somebody's gear and all four of them were puffing away on big stogies, blowing out the smoke as they stood about with their weapons, watching us. But not laughing or carrying on, as you might expect. No, they appeared serious and very calm in their manner.

"The tall colored man, Catlett, said something and the four of them began lighting the ends of the fuses with their cigars.

"Well, we began to pull and push against each other. We tried to reason—or maybe I should say plead with them by this time— seeing those fuses burning at eighteen seconds a foot, which seems slow, huh? Well, I'll tell you, those sputtering, smoking fuse ends were racing, not crawling, right there coming toward our legs. 'Stomp 'em out!' somebody yelled and all of us began dancing and stomping the ground before the burning ends were even close. The two colored men and the Apaches had moved back a ways. Now they raised their rifles, pointed 'em right at us and Catlett said, 'Stand still. You move, we'll shoot you dead.' "

Franklin Hovey waited, letting his listeners think about it.

"Which would you prefer, to be shot or blown up?" he said. "If you chose the former, I'd probably agree. But you would *not* choose it, I guarantee, looking into the muzzles of their guns. I promise you you'd let that fuse burn through between your feet at its pace and by then try not to move a muscle while being overcome by pure fear and terrible anguish. There was a feeling of us pressing against each other, rooted there, but not one of us stomped on a fuse. It burned between our feet and was out of sight behind us, though we could hear it and smell the powder and yarn burning. With maybe a half minute left to live, I closed my eyes. I waited. I waited some more. There was an awful silence."

And silence at the table in the Gold Dollar.

"I could not hear the fuse burning. Nothing. I opened my eyes. The four with the guns stood watching us, motionless. It was like the moment had passed and we knew it, but still not one of us moved."

Franklin Hovey let the reporters and listeners around the table wait while he finished the whiskey in his glass and passed the back of his hand over his mouth.

"The fuses," he said then, "had not been connected to the dynamite sticks, but burned to the ends a few feet behind us. It was a warning, to give us a glimpse of eternity. The tall one, Catlett, approached and said if they ever saw us again, well, we'd just better not come back. They hitched a team to the dynamite wagon and drove off with close to a thousand pounds of high explosives."

"That's it, huh?" a reporter said. "What was it the nigger said to you?"

"I told you, he gave us a warning."

"Just said, don't come back?"

Franklin Hovey seemed about to explain, elaborate, then noticed that two of the girls who worked in the Gold Dollar were in the crowd of listeners.

"He said something, well, that wasn't very nice."

"We see you again, we crimp the fuse on, stick the dynamite stick up your ass and shoot you to the moon . . . boy," were Bo Catlett's exact words.

3

A man by the name of Gean was brought down in a two-wheel Mexican cart lying cramped in the box with his new straw hat on his chest, both legs shattered below the knees by a single .50-caliber bullet. He said he felt it, like a scythe had swiped off his legs, before he even heard the report; that's how far away the shooter was. He said he should never have left the railroad. If he ever went back he would be some yard bull, hobbling after tramps on his crutches, if the company doctor was able to save his legs.

The one who had guided the cart down out of the mountains was Maurice Dumas. The Chicago Kid was tired, dirty and irritable and did not say much that first day. He took Gean to the infirmary where there were all manner of crushed bones from mine and mill accidents, some healing, some turning black, lying there in a row of cots. It smelled terrible in the infirmary and the reporters who came to interview Gean handed him a bottle and asked only a few questions.

Had Sundeen found Moon?

Shit, no. It was the other way around.

Moon was carrying the fight now?

Teasing, pecking at Sundeen's flanks.

Was it Moon who shot him?

Get busted from five hundred yards, who's to say? But it's what he would tell his grandchildren. Yes, I was shot by Dana Moon himself back in the summer of '93 and lived to tell about it. Maybe.

How many men did Moon have?

A ghost band. Try and count them.

What about the Mexicans?

They'd come across women and children, ask them, Where they at? No savvy, mister. We'd burn the crops and move on.

And the colored?

The niggers? Same thing. Few Indin women and little wooly-headed breeds. Where's your old man at? Him gone. Him gone where? Me no know, be home by-'m-by. Shit, let's go. But it was at a nigger place the sniping had begun . . . riding off from the house after loading up with chuck and leading a steer . . . ba-*wang*, this rifle shot rang out, coming from, I believe, California, and we broke for cover. When we looked back, there was one of ours laying in the weeds. After it happened two times Sundeen had a fit, men getting picked off and all you could see up in the rocks was puffs of smoke. But he took care of that situation.

How did he do that?

Well, he took hostages so they wouldn't fire at us. I was

walking up a grade toward a line shack, smoke wisping out the chimney, I got cut down and lay there looking at sky till one of your people found me and saved my life. Though I won't pay him a dime for that bed-wagon ride back here; I been sick ever since.

What else—how about Indians?

Shit, the only Indians he'd ever seen in his life was fort Indins and diggers. The ones rode for Moon were slick articles or wore invisible warpaint, for they had not laid eyes on a one.

The company doctor took off Gean's right leg. Gean said he could have done it back home under an El Paso & Southwestern freight car and saved the fare from New Mexico.

4

My, that Gean has the stuff, doesn't he? Tough old bird.

Maurice Dumas said to Bill Wells of the *St. Louis Globe-Democrat*, "Everybody was so taken with his spunk, or anxious to get out of there, they didn't ask the right question."

"About what?"

"The hostages. He said they took hostages, then started talking about how I found him and put him in the cart."

"What about the hostages?"

"They shot them," Maurice said.

He wasn't sure he was going to tell this until he did, sitting with Bill Wells in the New Alliance. Like one reporter confiding in another. What should I do? Should I reveal what happened or not?

Why not?, was the question, Bill Wells said. "Are you afraid of Sundeen?"

"Of course I am," Maurice said.

"We have power, all of us together, that even the company wouldn't dare to buck," Bill Wells said. It was a fact, though at the moment Bill Wells was glad they had come to this miners' saloon rather than mix with the crowd at the Gold Dollar. "Tell me what happened."

Maybe Sundeen thought it would be an easy trip: march up there with his hooligans and run the people off their land, burn their homes and crops, scatter the herds—like Sherman marching to the sea. Sundeen did have an air about him at first, as though he knew what he was doing.

But there were not that many mountain people to run off. And how did you burn adobe except to blacken it up some? Tear down a house, the people would straggle back and build another. The thing Sundeen had to do was track down the leaders and deal with them face to face.

But how did you find people who did not leave a trail? Even the cold camps they did find were there to misdirect and throw them off the track. Sundeen's men began to spit and growl and Sundeen himself became more abusive in his speech, less confident in his air.

They had burned a field of new corn when one of Sundeen's tail-end riders was shot out of his saddle. The next day it happened again. One rifle shot, one dead.

Sundeen came to a Mexican goat farm early in the morning, tore through the house and barn, flushed assorted women and kids, ah!, and three grown men that brought a squinty light to Sundeen's eyes. He tried to question them in his Sonora-whorehouse Spanish—no doubt missing his old segundo—and even hit them some with leather gloves on, drawing blood. Where's Moon? No answer. *Smack,* he'd throw a fist into that impassive dark face and the man would be knocked to the ground. The women and children cried and carried on, but the three men never said a word. Sundeen tied their hands behind them and loaded them into that two-wheel cart with a mule to pull it and had them lead his column when he moved on.

But then, you see, he didn't draw any sniper fire and that seemed to aggravate him more than having his men picked off.

Soon after taking the hostages they woke up in the morning to find half their horses gone, disappeared from the picket rope. Sundeen sent riders to Sweetmary for a new string. They came back to report the story of the survey crew being hit.

It was in a high meadow facing a timbered slope and a little shack perched up in the rocks above that Sundeen, all of a sudden, reached the end of his skimpy patience. It was no doubt seeing the smoke coming out of the stovepipe. Somebody was up there, a quarter of a mile away. And he was sure they were in the timber also, in the deep pine shadows. There was not a sound when he began to yell.

"Moon! Come on out! . . . You and your boogers, Moon! . . . Let's get it done!"

His words echoed out there and faded to nothing.

Sundeen pulled the three Mexicans from the cart and told them to move out in the meadow, keep going, then yelled for them to stop when they were about forty yards off. They stood in the sun bareheaded, looking up at the timber and turning to look back at Sundeen who brought all his riders up along the edge of the meadow, spread out in a line.

He yelled now, "You see it, Moon? . . . Show yourself or we'll blow out their lights!"

Nothing moved in the pines. The only sound, a low moan of wind coming off the escarpment above.

The three men, bareheaded and in white, hands tied behind them, didn't know which way to face, to look at the silent trees or at the rifles pointed at them now.

"I've given him enough warning," Sundeen said. "He's heard it, isn't that right? If he's got ears he heard it." If he's up there, somebody said. "He's up there, I know he is," Sundeen said. "Man's been watching us ten days, scared to come out. All right, I give him a chance, haven't I?" He looked up and yelled out once more, "Moon?" Waited a moment and said, "Shit . . . go ahead, fire."

"And they killed them?"

Maurice nodded.

"But if he knew you were a witness—"

"He'd forgotten I was along by then, other things on his mind."

Bill Wells was thoughtful, then asked, "Was Moon up there, in the trees?"

"Somebody was. Shots were fired and Sundeen divided his men to come at the timber from two sides. That was when Gean was shot."

"And you were considering you might keep it a secret?"

"I wasn't sure how I felt. I mean I've never handled anything like this before," Maurice said. "Though I know we're sworn to print the truth, letting the chips fall where they may."

"Or stack the chips against the company's hand," Bill Wells said, the idea bringing a smile. "Yes, I can see Vandozen squirming and sweating now."

THIRTEEN

1

There was a framed slate in the Gold Dollar, back of the bar, that gave the betting odds on a Sundeen-Moon showdown:

2 - 1 one week
5 - 1 four days
10 - 1 two days

It meant you could bet one dollar to win two if you thought Sundeen would track down Moon and bring him in dead or alive within one week. The house was betting against it ever happening. When a week passed and Sundeen hadn't returned, you lost your dollar. For shorter periods you could bet the higher odds that were posted.

When Sundeen returned a few days ago with four men face-down over their saddles and the rest of his troop worn raw and ugly, they erased the old odds and wrote on the slate:

4 - 1 one week
10 - 1 four days
20 - 1 two days
100 - 1 one day

A miner at the bar, who had not seen the new odds before, said, "I'd hide that thing was I you. Case he comes in here."

"Who, Mr. Sundeen?" said Ed O'Day, who ran the Gold Dollar and sometimes served behind the bar. "He wants to bet on himself we'd be glad to cover it. Or, he wants to bet against himself I'm sure there some takers. Making a wager isn't anything personal. The man is not gonna bet against himself and take a dive, is he? No, not in this kinda contest. So, he thinks he's gonna come out the victor, let him put up his money."

Ed O'Day was a known high-roller; he ran faro, monte and poker tables in the back of his place and would bet either side of an issue depending on the odds.

Bren Early stepped toward them, moving his elbow along the polished edge of the bar. He said, "You're betting against him finding Moon is all you're doing."

"Mr. Early, how are you? Sorry I didn't see you there. The usual?"

Bren nodded. The slight—not being noticed immediately— was as much an insult to him as the odds board: putting Sundeen against Moon and ignoring him completely. Bren had a hard knot inside his stomach. He wanted to cut this barkeeper down, level him with a quiet remark that had an eternal ring. (Something to do with, serving these miners and tourists, "What would you know about putting your life on the line?" Or, ". . . What would you know about facing death?") But he couldn't think of the words when he was on edge like this. God-damn it.

Pouring him a whiskey, Ed O'Day said, "Finding Moon is ninety percent of it, yes. If that ever happens it would be a different story."

"How would you set the odds then?" Bren asked, satisfied that his tone did not show the edge.

"Well, I'm inclined to believe they would favor Mr. Sundeen. I don't mean as a shooting contest. I mean if he runs him down the game's over."

"How do you come to that?" Bren asked the know-it-all, feeling the knot tighten.

Ed O'Day looked both ways along the bar and leaned closer as he said, "You take a person raised on sour milk and make him look dumb in front of his fellow man—You see what I mean? He ever sets eyes on Moon he's gonna kill him."

"You know that as fact," Bren said.

"No, but I'd bet on it."

"You heard right now that Sundeen had located him—you'd put your money on Sundeen?"

"I'd say it would be the safer bet."

"Turn the same odds around?"

Ed O'Day hesitated. "You said if he locates him—"

"Gets Moon to stand still and fight."

"Just Sundeen, or his men too?"

"His men, anybody he wants to bring along."

The miner standing next to Bren said, "Anybody or everybody? The way he's signing up people, he's gonna be taking a army next time—saying up at the works the next time's the last time. Though I don't want to mess up your bet none."

"That's talk," Ed O'Day said, but looked at Bren Early to get his reaction.

"No, it's fact," the miner said. "Sundeen sent to Bensons, St. David, Fairbank—twenty a week, grub and quarters. Most the miners want to quit and join up; but Selkirk told him no, he couldn't hire no miners. See, he's gonna take all the men he can find and not come back till it's done."

The miner's heavy mustache, showing fine traces of gray, reminded Bren of Moon. He wondered what Moon was doing this minute. Squinting at heat waves for signs of dust. Or tending his guns, wiping down Old Certain Death with an oil rag. Damn.

"I don't care how many people he raises," Bren said, "I want to know what odds you're giving if both sides stand to shoot and you want Sundeen . . . ten to one?"

"*Ten* to one?" Ed O'Day said. "Talking about if the two sides ever meet."

"No bet less they do."

"Doesn't matter how many men Sundeen has?"

"He can hire the U.S. Army," Bren said.

"Ten to one," Ed O'Day said and thought about it some more. "Well, it's interesting if we're talking about real money."

"Give me a Maricopa bank check," Bren said.

Ed O'Day went over to the cash register and came back with the check, an ink pot and a pen.

Bren leaned over the bar and scratched away for a minute, picked up the check, to blow on it, wave it in the air, and laid it on the polished surface again.

"Seven thousand Sundeen goes out and never comes back."

Ed O'Day, who wore the same expression drawing a pair of aces he did picking his teeth, said, "Is this the bet we been talking about all along?"

"I'm cutting out the only-if's and what-if's," Bren said. "Sundeen comes back for any reason after he leaves—if it's just to go to the toilet, this check is yours. But when he doesn't, and you learn he's dead, you pay off ten to one. Which is what?"

"Comes to seventy thousand," Ed O'Day answered, like it was no more than a day's take.

"This man here is our witness," Bren said. "Have him write his name on the check somewhere."

The miner looked from Bren to Ed O'Day with his mouth partly open. "You're paying him seventy thousand dollars if Sundeen gets killed?"

"No different'n writing life insurance," Ed O'Day said and winked at Bren—

Who felt good now and didn't mind at all the man's cocksure coyness.

"I'll even pay double if he gets struck by lightning," Ed O'Day said.

Bren let an easy grin form, as if in appreciation, though there was more grin inside him than out.

He said, "You never can tell."

2

"All the people," a reporter sitting on the Congress front porch said. You would think the circus was in town. It is, another reporter said; featuring Phil Sundeen and his wild animal show. Christ, look at them. Bunch of range bums and bushwackers trying to pass as Quantrill's guerrillas.

Bren found Maurice Dumas sitting in the lobby staring at nothing. When he asked what was the matter, Maurice said he was thinking of going home; watching innocent people get shot was not his idea of covering a war. Bren said, no, when men fought without honor it was a sorry business.

"But we're gonna teach them a lesson, partner, and I sure hope you're here to see it."

Maurice perked up. "You're getting into it?"

Bren nodded.

"When?"

"I'll tell you," Bren said, "this looks like it's gonna be my busy night. If you could help me out some I guarantee you'll be in the front row when the fireworks go off."

"Get what things done?"

"Find Sundeen first. Tell him I'll meet him at the Chinaman's, the Oriental in about an hour."

"You mean——"

"Unh-unh," Bren said, "that's what I don't want to happen by mistake, ahead of time. Tell him I got something important to say. No guns. You'll inspect him and he can have somebody inspect me if he wants. Tell him it's the answer to how to end this deal and that he's gonna like it."

"I don't know if I can stand to speak to him," Maurice said.

"Listen, you write this story they'll make you the editor. Don't let personal feelings get in your way. The other thing——" Bren paused, looking around the lobby. He said, "Come on," and led Maurice to the back hall where the first-floor rooms were located. The light from the wall fixtures was dim, but it was quiet here, private. Bren took a thick envelope from his pocket and handed it to Maurice.

"List of some things I'm gonna need and the money to buy 'em with. Open it."

Maurice did.

"Put the money in your pocket."

"Looks like a lot."

"Two hundred dollars is all."

Maurice unfolded a sheet of paper. It was Moon's "wanted" dodger.

"You'll see the notes on there I've written."

"Yeah?" Maurice read them, then gave Bren a funny look, frowning. "You serious? You want this printed?"

"Trust me and don't ask questions, it's part of the scheme," Bren said. "You'll see where to get everything; it's all on the list. The case of whiskey, buy something good. The pack animal and cross-buck, I wouldn't pay more than fifty dollars. What else? It's going on seven o'clock, how about we meet at the livery stable eleven thirty, quarter of twelve. Sound good?"

"I don't know if I can have everything by then." Maurice looked worried now.

But not Bren. He said, "Hey, are you kidding me? Anybody rises as early as you is a natural-born go-getter."

3

Vandozen, seated in the middle of the settee, seemed to blend with the room, belong: formal but relaxed in his light-gray business suit and wing collar; pinch-nose glasses hanging from a black ribbon, resting on his vest.

Janet Pierson said, "Mr. Vandozen is here." Saying it as Bren came through the kitchen and the two men were already face to face. "He's been waiting for you. I asked him if he'd like some coffee—"

"How about cognac?" Bren said.

Vandozen nodded. "A small one. Mrs. Pierson was kind enough to let me wait."

"I didn't know you were in town." Bren glanced at Janet.

Vandozen watched her go out to the kitchen as he said, "I built a place near Lordsburg, to be close to our New Mexico operations, some good ones just getting started." His gaze returned to Bren who was seated now in an easy chair, his hat off, coat open. "I can be here overnight on the Southern Pacific, but I hadn't planned on coming as often as I have."

"No, this kind of business," Bren said, "you don't plan its twists and turns, do you?"

"We're going to end it," Vandozen said. "I want you to go out, talk to this Moon. Tell him we'll make a deal with him."

"What kind of deal?" Bren said, taken by surprise. Jesus Christ, he didn't want any *deal*. Not now. He stared at Vandozen sitting on that velvet settee like it was his throne.

"You're going to arrange a meeting between this Moon and myself." Vandozen paused, his gaze moving as Janet came in with a decanter and two brandy snifters, and watched her as she served them, saying, "Very nice. Thank you."

Bren remained silent, edgy now. Damn. Seeing his plan coming apart. He said, "It's dark in here. Why don't you turn up the lamps?"

"It's fine," Vandozen said. "Though you can close that front window if you don't mind."

There were occasional sounds from outside, men's voices in the street: first-shift miners returning to their quarters, some of them a little drunk.

Jesus Christ, whose house was it? Bren said, "What do you want to talk for? Your man's going out again; he'll get it done."

"He's *not* getting it done," Vandozen said, with emphasis but more quietly than Bren had spoken. "This business should have been handled quickly with a show of force. Offer one choice, leave, that's all. What does he do, stumbles around, can't even find them. When he does, he ties up three Mexicans and shoots them with a newspaperman as a witness. Which is going to take some countering, not to mention money."

"It's gonna be over soon," Bren said.

"I know it is. Your bring this Moon to me and we'll make a deal."

"His name's Dana . . . Dana Moon," Bren said.

"That's fine. Go get him. Tell him we'll meet at his office or mine, I don't care. Criminal charges against him will be dropped. We'll pay for—no, we'll work out some plan of assistance for anyone whose home or crops were damaged. Tell him any future survey work will be done in isolated areas."

Bren said, "Ah, now we're getting to it. You haven't found the copper you thought you would, huh?"

"I can say test samples have been misleading, promising more than the locations would ever yield," Vandozen said. "But that's beside the point. I made an error in judgment, this business going on; allowed it to take on far more prominence—considerably more of my time than it's worth. So you and I are going to bring it to a halt."

"I don't believe it's part of my job," Bren said, "since I'm not a messenger boy."

Vandozen looked at him for what seemed a long time, though perhaps only ten seconds. "What *is* your job?" he asked.

"I don't know. Tell me."

"Isn't this Moon a friend of yours?"

"*Dana* Moon."

"You two, I understand, used to be close friends?"

"What's that got to do with it?"

"Don't you want to help him?"

"Dana can handle it himself."

"For God's sake—" Janet Pierson said.

The two men looked at her seated in the straight chair, away from them.

"I'm sorry," she said. "I didn't mean to interrupt."

"Mrs. Pierson understands," Vandozen said. "Or, I should say, she doesn't understand why you don't want to help your friend." Still with the quiet tone.

"I didn't say I wouldn't help him."

"Or why you don't want to help the company. You're a stockholder . . . making, what?, ten thousand dollars a year. Why would you knowingly act in violation of your contract?"

"Knowing what?"

"Well, doing anything that's not in the company's best interest. That's standard in any employee contract."

"The fine print, huh?"

"You don't recall reading that?"

Bren didn't answer. He sat with his cognac, looking at Vandozen, a question in his mind, but afraid Vandozen's answer would destroy his plan completely. Still he had to ask it.

"What about Sundeen? You call him off?"

"Not yet."

Bren let his breath out slowly. "When you gonna see him?"

"He's to see me first thing in the morning."

"So he doesn't know about this yet."

"He'll be fired five minutes after he walks in the office."

Bren sat in the deep chair another moment, comfortable, beginning to feel pretty good, yes, confident again. He finished his cognac and pulled himself out of the chair.

"Well, I might as well get going. You'll know something tomorrow."

Janet Pierson said, "Do you mind? It's stuffy in here."

Vandozen watched her raise the window and stand looking out, her back to him.

"Why does he have to go tonight?"

"Because he's childish," Vandozen said. "He has to go out and kick rocks, or run his horse till it lathers." He reached over to place his glass on the end table and sat back again.

"He is like a little boy," Janet said.

"Yes, he is . . . Why don't you come over here?" Vandozen watched her turn from the window. "Come on . . . sit here."

When she was next to him, on the edge of the settee, he put his hand on her shoulder and brought her gently back against the cushion. His hand remained as he said, "Tell him you're leaving."

She looked at his face that was lined but not weathered, the skin on his neck loose, crepe-like, in the starched white collar.

"I admired you when you admitted you'd make a mistake."

"Not a mistake, a misjudgment. Come to Lordsburg with me."

"Don't you have a wife?"

"In New Jersey. Not in New Mexico, Colorado or Arizona."

"I admired the way you never raised your voice, even when you said things with feeling."

"Yes," Vandozen said, drawing her against his shoulder, "in certain areas I have firm convictions and feelings."

4

Bren sat at a corner table in the Oriental. He let Sundeen take his time and look around. When Sundeen finally came over he pulled out the chair across from Bren and sat down.

"Now then," Sundeen said, "where were we?"

"They're trying to call the game." Bren sat with his hands flat on the table. "Vandozen says he's had enough of your monkeyshines. He's gonna fire you tomorrow, and all those hoboes you got riding for you."

Sundeen nodded, not surprised. "You would think he had something personal to do with this." He sat back in his Douglas chair saying, "Shit."

"There's hope," Bren said, "if you can get your misfits out of town before morning. He can't find you, he can't fire you, can he?"

"I don't know—don't many of 'em snap to as they should," Sundeen said. "There's some mean Turks, but most of 'em ain't worth cow shit."

"How many you need? . . . How many does Moon have?"

"Who in the hell knows? All I seen was women and little kids."

"Some Mexicans with their hands tied, I understand."

"And their eyes open. They knew what they were doing. I cut the ropes, let 'em hold their old cap-n-balls, they'd still be dead, wouldn't they? I lost men blown to hell from a distance. Are we talking about rules of some kind or what?"

"We're getting off track," Bren said.

"You're the one called this," Sundeen said, his snarly, ugly nature peeking through. "We can settle up right now, you want, and quit talking about it."

"You got spirit," Bren said, "but save it and let's do this show with a little style. You don't want to meet in some back alley; you got a reputation to think of—as poor as it is."

"Jesus," Sundeen said, on the edge now, hands gripping the arms of his chair.

Like working a wild stallion, hold him on the line, but don't let him break his neck. Bren said, "If you're big enough to handle your men, gather 'em and head up to White Tanks. I'll get Moon, whatever people he's got . . . You come up the draw and we'll meet at his place."

Sundeen said, "Through that steep-sided chute? You must believe I'm dumb."

"Scout it. Turn all the rocks over, you want. I'm talking about we meet at the top, have a stand-up battle like we had in Sonora. Quit this tracking around and do the thing right." Bren paused. Sundeen remained silent. "Unless you lack the gristle."

Sundeen said, "You don't need to prod, if that's what you're doing. I'm thinking." And said then, "Why don't we meet at White Tanks?"

"Moon won't do it, I'll tell you that right now. He'll fight for his home, but not for any government layout. He doesn't look at this the way you and I do."

Sundeen was thoughtful again. "It would make some noise, wouldn't it?"

"Hear it clear across the country," Bren said. "Get your name in the history book."

Sundeen grinned then, tickled. "Jesus Christ, is this the way it's done?"

"Why not? Better than maybe we meet sometime maybe we don't."

"Well . . . Moon's place then. I guess it's as good as another."

As Sundeen got up, Bren said, "Whatever happened to that old segundo of yours?"

"Ruben Vega," Sundeen said. "He tried to change sides and didn't make it."

"That's too bad. He seemed a good one for his age."

"Yeah, he was quicker than most," Sundeen said, "but in this game there ain't any second prize, is there?"

5

The sound jolted Bruckner awake: something dropped on his desk. Somebody standing there.

Maurice said, "The printer over at the paper asked me to give these to you."

"What?" Bruckner said. "The hell you want?"

Maurice stepped back from the man's stale whiskey odor. "You're supposed to post them around right away. Printer said it was ordered from the county."

Bruckner rubbed a hand over his face, opened his eyes and the squirt reporter was gone. He looked at his watch: twenty past twelve; heard horses outside and turned to his window.

Three horses out there . . . the squirt news reporter mounting and another fella already up, leading a packhorse with gear and a wood crate lashed to the cross-buck. Bruckner watched them head down LaSalle Street into darkness.

When he turned to his desk again he frowned and said out loud, "What in the hell—" Bren Early's photo was looking at him from a stack of "wanted" dodgers that said:

$5,000
REWARD

(Dead or Alive)

for information leading to
the arrest or seizure of

CAPT. BRENDAN EARLY

wanted for the killing of
P. Sundeen (and probably others)
Approach with utmost caution!!!

FOURTEEN

1

Kate said to Moon, "What do you need all those enemies for when you got a friend like Bren Early?"

Moon said, "How long you want to live in a line-camp and cook outside in the weather? It's a way to get it done and move back in our home."

"If you win," she said.

Moon said, "I don't worry about that part till I'm there."

"Do you think it makes sense?"

Moon had taken his wife aside for this chat, away from the others sitting around the tents and brush wickiups of the camp, one of the high-up Apache rancherías.

He said to Kate, "Don't look at it as a sensible person would. Try to see it through Bren's eyes first, the chance to do battle and win some medals."

"Who gives him the medals?"

"You know what I mean—add to his stature. He missed the war and he's been moaning about it ever since. Now he sees a chance to win fame and get his picture in the paper, big."

"At whose expense?" Kate said.

"You got to look at it another way too," Moon said. "Sundeen is gonna dog us till we put an end to him. I'd rather meet him across the wall than keep looking over my shoulder . . . worrying about you at home the times I'm gone."

"Now you make it sound like a just cause," Kate said, "but I believe the idea tickles you as much as Bren."

"No, not that much," Moon said, feeling itchy, excited, but trying not to show it. "Come on."

They walked back through the pines to the ranchería, past the children and the squat Mimbre women at the cookfires, to where Bren was sitting on his bedroll, Maurice Dumas next to him. The Apaches had sighted them early this morning and brought them up to the camp. The case of whiskey had been opened and a bottle passed around as they discussed this business of meeting Sundeen. The whiskey was good after nearly a month of sour corn-beer. The talk was good. The idea seemed good, too. But did it make sense? Or didn't it have it?

Bo Catlett was here and another former 10th cavalryman by the name of Thomas Jefferson. Eladio Duro, the son of Armando, was here with a heavily armed farmer named Alfonso who wore three belts of bullets. Red was here—it was his camp—with seven Mimbre Apache males who remained silent and let Red speak for them—as he was doing now in halting Spanish.

When he finished Bo Catlett said, "It seem that way," and looked at Bren Early. "Captain, Red say, do these people want to die? Or is it us want to die?"

"Tell him," Bren said, "these people will never stop hunting him as long as they live, or we let them live."

"He knows all about that," Bo Catlett said. "He wants to know, what is this standing and waiting for your enemy to come at you?"

"Tell him it's the way white men face each other with honor. I mean civilized people," Bren said to Bo. "It's the way we've always done it."

"Tell him *that*?" Bo Catlett said, glancing at Moon and back to Bren. "You gonna have to explain it to *me* first. Lest you plan to bushwack him in the draw. We got seven hundred pounds of dynamite could help."

"Artillery," Bren said, and was thoughtful a moment. "I told him he could bring his men up. Gave him my word on that."

Bo Catlett translated into Spanish and Moon watched Red and his Mimbres as they looked at one another.

"They think you must be drunk," Moon said to Bren. "Let me make a speech for a minute."

He spoke in Spanish, for the benefit of the Apaches and the Mexican farmers, though Bo Catlett's people were included. Moon said that some of this business with Sundeen was personal and he didn't expect anyone to fight because of something that happened a long time ago in Sonora. But Sundeen and his people also represented the company and the company wanted this land.

"Tell them it's a question of honor," Bren said. "Oh-*nohr*."

"It's a question of how you want to live," Moon said in Spanish. "My business isn't to hide and shoot at them the rest of my life. I have other things I want to do." He looked at Kate. "But I can't do them until I finish this. Can we win? I believe so. I believe the company will look at us and decide it isn't worth all the time and money and they'll go somewhere else for their copper." Moon's gaze moved to Bren. "In fact, I'm surprised the company hasn't sent somebody to talk to us—"

Bren didn't move; then shrugged; then tried to think of something to say.

"—but I believe the company will when they see we're determined to stay."

"That's it," Bren said. "This is the company's final show of strength. And when they see it fail, they'll cave in."

Moon seemed to accept this. He said, "Will some of us die?" And looked at Eladio and Alfonso. "Some of us already have. But I would rather face them now than risk being shot in the back planting corn. Maybe you don't like to fight this way. I don't blame you. But this is the way it is."

When Moon appeared finished, Bren said, "Did you mention honor? It didn't sound very inspiring."

Moon said, "It's their lives. It's up to them."

Following the trail down from the ranchería, Moon close to Kate, he wanted to talk to her, be near her. But Bren rode a length behind and told how Sooy Smith had entered Okolona and captured a big bunch of Rebel officers and men on furlough, February 17, 1864— Bren full of war again—February 20, 3:00 P.M., reached a point south of Prairie Station with two brigades and learned that Nathan Bedford Forrest was facing him with a force of 7,000. You know what Sooy did?

"What?" Moon said, interested.

"God—" Kate said.

Maurice Dumas watched and listened, fascinated.

Later in the morning the mountain people began to arrive at the stone house with the charred furniture in the yard:

Bo Catlett, Thomas Jefferson and two more in "US" braces and worn cavalry boots. Bo said they had flipped coins and the ones lost had to stay home with the families and the herds. They had a talk with Moon and Bren Early, got Bren to agree to an idea and the 10th Cavalry veterans went down into the barranca with two fifty-pound cases of dynamite.

Young Eladio Duro, Alfonso with his cartridge belts, and six farmers carrying old Ballards and Remingtons represented their families. (Others were scattered and could not be notified.) Eladio wore a green sash, a sword and a caplock Dragoon pistol his grandfather had carried at Resaca de la Palma. Everyone full of war.

Red and his seven Mimbres squatted in the yard with a clay pot of ochre paint; with bowls of *atole*, the flour gruel they would eat as their last meal before battle; with small leather sacks of *hoddentin*, the magic powder that would protect them from bullets; with cigars and tulapai, the corn-beer, and chants that reminded them they were the *Shis-Inday*, the invincible Apache . . . the chosen ones. Those not chosen for this—another twenty in Red's band—were in the thicket behind the house, up on the escarpment and watching the back trails. (Sundeen would have to come straight at them up the barranca, and not pull any sneaky tricks.)

Bren unloaded and reloaded his .44 Russians and his fancy Merwin & Hulberts and shoved a seven-cartridge tube into the stock of his polished Spencer . . . ready for war, brimming over with it, telling Moon how Sooy Smith had dug in to make a stand at Ivey's Farm against Barteau who had taken over for Tyree Bell, see, when Tyree Bell had become sick . . . confusing but, to Moon, a good sound; it matched the excitement he felt.

Maurice Dumas spent some time inside the smoke-blackened house with Kate, helping her as she baked about a dozen loaves of bread, but most of the time looking out the window at the Apaches and the Mexican farmers, at Moon and Early out by the adobe wall.

It was exciting and it was scary, too. Maurice wondered if he was the only one who felt it. Everyone else seemed so calm, or resigned. He said to Kate, "The thing is, they don't *have* to do this."

"Yes, they do," Kate said. "They believe they do, which is the same thing."

"Twenty-two," Maurice said, "against however many Sundeen brings. Probably twice as many."

"Twenty-three," Kate said, finished with the bread, loading a Henry now with .44's.

"*You're* gonna take part in this?"

"It's my house too," Kate said.

In a little while Moon sent Maurice Dumas down to White
Tanks to tell Sundeen he could come any time he wanted.

2

Someone had brought the Capt. Brendan Early dodger,
". . . wanted for the killing of P. Sundeen," and showed it
around. Sundeen read it and shook his head, pretending to be
amused, but did not think it was funny. The news reporters at
White Tanks quoted him as saying, "I hope there is money on that
son of a ———'s head, for I am sure as —— going to collect it."

Yes, the news reporters had finally come to the field, brought by
the message Maurice Dumas had left displayed in the hotel lobby:
*Come to White Tanks for final showdown, Rincon Mountains War.
Scheduled to begin around noon today!* Bren Early's idea. ("Why
do you want all them?" Maurice had asked him. Bren's answer:
"The more people there are who sympathize with our fight against
the giant company, the more likely the company is to back off."
Now it was *our* fight.)

When Maurice came down the mountain to White Tanks and
saw the crowd, he couldn't believe it. Riders, wagons, buggies, Indians, a few women, little kids playing on the fence around the
stock pen—there must have been two hundred people or more.
When he reached the agency buildings and began sorting everybody out, Maurice found that maybe half were spectators, gawkers, and the rest were in the pay of Sundeen . . . something like a
hundred armed men!

Had Bren Early counted on that many opposing them? Not by
half, Maurice recalled. Perhaps forty men at the most.

But one *hundred*—all hard-eyed cutthroats in a variety of getups:
derbies, straws, sombreros, dusty business suits and batwing chaps
. . . shotguns, rifles, six-shooters, all were armed with at least two
guns; they stood about talking, drinking whiskey, checking and fooling with their weapons . . . talking in loud, confident voices and finding, it seemed, a great deal to laugh about.

My God.

C.S. Fly was not present. Maurice learned the famed photographer had declined the invitation, saying he had pictures enough for
a fools' gallery as is. However there were others—among them A.

Frank Randall of Willcox and someone representing Beuhman & Hartwell of Tucson—busy taking pictures of Sundeen, groups of his cutthroats holding rifles and revolvers, and some of the White Tanks reservation Indians who posed, not having any idea what was going on.

Maurice had to push through a crowd on the porch of the agency office to get to Sundeen inside, sitting with his boots propped up on Moon's desk and telling the news reporters his riders would "bite shallow" else they would eat those people up in two minutes. Maurice waited for Sundeen to notice him, then said, "They're ready for you."

Sundeen eyed him. "How many people's he got?"

"I'm not at liberty to say."

"At *liberty*," Sundeen said, drawing up out of the swivel chair. "You little squirt, I'll free your soul for you."

"About twenty," Maurice said.

He turned and walked out. Should he have told?

Did he have a choice?

The least he could do was ride back up there and tell how many Sundeen had. God—and watch their faces drop.

The photographer from Beuhman & Hartwell caught him outside on the steps and said, "If you're going back up, I'm going with you." Then Bill Wells of the St. Louis paper and several other reporters said they were going too. Then a man Maurice had never seen before came up and said, "Maurice, I've been looking for you. I'll be in your debt if you'll present me to Dana Moon and Captain Early."

Maurice was certain he had never seen the man before this. For how could he have forgotten him? The gleaming store teeth and waxed guardsman mustache twirled to dagger points—

"Colonel Billy Washington, at your service, Maurice."

—the pure-white Stetson, the tailored buckskin coat with white fringe, the black polished boots with gold tassels in front—

"You've heard of me, have you?"

"Yes sir, I certainly have," Maurice said. God, all this happening at once. "I just have never seen you in person before."

"Well, you see me now," Colonel Washington said.

3

Bo Catlett rode up out of the barranca and crossed the open ground to the wall. He said to the people standing behind it, "They on the way."

"How many?" asked Bren.

"Say a hundred, give or take." Bo Catlett rode into the yard before stepping down, pulled his carbine from the boot and slapped his mount toward the smell of feed and water over in the corral.

"Five to one," Bren said, sounding pleased.

Kate looked at him, her Henry resting on the wall. Moon gazed down the slope, past the open ground to the trough of the barranca. He could see figures now, a line of tiny dark specks coming up the switchback trail, through the field of saguaro.

Bren raised the field glasses hanging from his neck and studied the enemy approaching. "Straggling . . . close it up there!"

Moon looked at his Apaches. They looked at him, faces painted now with streaks of ochre. He turned to look at the Mexicans lining the wall: Eladio with his sword and green sash among the farmers in white cotton.

"Tell 'em to get ready," Bren said, field glasses at his face.

"You don't have to stay," Moon said in Spanish. "No one is asked to fight one hundred men."

The Indians and the Mexicans remained at the wall, looking from Moon to the slope. They saw another of the colored men now, Thomas Jefferson, coming across the open ground and through the gate space in the wall.

"They dismounting, like to come as skirmishers."

Bren lowered his glasses and called out, "Come on! Take your medicine like little men! . . . Christ, what're they fooling around down there for?"

Moon said to Bo Catlett, "They'd do better to stay mounted and run at us."

"Man never soldiered," Bo said. "Can see he don't know doodly shit what he's doing."

The sound of firing came from down the slope now . . . the tiny figures spreading out, moving up slowly, dropping down to fire, waiting, moving up again.

"Christ, it'll take 'em till tomorrow," Bren said. The Mexican farmers were raising their rifles. "Not yet," Moon said in Spanish.

"If you shoot now I think they won't come close enough. We want them up there on the open ground."

"We get them up," Bo said.

"What's your signal?" Moon asked him.

"Three quick ones. My boys'll light the fuses and get."

Moon held his hand out. In a moment Bren noticed and handed him the glasses. Moon studied the figures coming up through the brush and fencepost saguaros. He raised his gaze to a high point on one side of the barranca, then moved across to the other side where the barranca narrowed and Bo Catlett's powdermen had planted the charges. The tiny figures dotting the slope were coming up through the narrowing of the trough and spreading out again, more of them firing now, the closest nearing two hundred yards. They could blow the charges now and wipe out about a quarter of Sundeen's men and send the rest running. But that wasn't the plan. No, Bren had promised Sundeen safe passage—one general to another. That was all right. Because the plan was to get them all up on high ground, in the open, then blow the narrows and cut off their retreat, prevent them from falling back to cover. Get them milling around in the open and shoot the spirit right out of them, blow Sundeen to his reward and close the book. That was the plan.

The first skirmishers were approaching a hundred and fifty yards now, snapping shots and moving up, feeling the excitement of it probably, feeling braver and with no one shooting back. Moon moved his glasses over them to pick out Sundeen. Not in the first bunch . . . there he was with his funneled hat and silver buckles, crossed gunbelts and a six-shooter in each hand, waving his men to come on, goddamn it, get up there.

Moon set the glasses on the wall and raised his Big-Fifty Sharps.

"Don't you do it," Bren said.

Moon said, "I'm just seeing how easy it would be."

"Let him come up all the way."

Pretty soon now.

The skirmishers were firing from a hundred yards and the tail end of Sundeen's men was moving through the narrows. The firing increased. Sundeen positioned a line of shooters behind cover, just across the open ground—about twenty of them, gave a signal and they all fired at once.

Seeing this about to happen, the people behind the wall ducked down or went to one knee. All except Bren Early. After the second fusillade he said, "At Fredericksburg, where Doubleday's Iron Brigade stood up to the Rebel guns, D. H. Hill sent a flag of truce over with his compliments to General Doubleday—"

Another volley ripped out from the brush slope. Bren tried not to hunch his shoulders.

"—saying he had never in his experience seen infantry stand and suffer casualties under artillery fire more bravely."

Moon said, "You have got something in your head about having to die to win glory. If that's the deal, I pass . . . Bo, let's close the back door. Give your troopers the signal."

Bren, standing, said, "Hold there," and picked up the glasses from the wall. "Some more are coming up behind."

Kate had said to Moon, "I'm not staying in the house; you know that." He said no, he guessed not. "But if you worry out there about me instead of yourself, you'll get shot. So think of me as another hand, not as a woman or your loved one." Moon had agreed because there was no fighting her. Though he had said, "If something happens to you, your old dad will kill me."

At the wall now Kate was alert, aware of being in the middle of men's business and would pick out little things that surprised or impressed her. The stoic look of the Apaches. Were they afraid? Was Eladio afraid? Yes, he looked it; but didn't leave when given the chance. Was Bren afraid, standing up to their rifle fire? Or was he beyond fear, playing his hero role? Bo Catlett and the other cavalryman—she thought of them as professional soldiers who would stand because that's what you did. Moon. Moon had good sense, he *must* be afraid. But his look was the same, his gaze, his unhurried moves, the hunk of tobacco in his jaw. She did not think of herself until the concentrated fire came from the slope and she crouched close to the adobe, feeling the pistol in the waistband of her skirt digging into her, clutching the Henry tightly and seeing her knuckles, close to her face, standing out white and hard. There was a feeling of terrible pressure. She could die on this spot . . . hearing Moon say if that was the deal he'd pass, saying it so calmly . . . all of them appearing calm as the rifle fire cracked and sang through the air. Determined, not resigned, but quiet about it. You'd better be, huh? Was it that simple? Run and they'd shoot you in the back. It was fascinating, even with the feeling of pressure. The ultimate, a life or death situation. Bren said,

"Hold there . . ." The firing stopped. They began to raise up from the wall.

"They're riding through Sundeen's people," Bren said. "They're not his. Some other bunch."

"That's your friend," Moon said. "What's his name."

"Maurice. Christ Almighty, one of 'em's leading a pack animal."

Kate could see the shooters who had been down in the scrub and rocks standing now, looking around, as this parade of single-file riders came through them led by Maurice Dumas . . . nine, *ten* of them, the packhorse carrying something covered with canvas, poles sticking out, bringing up the rear. They came across the open ground and now the second rider, wearing a tall white hat, drew even with Maurice in his cap. As Kate got a good look at the man she said, "My God," and turned to Moon who was staring at them and showing the first expression of pure surprise she had ever seen on his face.

The man in the white Stetson and fringed buckskin dismounted in the yard. Maurice, still mounted, was saying something as the others rode into the yard behind him. The man in the white hat raised his hand to stop Maurice. "No need," he said, and walked over to Moon and Bren Early.

"Gentlemen, I would know you anywhere. Even if I had not seen your renown C.S. Fly photographs I would know you are the famous scout, Dana Moon . . . and you, sir, Captain Brendan Early." He was taking something out of his fringed coat now—his false teeth and waxed handlebars agleam, something that looked like picture postcards in vivid colors, and said, "Gentlemen, may I present myself . . . Colonel Billy Washington, here to extend a personal invitation to both of you to join the world-famous Billy Washington All-American Wild West Show as star attractions and performers . . . *if,* of course, you get out of this jackpot you're in alive. What do you say, gents?"

Moon looked at Kate. Kate looked at Moon.

Bren was saying, "What—"

The man from Beuhman & Hartwell and his assistant were setting up their camera, both of them glancing up at the sun. The news reporters were looking around at the scenery and down the slope toward the skirmishers standing in the scrub, judging the distance with keen gaze, beginning to make notes . . . the Mimbres, the Mexican farmers, the two black cavalrymen looking at the reporters and the bill-show man in the white hat and buckskins, staring at them. Where did they come from?

Bren was saying now, "Will you all kindly move out of the way? Go inside the house. Go on." Shooing them, going over to the photographer who was beneath his black cloth now. "Mister, will you move out of the way—"

Kate kept looking at Moon. She said, "What are we doing here?"

Moon didn't say anything; but his eyes held hers until they heard the voice call out from the slope.

"What in the hell's going on!"

Sundeen stood with several of his men at the edge of a brush thicket, looking up at the wall, at the people they could see close beyond the wall and through the gate opening. Now he yelled, "Get those people out of there!" and waved his arm.

"Jesus Christ," he said to the man in the derby hat next to him, who had been with Sundeen since the beginning of this company business, "you believe it?"

The man didn't say anything; he was squinting in the glare, frowning. The man didn't seem to know what to think.

"Goddman it," Sundeen said, "give 'em a round."

When the man in the derby hat didn't move or raise his Winchester, Sundeen took the rifle from him, levered as he jerked it eye-level, fired, levered, fired . . . seeing them scatter now . . . levered and fired again, sending his shots singing off the adobe wall where some of them had been standing, then yelled, "We're coming up!"

He half turned and began waving to his men to come on. Not one of them moved. Sundeen pulled his hat off, stared, put his hat on again close over his eyes, pushed the rifle at the man in the derby hat, placed his hands on his hips and looked all around him at his mean Turks. They stood in the hot dusty scrub and shale watching him or looking up the slope.

Very slowly, Sundeen said, "What is going on?"

Before the man in the derby hat could answer—if he was going to—a voice from the yard yelled, "Hold your fire, I'm coming out!"

Sundeen watched the picture-taker and his assistant appear with their camera and heavy tripod, coming out of the yard and moving to a rise off to the side where they began to set up the equipment. Sundeen stared, pulling his funneled hat brim lower. As the picture-takers were getting ready, the man in the bill-show cowboy outfit appeared at the wall and called out, "Mr. Sundeen!—"

Sundeen let go, yelling now as loud as he could, "Get that fancy son of a bitch out of there!" Said, "Jesus," in his breath and started up the slope by himself.

Kate saw him first. She had begun to feel a letdown, a tired after-feeling; but now the pressure of fear returned. Looking around, she said, "Dana?"

No one was facing this way.

Only the young newsman, Maurice. Moon was over by the others, moving them toward the house. Kate thought, You have to hurry. They have to hurry. This is what they were waiting for. Bren was walking Billy Washington across the yard, the wild-west show impresario holding onto Bren's arm with one hand, gesturing with the other as he spoke, waving his arm in a wide arc to take in the world.

"Dana!"

Moon came around, alert to his wife's tone. He looked out toward the wall, his gaze holding as he came back toward the gate opening. He stood there, as if to greet Sundeen coming across the open ground.

Kate said, "Dana?"

He didn't look at her now. Kate turned to the wall where the Henry rifle rested on the flat surface, pointing out. She stood some fifteen feet from her husband.

Maurice stood between them, but several feet back from the wall. He didn't know if he should stay here. No one had said anything to him. Sundeen had reached the flat piece of ground beyond the wall. He was about fifty feet away now. Beyond Moon— and the group of Apaches and Mexican farmers spaced farther down the wall—on the rise off to the side, the photographer was fooling with his camera, the assistant holding open the black cloth for him to duck underneath. From Beuhman & Hartwell, Tucson. Maurice remembered that. He wasn't sure of the spelling though. Or how to spell the colored man's name—the two colored soldiers in their army braces and boots, off beyond Moon's wife. Sundeen's belt buckles glinted in the direct sunlight. Sundeen with a revolver on each hip, bullet belts crossed in an old-time desperado style . . . My God, was Moon armed? . . . Yes, the shoulder rig. He was in his shirtsleeves and wore braces and there seemed to be all manner of straps over his shoulders and around his back. Moon with a shoulder holster. Sundeen with his gun butts almost touching his hands hanging at his sides.

Did he say something? Mention Sonora?

Maurice could see all the hired manhunters waiting down there at the edge of the scrub. There was sky behind Sundeen's head and shoulders.

He said, "You first, Moon, then your friend. Where is he at?"

"He doesn't come right now," Moon said, "you'll never see him again."

This took place in moments, right before Maurice's eyes. Bren Early was somewhere behind him in the yard. Maurice wanted to turn around, but couldn't take his eyes off Sundeen . . . or Moon, he could see by shifting his eyes a little. He wanted to call out Bren Early's name, get him over here. But at this moment there was an awful silence. Two armed men facing each other. Was there a signal? Men shot each other from a distance or sneaked up or came into a place shooting if one wanted to kill another. Did this happen? Maybe it did, for it was certainly happening now, Maurice thinking: Before your very eyes.

Sundeen said, "Your move."

Maurice saw Moon's right hand cross his body.

He saw Sundeen's right hand with a revolver in it. Like that. He saw the glint of sunlight on gun metal.

He heard an explosion, a heavy, hard report and a quick cocking lever action in the echo . . . to his left, where Kate Moon stood holding the big Henry rifle at her shoulder . . . and Sundeen was stumbling back, firing with a shocked look on his face, firing wildly again as Moon extended his revolver and fired and Kate fired the Henry, the two of them hammering Sundeen with .44's and that was the end of him. There was a silence. Sundeen lay on his back with his arms and legs spread out.

Maurice heard voices, someone in the yard calling out, running this way. He saw Kate lower the Henry and look at her husband, first with concern, then beginning to smile faintly. Moon looked over at his wife, not smiling but with a calm expression. Moon shook his head then. Maurice turned to see Bren Early coming with a matched .44 Russian in each hand.

Bren saying, "You got him? . . . You *got* him!" At the wall now, pointing a revolver down the slope and yelling at his men, his Apaches and Mexicans and pair of old cavalrymen, "Now! Pour it into 'em, boys!"

Moon turned away. Bren looked at him, a dumb, bewildered expression.

"We got to finish it!" All excited.

Moon shook his head. "You're too late for your glory." He looked at his wife. "When did it happen?"

Kate said, "I think it was over before it started."

"I guess so." Moon said then, "You shoot good for a little girl."

She said, "I wasn't gonna see you die for no reason."

Bren looked at them, from Moon to Kate and back. His gaze moved to Sundeen stretched face up on the bare ground and beyond him to the men standing in the scrub, Bren full of desperate energy brought to a halt.

"His people are still there . . . *look*."

But with little conviction in his tone. A last, too-late call to battle.

Remember it, Maurice thought. All of it:

Bo Catlett sitting on the wall, lighting a cigar. The other cavalry veteran leaning against it, his back to the scene of battle.

The Mimbre Apaches—gone. Where? Just gone. The Mexican farmers and the young one with the sword, moving away, walking off past the newsmen and the bill-show dude standing on the porch.

Moon gazing in that direction—

He said, "Well, we've paid up and lived to tell about it."

The bill-show man in buckskins was coming out toward them now, getting important-looking papers out of his pocket.

Moon watched him. He said to Bren, "It wouldn't hurt to travel, see the sights, would it?"

Kate shook her head, resigned or admiring or both. She said to Moon, "You're the sights. You and your partner."

Maurice Dumas got out his notebook and started writing it all down as fast as he could.